JENNIFER M. WALDROP

Dedication

To my little sister, Kristen—

Thanks to one fateful night of extra chili bomb ramen, questionable life choices, and you letting me hijack your dating apps after two Sapporos, I was blessed with the idea of growing a lover out of Spam. You're the real MVP. And I'm so glad you finally found your James—no cloning required.

A Note from the Author

Hello lovely reader!

Thanks so much for reading my first dark romcom! This series gets progressively darker and there is some content in this book that you should be aware of before you dive in:

Plane crash; death; suicide (atmospheric); mentions of kidnapping and human trafficking; mentions of emotionally unavailable parents; mentions of euthanasia; medical assistance in dying (MAiD); and murder (kinda).

Please read safely, and I hope you have as much fun reading it as I did writing.

<3 Jennifer

Prologue – A Soft Landing

James

There are a few things you should know about what it's like to die in a plane crash.

First, it's important to note, as I've had plenty of time to consider this now that my memories have fully returned, that the experience is starkly different from dying of a terminal illness, in that it's abrupt. But not so abrupt, like dying in a car wreck where you don't see your death coming.

You get about five minutes on average—I know because I've looked it up—to sort through your life while the pilots desperately try and fail to solve the problem of your malfunctioning, thus plummeting, aircraft.

It goes like this. One moment you are rising to the pinnacle of your career, pleasantly buzzed off the twenty-year-old whisky served neat and amusing yourself with the latest ridiculous headline about the ethical limitations of your most recent business venture while soaring through the sky on a well-appointed private jet share. The next moment, there's a boom right outside your window. The plane violently jolts, and the lights go out. Maybe your head slams into the cabin wall, or was that your imagination? You hear the pilots through the open cabin frantically radioing the nearest control tower to locate a suitable airstrip to make an emergency landing. Of course, this is unrealistic, as the jet, whose engines are no longer humming, can only glide so far.

Here's what happens. Your normally active mind scrambles for something to do while you urge yourself to remain calm. You shoot the whiskey you've managed to hang onto, for good measure. What should you be thinking of? What can you do? You know nothing of aeronautics, so you're of no help there. *Perhaps you could make a lucrative deal with God*, a disembodied voice says, and you glance in the direction it came from only to see the blinking electronics panel by the emergency door. Your head pounds, but you shake it off.

People! Surely that is what a normal person would think of in an emergency. But you can't remember the names of anyone you've ever known. Somehow, however, your name is crystal clear. *James Alexander Fletcher* lights up in your mind like a neon sign. Then a résumé of your life's accomplishments flashes across your mental landscape, from the day you graduated Dwight with honors to the first condo unit you closed on. The day you started your company and your first major acquisition. At first, a swell of pride overpowers your terror. But then the résumé changes.

You had a younger sister. Well, technically, you still have her. At least for another three minutes. What was her name? And more importantly, why hadn't you been able to make it to the hospital for the birth of her first child? You were in Chicago to meet with an investor. It seemed very important at the time. Then there was the child's christening that had inconveniently been scheduled at the same time as that speaking engagement for the Young Entrepreneurs of America. Surely, the impact of your talk on networking outweighed the need for your attendance at the church. The baby wouldn't have known if you were present or not. *But your sister would have*, your laptop mutters.

Her name was Abigale, you later remember. She'd brushed it off. There'd been an aloof edge to her voice when you gave her your regrets. But the same people raised her. Business First—it might as well have been your family motto. But the next time you saw her, she'd been a little colder than normal. You, being the idiot you were, took it as the strain of being a new mother. You weren't close as children. Not really.

Side note: I've discovered this is when I started anthropomorphizing electronics, if you haven't figured that out. An apparent side effect of the trauma of my impending death. Exciting, I know.

Hey asshole! the oxygen mask shouts as it pops down from the overhead. *You're probably dead anyway, but you should put this on—just in case.* You obey, not thinking anything of it until your phone, which you didn't bother to put on Airplane Mode, buzzes in your pocket.

Now your cell is speaking to you, too. *Care to make any final calls? Any loved ones who will give a shit that you're dead?*

Would you really call your mother in a situation like this? What would you say? The words *Sorry for missing your surgery* auto-populate in your mind. Where had you been that day?

You have two minutes left. There are flashing lights and the ground seems uncomfortably close. The woman in the seat next to you is crying now, and the man behind her has leaned forward to shut her window.

You stare out your own window at the quickly approaching ground. Outwardly, you appear calm. Steady, able to handle anything. Exactly as you've trained yourself to be. Inside, your heart is thumping wildly.

"I'm afraid we're going to have to attempt an emergency landing . . ." the pilot says over the intercom.

You grip the armrests as the intercom asks, *Why did you miss your mother's surgery? She almost died. Just like you're about to. And you weren't there. Selfish prick.*

No, that isn't true. You try to remember something good you did. Those young entrepreneurs . . . surely, they got something from your talk. See, your life had meaning. But your mind only wants to flash every single deficiency, every shortcoming before your eyes. Every meaningless moment you spent in pursuit of success and everything you missed because of it. Every family gathering. Every Christmas party. The girl you dated in college who you broke up with because she wanted you to put her first instead of chasing investors.

As your remaining seconds dwindle, the adrenaline pumping through your bloodstream washes through your system and numbness takes over. An eerie mental clarity strikes you like the clouds parting—a terrible analogy, considering your current circumstance. Outside the window, the angle of the ground is too sharp. You will not survive this. Somehow, that hadn't directly occurred to you until this point. In concert, all the mechanisms of the plane shout, *You're going to die!*

Your sweaty palms slip off the armrests, and you stare wildly at the other panicking passengers. Then you scream, "I don't want to die!" It bursts unexpectedly from your normally controlled façade. Sweat cascades down your temples in rivulets. You dab at it, but your hand comes away stained with blood.

The pilot announces something about the safety card and assuming the brace position over the chaos. You glance at the card in the seat-back pocket. Instead of picking it up, you scream again, "I don't want to die," more vehemently this time, but no one is listening. Every plan you've made, all the things you're striving for—it's all over. In seconds, there will be no more James Alexander Fletcher. This is it. Your life will be gone in a blink.

Maybe your parents will put your name on a building, the dormant engines suggest.

You're torn between throwing up and screaming again, but the engines' commentary forces out a crazed laugh. "Yeah, maybe."

Screaming fills the cabin. The pilot doesn't bother using the intercom as he shouts, "Brace for impact!"

This is where my story is going to diverge from the standard death narrative you might be expecting. Instead of the lights fading to black or an in-person meeting with my maker, I open my eyes and see that I stand face-to-face with the most beautiful woman I've ever seen. Retrospectively, had I retained all my memories, I might have thought the glowing lights illuminating her angelic form meant she *was* God.

But that's the thing. I remember nothing of how I got there. Not the falling plane or my brief but meaningful existential crisis. Nothing that could place me in the room with the woman.

My mind whirls as my heart thunders wildly. *Where am I?* This woman and whoever she's working for have abducted me and are holding me for ransom. That is the only reasonable explanation. My wealth makes me an attractive target—and someone is after the money I'm certain I have.

I fix the woman with the most authoritative stare I can muster and boom, "Where the fuck am I and who the fuck are you?"

1 – Say Yes to Manupartners

K8

September 21, 2390, before.

Modern times are lonely; the future may be worse.

K8's doorbell pings, drawing her attention away from the eerily accurate Old News article she was reading dated September 21, 2030, exactly three hundred and sixty years ago. Jett breezes into her unit carrying a to-go bag from Say Yes to Noodles.

"Lessa says you're being weird again." He hands her the package.

She scoffs. She isn't being weird. Certainly not again. In fact, she's never weird. K8 is perfectly normal. Just an incredibly ~~lonely woman~~ important particulate pollution scientist who ~~pathetically lives by her-~~

self maintains a very nice unit in C Quadrant. So what if she hasn't left that very nice unit since her birthday a week ago?

Before she can come up with a viable excuse, he frowns, scolding, "K8-nine-ten, if you continue to isolate yourself like this, how am I supposed to do my job as one of your FRIENDS?" He holds out his device for the retina scan. "Speaking of, let's verify before we forget." She leans forward and it pings. Then he does his own. *Lunch encounter verified. Only two more encounters needed to complete your September requirement*, the device confirms.

Jett is the one of her three government-assigned FRIENDS who she's closest to. Close isn't the right word. Surface level is a better description. He's better than the other two.

Today he's wearing his strip of icy blond hair slicked back over his head, so the shaved sides stand out. The severe style makes his sharp cheekbones and the deep hollows beneath them pop more than usual. With his heavy brow and deep-set eyes, he looks as if someone's placed a charcoal bias-cut tunic and pair of leggings on a marble statue. A statue that has black eyes and an iridescent black snake scale tattoo peeking out of the edge of his collar to wrap around his corded neck as a cuff. He purses his pale lips as he studies her.

"I'm not being weird." She sets the two boxes of noodles on the coffee table along with a water and VitaShot for each of them. "It's only that I had a dream about my parents again and it got me thinking."

Jett gives her a dramatic eye roll as she passes him a water. "Not this again. They were born in the late 2000s. You can't expect things to be how they were back then. You're a scientist, for the love of Zorg. Be logical."

"But it would only take one other person who feels the same. Then I could have what my parents did." She knows exactly where this conversation is headed, but she's powerless to steer it in a different direction. The logical reality is that in all her eighty-six years, she's never met a single person who wants the same thing as her: companionship. *With another human.*

"I'm telling you," Jett starts, but she parrots him as they finish together, "you should get a manupartner."

They both chuckle because this isn't the first time they've had this conversation.

She opens her mouth to speak, but Jett cuts her off before she can. "Please, not another diatribe against manupartners."

She huffs, feeling defeated by the prevailing attitude of her time. She can practically see the GROW slogan in fresh, grass-green letters as if it were a banner in her mind: "Love Has Never Been Easier."

"I'm serious," she says. "I don't get the point of them. Why pay unicoin for something you can have for free? They're not even real. Just biologically identical dupes. Don't you find it a little gross that you're having a romantic relationship with a clone?"

Jett snorts. "You usually say flesh robot. You must be serious this time."

She can almost rationalize why Jett and every other member of her society choose manupartners. The man who invented them, Res6, is a modern-day hero. The *flesh robots* provide an easy, no-strings-attached option for companionship. Eager to please and disposable. Sounds great, right? But something in her refuses to give in. It's what her ~~heart~~ brain wants. "I just can't stand it anymore."

"Think of it this way; they're like having a dog that you get to have sex with. You get companionship during the day and something to warm your bed at night." Jett smirks, seemingly amused at his cleverness.

K8 imagines the small furry animals that lived inside people's houses. She thinks of her own dog. How petting its soft fur has been such a comfort to her at low points over her life. But having sex with one . . . "That's disgusting. People didn't have sex with dogs."

Jett chuffs, breaking the seal on his box of noodles. "I know that. But you get my point."

"I think someone should start a dating service. Like a system where the algorithm suggests potential partners based on personality and similar interests. You can narrow down the pool of potential candidates based on—"

"Society has already tried and failed with those applications. Not to mention the Northern Hemisphere Organizational System's Community Protection Bans. I'm fairly certain dating platforms are on the list of prohibited online activities."

K8 huffs, flicking an irritating lock of hair over her shoulder. "But it might be different now. What if you could check boxes, like how you do when you order a manupartner, but instead of a flesh robot, it gives you options for real people? If I could get enough signatures, I could convince the NHOS Intra-society Network Monitoring Agency about the substantial benefits for the modern world."

"There's no way NHOS will make an exception. It's well documented that programs like that created the societal malaise that led to The Great Equalizer. The latest literature points to 'interested parties' conditioning society through various social platforms. People became apathetic."

The catastrophic event had ultimately benefited society. So what if it took hackers programming AI bots to wipe out the financial systems in a single night? They effectively did away with the "interested parties," a.k.a. the faceless entities ~~controlling~~ destroying the world.

"Look at how good things are now. These delectable and nutritious noodles are affordable to every citizen. Advancements in medical care mean that we can live several hundred years, maybe even more. Our choice of entertainment is at our fingertips. Want to go rafting down the river or lie on the beach at a luxury resort? Anyone can step into a simulation chamber and experience it—regardless of the pay bracket."

Jett shakes his head. "Wiping out all monetary records means good people lost everything, too. It sent the world into chaos. Food and supply systems failed, setting humanity back, by some estimates, nearly a hundred years. Maybe more."

"But that was about money and power," she argues. "Not about connection and, dare I say, love."

"It's a slippery slope."

She really should listen to Jett. As a chronologist, this is his field of expertise. "There are markets on the network for everything one might need. Why can't there be one for a real human partner? I could approach the Consumer Rights Protection Agency. Don't we have a right to such a service?"

Jett sighs. "You're just being stubborn now, K8. If they didn't work then, they certainly won't now. Think of everyone you know. Besides Oro1's misguided attachment to Purpl, what's the longest anyone's kept a manupartner?" When K8 doesn't speak, Jett answers his own question. "A year at best before they get bored and crave something new and exciting."

K8 picks up her spin-o-stick, poking the pronged end into the box and squeezing the handle of the device. The two metal forks at the end spin, gathering a delectable bite-sized wad of noodles, which she then stuffs into her mouth, moaning at the delicious spice.

She wants to tell Jett the reason they don't last is because the manupartners aren't real. How can you connect with something whose only purpose for existing is to please you? But they've been the standard since they came on the market almost a hundred years ago. Manupartners are easy. Safe. Disposable. If she lets the conversation continue, Jett will ask her how many people she knows in a human-human relationship. She'll say zero. Then he'll give her a smug smile, as if that somehow proves the point.

No. This time she isn't letting it go. She is tired of everyone telling her she's wrong. That her sense of things is off. She can't be the only one who feels this way. Jett, of all her FRIENDS, should be the most likely to understand. She only needs to try a different angle.

"Picture this, Jett. You could live here with me. We could wake up together. We'd drink our morning pick-me-UP nourishment packets together. After work, you could tell me about your day. Then at night—"

"Is this your way of propositioning me for sex, K8?"

K8 groans. "I'm trying to get you to do a thought experiment with me. I'm describing companionship." Even she isn't brave enough to speculate about *love*.

He gives her a quizzical look. "I don't get it. Everything you're describing you can get with a manupartner."

"But it's not the same. You argue with me. They only compliantly agree. Aim to please, and all that. Yansy is currently driving Lessa crazy. I bet they'll call any day needing me to go with them to the recycle station."

"So add contrary and argumentative to the list of traits. They'll program your GROW manupartner, then you'll have exactly what you're looking for. Besides, I didn't think we were each other's type." With his spin-o-stick, Jett points to her box of noodles. "They're going to get cold."

The distraction is good because the argument is moot. As a scientist, she can admit the technology is incredible. A little frightening, if K8 is being honest with herself. But she's never going to agree, and she's certainly never getting a manupartner. Not that she hasn't logged onto the website after one too many glasses of Vine and dreamily clicked a few boxes, imagining the perfect partner in a moment of weakness. Their marketing was that good. The point is, she's never followed through. Never once clicked Purchase. A point she prides herself on.

Right as she stuffs a bite into her mouth, the smartwaiter built into the exterior wall chimes. When did she order something? The only block of time she has trouble recalling is the few hours before she dozed off on her birthday. How many Spiral Apples did she have?

Shopping! That's it. She'd spent several hours spending her unicoin on whatever whim struck her fancy. Glorious. Satiating. Coin-dropping. What a delightful realization. If only she knew what she purchased.

Shoes! Hopefully, inebriated K8 bought the several pairs she's been eyeing. The pay bracket for being an air control officer pays her well enough; still, she rarely splurges. K8 reserves her few indulgences for her birthday and Holiday. Well, and when a new designer puts out something fabulous. And for her FRIENDS' birthdays, obviously. The scientist in her sees her inebriated shopping as an experiment of sorts. A way to discover her subconscious desires. This isn't her first experiment. A fact that makes her fairly certain she's purchased ~~a sex toy~~ shoes.

K8 doesn't give the lukewarm noodles another thought as she rushes over to the smartwaiter, pressing her palm to the lock pad. The chamber hisses, unsealing. Technically, she doesn't need more shoes, but that doesn't dull her excitement. What else would she have bought?

She lifts the lid, reaching inside the shadowed space, tugging two boxes toward her. She carries them over to the counter and unwraps the first one. *Well, this is no surprise.*

"A GROW manupartner would be far superior to this contraption," Jett says, coming up beside her and running fingers over the slick box.

Across the front in bold bubble letters is the word "PUSSYzapper3000." Next to the logo is a picture of a woman wearing an opaque virtual reality headset. Her head is cocked back, and she appears to be mid-gasp. The smaller text below reads "Download your FREE virtual catalogue now!"

Jett flips over the box as K8's face flames. "It looks like a sea creature. What were those flat ones with the wings called?"

K8 snorts. "A manta ray?"

"Yes!" he exclaims. "Looks like our K8 is going to have a good time tonight."

The sea creature–shaped sex toy came highly rated. Apparently, once strapped in place, different protrusions emerge from the flat surface, vibrating, nudging, and penetrating in response to the user's reaction, both physically and chemically, through highly sensitized detectors.

"Can we please talk about something else?" K8 snatches the box out of Jett's hands. "Let's open the other one. I'm sure it's shoes!"

She makes quick work of the packaging, but her heart catches in her throat as she sees the glossy black and green letters. "It can't be."

Jett makes an excited, strangled sound. "Oooohh! This is so much better than the first one. Happy birthday to you!"

If only she'd been alone when the delivery came. Then she could hide the box in her bedroom until she had time to return it. What is she thinking? The kits probably aren't returnable.

"I'm feeling a little weak." This can't be real. But the truth is in her trembling hands. All thoughts of collapsing societies and dating services flee from her mind.

The logo on the sleek black box is unmistakable. Grass-green block letters scream at her from the lid: "GROW!"

2 – A Sudden Break from Sanity

K8

To K8's horror, Jett takes the box from her, excitedly carrying it to her desk. "I think this is fantastic." Like a robot, she follows his bobbing blond head and stares blankly as he opens the box and pulls out the memory chip. "Let's see what Drunk K8 ordered."

He's enjoying this far too much. He waggles the chip in the air as if she might try to snatch it from him before plopping it down on the reader disk. ~~Because she's intensely curious~~ Knowing her resistance is futile, she watches her system scan his retinas. The light-bars spring to life as she peers over his shoulder. Then the blue scanner activates the moment it touches the surface, and K8 stifles a gasp. A database pops open on the main screen. Using his embedded m-volt synaptic transistor, Jett selects a file labeled "GROW Unit 3542-MSP-XXXXX-00023468 Three-dimensional Model." K8's stifled gasp escapes as the rendering appears.

"Zephyr, K8. He's very rugged. You must have been in quite a state when you ordered him." Jett must think the command Rotate, because the image of the manupartner spins slowly.

Nearly black hair that appears ridiculously soft. Dark lashes over closed eyes. The specification says she selected blue. It has full maroon lips, a day's worth of stubble, veins snaking up its toned forearms, and—those hands!

"Wow," she mutters.

"Do you think I could get my thighs to look like that?" Jett asks.

K8 glances down at Jett's legs, which are solid, wiry muscle, yet a bit on the slim side. "Probably. You aren't going to call me a hypocrite?" She braces for his reply.

He only gives her a sympathetic look. "I can't believe you finally clicked Purchase."

Maybe she didn't. She wouldn't put it past her FRIEND Lessa to press her thumb onto the signature pad on her behalf. "Let's look at the contract."

Jett opens the file and scrolls all the way to the bottom. There is the evidence. Her identification number in block letters forms a circle around her thumbprint, next to an image of her face, grinning for the retina scan. No Lessa in the background to pressure her.

"You're going to love him. Everyone's going to want to know how far back in the DNA samples you went to find this specimen. I'll have to get the year for when I replace Decci."

Jett's words barely register as K8's reality settles around her. "What do I do?"

"Oh, I forget you've never activated one. The instructions are simple. There." He points to the owner's manual file.

"No. I meant do you think I can return it? I certainly can't keep it. It's not like I have the unicoin to waste—Incredible Bill's new Inside for Winter collection will be out soon. There are several pieces I must have!" K8 swallows the anxious lump in her throat.

How does he not seem to notice the emotional crisis she's been thrust into? Imagine if she were to activate the thing? After holding out on her dream of real human companionship for all these years—what type of person would that make her? It seems all it took was one drunken night of desperation and she cracked. If there were only one person who wanted her . . . but in eighty-six years, there hasn't been anyone. Not for the first time, K8 works her way through the mental list of why this is the case. It always comes down to one thing: K8 must be unlovable. The GROW manupartner kit on her desk is the final, glaring proof.

Her jaw clenches. She is stronger than this. She can still find some-one. Tomorrow, she will take the kit to GROW and demand her money back. Blame it on their manipulative advertising or—well, she doesn't know, but she'll review the contract and think of something.

"I can see your wheels turning, K8. You are not returning this beau-tiful specimen. If I had more time, I'd stay and force you to begin the grow process right now, but I have a Cell Tech facial scheduled." Jett takes another moment to stare in awe at the ~~atrocity~~ manupartner she's purchased before heading for the door. Before it closes, he says, "I'm calling Lessa. They'll make you activate it. Don't have a meltdown!"

When the door clicks shut, she's left alone with a single awful thought: *What have I done?*

After an hour of ruminating, K8 meets Lessa and their manupartner, Yansy, who stand by the airlock elevator doors that will take them down to the B level SAT garages for Tower CA25. Thank Zorg no one else is waiting in line for the building's shared transports. The sooner this is over, the better.

When Lessa messaged, they didn't mention K8's misguided purchase, so when they asked her to accompany them to the GROW recycle station, K8 agreed. Better to keep busy. Knowing Lessa, they were probably so focused on recycling their manupartner, they didn't even read Jett's message announcing ~~her sudden break from sanity~~ her GROW purchase.

"Hi Yansy," K8 says, wondering if Lessa has told it where they're going. She knows Yansy will have no feelings about its fate. Still, she feels awkward riding with what appears to be a human to their ~~death~~ decommissioning.

Yansy gives her a lopsided smile. "Hi K8. I had a great time at your birthday last week." It turns to Lessa. "My, you look delicious."

Overeager indeed. A flaw in the design, she supposes. That is to be expected with some of the lesser quality manupartners, but not a GROW. But she's heard a rumor that the company has been tinkering with its processes, trying to get a more realistic, emotive product. An edge that would elevate them above their two biggest competitors, ManuMATE and CHOICElover. Perhaps this minor flaw is a side effect of that tinkering.

Lessa arches an eyebrow, giving K8 a *See what I mean* look. They obviously checked the friendly and agreeable boxes when they ordered it. Yansy doesn't register Lessa's irked expression, however. Each manupartner is a bit of an experiment. The consumer selects the general qualities, then hopes for the best.

The scientist in her wonders what the kit in her unit would produce. She can't believe the specimen she picked could act eager, but they say a manupartner's traits and build are completely distinct.

Yansy guides them into the airlock elevator. "Something the matter, my love? Are you unsettled about your decision to recycle me?"

K8 bristles. *No, K8. It's not a real person.* It is almost painful how often she has to remind herself of that.

"Of course not." Lessa notably looks anywhere but at their manu-partner.

K8 spots their half-lie, knowing the twenty percent of them still clinging to it will fade away in a few days' time.

"I only want you to be happy." Yansy stares dreamily down at Lessa.

"Yes, I'm quite aware of that," they say.

K8 doesn't speak, letting the soon-to-be not-couple have their moment. The airlock elevator they entered comes to a halt. Inside, green light bands running the circumference of the space at regular intervals from floor to ceiling alert them that the area is safe to enter. The pressure shifts, hissing, as the doors slide open. K8's ears pop as the carefully managed air depressurizes. As she steps into the SAT garage, the air between the four rough concrete walls feels perfectly still, like her favorite antigravity-antiaging chamber.

The next available Sealed Air Transport rests on a low platform in the center of the room. Like all SATs, its body is constructed from an acid-resistant black fluorocarbon. A thick band of purified aluminum makes a loop around the middle. Two matching stripes run the length of the underside. Environmental exposure etches the smooth met-al, creating little pits which must be filed down at regular intervals. Eventually, the entire magnetic strip becomes so thin it will no longer respond to the MagTrack lines. Then the old metal is stripped off to be reprocessed, and new ones are put in their place. Fortunately, this one appears to be in good shape. The older ones always make her nervous.

Above the aluminum band, safety lights encased in glass flash in the Ready-Welcome sequence. Yansy rushes around opening their doors before sliding into the back. K8 places her palm on the panel to activate the machine. It springs to life. The magnets produce a faint but high-pitched humming as it lifts off the ground. Whirling lights click on.

The system, in a perfectly human sounding voice, confirms, "Passenger C-K8lyn-MSP-00023468. Please register all passengers." Little screens with handprint outlines light up in front of Lessa and Yansy's seats. They comply, placing their palms on the scanners. A moment later, their NHOS identification numbers flash on the screen. K8 taps the screen to verify the information is correct.

"Input your destination," the system instructs.

K8 gives Lessa a sidelong glance before saying, "GROW Recycle Station. Tower MM10."

Lessa reaches over, squeezing K8's hand. Probably more for her benefit than Lessa's. After the SAT's display confirms its air seal has activated, the two metal doors of the garage wheeze, sliding open. Red lights illuminate the room as the sooty outside atmosphere whooshes into the chamber. Heavy brown particles mix with the purified breathable air. K8 studies the difference in consistency as the lighter wisps of clean air escape. Looks to be a bad air quality day. Worse than she predicted a week ago in her official ledger. That usually means two things. Fewer people will be out and about, and there will be more atmosphere-assisted suicides this week.

The SAT travels along a MagTrack line out of her tower, entering the flow of SATs zipping along carefully planned routes. They move up and down interchange paths to pick up different connections. Half an hour later, they've made it into the M Quadrant of Minneapolis–Saint Paul, or MSP. At the recycle station receiving garage, there are a dozen SATs in line.

Another half an hour passes before they make it to the front of the line. The garage doors open. The SAT inside zips out, turning in the opposite direction they came from. Through the thick glass, K8 sees a woman chatting animatedly with her passenger. Like always, the entire process strikes her as unfeeling, callous even. Unsettling to see someone moving on so flippantly from whatever this is. *Disposable.* As the word flashes through her mind, her chest tightens.

The attendant, wearing a full-environmental protection suit, stands inside the doors, waving a blinking wand to usher them inside. Once the SAT parks on the platform, the garage doors slide shut, sealing with a loud clack. The attendant steps into a smaller chamber as the air inside the garage rattles the SAT. After a few minutes, the red lights switch to green. The attendant exits the smaller room, approaching the SAT. Lessa steps out, already pulling their device from their bag.

K8 watches from beside the SAT as the attendant says, "Documentation," as a matter of greeting, holding out a tablet.

Lessa taps the screen a few times and both of the devices ping. The attendant reads over the information, then looks to the backseat of the SAT. With a hand, he waves Yansy out. Looking unfazed, Yansy strides around to stand beside Lessa.

"Hand, please." As the manupartner lifts its hand, the man pulls out a little cylindrical silver device from his pocket and presses it into Yansy's pointer finger. Then he lowers it over his pad, depressing the button on the top. A few drops of blood fall into the receptacle. Neon colored lights illuminate the tablet.

The attendant nods, approving of whatever the tablet shows. "Please sign here to confirm the identity of GROW Unit 2460-MSP-Yansy-00023287."

Without hesitation, Lessa presses their thumb into the pad, then uses their own stylus to scratch their NHOS identification number around it in a circle. "You understand this ends your contract on GROW Unit 2460-MSP-Yansy-00023287?"

K8 tunes out as Lessa completes the uncomfortable process. If she activates the kit in her room, this will be her in three months' time when her lease expires. Unless she can afford an extension, which is doubtful. No point in even thinking about it. The best plan is to return it. Even if they don't give her unicoin back, at least she won't be responsible for dropping one off for recycling.

Finally, Lessa turns without looking at Yansy and approaches the SAT. "Ready?"

K8 watches as the attendant leads Yansy through the airlock doors to the interior of the building. It never looks back. Neither does Lessa as they enter the SAT.

As they pull out of the garage, Lessa carries on about what a relief it is. A weight off their shoulders. Feels so much lighter. Etcetera.

"Want to get lunch? I know this great little place near here. And since we're in this area, we could hit a Regen Room. With the weather, I doubt we'd have to wait long. Did you hear they're putting in a juice bar in your tower?"

K8 makes eye contact with the passenger of the SAT waiting next in line outside the garage as they pass. She can't tear her gaze away, her neck twisting as she holds the woman's stare. Not ten minutes prior, she was in that woman's position, watching a pair exit the garage, chatting mindlessly as if nothing strange was occurring. What does the woman think of her now? Are her thoughts similar to K8's? And why is she reacting like this? It's not like this is the first time she's been in this very garage doing the very same thing with one of her FRIENDS.

What is it about this time that strikes her so differently? Because she's tired of being alone? Normally, that would be her determination. This time, however, her mind drifts to the temporary solution back in her unit waiting for her to GROW, then activate it.

"K8," Lessa says, getting her attention.

She shakes the swimming thoughts from her mind. "Sure, lunch. I need to pick up a few extra task orders after that, though."

Lessa huffs, slumping back into their seat. "Fine. I'm going to the Regen Room after." They flip their tablet into mirror mode, inspecting the nonexistent lines around their eyes. "I think I need a full refresh. Look at this . . . right here."

K8 leans over, trying to see whatever they're pointing to. "Lessa, I see nothing. Wait, I think that's a speck of dust." K8 brushes it away. "There. All better. You don't look a day over one hundred."

Lessa beams. Shining, unnaturally potent chartreuse eyes. Dewy, glowing skin, every flaw long since lasered off. Cheeks expertly plumped to the latest fashion. Perfect teeth gleaming within a perfectly altered smile. Not a single gunmetal strand of hair is out of place. "Thanks, K8. You're the best."

Is she, though? How can she be when all she can do is sit here and think, *Is any of this real?*

3 – Loneliness Ends Now

K8

September 28, 2390, Day 90.

K8 leans across GROW's customer service counter, locking eyes with the agent. "Your website claims, 'If you're not completely satisfied with your purchase—'"

The woman cuts in, repeating, "We would replace your unit for free."

"But I don't want another unit. As you can see, I haven't even activated this one," K8 patiently explains.

The agent pushes the GROW kit back across the counter. "Then how do you know you aren't satisfied?"

"Like I've repeatedly told you, I hate the very idea of a manupartner and I refuse to activate it." K8 turns her device toward the agent, whose dark eyes flash with irritation. "If you would just revisit point four." She gives the agent a moment to scan the text before continuing. "Is GROW no longer committed to the best manupartner experience for all their Valued Customers? How will the Consumer Rights Protection Agency feel about your false advertising?"

The agent releases an audible sigh. "How would this be considered false advertising?"

"I don't want a manupartner, and having this kit is making me miserable." K8 tries her best to keep from whining. "So," she continues in a calm, professional voice, "you might as well give me my unicoin back."

"We've reviewed our policy with you four times already, Valued Customer K8. Plus, each of the fifteen bullet points you emailed our team. Unfortunately, we are unable to issue you a refund at this time."

Heat crawls up her neck and she's sure her face is flushed. All this arguing . . . No wonder she avoids confrontation at all costs. This can't be good for her complexion. It seems there is only one way to solve this. "May I please speak with someone more interested in hearing my concerns?"

The agent grins. "Excuse me?"

K8 shifts uncomfortably. "Who do you report to?"

"You would like to speak with my manager?"

K8's voice is sheepish as she says, "Yes."

"Go wait in the lobby. And don't forget your GROW kit." The agent shakes her head as she walks away.

Shame heats K8's cheeks as she snatches her kit off the counter and makes her way to the lobby. *Zephyr, please don't let anyone I know be here*. She's sure she's never been so uncomfortable. If she tucks herself into the corner between the wall and a vending machine, hopefully no one will notice her.

This will all turn out fine. She will talk to the manager—*the horror*—and convince them to take the kit and refund her. Then this entire awful experience will be over and she can get on with her life. Maybe she'll even go out and try to meet someone. Take the refund and start a savings account. Well, nothing drastic. She'll invest in Incredible Bill's collection, then start saving.

K8's email alert pings, drawing her attention away from the momentary blip her last week has amounted to. She sets the GROW kit down at her feet, fishing out her device. The subject reads:

NHOS: Project: Loneliness Ends Now Annual Survey

Why NHOS sends out these mandatory surveys is beyond her. After the first ten years in her current FRIENDS group, she started copy/pasting the same saved answers. That the agency accepts them every year without question suggests no one evaluates the answers unless there's a glaring red flag. Still, she dutifully skims the body of the ~~welcome distraction~~ necessary email.

Good morning, Citizen C-K8lyn-MSP-00023468,

As a requirement of Project: Loneliness Ends Now (Project: LEN), the Northern Hemisphere Organizational System (NHOS) requires you to complete this year's annual survey for the following Project: LEN issued FRIENDS:

B-Lessa-MSP-00023287

B-Oro1-MSP-00022039

C-Jett-MSP-00022978.

As you complete the survey, remember your NHOS issued FRIENDS are a vital:

First Response to Isolation via Engagement with Networking as a Deterrent System.

Our research supports the many Citizen benefits of maintaining three FRIENDS, such as increased life expectancy (24.76% on average). Not only do FRIENDS help decrease loneliness, FRIENDS are an effective step in each Citizen's Fight Against Aging!

But for Project: LEN to work effectively as designed, all three FRIENDS must be performing optimally. Your answers below will not be shared with your FRIENDS, and if needed, we may issue new FRIENDS. Project: LEN is committed to the maximized happiness of each valued NHOS Citizen.

K8 rolls her eyes, wondering if any of the government employees working for Project: LEN believe the nonsense they're purporting. What would they do if she failed to check in for her group's weekly drinks appointment? Or worse, added a fifth member to the FRIENDS group, throwing off the optimal balance.

Not that she would do such a thing. She is rather fond of this group, which she's been a part of for almost forty years. Granted, most of their interactions revolve around superficial things, like MediSpa appointments and visiting new eateries. Yet she wouldn't trade them. After the first twenty years, she grew an affection for them. That's not to mention how awful her first three FRIENDS groups were.

In her last group, a woman named Ammee wore a salted palm nut perfume that was so strong, the pungent fruity scent made K8's mascara run. Then there was that person Billi who insisted at each meetup they play multi-level board games, which carried on until she felt as if she might publicly weep. Weeping would cause wrinkles, to say nothing of distress. Two things to be avoided at all costs.

Therefore, she had no trouble filling out the surveys those years until she finally landed in her current group. It's concerning to think that Lessa, Jett, or Oro1 might be unhappy with their FRIENDS group and respond to their surveys negatively. This prompts her to paste the same benign answers every year, hoping for their mirrored consistency. Her chest constricts as she selects the answer to the first question.

Q1: When is the last time your FRIENDS listened and showed genuine interest when you expressed yourself?

K8: *At my birthday dinner just last week, we discussed my deep-seated fear of sagging skin. They each listened with great empathy and understanding.*

Q2: How do your FRIENDS show you they appreciate you for who you really are?

K8: *By demonstrating interest in the things that are important to me, like my vital work as a particulate pollution scientist.*

Q3: Can you have meaningful conversations with your FRIENDS?

Yes and no. See, the truthful answer is only to a point.

K8: *Yes, of course. Recently, we discussed the merits of voluntary end-of-life procedures.*

They discussed the 301-year-old woman on K8's floor who opted for the SAY GOODBYE Peaceful Passing Procedure just last week. The focus of the conversation, however, was who she might gift her collection of multicolored light-up wigs to.

Of course, they've never discussed such sensitive topics as the societal impact or ethical considerations of the procedure. She might mention her and Jett's regular argument about manupartners, but at this point that would feel a little too hypocritical since there is one that she bought and paid for currently resting at her feet. Also, it might alert the people at Project: LEN that her FRIENDS did not fulfill every emotional need in her life and that might garner unwanted scrutiny. The last thing she needs is for them to replace her FRIENDS.

Q4: Do your FRIENDS meet your needs for companionship?

Now here is where it gets stickier. Her FRIENDS provide a certain amount of companionship. But—and this is a big but—they don't. It's oversimplifying this gnawing ache in her chest down to her government prescribed network as if she should be satisfied with *enough*. While she cares for them and she should be grateful for the NHOS initiative and the research that went into it, she wants something more.

Sure, she spends time with her FRIENDS, and often. It's ~~enough~~ great most of the time, but one of them usually has a manupartner in tow.

She glances up from her device to the rotating advertising banner on the opposite wall. It pauses on the GROW logo, which glows in the center of the particle pane. Beneath it is their customer promise: "Providing Customers Premium Companionship Since 2304."

Companionship. What utter nonsense. Instead of dwelling on the true answers to the remaining survey questions, K8 copy/pastes in the not-quite lies to questions four through ten before submitting the survey. She's sorting through her inbox when she hears his voice.

"Hello, lovely creature," he says, making the hairs on the back of her neck stand on end. Even though it's been over fifty years, she would know that tenor anywhere. It's the man whose name she never caught, but who rarely leaves her thoughts for more than a week or two.

She peeks out from her hiding spot, expecting to see the pale skin and copper hair imprinted in her memory. Instead, he's wearing it longer and blond, which doesn't complement his skin quite as favorably as the copper did. It also seems he's had the shape of his eyes altered. He's still attractive, but not as glaringly as she remembers.

She stuffs her phone into her bag and picks up the GROW kit in case she needs to suddenly flee.

"If you're between manupartners, might I offer myself to occupy your time?" He offers her a coy grin.

K8 blinks as she scans his uniform. "You work here?" she squeaks. *Zephyr, get it together, K8.* She never expected to run into him again. Especially after all those failed attempts at searching for him. She even went to the same club night after night following their encounter, hoping to see him. She never did. Now here he is, evidently working for GROW, and propositioning her like he did all those years ago.

"I do. In the advertising department," he proudly offers. If he only knew how vile she thought the flesh robots were, not to mention how ironic it was that he worked in the very department she blames for tricking her into ordering the kit she now clutches to her chest like a shield.

All she can do is stupidly say, "You've been here the whole time. In M Quadrant?"

"Do we know each other?" His eyes narrow.

She gasps as if struck. "Firelight?" she tries, thinking the nickname he gave her might jog his memory.

"Is that your name, lovely?"

"Zephyr, you really don't remember me."

He chuckles. "It seems I made quite the impression on you. What do you say we do it again?"

K8 grips the box for dear life as the memory of their encounter washes over her. She'd been in her late twenties and wearing a backless dress when she'd first heard his voice. A low, smooth tone whispered into her ear, "Hello, mythical creature. You've caught my eye, and I can't seem to look away."

K8 shivered as she felt the heat of his hand hovering against her exposed back. "May I?" he asked.

She said, "Yes," without even seeing his face.

"What's your name, Firelight?" he asked.

"Firelight?" she replied.

His fingers grazed her spine. "Your tattoo. They're dragon scales, right?"

As she turned into his arms, meeting his gaze, her heart lurched. He was beautiful. Lustrous copper hair, matching eyes ringed in violet, and smooth, pale skin that her fingers itched to touch. "K8," she said, a little afraid she'd fallen in lust at first sight. An unsettling proposition, considering how dangerous such strong feelings were. But the way he was looking at her . . . could he be feeling the same thing?

Her pulse skittered with excitement when he asked, "What can I do to set your world ablaze?"

He was stroking her back now, slipping inside the fabric of her dress. His tantalizing fingers teasing, leaving little sparks of anticipation for what was to come.

"A fantasy?" she yelped. Zephyr, what was this man doing to her? She needed to get it together. Think about it rationally.

"Tell me your deepest desire, Firelight," he urged.

What was her greatest fantasy?

"Tell me and let me give it to you. Anything you ask is yours." He leaned down to graze his lips against the shell of her ear.

What did she want? It struck her suddenly. "I want a boyfriend. A real human one like they had in the old days."

The man's posture stiffened for a moment, but then his body eased against her. "I think I understand what you're looking for. I'm glad we met because I want that, too."

From that moment on, her heart latched on to every word he spoke. She led him back to her unit, and all the while he said increasingly romantic things that filled her chest near to bursting.

When they were finally behind her closed door, she was aching with need.

The man took his jacket off, draping it across her desk chair. "So this is home," he said, and her stomach flipped. Noticing her reaction, he drew her into his arms. "It could be our home."

Her knees went weak. He chuckled as he caught her and carried her into the bedroom. He slowly undressed her, whispering about what a rare treasure she was and how he'd been so lucky to see her that night.

Then he crawled over her, never once breaking eye contact. When his fingertips brushed across her stomach, her chest squeezed in a way it never had before. "Maybe one day . . ."

Her pulse hummed. "Go on."

"Maybe one day, your belly will swell with my child," he finished.

She remembers whimpering, and he rewarded her by sliding inside. She doesn't remember much after that. Only that right as she was about to climax, he asked her to marry him. "I think I fell in love with you the moment our eyes met," he said.

Retrospectively, it was a ridiculous notion as marriages were no longer legal, but she said yes, then fell into unmatched bliss.

It was what came after that she remembers the most clearly. Within seconds of him rolling off her, he picked his trousers off the floor and slipped into the bathroom. He came out with a warm cloth, handing it to her. There was something off about his demeanor even before he said, "Will you need anything besides this before I go?"

She took the cloth with a trembling hand and said, "But I thought—"

"Listen, I have a manupartner kit at home halfway through its activation that I haven't watered since I left. You know how finicky those things are." He leaned forward, reaching toward her, but then he jerked his hand back and stuffed it in his pocket.

She stared at his tucked away hand, blinking. His initial reaction had seemed instinctive. Like reaching for her had been natural. They were engaged, after all. But for some reason he stopped himself.

She can see herself sitting on the bed, clutching the crumpled sheet to her chest as her heart caught in her throat. Almost feel her mind swimming as it did back then.

She opened her mouth to ask him how they might reconnect, but he said, "Enjoy the rest of your evening," before turning and leaving her speechless.

She thought since he knew where she lived, he would come to her, but he never did. So she searched until she felt vacant and exhausted. The day she realized her efforts were futile, she wept. Why had he forgotten her so easily? They had shared something, hadn't they? Sure, it started off as a fantasy, but it felt real.

Her flood of memories makes her clutch the GROW kit tighter, causing the box's hard edges to dig into her skin.

How could she have been so stupid to confess such a vulnerability as a desire for a real human boyfriend to a stranger? Back then, her embarrassment almost made her delete her Old News subscription, foolishly blaming her fondness of the old articles for her romantic notions.

A little chuckle escapes her as she stares at the attentively waiting man before her. His copper eyes glitter as he studies her like he did all those years ago.

"Something funny?" he asks.

"Yes, but you wouldn't understand."

It was never the Old News articles—her desires went much deeper than that. For her first twenty years, she watched her parents' dedication to each other. So unshakable that they held hands the day of their Peaceful Passing Procedure. They'd been 220, telling her they'd lived long enough. They came from a time when their life expectancy had already doubled. Her mother once told her they'd planned to do it a few years before she was born, but the morning of the appointment, they found out they won the birthing lotto. They continued living for a while longer to have her, postponing the procedure until after she was grown.

For that, K8 had been lucky. Living without them was difficult for the first few years, but their memory and the knowledge of their connection had helped ease some of the grief. But now she resented having to bear witness to such a pure connection because it only made what she'd never have so heartbreaking.

But it wasn't her parents' fault. Surely in eighty-six years she'd have found one person . . . Something was wrong with her. She was the one that didn't fit. The oddity, the outsider. As though her programming had glitched at birth, like a faulty, twitching manupartner.

K8 shakes her head, anchoring herself to the present. She can't let those thoughts seep in. Not in front of him. Not after how easily he forgot her. In all her life, she's never felt so insulted. All those years ago, he didn't want her. Made her feel like he chose her, only to have been faking it for a fantasy she was stupid enough to request. He offered her everything she wanted, just like she asked him to. But it was only a role—and like a helpless fool, she hoped it was real. Believed it. Tears would fall if she didn't get it together.

"Even if you activate your kit today, your manupartner won't be ready for a week. I'm free tonight," he presses, interrupting her thoughts.

If only she could be satisfied with one of the flesh robots like everyone else.

"What's your name?" she asks, because she needs to know.

His grin reappears. "Viper."

Viper, really? The man she's been pining for all these years is named Viper? Zorg, strike her down now. This situation can't possibly get any worse.

"Valued Customer K8, the manager is ready to see you," a voice calls over the intercom. K8 cringes, praying the shiny white tiles of the lobby floor will swallow her whole.

Viper's brows twitch like they're trying to lift in concern.

But when she sways, and he doesn't even reach out a hand, her humiliation dips to a new low. No wonder she is in her current predicament. Yet she refuses to cower in front of this man.

She marches away with her chin held high. Before she makes it to the counter, Viper calls, "About tonight?"

The arrogance. Without thinking, K8 spins, holding the manupartner kit between them and throws everything she's learned during years of Respectful and Considerate Conduct Courses in the recycle bin. "I would rather wait a lifetime for this manupartner to GROW than spend a single night with you."

Gasps come from the several bystanders waiting for their turn with customer service. Viper's mouth drops open, and she's fairly certain he doesn't know what he's done. That doesn't dampen her triumph as she turns toward the counter to find the original agent along with her manager, who is smiling pleasantly.

The manager says, "What excellent news to hear that you've reconsidered. We are pleased that you've decided to keep your GROW kit."

Her eyes widen as she realizes her mistake.

The first agent chuckles. "Bye now. Be sure to let us know if you need help with the activation process."

K8 makes her way home with the details of her failed mission clashing in her mind—her anger toward Viper seeming to win out every time. How dare he? She spent fifty years thinking about that night. About what she must have done wrong and why he left without ever giving it a second thought. How had it all seemed so real?

She determinedly unboxes the grow kit, positioning it in the center of the floor in her sparse spare bedroom. She'll activate the thing out of spite.

Oh Zorg, is she really doing this? She grits her teeth. She should behave like the rational scientist she is and make a pros and cons chart, but here she is. Not only is she doing it to erase the memory of Viper from her mind once and for all, it's time to see what the fuss is about. Why everyone is so crazy about these monstrosities. If that means she'll have to make a trip to the recycle center, so be it. In a way, it will be the walk of shame she's earned.

As she tosses her head back, lifting the slab of biological material to the glowing lights of her ceiling, it still feels like surrender. "You win!" she shouts to no one in particular.

She slams the flesh patty onto the center of the GROW Pad, then peels off the protective gloves and discards them in the pile with the rest of the packaging. Her hand trembles as she holds the bottle over the water slot. The instructions say a single drop will start the process. Then the light will turn green when it's full. When it turns red, an alarm will sound, and you repeat the process.

Before she can let her better sense talk her out of it, K8 tips the bottle and watches in a mixture of wonder and horror as a steady stream of water pours into the slot. When she finishes the entire bottle, she holds her breath. There's no going back now.

A few tenuous seconds later, the light turns green.

4 – He's Not Real

K8

October 5, 2390, Day 83.

After an arduous week spent pouring little bottles of water into the slot at regular intervals, K8 stands before her fully formed GROW a little dumbstruck. "Gorgeous," she mutters, walking a full circle around it. The *man*, with its chiseled muscles, hard jaw, days' worth of stubble, and smooth tan skin, does not compare to the 3D model.

K8 can't resist. Its fingers twitch as she runs her fingers across its palm, noting the calluses there. A shiver works its way down her spine in response. Positively rugged. Delectable.

In fact, her GROW might be so rugged that it'll draw unwanted attention. Jett has already messaged her three times that morning to see if he can swing by to see it. Perhaps this is a bad idea.

No. *Good idea. Remember?* She's gone through the same series of affirming thoughts a dozen times in the last forty-eight hours. It's like the advertisement states: "Companionship is at your fingertips. Time to take control of your destiny and get a manupartner today!"

That's what she's done. Bought herself companionship. Like a ~~desperate loser~~ normal person. She is, after all, a high-powered scientist. Nearly ninety. And deserving of whatever pleasure she can gain from this ~~strange experience~~ fully formed manupartner standing before her. She's convinced herself that after a week with it, her memory of Viper will be erased once and for all.

Maybe running into him and being forced to keep the manupartner means she's lucky. Reframing her circumstances is so much better for her self-care prerogative. Maybe that means she'll win the birthing lotto too. The old dream flashes through her mind as a series of snapshots. Getting the selection email. Choosing a donor—she'll only pick someone who wants involvement with her and the child. They'll get to know each other as the baby grows. They'll see how excellent she is at child-rearing—because she's naturally excellent at everything she puts her mind to. Then they'll be so impressed, they'll agree to be her companion. Maybe even move into her unit!

It's a silly dream. With the increased population restrictions, winning the lotto is highly unlikely. Nothing she should concern herself with. Especially not when she has a manupartner to activate. But since things are going her way, she might as well aim her wishes in that direction.

Holy Mother Zephyr, I'm ready for the companion of my dreams. After I turn this manupartner in, she clarifies.

She stands on the tips of her toes to get a closer look. Are those . . . *wrinkles?* Three fine lines run across the forehead. Her head cocks to the side. She hasn't seen anyone with a wrinkle since . . . since . . . well, she can't remember when or who it might have been.

Somehow, the lines and the slight curve at the bridge of its narrow nose make it more, not *less*, attractive. Not to mention its sizable asset. His. *His* sizable asset. She swallows the lump that's formed in her throat as she unabashedly stares at it. Delectable indeed.

K8 wipes the corner of her mouth. Before she starts touching things she really shouldn't—yet, anyway—K8 takes the towel from her shoulder and wraps it around *his* waist, tucking it so the muscles narrowing into a V peek out above the fabric. Once satisfied, she reaches down to place her fingertip on the final button on the GROW Pad. She takes a deep breath, pressing before she can hesitate. The pad beeps in the sequence she's read indicates that all has gone smoothly. As a series of white lights around the pad flash on and off, her stomach does a series of flips, seeming to coordinate with the pad's electrical current.

Her GROW takes a sharp inhale, almost making K8 jump out of her skin. How has she never invited herself to watch one of her FRIENDS' manupartners activate? Of course, she's seen the videos online, but seeing it in real life is something else. The GROW's breaths now come in a steady rhythm as the electrical connection between the brain and body is made. The manual says this will take about ten minutes.

Once the unit's eyes open, it will be ready to have a name programmed into the pad. Then one more button and it'll be released. Ready to get dressed, then go downstairs with her for their *meeting*.

After much deliberation, she selects the perfect location for it to happen: an eclectic teahouse called Bird Tea on the third floor of her building. She'll plant the unit at the standing table in the back beside a large cage that holds a pair of rare love birds. Then she'll slip up beside it. Perhaps say something about twittering. It'll fall helpless to her charms. They'll enjoy their tea before heading to her unit to test out that impressive *equipment*. Anticipation has her belly clenching with excitement despite any residual misgivings.

Then ... Well, then comes the *companionship* part. They'll get ready for bed. Tuck in side by side and discuss the latest Old News article she read before drifting off to sleep. In the morning, they'll go meet Jett and his manupartner, Decci, for breakfast. Lessa will show up ready to lament about missing Yansy until they see K8's manupartner. Then they'll be off to order one just like him, their status in pay bracket A allowing them to afford a regular premium manupartner. That and their willingness to wear last year's designs, something K8 could never do. After breakfast, maybe she'll take her manupartner to a simulation chamber. They can walk by the lake, holding hands. He'll ask about her FRIENDS and she'll tell him that even though they're not perfect, they're the best FRIENDS she's had.

The unit's fingers flex, drawing her attention from her fantasy. Those hands, those calluses, will roam over her skin in a matter of hours. Now, if she wants. A tantalizing thought. No, better to drag out the first time for at least an hour or two.

As she stands before ~~it~~ *him* in his fully formed state, she resolves to enjoy *him*. Admittedly, she's still working through the mental gymnastics required to swallow her hypocrisy. Think of it as a real man. Believing the fantasy shouldn't be too hard. It is a *he*. The GROW is a *him*. And if she's going to enjoy it, she had better start thinking of it—no, *HIM*— that way. Besides, she's already spent the unicoin.

As the timer counts down to six minutes remaining, K8 considers the options she selected. Assertive. Kind. Confident. Passionate. Open. Adventurous. Playful. Present. Devoted. Independent. Interesting. Unlike Lessa, and perhaps because she ordered the kit after she spent a night with them and Yansy, friendly and agreeable are not on the list.

An uncomfortable sensation washes over her. Like she is seeing something she shouldn't. Is it really appropriate for her to be standing here while he comes to life? Is that considered rude? K8 clamps her eyes shut. *He's not real. This thing doesn't give a care about what you do or don't do. Literally.* She can bring someone else to her bed without mentioning it and he won't blink. She can return it to the recycle station tomorrow. It doesn't matter.

Of course, she won't do that. The standard contract is for three months paid upfront, a substantial investment. Then the contract can be renewed on a monthly basis as required by the user. If you don't pay, they can come to repossess your unit. She's only ever heard of that happening once, though. Usually, you get a string of angry emails before they show up at your door.

When K8 opens her eyes, the darkest pair of slate irises stare back at her. They are supposed to be blue, but all she can say is, "Wow." It comes out as barely more than a breath. She'll take the deep color of his eyes as a happy accident. Two swimming pools, seemingly depthless, full of swirling emotion more intense than she ever expected from a manupartner. One could get lost in them for days and be glad for the escape. Maybe GROW's tinkering is working.

Jett might be right after all. This is exactly what K8 needs. Right as a grin is about to sprout, her manupartner's mouth opens.

A rough voice booms, "Where the fuck am I and who the fuck are you?"

K8 takes several wary steps backward. The fine hairs on the back of her neck stand upright with alarm.

Her unit tries to lunge forward, but the GROW Pad holds him in place. He won't have full motor control over his body until she programs a name and pushes the last button.

Suddenly, the swirling depths of his eyes take on an irate sheen. "Can you hear me? Or am I talking to myself?"

"I hear you." K8's unsure of how else to respond. Did she check the wrong box? She was quite drunk. Or should she have used more care selecting his traits? She doesn't think this is how the activation is supposed to go. Thank goodness he remains stuck to the pad.

"Then answer my questions. And why can't I move?" His voice comes out as a growl.

K8 scours her mind, trying to recall what he asked. And why is her heart beating so frantically? Fear? Exhilaration? "Calm down," she instructs them both, but he is practically vibrating with anger now. Her words only seem to heighten his agitation, so she quickly supplies, "I'm K8. You are in my unit. The spare bedroom. You can't move because I haven't programmed in your name."

There. Now he will be pleasant.

His eyes narrow. "If I tell you my name, you'll release me?"

K8's head tilts to the side in confusion. Hopefully, he isn't malfunctioning. Since GROW won't refund her unicoin, that would mean she'd have to go through this whole awkward process again—something she'd prefer to avoid at all costs.

"The pad will. Not me." She points to his feet, but it's of no use. He can't look down to see. "There's a pad that you're connected to at your feet. It's what is holding you, but once I name you and program it, then yes. It will release you."

She offers him a smile. Probably another side effect of GROW's tinkering. "Don't worry. I only need to think of a name." His brows furrow, the space between them creasing unnaturally. She taps a finger on her lips as she contemplates which name suits him. "What about Lucal? Or Bensy. No, that's too close to Yansy. Echo?"

Her eyes widen as she finds herself genuinely interested in his input. She can only guess at the analytical process Drunk K8 employed to select his traits. The scientist in her is more than curious about this experiment. Riveted. Now that she's committed to it, that is. And provided he isn't defective.

"Those names are idiotic. And I already have a name," he barks.

Oh my. What an odd development. He stares at her as if she is crazy.

Could playful possibly be interacting negatively with assertive? Or independent? Oh, maybe this is some sort of game for her benefit. Interesting. At least he has visibly relaxed and isn't twitching like Purpl. A little tension is probably a side effect of waking up that she missed in the literature. Well, her GROW is already poised to keep her on her toes. Somehow, she wouldn't expect it any other way. She only needs to change the lens. This will be fun!

She releases a breath, her smile returning. "Okay, then. Let's hear it." Maybe GROW has done it with this latest batch of programming. How exciting!

The GROW gives her a snide smile, then bites out, "My name is James Alexander Fletcher."

5 – J-A-M-E-S

James

"James Alexander Fletcher," she repeats, grinning up at James. "*How unusual*. I love it. Very creative, too, but your identification number only has room for five letters, so we'll go with James. J-A-M-E-S? Is that how you spell it?"

She kneels at his feet to do what? Program his name into some device?

Though he can't shift his neck, James scans the edge of his vision, assessing surroundings he doesn't recognize. Besides the top of the woman's head, all he can see is a door and three stark white walls. The still air is slightly warm, but uncomfortable. Nothing else that might suggest his location. After several moments racking his brain, he realizes he has no clue how he got here. He remembers being at dinner with someone—a client, maybe? Then the bar, but he didn't drive after. He has a vague image of his driver waiting outside and getting in the town car. They were heading somewhere—was she with him? She couldn't have been. He had a flight . . . so this woman must be a flight attendant. Finally, a break in his mental fog.

Dread, like a punch to the gut, sends him reeling. She drugged him! He's been abducted! He's being held for ransom. How much does she want? Why can't he remember her from the plane? She's uncommonly beautiful, if a bit odd. Surely he'd remember someone who looked like that.

He collects himself quickly. He shouldn't be too surprised. There are dozens of accounts of successful men being held for ransom—he feels almost proud to be counted amongst their ranks—though his mind is fuzzy about why. Or how he knows he's supposed to initiate an action plan as soon as possible. His urge to do so is almost robotic. Once he can move, he'll find a phone, assuming he can't find his cell.

A trickle of sweat runs down his side. The room is becoming warmer.

Focus.

He is supposed to call—numbers flash across his mind. At first he thinks they are his number, but then a name pops into his head: Worldwide Rescue Services. How prudent of him. If only he could shake the clouds from his mind.

Why does he know this? It feels important.

The air conditioner kicks on, sending a gust of cool air nipping over James's bare chest. Bare. As in naked. Not only locked up in this odd woman's barren room, he's naked. Is this some sort of sex thing? "Yes, that's how you spell it," he finally answers her. "Where are my clothes?"

"I wrapped a towel around your waist," she says, like it isn't a viola-tion that she's undressed him. "You can get dressed once we finish your programming. Then I was thinking we could arrange a chance meeting at the teahouse downstairs." The woman, *Kate*, seems more settled than she did moments earlier as she fidgets with the device. "I would like this to feel as realistic as possible. I never wanted a manupartner, but either way, you're here, so I might as well use you. I probably should have had Lessa activate you and arrange our meeting, but too late for that now. We can pretend!" Her voice is unnaturally chipper.

How is she so nonchalant, and what about the threats? Isn't she supposed to be demanding money? And what's a *manupartner*?

He is about to snap at her when white-hot pain flashes across his feet. An undignified sound hurtles from his throat. Able to move his limbs, he high-steps across the room as if he is dancing across coals.

"Did that hurt?" Kate's dark eyes fill with concern, like she's surprised.

He lands on the one piece of furniture in the room, a small bed draped with a light gray blanket. No pillows. No side tables. The firm mattress creaks as he adjusts his position so he's sitting perched at the foot of the bed next to a small package of what he hopes is his clothing. He crosses one leg over the other and angles his foot to inspect the sole. There's a mark tattooed in red ink, similar to a QR code but with characters he doesn't recognize. His feet no longer hurt, so he runs his fingers over the ink to see if the odd brand has any texture. The skin appears to be perfectly healed and smooth. An identical mark is on the opposite foot.

"Yes, it fucking hurt," he barks. "What are these marks?" Though the pain has evaporated completely, his irritation lingers. He holds it in. Most of it, anyway. He needs to see how much information he can get from the woman who's holding him hostage and has branded him before he tries to get away. Surely he can overpower her, but who knows what lies beyond the door.

Kate gives the little square scale-looking thing he was standing on a quizzical look. "The shock must have come from the disconnection to the electrical charge. Now that your body is performing its own electrical functions, you no longer need it. The tagging laser shouldn't have caused you pain."

The woman gave him a minor electrical shock? A submission tactic? She makes quite the actress, standing there with her pouty lips turned down and her large, sparkling brown eyes blinking innocently at him.

He's aware he's gawking. The way her black bodysuit highlights every sumptuous curve—those fucking tits alone. They are too perfect to be her originals, but . . . they look *real*. The material looks like it's sprayed onto her. He can't even detect a seam. If this is a sex thing, there would be no reason to drug him. Too bad she's abducted him. And is, apparently, a sadist.

Kate gives him a lazy smile, as if she's noticed him studying her and knows she's pleasing to the eye.

"Listen, lady," he says. "I don't know what game you're playing at, with your sexy cat suit, those ridiculous boots, and the little insignia on your chest like you're some sort of Avenger. What does that say?"

She takes a few steps closer, leaning forward so her chest is eye level. " 'Sector C Air Control Officer.' I worked this morning. Didn't have time to change before your alarm sounded."

"Air control?" He was right. She works for the private jet share company—though that is a fancy name for a flight attendant.

"Mmm . . . yes. A very important job. It puts me in pay bracket C. That's how I can afford this place. And you." She winks as she boasts, as if what she's saying means anything to him. "You should get dressed. I'll do the same. Then we can head downstairs and I'll tell you whatever you want to know."

Downstairs, possibly with other people. Who else is involved? He hears nothing from the room beyond. His focus turns back to her. He's got to get out of here and back to his life—whatever that entails. Somehow, the urgency he feels makes him think it must have been important. *He* must be someone important. Why else would he have had the number for a global rescue service memorized—practically embedded into his subconscious—if he hadn't thought he'd need it one day?

James watches her slip out of the room, seeming pleased with herself. Her long auburn hair swishes behind her as she leaves.

Wait. She thinks her pay bracket afforded him? She already said she plans to use him . . . how precisely does she intend to use him? A chill that feels a lot like intuition dances across his skin.

No reason to panic. Things could be worse. He could still be immobile. Someone could be pointing a gun at his head, making an astronomical demand.

James takes a calming breath and grabs the package, tearing open the closure. Not a zipper, more like a smooth magnet? Inside, he finds a fitted pair of pants—uncomfortably, revealingly fitted—and an asymmetrically cut knit shirt. Both are a deep navy with a subtle sheen to them. No boxers, or even briefs. Not that they'd fit under the second skin he's squeezed himself into. At least he isn't naked.

He scans the room for footwear, eyes catching on a pair of military-style boots that would rise to mid-calf. No socks either. He sighs as he struggles to figure out the clasps, eventually discovering the gunmetal buckles are only decorative. Giving the shaft a tug, like the package, a practically invisible seam opens down the center. A smooth sock-like material meets his bare foot as he slides it inside. As he does, the boot seals itself over his ankle, cinching to match its circumference perfectly.

They are a strange style. One he'd never wear. Like something from a costume shop selected to match the weird outfit the woman wears. But they're his only option and seem sturdy enough. He shakes his head as he tugs the other one on before rising to his feet, finding the odd boots surprisingly comfortable.

He approaches the door, which doesn't have a handle. He runs his fingers along the gap between it and the wall until the door clicks, then swings open to reveal a minimalist apartment. The stark concrete walls and floor lend it an eerie, sterile feel. The solid material of the ceiling glows, brightly illuminating the space. Yet the light is soft enough to stare at without irritating his eyes. An elaborate computer desk sits in the center. Or at least what looks like a computer out of some futuristic movie. The giveaway is the keyboard stationed between the six of what must be screens. Except they are metal bars suspended on stands, each emitting a field of black light, shooting upward into paper-thin rectangles. He assumes that means they are asleep. Other gadgets James can't identify litter the desk.

Across the room, an L-shaped couch wraps around the corner of the room. Conveniently placed tables sit around it, along with a few footstools. An embarrassing gasp escapes his throat as his eyes land on the windows. Though Kate mentioned she worked all day, it still appears to be light outside. Wherever this apartment of hers is, a deep, dense green forest surrounds it. Pine and fir trees fill two of the three windows. Outside the third, a rugged peak climbs to the sky in the distance.

"Beautiful, isn't it?" she muses, her soft voice drifting toward him from behind.

James staggers back. Where this could be? Canada? Russia, depending on how long he was out. Where has she taken him? And why haven't his memories come back yet? His head feels clearer by the minute.

"I know. This is one of my favorites. I'm glad you like it too." She stares dreamily at the scene in the window. "Tomorrow we'll try a different scene."

"You mean go somewhere else? Do you have a private plane too, Air Control Officer Kate?" He means it sarcastically, but she doesn't seem to take it that way.

"No, silly. They're particle panes, though I'm surprised you don't know this. The literature says you're supposed to come equipped with a certain base knowledge of the world."

It takes no slight effort to tear his eyes away from the scene in the windows. Escaping this woman is becoming more daunting with each passing minute. "Jesus!" His eyes land on the pale pink floor-length gown she wears. A completely sheer gauzy material drapes across her languid curves. Her barely concealed, dusky pink nipples beg for his attention. Against his better judgment, he obliges, fixing his gaze to her perky breasts. He tries to tear it away. He really does. Once he notices her strange tattoo, it's easier. Iridescent pink and red scales that complement her auburn hair peek out over her shoulders and sides.

Seeing where his eyes have traveled, she spins, lifting her hair so he can take in the artwork adorning her body. "Dragon scales," she offers. "To honor my ancestry."

The tattoo runs from the top of her spine to its base, with only wisps reaching toward her front. Otherwise, her body is perfectly unmarred. A delicate thong and an equally delicate pair of high-heeled sandals are the only other clothing she wears. James tries, but he can't spot a single imperfection as she turns toward him.

"This is too fucking surreal," he mutters.

"I'm pleased to see the clothes I got for you fit. Tomorrow we can go shopping for some additional pieces." She runs a hand possessively down his chest. "I want you to be as comfortable as possible."

If she wanted him to be comfortable, then she'd have provided him with a suit, like he's used to wearing. The thought triggers a memory of him standing at the head of a table in a boardroom. He's saying something about combating rising operating expenses on a portfolio of multifamily assets. On the wall opposite him there's a logo for a company called Tiger Capital. Does this mean he was a businessman—a developer? The group in the room nod eagerly, as if they agree with his strategy.

"Ready?" she asks, interrupting his memory. She walks toward the door as if she expects him to readily comply.

Letting her take him out of her apartment is a gamble. He might get the chance to run, which would put him closer to finding a phone since he can't see anything that resembles a telecommunications device in her apartment, but she might have armed guards right outside the door. Better to stall and try to get more information. "But . . . you can't go out in that. I can see your . . ." He waves his hands in the general direction of her chest.

She hesitates for a moment, seeming unsure, before smiling coyly. "I'm pleased you like them. You can touch if you like. That *is* why I bought you."

Before he knows what is happening, her hand wraps around his and she's lifting it to her chest. James jerks his hand away so fast, the woman startles, stepping back. "You bought me to touch your—breasts?" He covers his face, massaging his eyelids. "This can't be happening."

"You don't wish to touch me?" Her eyes widen.

"No, I don't wish to touch you." That isn't entirely true. Her breasts are very nice, and he is typically down for a casual fuck. Well, he was before he turned thirty-five and decided to stop fooling around so he could find a wife. For her, however, he might have bent that rule. But no, this is against his will. A slimy sensation slithers down his spine, eliciting a shiver. Suddenly, he's a little more defensive of women everywhere. But surely he's never been the type of sick fuck to cause a woman a sensation like that.

The revelation causes him to grimace, an expression he directs at his captor. "Someone abducted me, brought me to this strange place," he points to the window, "and sold me to you. I only have vague memories of who I am, which tells me whatever they drugged me with is still in my system. What do you want from me?"

"I . . ." she hesitates, cocking her head to the side. "I don't know what you mean. Is this some sort of game?"

"I've been in your *unit* for half an hour. I have no recollection of how I got here. I'm wearing this strange outfit. You've offered to let me fondle you. And now you want to go to dinner to role-play or something and do all of this in the middle of goddamned nowhere! What do you want from me?!" Losing his temper like this is uncharacteristic of him, but his patience is dwindling.

She lifts her hand and covers her open mouth. Her eyes shift from bright and interested to glassy in the span of a few words. "I want . . ." She hesitates as she steps back. Tension hangs in the space between them as he waits for her to reply. Instead of finishing her sentence, her stare takes on a faraway quality, like she's lost in some internal world.

"Listen. I don't mean to upset you," he says, placating her as alarm bells sound in his mind. Something about this feels off. Very off. Disturbingly off. It feels almost like a negotiation, and he understands he needs to coax this woman into telling him what she knows, then figure out how to get to a phone. "Please, just tell me how I came to be here. I can assure you that however it happened, I wasn't a willing participant." She doesn't speak, so James presses. "Are there more people outside this door?"

She glances at the door opposite the windows, which he assumes leads to a hallway outside her apartment. Her voice is thin with fatigue as she says, "Of course there are more people out there. It's Minneapolis–Saint Paul. There are people everywhere."

He's fairly sure there aren't any evergreen forests anywhere near the Twin Cities. She's lying. He tries another angle. "Who sold me to you?"

At this, a single tear rolls down her cheek. "The people at GROW, obviously. I knew this was a bad idea." As she shakes her head, disappointment rolls off her in waves. Acquiring abducted people usually is a poor life choice, so he doesn't feel *too* bad. She mutters under her breath something that sounds like, "Probably should have read the fine print."

A second later, she's seated at her desk and has two of the six screens illuminated. Her fingers fly over the keyboard as she intently reads the screen. Five minutes pass by in silence before his frustration gets the better of him.

Noticing her chair is on rollers, he hooks his hand over the back of it, tugging her backward, intending to make her face him, but something on the screen catches his eye.

Loneliness got you down? Struggling to find real connection in the modern age? GROW your own manupartner today! Love has never been easier.

Manupartner. There's that word again. James jerks his chin in the screen's direction. "What the fuck is that?"

"You say that word a lot," she observes, frowning.

"I'm very fucking frustrated and more than a little confused." Not to mention a little frightened—not that he would share that. "You would be too if you were abducted and thrown into this weird parallel universe with a disturbingly hot yet clueless chick who refuses to give you any answers. Who acts as if they're the only one being slighted here. Didn't get what you bargained for? Well, I certainly—"

She lifts a single digit, silencing him. "Let me think." Her eyes go distant again.

Fine. He'll think, too. *Manupartner.* Does that mean what he thinks it does? Somehow that little scale thing he was standing on, which electrocuted him, should have brainwashed him into becoming some sort of lover for this woman? And now she's upset that it hasn't worked?

Another five minutes pass before she rises from her seat. Kicking off her heels, she pads to an adjacent room. James follows her into a small kitchen. She reaches inside an odd-looking refrigerator and pulls out a dark glass bottle. She twists the cap off and tosses it into a waste bin, then takes several large gulps and offers it to him. "Don't worry. The bottles are sterilized then refilled. Vine?"

Why would he care if she recycles? When he doesn't immediately take the bottle from her, she opens a cabinet and fishes out two glasses. After pouring them each a healthy serving, she sets his glass on the counter before him. She returns to the living area, unceremoniously dropping onto the couch, breasts still on full display. Reluctantly, he picks up the glass and follows, taking a seat opposite her, because at this point, he has more questions than answers.

Kate breaks the silence, saying, "There's something wrong with you. They've been tinkering with the process, but you seem to be an unintended result."

Repressing an indignant huff takes considerable restraint. As if he is the one with something wrong with him. He sucks a breath in through his nose, releasing it slowly. *Play the long game. You don't know what is waiting outside for you.*

He should take a sip, but he's wary of the deep red liquid. She seems willing to talk now. He can coax out a little more information. Maybe with another glass of—what'd she say, *Vine?*—she'll be more pliable. "An unintended result of what?"

"The tinkering," she says, as if James is the idiot. She takes a sip as he watches her intently. "It's not poisoned, if that's what you're thinking."

"Clearly, I was drugged, considering I don't know how I got here."

She rolls her eyes. "No one drugged you." As if to make her point, she reaches forward—never mind the view it gives him—and takes his glass. She takes a demonstrative sip, swallowing the liquid before placing the glass back before him. When she leans back, her shoulders hunch. It is clear she's just as exasperated as he is.

It's his turn to frown as he picks up his probably-not-drugged Vine. Like her, he could use a drink. Just a little something to take the edge off. The thick red liquid goes down with a burn. James has to unscrew his face from the pinch the tart drink creates. "Please elaborate on the tinkering."

"You think someone's abducted you. You think you have a name already. There's something wrong with your nose. And you have wrinkles. And you're talking back. And you don't want to touch my breasts. Shall I go on?" She lets out something between a gasp and a sob as if this is all her bad luck.

"I broke my nose boxing when I was seventeen. As far as the wrinkles go, that's what happens when you're in your mid-thirties, sweetheart." She scoffs at this, but he continues. "I'm talking back because that's my prerogative, and my parents gave me the only name I've ever had. I already addressed the abduction. Shall *I* go on?"

A sheepish grin lights up her pretty features. "You didn't address my breasts."

"While your breasts look very touchable, I'm not going to because this is insane. Furthermore, I would appreciate it if you would go put on some appropriate clothing."

Kate's eyes narrow as if she's picked up something from their exchange that she can use for leverage. James almost releases an audible groan as she says, "No. I don't think I will."

He sighs, refusing to take another glance at them, no matter how tempting. "Very well."

She takes another sip, emptying her glass. "I have a hypothesis."

"Enlighten me." He shakes his head, wondering if he'd be better off running for the door now that she's relaxed than listening to whatever her hypothesis is.

"See, I'm a scientist."

He almost chokes on his Vine. An air control officer is a scientist? So not a flight attendant. It's enough to convince him he's in an alternate reality. Or a dream. No, this feels too real. He eyes the door, inching forward in his seat. Hoping she won't notice. Being a scientist means she's probably smart and calculating. Unless she's lying about being a scientist.

Kate continues. "To prove theories, scientists ask questions. So, if you'll allow, I'm going to ask you a series of questions."

James takes a deep breath, nodding. Okay, this is a path forward, and he doesn't feel like he is in immediate danger. Sure, he can try to flee from this apartment, but how far will he get? Will anyone outside speak English or come to his aid? That can be Plan B if the next thing that comes out of her mouth is utter nonsense.

"Go on," he instructs her.

"What year is it?"

He blinks. "Twenty thirty-five."

She nods. "Where do you live?"

"New York City." She's hitting him with straightforward questions to test his sanity. Good so far. He takes a sip of the red liquid that is growing on him with each taste.

"How did you die?"

He spits the Vine across the room. "What did you say?"

Kate repeats the question as if it's innocuous. "How did you die?"

6 – A Disturbing Turn of Events

James

The question is so startling, it cuts short all thoughts of running out the door. James holds out his arms, showing her his living, breathing flesh. "I guess I don't understand the question."

A pitying expression weighs down Kate's bright features. "James, the year is twenty-three ninety. New York City is underwater. You're not the James Alexander Fletcher you used to be." She pauses, jumping up mid-thought, rushing to the room he awoke in. When she comes back, she has an empty box in her hands.

James recognizes the logo from the website she visited earlier. And there's that word again: manupartner.

"A week ago, you were nothing more than a DNA sample attached to a GROW Pad," she says.

The information whirls through his mind. She's implying that he was in a petri dish? And in one week he became him—a fully formed human? Like a clone? Not only is what she is saying impossible, it's implausible. He can imagine a future world with advanced medical technology, but what she's describing can't be real.

He must look incredulous because she braces herself, like she's preparing for something.

"Manupartners—flesh robots, as I call them—are biological products genetically programmed to grow into an adult human body. While they come from human genetic material, as in people who actually existed once upon a time, they aren't those people. They have no memories, no hopes, no dreams. They are programmed to be shells, ready for their owner and the production lab to imprint whoever they want them to be onto them."

"No fucking way." He scratches his head as if it will keep his mind from imploding.

"It gets worse. All the consumer has to do is check a series of boxes representing traits, and voilà! Their GROW Your Own Boyfriend or Girlfriend Kit will arrive to their delivery box ready to morph from a small sample of organic material into a fully formed human, capable of eating, drinking, laughing, and, of course . . ." She hesitates, glancing around like she might find the correct word sticking to a wall or drifting past the window.

Understanding, and unwilling to use a more comfortable euphemism, he fills in the word for her. "Fucking."

"Right," she agrees, biting her bottom lip.

At least he was right about one thing. But if what she's telling him is true—if he is one of these clone things—then how does he have his memories? Or some of them at least. If she's suggesting he's a manupartner, could that explain the incomplete picture he has of himself? Suddenly, his body feels as if someone's dipped him in an ice bath.

He shivers as an image of himself at sixteen, submerged in a metal tub surrounded by floating chunks of ice, pops into his head. He latches on to the memory, trying to unfurl as much of it as his mind will allow.

A man looms over him. The name Jimmy feels right. James had gone behind his parents' back and hired a boxing coach. They'd forbidden it when he expressed his interest, saying boys like him didn't take up sports like that. Why couldn't he choose something dignified like polo or golf? But Jimmy's voice sounds in his head, overriding his parents. *If you're determined to get that silver spoon out of your mouth, it's going to require a few scars, son.* He'd been taking secret boxing lessons for years at that point.

"You're having a memory," Kate astutely observes.

"I used to box," he says, diving deeper into the memory. The first day he'd approached Jimmy at the old club on the North Side, the coach rejected him outright. *No trust fund kids in my club.*

"My father's expectations made me want to punch things, so I went to a club to take lessons. My parents forbade it, and even my coach, Jimmy, turned me away at first. I figured out he was testing me, trying to see what I was made of. It worked, and I showed up every day for two weeks, giving him new reasons to accept me." He chuckles, running his hand through his hair. "I have no idea why I'm telling you this."

"Did Jimmy finally accept you?" She leans forward like she's truly interested.

"Yes." He hopes his one-word answer conveys that he has no desire to share anything with this woman.

Still, the memory continues to unfurl. Every day he would crawl into the town car, defeated. Eventually, his driver knew where James would ask to go after school before he'd even asked. Then finally, one day, Jimmy gave in. James remembers exactly what his argument to Jimmy had been that day as clear as if he said it yesterday: *I want to feel like I can become somebody on my own.*

It's ironic, considering that he's sitting in a strange woman's apartment, stripped of his autonomy. Momentarily powerless, but not for long. If boxing gave him one thing, it was the confidence to meet challenges head-on. An abduction is no different.

Beside him, the couch shifts. When did she move so close?

"I'm sorry. I know this must be difficult." She places a hand upon his, but he jerks back, jumping to his feet.

James bites down on his knuckle. "I don't understand. You're lying." He throws the accusation at her as he stares at the GROW box as if he could contract something from it, like ringworm or whooping cough.

Kate reaches behind the couch to the window ledge, picking up a remote. A moment later, the windows flicker. Flicker! Then, from the top down, the image dissolves. Outside, not forty feet away, another building stands. A bland, filthy-looking structure. "God," he shouts, jumping back, nearly colliding with the computer desk as a car-like thing zips by at breakneck speed.

"That's a SAT. It stands for Sealed Air Transport. We have more impressive technology now, but the SATs are the most pollution-efficient mode of transportation. Plus, they require very little maintenance once in operation because of the alloys available now."

Three more zip by in quick succession. He approaches the window and braves a glance down, unable to see the street below. "How high are we?"

"Floor one hundred and sixty-three. This tower goes to two hundred. Most of the ones in C Quadrant do."

"I see." Outside the window, across the open expanse, the SATs slow to move up and down along a track. Kate's warmth slides up beside him.

"That's the MagTrack interchange. During your time you would have had the Maglev in China, I think. Did you ever ride it?"

James clears his throat. "No."

A dazed sensation settles over him. He mindlessly wanders to the computer. Seats himself. Points to the screens and the little keyboard-shaped block, which seems to be stuck mid-flip between two sets of alphabet characters.

"Three-way-keyboard, or 3key," Kate explains. "It has three sets of characters to choose from: the standard Hanzi characters, the Latin alphabet, and one of digital symbols like emojis, but more sophisticated." She reaches forward, forcing the mechanism to settle on the Latin alphabet. "What did you want to look up?" She asks the question gingerly, like he's a fucking child.

But she's right to be cautious. Saying the words makes James's stomach swirl. There is no helping it. "If what you're saying is true, there must be a death record."

Kate crosses her arms, face pinching in concentration. "I don't remember how far back the digital records go. But, I think so. Yes. Sometime in the early 2000s, they digitized everything. It might take some digging, but we should be able to find something. If not a medical record, the news subscription papers you had?"

"The obituaries," he suggests.

Her face brightens. "Yes. Those. I keep an account because I'm fond of reading about the past through the editorial section." Her chest brushes against his shoulder as she leans over him to activate the screens. She nods to the network portal on the center screen, where an article from January 15, 2028 is open:

> Dating coaches recommend women fulfill more traditional gender roles to attract a partner.

"Regressive, right?" A moment later, she opens an app called Old News, which appears to be the database she referred to, and the cursor is flashing in the search bar. "When did you say you were born?"

"Two thousand."

Without confirming, she types "James Alexander Fletcher dies death obituary, New York City 2000 2035" into the search.

The screens flash as results populate.

Headlines. Dozens of them.

Infamous vulture capitalist James Fletcher's plane falls short in landing attempt.

Plane crash kills six, among them up-and-coming equity broker James Fletcher.

Entrepreneur James Fletcher lands in hospital after biggest deal of his career.

Fletcher, James Alexander dies at thirty-five.

Fletcher's friends and family mourn.

James Fletcher pulled from plane's fiery remains. Dead hours later.

Entrepreneur James Fletcher donates remains to science.

Fletcher's big bet pays off.

Fletcher poised to join the Forbes Real-Time Billionaires list.

Fletcher's untimely death instigates federal investigation.

With each headline, James becomes greener and greener. He places his clammy palms flat on the cool desk as if it might steady him. It doesn't. "Make it stop," he pleads. By the time Kate shuts down the screens, he is certain his flesh resembles a stagnant, algae-ridden pond.

He died. *Died.*

Bile swirls in his stomach, bubbling up to sting the base of his throat. "You've got to be fucking kidding me." What type of sick joke is this?

He pushes past Kate, racing for the kitchen. The few sips of Vine he drank come up, coating the sink.

She rushes up behind him. "Oh dear. I suppose I should have fed you before the Vine."

Another dry heave. Another wave of violence. James can't remember the last time he cried. A surge of emotion he is wholly unprepared for gushes to the surface. A tearless sob wrenches itself free. Another. And another until his fingers come away wet as he brushes them across his cheeks.

No. NO! This isn't happening. It can't be. He refuses to accept this reality.

He stands, gripping the sink, gasping for an indeterminate time. Hyperventilating, really. Then he gathers his senses, stepping away from the counter. Kate hovers near, quietly observing his meltdown. His implosion. He died almost four hundred years ago, if the woman beside him is to be believed. On the cusp of something he could no longer conceptualize. Success. Wild success. *Billionaire*, the headlines read.

Suddenly, he remembers exactly who he is. He's the founder, president, and CEO of Tiger Capital, an up-and-coming private equity brokerage in Manhattan. *Not anymore*, a disembodied voice says. He looks around for who it came from, only to find the 3key seeming to chuckle at him. *You're in the future and you're losing your mind*, it says. *Where did all that money go?*

He blinks, considering the question. If he's truly in the future, does his money even exist anymore? If he had ancestors, maybe they'd have it, but he never had kids, much less a wife. Some people who were born to privilege dedicated their life to building family legacy, philanthropy, or a hobby like alpine exploring. But he'd been so focused on amassing as much wealth as possible. No matter what he had to do to get there. His drive had been singular: make it on his own.

There'd been a moment at thirteen when the idea crystallized for him. He hadn't quite grown into his looks, but that hadn't stopped him from asking Amelia Beckett to the annual Dwight Spirit Day carnival. Amelia had bouncy blonde hair and the prettiest smile of all the girls in his grade. He might have been intimidated, but he was a Fletcher, and that gave him an innate confidence. So he asked, and she said yes. But when he showed up with her, the boys, who he now understood to be jealous, were relentless in their teasing.

Imagine asking an innocent thirteen-year-old girl how much she got paid to go out with him. His classmates were ruthless when they wanted to be. As if his overly proud father would have agreed to bankroll such a thing. Plus, their accusation was hypocritical, considering all their parents shelled out ridiculous funds for the prep school, too. Admittedly, his family was elite among the elite. But teenage boys didn't consider those things, and Amelia, embarrassed by all the negative attention, never spoke to him again.

Over the years, he was met with the same brand of scrutiny until he resolved that he wouldn't rely on his trust fund. It's what drove him into the boxing gym that day. He channeled that adversity into a determination to prove himself, and never looked back.

They say the first billion is the hardest—he can attest to that because he finally crossed that threshold. From there, the possibilities were limitless.

Kate rubs a soothing hand across his back. A normal person would think of their parents. Grieve for them. James imagines much of his father's disappointment would be about the abrupt end to his legacy. His chest tightens at the thought, but the memories keep hitting him one after the other. His now dead Irish Setter, Barney. His billion-dollar net worth. The handful of acquaintances he kept. All that success. The woman, Blythe, he took out a few times. The opportunities his death cost him.

You could try and do it again, the 3key suggests. *That would really prove something.*

The idea sparks something deep inside him. He'll have to start over. Build a business and a name for himself from scratch. The thought releases an anticipatory flutter in his stomach. Can he do it again? He can hardly live off this woman for the rest of his life. If this is truly the future, he has no other choice. Now the flutter feels a lot more like excitement. What *if* he did it? What better way to prove your capability than making it twice? He knows no one in this world, so no one could ever claim he made it because of his heritage. This time would truly be on his own. His adrenaline surges at the unbridled potential he feels.

She said the year was 2390. Everyone James knew would be long since dead. All his contacts. His business partners. How does the world operate now? What does the global economy look like? His stomach pitches.

James runs out of the kitchen to the windows. The SATs flying by only make his head spin faster.

No, his momentary excitement at making it again was just his nerves talking. Besides, it won't be necessary. He couldn't have died. He doesn't *feel* like he'd died. He feels exactly the same as he did the day before. That means the woman is lying. He is sure of it. And this has to be some sort of weird simulation. For all he knows, the current scene displayed in the windows is the false image.

Yes, that's it. He remembers his buddies talking about hazing. The ultrawealthy were an elite club. Like a fraternity with unlimited re-sources. He remembers the tech tycoon—what was it—Chip? Yeah, Chip, telling his hazing story to the group of them at one of the prestigious political fundraisers he often attended. After Chip's first billion, his friends rerouted his private helicopter to land on a yacht in the Mediterranean. Of course, his closest business associates were there, along with all the cocaine and Croatian hookers he'd ever want. Not James's taste, but to each their own.

The guy seemed like a real dickhead anyway, but at the time, James fondly considered what his eventual welcome into the club would entail. That must be what's happening. What an elaborate effort. He almost grins when he remembers his vomit still coating the sink. How embarrassing. But if he's clever and can get the fuck out of here on his own, he can use the story to impress potential business partners, much like Chip did. In hindsight, he'll remember it fondly. Laugh as he relays the misadventure. Possibly impress potential business associates with the tale.

He shoots the woman a last withering glare as he darts for the door.

In his periphery, he catches her alarmed expression as he slips out. Footsteps chase after him as he sprints down the hallway, trying each door until he finds a stairwell. One hundred and sixty-something floors down is a long way to flee. Suddenly, a door at the end of the hallway slides open. He rushes toward it, brushing past the exiting people. He furiously punches the number one as Kate attempts to catch him, her bare feet clapping against the cement floor.

"Wait!" she cries as the elevator closes in her face.

A minute later, the doors reopen to a buzzing lobby that cuts short his victorious feeling. People swarm the space, weaving through brightly lit three-sided signs. Advertisements blink and flash, attempting to win the attention of passersby.

Individuals as vibrant as the signs wear clothes spanning the gamut from sheer slinky pieces, like Kate's dress, to utilitarian uniforms, and everything in between. All attractive, yet not as precisely so as his captor. Hair in various shades and styles. Does that woman have a metal arm? Upon closer inspection, her skin has been tattooed, like Kate's dragon scales, to resemble the texture of metal bands, glinting as if the artist mixed a metallic powder into the ink. Fucking weirdos.

The visual stimuli overwhelm him. Several people enter the elevator as he stumbles out. A man walks by, knocking into his shoulder.

"Careful," the man barks.

James whips his head around to get a good look at him. Red irises stare at him as if his mere existence is annoying. He spins, searching for the exit. Beyond what appears to be a recessed food court, tall windows with a few revolving doors span the wall. He hurries toward them, clipping people as he goes. He doesn't bother apologizing as their aghast faces alternate between affront and intrigue.

"James!" Kate calls from further back in the crowd. He picks out her voice from the commotion he leaves in his wake. Shit. He has to get away from here. From her.

Aside from being a haven for the alternative, this building seems relatively normal. This gives him further reason to believe she's lying. This isn't the future. He's sure of that now. What did she say? Year 2390? Definitely not.

Yet this place feels different from a typical apartment building, almost like a shopping mall. Maybe it's an experimental project, like one of those Vertical Cities where an entire community exists in one building. Where do they have those? Dubai? Of course, that's where his friends sent him. That means he's in the Middle East. A dust storm, then, and not smog as he assumed. It still doesn't explain the scantily clad people. Or the hovering cars.

Right as he has the thought, one of them zips by the window, reminding him of the car from *Back to the Future*, but sleeker. Across the street, a storefront displays a phrase spelled out in four distinct languages. He suspects they all express the same meaning of the one he can read: Police Station.

Relief washes over him as he makes for the revolving door. He stands in the short line waiting his turn, agitatedly glancing over his shoulder. The practically nude woman edges closer, waving her hands frantically. He has to get outside and over to the station. The police will sort this out. Surely someone there speaks English and can take him to the embassy. Then, with a few calls, he'll be on a private jet, heading home. The joke will be on them.

"James, wait!" she cries again.

He half considers dragging her across the street with him. She deserves a fine, at minimum, for the agony she's put him through. It doesn't matter if his friends paid her handsomely. She's complicit as far as he's concerned. Probably a common criminal. Or an adult film star for hire, more likely. Scientist his ass.

He needs to get the hell out of here. He can only imagine the mountains of work he'll have by the time he gets back stateside. If only he had his cell.

He darts into the next available slot. The door moves him forward, sealing him in his piece of the pie. But unlike any revolving door he's ever been in, it pauses. He tries pushing on the glass wall that will lead him outside, but it doesn't budge. Instead, it makes a series of hissing sounds. The air in the tight space blows down on him, rustling his hair wildly. Then the pressure equalizes, moving him forward into the next position. The process repeats.

James draws in a deep breath as his lungs tighten. Is the door somehow making the air thinner? And why is it taking so long?

Behind him, Kate pushes her way inside the revolving door's next opening and is beating on the glass with vigor. He glares at her as the door operates. The panic in her bulging eyes seems oddly . . . *genuine*. And what is that thing she wears over her mouth? It should signal something to him. It's at the edge of his reasoning. Something isn't quite right. But in his increasingly altered state, he grins at her, pointing over his shoulder at the police station. She shakes her head, jerking her hand toward the building they're exiting.

James feels so much lighter now that he's stolen back control, and she is the one panicking. *You're caught*, he mouths slowly enough that she'll be able to read his lips. Thank God this disaster is finally over. Perhaps he'll donate a portion of his wealth to victims of human trafficking now that he can personally relate to the horror. Even if this is only an elaborate prank.

He steps out into the fresh air as a lightheaded sensation sweeps over him. He tries to draw in another breath, but it catches. No, it *burns*. Fire scorches through his lungs.

James's mind clears. His eyes dart around, taking in the strange new world around him, finally landing on Kate. A stark clarity hits him with each painful inhale. His belief perseverance can persevere no longer. His perceptions shift. She said something about the outdoors being uninhabitable. This isn't just smog or a dust storm. The air is toxic. Exactly like she said. She isn't lying.

This. Is. The. Future.

If that's true . . . it means. He can't think about what it means. Still, the truth confronts him with every aching inhale. Nearly four hundred years ago, he died. By some miracle of fate—more like futuristic medical technology—he got a reprieve from death. Now, he's about to die a second time. He tries to take another breath, tries to crawl forward, but his lungs seize. His hand grasps at his chest. The burning is agony.

Kate's fists pound on the glass. From his knees, he stares up at her, utterly helpless. She's taken her mask off to yell, "HOLD YOUR BREATH! I'M COMING."

He obeys, though as the seconds drag on, the burn transforms into a pleasant sort of vacant sensation. Behind him, a few people have exited the door for the opposite building, each wearing a mask like Kate's. They go about their day, only sparing him a passing glance. A new tugging sensation bites at his aching lungs, getting stronger by the moment. He's lightheaded from the oxygen deprivation and the invisible toxins floating in the air. How much longer can he hold his breath?

When he turns back to see what is taking Kate so long, she's rushing toward him. Spots color his vision as she lands on her knees. She takes a spare mask and places it over his mouth. She's already replaced hers and her voice is muffled as she says, "Breathe."

He sucks in the filtered air, his lungs filling like a vacuum seal failing. He gasps down several delicious gulps before the coughing starts. Kate pats him on the back, urging, "That's it. Get it out."

By the time the coughing fit ends, his lungs are raw. He blinks at Kate with watery eyes.

"The coughing is normal," she says. "It helps expel the toxic particles you inhaled. I'll have to get you a lung treatment to help your body filter out the rest through your bloodstream." She stands, reaching a hand down toward him. "Come on. Let's get you back inside."

James allows Kate to draw him toward the building. As they enter hand in hand, he notices the onlookers gathered, gaping at the spectacle he's made. That's when he hears a man with a shock of spiky white hair mutter, "Zorg, there goes another one."

Tracing the man's line of sight, James catches a lavender-haired woman as her knees hit the pavement. His first instinct is to run outside to give her a mask like Kate did for him. He knows what the air will do to her lungs. But he only has his mask, and he isn't sure his lungs can take another dose of the atmosphere. He quickly scans the lobby, trying to figure out where Kate got the masks. A rack clings to the wall on his right. There are two bins. One label reads Sanitized, and the other, Used. He makes to rush over to them when Kate's hand wraps around his forearm.

"She knows what she's doing." Her tone isn't even somber. As if this is a regular occurrence.

The words ring through him. Does she mean suicide? By now, the woman has staggered over to lean against the opposite building. A couple wearing the issued masks walk by her, holding hands, not paying the woman any mind.

James's body gravitates toward the window. Moments later, he finds his hands and forehead pressed against it as if he is a small child. He stares at the woman, unable to blink. Then he feels Kate's presence next to him. As the last bricks of his denial collapse, he whispers, "Why?"

The woman seems peaceful now, but James can't shake the horrific sensation watching her die gives him. His nerves are bruised and bleeding. He doesn't think he has a weak constitution, but the last—what, hour?—has been the most disturbing and stressful of his life. He has no stoicism left to draw upon.

The woman's head lolls to the side. Then a last exhale, and her chest stills. "She's dead," he mutters. Just like that, the woman has breathed her last breath. A shudder wracks its way through him. Behind him, the lobby continues its chaotic swarming, while an eerie silence takes up residence in his mind. From a door a little further down the road, two men in what appear to be full hazmat suits come out carrying a stretcher. They place it next to the woman, then ease her body onto it before lifting it and taking it back into the building where they came from.

The entire scene is *business as usual*.

"Let's go back upstairs." Kate tugs his arm toward the bank of elevators. Finally, he peels himself away and follows her. He needs something to numb his emotional discomfort. He needs Vine. A bottle or two.

As they tuck into the elevator alone, she addresses his earlier question. "Now, people live well into their second and third centuries. That much time . . . it's too much for some."

As if people aren't meant to live this long, he muses. She explains the woman's death as if it were that straightforward. Even at her age, didn't she have a reason to live? James can think of plenty. Well, one specifically: he can and will make something of himself. Again. If he really died tragically at thirty-five, then this is an opportunity. As soon as he can, he'll take back his autonomy and separate himself from this woman who planned to use him for—he doesn't want to think about that. The point is, he will accept no less from himself. He only has to figure out how to navigate this new strange future where people choose to take their own lives because they've had enough living.

"Wait, the woman didn't look that old." He thinks of Kate finding the lines creasing his forehead novel. Now that he is mentally sorting through the various bodies in the lobby, he doesn't remember anyone looking over the age of thirty.

"Medical technology is far superior to what it was during your time," she explains. "Traits can be selected for before a zygote is created. This practice means most inferior genes have been effectively eliminated from the pool. What isn't caught before implantation can be corrected with cosmetic and medical advancements. If I had to guess, that woman was well over two hundred."

How can she tell? The beautiful woman leading him back to her apartment embodies a clinical, detached scientist, as she claimed. Had her parents selected those traits when designing her? Did she even have parents or are humans now grown in tubes like in the movies? Depending on the answer, the idea of Kate ordering a cloned lover might seem more plausible.

It would also frame the dead woman in a new light. She must have no friends or partner to mourn her or be there with her as she passed. He was fortunate enough to grow up in a nuclear family with a healthy social circle. Is that a thing of the past? Is that a bad thing? He always envisioned that one day after he amassed his fortune, he'd find a suitable partner and have a family of his own. If for nothing else than to have someone to pass on the fruits of his labor to. A legacy, like what his father wanted. He'd deliver the expectation to his children differently, however. He'd give them a choice about how they wanted to continue that legacy.

As they step into her apartment, he rubs his aching chest. He's never emoted this viciously. Considering his snowballing experience, he's certain feelings of such magnitude aren't for him. Because to his mind, he witnessed a tragedy. Hell, he's experiencing one: his own death. The knowledge of it makes him feel ill. Out of control. Untethered from a normally solid foundation. He despises it.

This future world is a bitter pill he will have to swallow. Still, he can't get the image of the woman out of his head. That might have been him if Kate hadn't got to him. He doesn't want to think of that possibility.

"So, they commit suicide and no one does anything?" James knows suicide rates were on the rise during his time. Why does he expect it to be any different in the future?

Kate shrugs. "Some people prefer the assistance of a physician, but the atmosphere does the job as easy. It only hurts for a minute. And it's free. She probably wanted to spend all her remaining unicoin on one final goodbye blowout."

He knows he's giving her strange sidelong glances when she says, "Don't worry about it, James. She got to choose her time after a long and most likely satisfying life. People will miss her, but it isn't the tragedy you think."

So far, James doesn't like the future. At least during his time, the taking of one's life was viewed as a catastrophe. He is alive now, though, and James Alexander Fletcher is a capable man. Despite the superficial and callous new world he's found himself a part of, he plans to make the most of his accidental escape from death.

If only he understood *why*. Why him? Was it truly chance that led Kate to select his DNA, or is there some greater purpose he's meant to fulfill?

Fate must have its justification to unfurl in this manner, but he's never been one to waste energy on impossible philosophical questions. He certainly isn't the type to waste an opportunity—because ultimately that's what this is. He'll do whatever it takes to make something of himself a second time. Now, he has no other choice.

7 – Report a Dangerous Product

James

"Here, breathe through this. It should help." Kate holds out a little device that looks like an inhaler. "For your lungs. I'll order some food."

He takes it from her and draws in deep breaths through the mouthpiece. As she goes to check an exterior delivery compartment in her wall she refers to as a smartwaiter, he rummages around in the refrigerator and finds a bottle of plain water. After a few sips, the chalky taste from the inhaler vanishes.

He follows her into the other room with a million questions banging around the hollowed-out cavern of his mind. The food she ordered arrived and she's busy arranging two benign-looking boxes of what resembles fried rice on the coffee tables. Seems like as good an opportunity as any to get started learning about the world now. "You said New York City is under water. Why?"

"The Great Warming."

"You mean climate change?"

"Yes. But it played out over a period of several hundred years due in part to the industrial and technological revolutions. From this historical vantage point, we can see it more clearly than you did in your time. Now it's known as The Great Warming."

"Does the United States exist anymore?"

"No. Out of necessity, the countries that existed then banded together under one centralized government called the Northern Hemisphere Organizational System, or NHOS. It's run by the Board of Commanders, which includes three randomly selected representatives from each major population center. They serve for ten years each, before the next lottery."

Kate must notice the melancholy washing over him because she says, "Paris still exists, though not as you would have known it. Mexico City is a big one. Let me see, Dallas–Fort Worth is coastal, and the air near the ocean is even more uninhabitable than it is here."

"I see." James takes a moment contemplating the state of the new world he finds himself alive in. He glances through the windows toward the grimy building across the street. "Wait, you mean to say the outdoors is uninhabitable everywhere? Not just here. What about plants and animals?"

Kate picks up the same remote she turned the screens off, pressing a few buttons. A tropical beach appears outside the window. When James's nose wrinkles, she says, "Too much?" She settles on a cityscape that might have existed from a high-rise penthouse in any major western city.

"To answer your question, yes, to go outdoors anywhere on Earth now, a respirator is required. A full protective suit in some areas, or for people whose job regularly exposes them. Even that isn't advisable for extended periods. It's common knowledge that planetary atmospheres change. The emergence of life on Earth is one example. The impact of human progress is another, though it happened many times before those two instances from modern history. Maintaining an indoor equilibrium designed for human habitation is incredibly important. Hence my line of work and how it affords me all this." She waves her hand around to her stark unit. The *and you* is implied this time.

Her space looks a little sterile to James, but he keeps the observation to himself. She doesn't seem to see it that way. "No stock market, then?"

She shakes her head.

"Money?"

"Unicoin is distributed by the Centralized Worldbank."

So, a government currency. "Is Worldbank owned by NHOS?"

Kate nods. "*Owned* isn't really the right word. But it is run in cooperation with SHOS, the organizational system in the southern hemisphere. I'm not sure where your line of questioning is going, but I have a suspicion."

Somehow, he doesn't think that this new world will allow this reincarnated version of himself, a manupartner, to go on existing without it causing a stir, and he refuses to become the subject of an investigation, scientific or otherwise. He elects to keep these thoughts to himself. For now. He needs time to learn about this world and consider his options. To come to terms with his new reality. "We can talk about it tomorrow. Is there somewhere I can stay for the night? A shelter, maybe?" The sound of that makes him as uncomfortable as she looks.

Kate's brows don't seem to be able to crease, but her expression suggests she is rife with concern. "A shelter?"

"It's a place where people without a home can stay—"

"You can take the spare room for now. We'll discuss what happens next in the morning." She leaves no room for argument.

After cleaning up, she ushers him back to the bedroom he woke up in. She takes away the GROW Pad, then brings a pillow from her room and places it on the uninviting bed. Shows him where the bathroom is and how to operate the knobs and switches, then leaves him.

James crawls atop the bed fully clothed. It's only as he lies staring up at the ceiling, unable to sleep, that he realizes this room wasn't intended for him. She expected him to sleep in her bed tonight. Maybe she expected more than that after the staged meeting she referred to. After all, she expected him to be a fully functional sex doll. He closes his eyes, letting his mind wander. He really should start thinking of a strategy to find an income—a methodical approach—but another question nags him. Who is Kate, and why did she feel so desperate for a warm body that she needed to purchase a clone to be her lover?

The bed creaks as he flips to his side, considering moving to the couch. The closed door gives him space to think, however, so he stays put, letting his mind drift to the strange woman on the other side of the wall.

October 6, 2390, Day 82.

James doesn't rise until long hours have passed. Shuffling comes from the living room. Then clacking on the keyboard. He hasn't come to any definitive conclusions about Kate or a potential source of income. A sense of bitterness at his rotten luck creeps in, but he's never liked the taste of that emotion. It serves no purpose. Especially when one has such a monumental task ahead.

Still, to come so far, to have worked so hard, for the sense of entitlement to have buried itself so deep in his psyche that a part of him wants to cling to the past . . . How does a man cope with the news that he'd finally hit the billionaire milestone he'd been chasing since his youth, only to die in such an unexpected and tragic way? For it to all be for nothing. He rubs at his temples. There's no point wasting time going down that road. Despite the complete lack of control he feels, he needs to take action.

Overnight, he realized he has a lot to come to terms with. Yet, in the fresh hours of the morning, if he considers his situation objectively, which plays to his strengths, he can see that he's gotten a second chance for a new, more challenging rite of passage. That is how he will think of it. Eventually, he'll feel some semblance of control. He only needs to find a path, make a plan, then follow the steps. He's done this dozens of times before. Sure, the process isn't foolproof, but few people are more experienced at brokering difficult deals than James. He will simply put those skills he learned in all his years of business into effect.

After relieving himself and freshening up in the compact bathroom, he emerges with a sense of determination. Kate sits at the computer desk wearing the same black superhero catsuit as she did the day before. She's opening and deleting what look like emails on one screen. On another, a browser displays the list of headlines. A third shows some type of survey. The fourth, an email with a subject that reads:

URGENT: GROW SURVEY NOTICE.

James's heart skips a beat. That means him. This can't be good. "What is that?" He gestures to the offending email.

"It seems the manufacturer knows there's been an issue with the latest production sequence." Kate doesn't so much as glance at him as her fingers dance over the keyboard.

He searches for the cursor, finding it on the survey. Words quickly form. *Unit seems to have embedded memories from man named James Alexander Fletcher, year born 2000.*

He scans the form. Above her damning answer, she's checked Yes to the question "Has your GROW exhibited any unexpected behavior?"

Yes to the question "Do you have any reason to believe your GROW is faulty?"

Her emerging paragraph responds to "If yes, please explain."

There isn't a clicker and he can't see how she's moving the cursor around. He pokes at the screen, but his fingers go through the image without effect. At least the keyboard is familiar enough to recognize the enter and backspace keys.

"Make the cursor move to the last question," he commands.

She does, and he watches to see how she's controlling it. The cursor moves, but she hasn't.

"What the—?"

She lifts a sheet of hair to show him the space behind her ear. A small metal disk is embedded into her skull, almost flush with her skin and almost the same pale golden-brown. "It's a neuroelectric communications device called an m-volt synaptic transistor. It connects to my device, too. For work, I like the tactile sensation of typing on a keyboard. Helps me think."

Thank God for that. If it weren't for the keyboard, he'd have no chance at controlling her computer. At this rate, he might as well add *operating computers* to his growing list of challenges. He reaches down, pressing the backspace key until her sentence disappears.

"Next one," he directs.

"But—" she protests.

"Just play along."

He gets her to check *No* on all the boxes and delete the damning text. When they've reached the bottom of the survey, he taps the enter key, hoping it suffices to submit the survey before she can intervene.

"Wait!" she cries, but it seems to have worked. A new window pops up and a red light on the bar of the center monitor lights up. She groans. "Please move. I have to do the retina scan." When the scan is complete, an image of Kate appears on the screen with a green checkbox beside it, then disappears. She turns to him. "Why did you do that? Do you have any idea how much trouble I could get into for reporting false information?"

He shakes his head, trying not to be agitated by her lack of consideration. "What would they do with me if they found out I retained the identity of the DNA used to formulate your . . ." He hesitates, mouth puckering with disgust as the word tumbles from his mouth. "*Manupartner?*"

"They would probably have me bring you to the GROW facility."

"Why?" He wants her to come to the realization on her own.

Her pretty face blanches.

"Would they let me live?" he presses.

"I . . . I . . ." Now Kate is the one with words lodging in her throat. "I suppose they would want to study you to see what went wrong."

"Then what? When they were done inspecting me for faulty wiring, what would they do with me?"

"They'd probably send you to the recycle station." She sheepishly sinks back in her chair.

"Recycle station?" he parrots, his blanch now mirroring hers.

"Organic material is a premium product. Nothing is wasted. Biological material is repurposed every time a GROW is decommissioned or even when a real human dies. Same if food is discarded. You get the gist. Though considering your sentience, the ethical implications are unknown. I didn't think of that."

"Well, good thing I did."

She deflates further.

Shit. Now that he knows she didn't abduct him and seems to have no ill intentions besides having intended to use his body for sex, he really doesn't wish to upset her. "Listen, I know this isn't what you planned for me, but it doesn't negate the fact that I'm a real man. Unfortunately, in your possession, so it seems, considering you've paid for me. At least until I can figure out a solution. Dying again so soon isn't it."

Somewhere in his monologue, Kate's eyes widen, as if something he's said intrigues her. "You're real," she observes. Awe is unmistakable in her tone.

James's brows shoot up, furrowing for good measure. "Yes, I'm quite real, sweetheart. I don't plan on getting recycled." A shudder rolls through him at the dooming word. "So, like I said, I need to find somewhere to stay until I can figure out a way to make an income."

She glances toward the room he slept in. "If you need another pillow, or different bedding—"

"It isn't that. I don't expect you to foot the bill for my expenses. I'm used to being self-reliant. Usually, large cities have services for those between homes. It would be better than depending on . . ." He can't seem to bring himself to say the word *you*. "Someone else."

It wasn't her personally, either. Granted, the sex clone thing makes him feel massively uncomfortable. While he doesn't see any other obvious flaws—she appears normal amidst the sea of oddities in the lobby yesterday—there must be something wrong with her that she needs to resort to such a thing.

"James, this is the future. There's no need for services like that now. Besides, as you said, it's not as if you can tell them who you are, since you technically aren't supposed to exist. That little tag on your foot isn't the same as the identifier I have."

"I'm a product." Suddenly, his fledgling agency flies out the window—more like falls out of the nest. Not only does he not own anything, someone owns him. He's even tagged with a bar code, like a box of cereal or a football jersey. Great. Another thing about the future to hate. This is going to be much more difficult than he imagined. "What am I going to do?" He voices the question aloud, more to himself than her.

Kate's Scientist Face appears. The one where her brows fight her frozen forehead, attempting to pinch together, as her eyes take on a faraway quality. Her lips purse slightly, which makes her cheeks hollow and her cheekbones stand out more dramatically. It makes her sharper, somehow. As if her intellectual capacity turns her into a predator and her beauty is nature's warning. James can think of several beautiful but deadly creatures to compare her to. If she were an animal, it would be easier. But with her, he's unsure of what precise type of danger he should be wary of. As he watches her think, he's certain he should proceed with caution.

He's said something she hasn't considered. The smile she gives him thrills and alarms him simultaneously. He's won an ally in her, but the cost remains unknown.

"Obviously, the simplest solution is that you stay here with me. Until we can figure out your identity problem, we'll have to act as if you're like every other manupartner. I think we should carry on with my original plan. Have breakfast out, then go find you some clothing, as if nothing is wrong with you." She winks, and his stomach flips.

"There isn't anything wrong with me," he grumbles, intending to resist her charms. But then a thought occurs to him. "Why are you so willing to help me? I accused you of abducting me, then you had to save me from the atmosphere. I'll take up space and cost you money."

One corner of her lip quirks upward. She's staring at him like she pities him, and he wonders if what she's about to say will be the truth or part of the scheme she's clearly concocted. "The ethical considerations, like you pointed out. It's my fault you are here, so I feel like I'm responsible for—" She pauses, and he can see her debating how to word it.

James sees it plainly. She may be unwilling to voice it, but he isn't. "You feel like I'm your burden now. This is exactly what I wanted to avoid by going to a shelter."

Kate looks like she wants to throw her hands in the air but is controlling her frustration. "The shelters you keep referring to don't exist. The way I see it, you don't have a choice." Hurt flashes across her eyes. "I'm the best you've got." She glances away, seemingly unable to meet his gaze.

There's more behind her words. He doesn't know any other future people, but she seems decent enough. She's certainly beautiful enough. It's only that he doesn't like depending on others. If he accepts her help, can he really claim he did it on his own? But if there isn't a shelter like she claims, he really has no choice but to agree. "Fine. If I stay here, we'll keep a tally of every expense. When I'm able, I will pay you back, plus substantial interest. Is that agreeable to you?"

She waves, brushing him off. "Fine. Fine. If that makes you happy, then I'm happy to agree to it. I'll get you a tablet and you can keep track." She hesitates, and his instincts tell him she's about to say something he should really pay attention to. Something highly consequential. "We have one other minor thing to consider."

"What's that?" He's more than a little wary.

"Nothing to worry about yet. Only that we might consider solving that problem before your lease is up."

James coughs. He isn't sure what that means, but a lease seems bad. "You don't *own* me?"

"Technically, you're leased. Shouldn't be a problem, though. We just need to either make an extension or figure out how to get you an identity that doesn't tie you to GROW. Which might be a little difficult, considering . . ." Her voice lowers until she trials off entirely.

"Kate, how long is my lease, and what happens when it expires?" He's pacing now.

"Ninety days, which began last week when I started the activation. If for some reason we weren't able to cover the extension, which shouldn't be a problem, I mentioned recycling, right?" She shrugs, pressing a button on the 3key that deactivates the monitors. "Interesting process, I'm sure, but nothing we need to know the details of. Anyway, now that uncomfortable conversation is out of the way, we should focus on something that makes us happy. My friend Jett, who's been dying to meet you, will meet us for breakfast."

His stomach grumbles at the thought of food.

"Then," she continues, "I know what we can do that will make us both feel better about this interesting situation we've arrived in."

The rate with which she jumps topics makes his head spin. Like she didn't just mention that if they can't pay, he'll be recycled—a word that is easy to interpret as eliminated, or worse, *killed*. Still, she sits there waiting for him to ask, so he obliges. "What's that?"

She beams. "We'll go shopping!"

8 – Breakfast is Served

James

"So, is there anything I should know about manupartners before we step out in public?" he asks, following her into his newly assigned bedroom.

She ignores his question, waving a hand at the attire he hasn't removed since he put it on. "Take that off. I need to refresh it so you can be seen in public."

Reluctantly, James swaps his clothing for a towel. Kate uses a hand-held gun-shaped device labeled Fabric Renew to run several passes along the garments. Perfectly smooth and crisp fabric is left in the wake of the blue light the device projects. By the time he puts the clothes back on, they look and smell as fresh as if she freshly laundered them. Then, she sits him on the bed and goes about applying a series of creams to his face, running them over each fine line.

"This we'll have to explain." She taps the slight imperfection at the bridge of his nose. "And here." She taps the creases at the corners of his eyes. "I think it's best if we tell people I made a special request to make you as authentic to the time you came from as possible. Most people who know me will believe it since it's well-known that I'm one of the last to give in and purchase a manupartner."

"Care to explain?" Suddenly, he's immensely curious, this new piece of information making her seem like more than a pathetic, lonely woman. In fact, the more this she speaks, the more intrigued he becomes. She is clearly intelligent, if a little odd.

"Not today. I'm sure you can imagine this isn't how I planned for this to happen. Actually, until now, what's happened with you is unheard of. But we're going to make the best of it. Remember our plan for happy times?" A ping sounds from the clear rectangular box in her hand, which is like a futuristic smartphone from his time, though not as advanced as he might have expected. She lifts it and reads the screen.

He steps beside her, watching as a sentence—her response—appears on the screen. The device pings again. "Jett is already at the food court. He's almost as eager as my other friend Lessa's last manupartner, Yansy."

James follows his new roommate to the door. Her other friends have sex clones too? Perhaps they're more common than he guessed. She pauses before they exit.

"To answer your question from earlier, there are a few things you need to know. You can't argue with me in public, and you need to act as if you wish to please me. Based on what I've observed of your personality, that might be difficult for you, but if we're to keep your true nature a secret, then everyone will expect you to act like any other manupartner. Smile, and try to act pleasant, as if you're happy to be here. Think you can do that, James?" She gives him a coy smirk.

Is she flirting with him? Even if she's not, she's adjusting to their new circumstances faster than he is. She is from this time though, so it's no knock to his capacity. At least she's come up with a positive perspective about their calamity. He might as well do the same.

"It will be a struggle, but I'll do my best." He returns her playfulness with a smirk of his own.

As they step into the elevator, he can't help but notice the grin she can't seem to repress. "You're enjoying this, aren't you?"

She shakes her head as if she can't believe her luck. "I think I am."

"Kater, Sexy Alligator!" her friend Jett exclaims, rising to greet them, pressing a kiss to the corners of Kate's mouth before turning to assess James. The pale-haired man circles him, poking and prodding, expressing delight in his *rugged, masculine look*. By the time he finishes, James feels ready to be thrown on the grill. Typically, he doesn't mind appreciation from any of the sexes. Knowing his intended purpose as a manupartner, however, sours this appreciation.

They sit at the table Jett has reserved. The man leans forward, lowering his voice as if James isn't there. "Have you had him yet?"

James can't hide his authentic reaction, which is to chuff, then stare aghast between them. Did this friend of hers, Jett, just ask if she had relations yet with her mail-order sex clone? He's been alive for less than twenty-four hours. And that's personal. Surely Kate will rebuff the man.

She ignores his reaction entirely. "We're still in the foreplay phase of my plan." A wicked grin lights up her face. Her acting skills surprise him.

Jett lets out a robust laugh. "Leave it to Scientist Kate to chart her sex life."

Abruptly, Jett turns to him. "I assume you've already reviewed and memorized the plan? Care to spill any details? It would make Kate very happy!"

That Jett speaks to him as if he is real confuses him. He needs to make Kate give him more details about the particulars of manupartner social interaction before they go out again. This whole encounter is beyond strange, but Jett seems harmless, so he isn't all that concerned. This plan his new roommate obviously made up on the spot is more immediate. "It's an elaborate spreadsheet."

"What's a spread sheet?" Jett looks to Kate. "Is that a sex thing I'm unaware of?"

Shit. No more spreadsheets in the future. *Note to self: don't mention past technology in front of strangers.*

"Get it? Spread. Sheet!" Kate fakes a laugh. "Remember how Yansy was overeager? I think this one tries too hard to be funny. Oh well," she says, sighing.

It's a decent cover, but he doesn't like that she has to cover for him at all. The less he owes her, the better. He reaches out and wraps his fingers around Kate's. The way she blushes as if she were indeed enjoying this suddenly gives him the urge to ruffle her feathers. He turns to address Jett. "I'm eager for day four, when I'll get to please her with my mouth. Between her legs," he adds for additional clarification, as if it weren't obvious.

Jett spits the water he's sipping across the table, narrowly missing Kate. It takes him a moment to finish spluttering. "Well, that's wonderful. Isn't it, Kate?"

For James's part, he lovingly stares at his new roommate. Serves her right for intending to use him as a sex doll.

Kate glowers at him. Then her eyes brighten. "Yes, it's true. After I saw what limited equipment I had to work with, I incorporated more oral sex into the program." She pats the back of his hand. "He's almost perfect."

James grimaces, and Jett breaks into all-out laughter. At his expense. Though he knows Kate intended the comment as a retort to his own, he can't help but feel a little emasculated. After all, she had God knows how long to get an unbridled view of him naked. Not that he is lacking. His gaze slides to her. She seems nice enough, but did she touch him? Take liberties? Surely she isn't that desperate. Even amongst the people he's seen so far, Kate's beauty outshines them all. She wouldn't have any trouble finding a partner. But if that is true, then what is his purpose?

Jett sighs, relaxing back in his seat. "You seem happy. You're glad you went ahead with the activation?"

Kate clears her throat, and this time James is sure she's faking her smile. "You're right. It isn't nearly as weird as I imagined."

Jett's eyes gleam with barely contained delight. "See, I told you—"

"But I'd still rather have a *real* partner," she interjects. "One positive encounter isn't going to convert me. You know I only activated him because GROW wouldn't give me a refund. Ahh, here's Decci!"

Now James is sure there's more to the story, which he's suddenly very interested in getting to the bottom of. Unfortunately, there isn't time to follow that thought. A lithe man steps up to their table. Severe, shiny black hair hangs past his shoulders, and a matching liner circles his green eyes. A fine film of powder makes his complexion milkier than it might have been otherwise. For a man, James can acknowledge he's beautiful in an austere way.

The newcomer places his ring-bedazzled hand on Jett's shoulder, waiting to be acknowledged. A sinking feeling causes James's stomach to dip as he realizes what this other man is. Jett absently grazes his fingers over the man's hand before turning to him. "Decci, this is Kate's first manupartner, James."

James isn't sure what he is supposed to do, so he lets his instincts take over, rising to reach out his hand. Decci only stares at James's outstretched palm as if it is a curiosity. Noticing the lingering moment, Jett directs the manupartner. "I think he wants to hold your hand, silly." Decci puts the wrong hand in his, which James quickly releases, adding *don't shake hands* to his growing list. Jett turns to him. "Decci is my latest partner from CHOICElover."

James bites back the words *I gathered that* while trying to plaster a compliant, if not serene, expression on his face. "Wow."

Jett chuckles. "It's been a while since I've had a GROW. He seems genuinely surprised. I guess their recent adaptations are really panning out."

Kate smirks at James's apparent failure, patting his hand. "Yes, it seems so. They're still abominations."

Relenting, Jett sighs. "Decci, take James and show him how to operate the CaféPress. I'll take a flat white with sea salt foam, a pick-me-UP nourishment packet, and . . . let's see," Jett taps his finger to his mouth, "three rice cakes with red berry jam."

Kate rattles off her order much more quickly. He does his best to memorize it, but the jumble of words gets lost in his scrambled thoughts. Hopefully, the manupartner will remember. Otherwise, how many options can there possibly be? Surely, he'll get close enough. Or he could completely screw up the order and enjoy watching as Kate pretends like she's pleased with his selections. But that could backfire. She is doing him a favor by not reporting him. Notwithstanding the ethical implications that she acknowledged, which give him a shaky sense of security.

Decci directs him through the lobby, which is less crowded than it was the night before. In the corner sits a vending machine like you might see in a hospital waiting room that distributes coffee and a handful of other machine-produced drinks. As they walk, he considers what else he might learn from the manupartner. And how safe that might be. He figures it has to be relatively safe because the thing that looks exactly like a real man doesn't really have a vested interest in what James is.

Decci points to the touchscreen on the CaféPress. "You put your partner's unit number in first, and then you select the items required. It's easy. Watch and it will make sense. Us manupartners have to stick together." Decci gives an uncomfortable laugh as if that was a programmed line he recited.

James forces a chuckle and nods, watching Decci demonstrate. A moment later, the machine starts making whirring noises and then a claw hand drops three metal cups and two muffins onto the tray below. Decci takes the tray and nods toward the machine. "Your turn."

"Shit." Kate's order has officially drifted out of his memory. She really should have spent more time debriefing him on what to expect before they went out in public. "I'm afraid I don't know Kate's unit number."

Decci, unfazed, recites, "CA25-163-11."

Before he forgets, James punches the number onto the touch screen, then makes a last-ditch effort to remember Kate's order. He gives Decci another helpless look.

The manupartner happily grins as it supplies, "A pick-me-UP nourishment packet, a Café Italia, double XPRESO, double foam, and two bean puffs. And of course, whatever you choose to fuel."

James figures it added that last part despite its waning solidarity.

Behind them, another manupartner set on a mission to do its master's bidding says, "I'm happy to wait, but my Lolla needs her order. Will you please hurry faster please? Excuse me."

After the twenty-four hours he's had, he doesn't give a shit. He shoots the woman-shaped thing a masterful glare, wondering how many of the people he sees are manupartners and how many are their owners. If he really is Kate's first one, that says even more about the woman he's agreed to live with for the time being.

Decci explains, "She is a PickMe Partner. It's a generic brand and probably an older model. Not a premium manupartner like CHOICElover." This time, James is sure the line is implanted.

He shakes his head before turning to search for the items on the list. Decci only has to correct him twice, which he is rather proud of. As he swipes, he looks for eggs, bacon, or even a cup of yogurt for himself. It seems future people really enjoy their carbs. He needs something though, so he edits the order to include two of everything. Later, he'll talk to Kate about getting some meat and vegetables.

The machine whizzes and buzzes like it did before. When the tray is filled, he picks it up, turning to follow Decci. He clears his throat. "How long have you . . . err . . . serviced Jett?" Internally, he cringes, but he can't think of a better way to say it. And it was, after all, the thing's purpose. It was in the name. *CHOICElover*.

"I've been Jett's companion for over four months." Decci stares blankly ahead as it answers.

"And do you like it?" James presses.

Decci stops, slowly turning to look at James as if his question has caused the thing to short circuit. "Can you repeat the question?"

James figures he's already committed at this point, so he repeats, "Do you like servicing Jett? You know, do you enjoy what you do? Waiting on him, and other things."

The manupartner tilts his head to the side quizzically. "When Jett is happy, then I am happy."

"I see." He isn't going to get anywhere with this creature, is he?

A grin brightens Decci's face, as if it's pleased it answered correctly. Then it inclines its head and asks, "Do you like servicing Kate?"

It seems the programming to make it polite is working. "I haven't serviced her yet, but the prospect is thrilling." He assumes the manupartner won't pick up on his sarcasm. It is hardly more than a glorified robot. Ah—that's where Kate gets the term *flesh robot* from. He knows she's intelligent. She proved that when she quickly figured out that he's from the past. It seems she's witty too.

They set the trays on the table, offloading them as he studies her. Then James follows Decci over to a bin where they discard them. He arrives back at his seat in time to watch Kate's pink tongue dart out and lick the foam off her upper lip.

"Mmm . . ." she sighs, nodding at his identical order, and winks. "Good selections."

Decci picks up on their little interchange, brightening. "James is very eager to service you, Kate. He told me and I thought that would please you."

James chokes on the sip he took, while beside him, Kate drops the metal cup of coffee. It clangs as a bit of brown liquid sloshes on the table. The manupartner and Jett wear very different grins.

Kate gathers herself quickly, shooting Jett a knowing glare. "If I'd known he was so eager, I'd have rearranged the plan." Slowly, she turns to face him. "What do you think, James? Shall I have a ride tonight?"

He knows the flirting is an act for Jett's benefit, but his stomach jumps all the same. The word *ride* evokes thoughts, namely of certain body parts bouncing, that he doesn't want to be having. Therefore, he resolves to keep his head down, murmuring, "If that would please you." He'll survive the rest of breakfast, making as little eye contact as possible until they make it back to her unit. Once there, he'll sit her down and set a few boundaries. Just another item to add to his growing agenda:

- Set some boundaries.

- Learn about the future so he can find a way to make an income. Plan and execute.

- Become self-sufficient so he doesn't have to rely on Kate.

- Pay Kate back with interest.

- Figure out what Kate's problem with the manupartners is, why she finally got one, and why she can't seem to get a real partner.

Granted, the last item is only for the sake of his curiosity. In reality, Kate and whatever led her to get him doesn't have any bearing on James or his future plans. Still, that doesn't stop him from wanting to know.

9 – Her New Roommate

K8

James Alexander Fletcher. K8 repeats the name in her mind until it seems normal. What a strange thing, to have three names. And no numbers at all. How would the system know which municipality he belonged to? Or where to apply his charges?

Her ~~manupartner~~ new roommate, James, steps out of the dressing room. "Ooohh!" she exclaims, clapping her hands appreciatively. She knew the fitted orange slacks with the metallic glint would enhance his form. Zephyr, those thighs—Jett was right. And the bias-cut black T-shirt is simple, but clings to his chest in a way that makes her want to rub against it. But the slacks . . . "Those look—"

"Ridiculous. I'm not wearing these." James turns to the willowy shopgirl, 4Ally. "Do you have anything more understated? Looser perhaps?"

4Ally gives him a thorough sweep with her lusty yellow-gold eyes. "I think those look fine."

"Looser and darker," James demands, dropping manupartner the pretense. 4Ally doesn't flinch, so K8 holds her tongue.

She can't see why he doesn't like them. He'd be the height of fashion, and they are minimal, like he wanted. K8 leans forward, whispering to 4Ally, "We'll take that outfit. But see what else you can find. Maybe something with some give?"

She taps the screen a few times and the rota-closet spins. Multi-colored outfits blur as they zoom behind the glass pane. When 4Ally slips behind the screen, James steps up to the tablet. He spends a few minutes tapping the screen, eventually saying, "This is more like it."

4Ally reappears and glances around his shoulder. K8 moves to do the same. He's found the vintage section. K8 should have guessed he'd like that.

Shaking her head, 4Ally retreats again, then comes back with the tenth stack of outfits she's brought out. "Try these."

James looks at what 4Ally's brought and sighs, giving K8 a *Must I?* look.

A minute later, he comes out in a full moss green jumpsuit that, to K8's taste, is very plain. But stretchy. Surely he'll like this. K8 makes a spin gesture with her finger and James obliges. Then he sees his reflection in the mirror and runs an exasperated hand across his eyes.

Meanwhile, 4Ally is tugging on the material at the tops of his thighs. "Maybe a size smaller?"

James grumbles something K8 thinks is, "I'm in hell."

Apparently, a mere two hours of shopping is his limit. He motions for 4Ally to join him at the shop's tablet. "No on all of this, including the last one." He points to the screen. "You have my measurements. This is what I want."

She frowns deeply. K8 watches as he points at the screen, barking orders at 4Ally. Occasionally, she's brave enough to give her opinion, but James is decisive. There's no argument. He's so direct. And firm. Bordering on unkind, as if he views the shopgirl as an object to serve him. K8 isn't sure he is aware he's doing it. Or that 4Ally is seconds away from bursting into tears. Does he not see the effect he's having on her?

K8 brought him here because this particular shopgirl is excellent. K8's favorite, and truth be told, everything she's picked out for James works perfectly. If only he weren't so picky and demanding. Some interpersonal skills would go a long way. People during her time may not form long-lasting romantic partnerships, but each member of society holds a valuable place. Regardless of the profession or pay bracket. Respectful and Considerate Conduct Courses are compulsory, taken yearly during primary school and when one begins their first job. Then every ten years thereafter as social customs evolve.

The courses always bring up fond memories for K8 as she excels at all things pedagogical, not to mention respectful and considerate. Well, except for one particularly tenuous period when she was around nine. A lively debate had sparked up between a few pupils and the instructor, discussing the outdated concept of sharing. On the surface, the concept seemed to fit in with the course mantra: Each Individual Experience is Important. But the instructor quickly clarified, "In modern times, there is no need to take turns when everyone deserves the right to have their experiences met with equal consideration. Always remember, your needs are important!"

The explanation felt rather contradictory to K8, so she stood to ask for clarification about a few nuances of the rule. "How does waiting in line relate to our subject?" Little nine-year-old K8 felt very proud of her pertinent question. "For example, sometimes recess ends before everyone in line at the swimming simulation tank gets a turn."

She distinctly remembers the instructor's frown. "Well, you see, each individual deserves a right . . . Well, you see if the tank was full . . ." The man trailed off, stalling. Retrospectively, K8 felt surprised that her nine-year-old self could dumbfound an instructor, but it showed how little people thought to question things. Still, there were many valuable lessons to learn in the courses. Many she still applied to this day.

The instructor was still sputtering when K8 saved him, offering, "I think if we determined how many students could enjoy a swim session during each recess period, we could make a sign-up. Or if everyone wanted a turn, maybe a weekly rotation—"

Mid-sentence, like she was invisible, a girl from A Quadrant—Trssh, she recalls—stood up from her desk, raising her hand.

Trssh said, "In anticipation of today's lesson, I wrote a poem called 'The Sharing Fallacy.' May I read it for the class?"

This was met with eager nods and rapt attention from both students and instructors. Trssh began reciting:

"One for you, one for me, but none for you means two for me,
If two for me gives me glee, then why make two less one for you?
One plus one is so much fun—"

"I was speaking," K8 whined. "She interrupted me." Heat climbed higher and higher up her neck, and she gave serious thought to stomping. "How does that show respect—"

"Now, K8, don't you want to hear Trssh's poem? I bet she worked hard on it. Class, please show Trssh respect for her wonderful efforts." Even though Trssh had yet to read her entire poem, the class erupted into applause, with a few students even dancing in their chairs.

Now, K8 saw that the instructor had been happy to have attention diverted away from a question he couldn't answer, but at the time, she couldn't understand how she had been so easily brushed aside. It had a deep impact on her nine-year-old self, and she often thought of that day. K8 had studied the girl, trying to figure out what made her more important. Was it because she was from A Quadrant? Was it her pretty blonde hair? Or the way all the boys wanted to sit next to her? Or was it simply something about K8 that meant she didn't warrant the same consideration?

K8 watched the other children celebrating their classmate, but she couldn't force herself to join in. Of course, Trssh, noting her failure to clap, started blubbering. She pointed at K8 and asked, "Why isn't she clapping?" in a pouty voice only a child could manage.

K8 can still picture the instructor's deep frown as he asked K8 to leave the classroom until she could demonstrate a little more consideration for her fellow students. "You should be ashamed of yourself," he told her in front of the entire class. A dozen pairs of disapproving eyes followed her out of the room.

After that, K8 decided to never attempt sharing. She made a motto to avoid such uncomfortable confrontations: "When in doubt, just do a little dance, smile, and remember: Each Individual Experience is Important." Fortunately, no one seemed to remember her mistake the next day, but the lesson had already sunk in.

"Two of the black," James barks.

4Ally must be stronger than she looks. She doesn't even blink as she answers, "Yes, of course."

K8 offers 4Ally a sympathetic smile, which she accepts gratefully before returning her attention to James. They'll have to work on that.

She hates to make excuses for him, but maybe things really were that different during his time. The obituaries said he was a *billionaire*. That amount of money was extraordinary. He would have been akin to a king. Someone used to being served. Giving an order and having it done without question. Someone surrounded by people willing to do this. The whole concept feels strange to K8, but she's trying to understand.

After ten minutes of 4Ally taking notes on her tablet and James swiping through the catalogue, they appear to be completing the order.

A billionaire's equivalent doesn't exist anymore. Occasionally, someone will invent something and start a company. They'll make it into the rumored "A+" pay bracket. There are loopholes and secret markets that afford some a greater surplus of unicoin and the perks that come with it. But it's nothing compared to what James was during his time. That much she's researched. Yet there is still more to learn if she has any hope of understanding him. And she wants to. Because maybe this man from the past is her chance to build something real.

Holy Mother Zephyr gifted her James, someone who doesn't know how things are in her world. He obviously finds her attractive, so they are off to a good start. If most people during his time were in partnerships with other people, then he won't know how things are. He won't have the same relationship expectations as people do now. He might desire a monogamous partnership like her parents had. Her chest fills with hope. Could James be the answer she's been searching for?

She's practically buoyant when 4Ally says, "That will be three hundred forty-five million unicoin."

James wanders into the hallway to wait on her. K8 glances between 4Ally and James before leaning in. "We'll take the last two outfits he tried on, too. And I agree. Smaller would definitely be better on that green number. Zorg forbid we waste an ass like that."

The shopgirl gives her a conspiratorial giggle, adjusting her total. K8 types in her NHOS identification number and lets the camera get a retina scan for confirmation. Then she breezes out.

A few hours and a few shops later, she runs across the most divine pair of silver synthifiber sandals that would go perfectly with the dress she bought last week.

"I'll just pop in here," she tells James. She tries on the shoes, and they are as perfect as she imagined. When she enters her payment details, she has to withhold a grimace at the staggering sum that is nearly half of James's entire wardrobe. And there is his lease to consider. She should probably put them back, but when will she find something that goes better with that dress she bought last week? She's already made the investment. To not buy them would be a waste.

Thinking of it that way, K8 happily signs for her purchase, which will be delivered to her unit by the time they return.

James narrows his eyes at her as she drifts back into the hallway. "I guess being an air control officer is a pretty high-paying position?"

K8 shrugs, half intending to ignore the question. It is a high-paid position. But the spring lines this year were impossible to pass up. And when she wore that reflective lime catsuit, she got a dozen compliments.

"K8?" James presses. "You can afford all this plus my lease, right? At least until I figure out a way to pay you back?"

"Sure." She turns away from his prying gaze. Perhaps she should take a look at her Worldbank account now that it's come up. The thought makes her stomach swirl and dip. What she really needs is a distraction—for both of them. "Oooohhh!" she exclaims as they walk past a shop called Proclivities, which sells adult products. The gold spiked collar in the window is what catches her eye. Why didn't she think of it sooner? "I need to feed Broccoli! I'll introduce you. Come on."

"Who's Broccoli?" James asks, and she can tell he's intrigued. Plus, he's distracted from the money issue. Both things please her.

Perhaps this will go better than the clothes shopping. And she's missed Broccoli. She's been so preoccupied, and it's been years since she's seen him. What an opportunity. "My dog!"

10 – A World Without Dogs

James

The dog parks are on floor CA25-122. At the very end of the main hallway, there's a storefront with images of futuristic people hugging and petting all manner of dogs. James doesn't recognize a single breed. The dogs are different colors and sizes, but as they get closer, he sees they all seem to be an amalgamation of many breeds. As if *dog* comes in medium and white. Or small and speckled. But only one shape.

They enter, and Kate steps up to the counter, bouncing on the balls of her feet. "Hello."

"Hello," a man with a poorly bleached bowl haircut replies. He wears a completely see-through vinyl tube held up by two thin hot pink canvas straps. James dares a glance down, instantly wishing he hadn't. Is that supposed to be a fig leaf?

Kate, noting James's horrified expression, reaches forward and runs a glittery nail across a strap. "This is amazing! You must tell me where you found it." The man blushes, and Kate gets out her device to take down the information and snap a few pictures of him, which he eagerly poses for.

"It gets better!" The man reaches to the trim at his chest, pinching the material, and the whole dress lights up like a movie projector screen, playing a scene of a man standing under a fruit tree, holding up a red sphere and considering it. A woman struts over to him and plucks it out of his hand. She takes a large bite and they both start dancing, then the whole scene repeats.

Kate squeals in excitement, breaking out in her own little dance, which the man mimics.

James's temples pulse to the imaginary beat. How is this his life now? He's ready to go back to her unit and lock himself in the spare room for a few hours to escape the chaos that is the future. But a dog—maybe that will offer some semblance of normalcy in the sea of insanity he's wading through. Barney, his Irish Setter, was one of the few things that could mellow him out when his mood was getting the better of him. Maybe they could even take Broccoli back to her apartment. It's strange that she didn't already have it at home, but she might have boarded it to get through the manupartner activation process.

It's what he did with Barney before he left on that last fateful trip. When he never came to pick Barney up, did the vet contact his parents or his sister? A sick feeling tightens his stomach. Barney was a great dog. Someone would have found him a good home and taken care of him.

This is the last thing he should worry about. His goals should be his focus. But so far in this world, he's only encountered businesses that would be categorized as consumables or aesthetic services. But surely there is a financial services industry. He makes a mental note to ask Kate about this later.

When the dance party seems like it's never going to end, James interjects, "Excuse me. We're here to see my friend's dog." James raises a brow as the man shifts his attention to him.

They both stop dancing abruptly. "Yes, okay." He somberly returns to his tablet. "ID Number?"

Kate gives him her information and signs a digital ticket. "Would it be possible to get stall twenty-seven? It's my favorite."

Naturally, after the dance party, the man is all too happy to relocate its current occupants so Kate can have the spot. When he comes back, he proudly leads the way to the stall. All the while, the biblical scene on his dress replays over and over.

When the man finally leaves them, James glances around the small cube. His eyes land on what might be a dog-shaped hobby horse. Except it lacks detail. He glances at Kate, waiting for her to tell him this is some type of joke, but she's handing him a crystal VR headset. He takes it, then she puts hers on and drops to her knees next to the furry stick thing.

"Who's my good boy?!" she croons. "Yes, my Broccoli is so happy to see his momma. Does Broccoli want a cookie?"

James watches with something that feels a lot like horror as Kate lifts an invisible cookie to the stick thing, petting the faux fur with her other hand.

"Yes, that was so good, wasn't it? Such a good boy."

Kate strokes it, happily bobbing with each bit of praise she delivers. Her joy is so pure as she plays with the fake animal. The picture before him makes her seem untainted by the callous reality he's experienced. It's a mind-bending juxtaposition with the way she oozes sex appeal. His brain hurts. He needs a drink, or a bed, or both.

"James," she says. "Don't you want to meet Broccoli?"

No, James doesn't. He wants to run out into the atmosphere and end this nightmare. But he remembers how his lungs felt, and the fear of dying hits him a second time.

He's landed in purgatory. He knows that it's not quite hell because his clothes don't itch and the song playing lightly overhead has a folksy feel to it. It's well-known that hell plays 2000s country music and provides wool onesies.

Yet, a world without dogs? Because that's what this means. No dogs. Probably few or no other animals, too. He can't wrap his mind around the far-reaching implications, like the food system or forest ecosystems. Are the oceans dead too? He's going to be sick if he doesn't get some air. But that isn't even an option. Are the walls getting nearer? He wipes a sleeve across his brow, collecting the moisture beaded there. Since he woke up, he's been slowly adjusting. But to think so many things he loves about the world are gone . . . Warm rays of sunshine on his skin. Barney's soft copper fur. His happy brown eyes. The scent of a pine forest or a crisp winter day. A dip in a brisk ocean. All of it, gone.

For the first time, the true nature of his reality hits with a force that nearly sends him to his knees. He's trapped in the future and he doesn't have a lifeline.

"James?" Kate's concern softens her voice.

James eyes the hallway that leads to the exit. "I'm sorry, Kate. I can't do this. It's too much. I'll wait for you in the hall."

Then he turns to flee.

By the time they make it back to her unit, the packages have already been delivered. The smartwaiter is full and each time they empty it, it refills.

James is exhausted. Ready to retreat into the four concrete walls of his barren room in an apartment he doesn't even own, a feeling that seemed impossible only yesterday. Yet as he grabs a few boxes and heads to his room, his shoulders loosen. They'd loosen even more if he could get out of this ridiculous fitted ensemble. If he has to spend another minute wearing it, he'll lose it. His temper is already precariously close to snapping and his cheerful companion isn't helping.

"What happened back there? Visiting the dog park always makes me feel better when I'm upset. Do you not like dogs?" When he doesn't respond, she adds, "Maybe we'll try something else tomorrow."

All day, her cheerfulness has seemed to compound, as if to combat his foul mood. He's not sure how much more he can take.

"James, what do you like to do?"

He stops, slowly turning to her. How can he possibly explain what he's experiencing to this woman? "Everything about today has been incredibly unsettling. From meeting several manupartners, to walking between buildings with a respirator. And this awful outfit."

"And dogs?" she presses.

James eyes her as she frowns. Not wanting to be cruel, he's reluctant to mention why the dog park nearly sent him over the edge. The modern human experience is so vacant that people have to resort to a simulation of a pet. Despite his reputation as a ruthless and single-minded entrepreneur, even he had a pet dog.

He grimaces, and Kate studies him intently. He can't handle being coddled, so he waves her off. "It's fine. I had a dog in the past." *Go ahead, make your assumptions. Let's leave it at that.* "I just need to get into something more comfortable and get some food. Then sleep and pray this all was a nightmare."

Kate's lips form the shape of an O that she covers with a hand. "Wow, James, I didn't know. Seeing Broccoli must have upset you. I imagine if I'd woken up in your world, I'd be feeling the same. But think of the bright side—"

"What do you think the bright side is for me, Kate?"

She only stares at him, mouth snapping shut.

"Yesterday I discovered that at thirty-five, which at the time would have been considered my prime, I died when my plane crash-landed on a bluff. Then, by some magical twist of fate, a drunk woman ordered my DNA to be injected into a manupartner kit, which malfunctioned and brought me back to life. Now everyone I know is dead. Everything I had is gone. And the future is so bizarre it's making my fucking head spin. But believe me, I'm trying my fucking hardest to make the best of it. I've been given another opportunity to try to make something of myself—I know that—but don't act like you have any idea what I'm going through." He steps into the spare room, slamming the door in her face.

He realizes she's only trying to help, but he needs a minute alone to gather his composure. But first, change. He peels his way out of the clothing, discarding it in a pile in the corner. A minute later, he has a loose pair of pajama pants on. He sorts through the items he unceremoniously dumped on to the bed. There are a few other pairs of pajama pants, along with some boxer briefs, but no T-shirts. They must be in another package. He eyes the door as if it's an affront to his person. He'll have to venture out to retrieve the rest of the packages. God, the thought of having to confront her smiling face again. She'll have probably thought of a clever retort by now.

Bracing himself, he exits the room, making a beeline to the stack of bags and boxes. He feels Kate's eyes on him before he even turns to confirm. As he addresses her with an annoyed glare, her eyes dip to the waistband of the pajama pants and lower.

She swallows before redirecting her stare to meet his. "Those are nice."

A pink flush crawls up her neck. Then she looks away as if she knows she's violating some unspoken agreement.

If he's being honest with himself, which he is without fail, he can acknowledge that an attraction lies between them. Purely physical. But inappropriate. Even if he gave in to the attraction only to relieve a little stress, which he's pretty sure she'd be willing to do, she'd only be letting him because that's what she originally intended to do with him. Because she's desperate for anyone who will ease her loneliness. But he's a real man, not a sex doll or programmable companion. And it's not like she'd be picking him for him.

What is he saying? Even if she was picking him, James wants nothing to do with this woman, considering she's become the symbol of his plight. He can't even look at her, with her unnaturally bright eyes, and perfect—well, *everything*, and not see his unwanted reality.

Part of him is desperately clinging to this new opportunity he's been given. Another part mourns the life he's left behind. Not only the money. The comfort. The control. The familiarity of his world. Being able to expect what comes next and the sense of ease he took for granted. Hell, he even misses his Social Security number. So much better than the awful tags on his feet, which are nothing more than a product code. He clenches his jaw, refusing to let these feelings overpower his resolve.

"I can help carry these to your room," Kate offers, drawing him out of his momentary lapse into self-pity.

"No," he barks, wincing at the unnecessarily aggressive tone. He doesn't want her in his space. Her eyes become glassy for the second time since he's known her. He sighs, unable to apologize. More like unwilling. "I've got it."

Kate reverts to the quiet, observant woman he first met as she watches him move the packages to his room. She isn't gawking at his physique anymore. Only observing as if he's some sort of lab rat. Or an experiment she's trying to understand. He almost prefers the excessively chipper version of her from the dog park. It feels less foreboding, at least.

Before he shuts the door once more, she says, "I'll order us some food."

Shit. He was supposed to talk to her about that. "Okay." He winces, hoping to God it won't be another box of bland rice.

When James finally emerges with a slightly clearer head, he spots a takeout container waiting for him on a coffee table. Kate has opened the lid and set a glass of Vine and a VitaShot next to it. The pangs in his stomach are at odds with the revulsion he feels toward the food. Triangles of a spongy bread sit in a neat stack next to what appears to be cubes of sautéed tofu in a brown sauce. At least he'll get some protein.

He sighs as he takes his seat. "Listen, Kate, we need to discuss a few things." He'll ease into the conversation with something simple, like dinner. Build some resolve. Then set some ground rules about their dynamic and clarify expectations. "I appreciate you taking care of our dinner, but we're going to need to get some proper food. I can't survive on"—he waves his hand at the spread before him—"whatever this is."

Her brows twitch, but stay mostly frozen. "This *is* proper food."

"No, I mean I need some chicken and vegetables, or steak. A salad would be fantastic. This is just..." He takes a bite, trying not to grimace as he chews, then swallows. "I mean, I don't know how people stay so fit if this is all you eat."

Kate gives him a slow nod. "I see. I'm afraid this is something else you'll have to come to terms with." She scratches her head. "I'm trying to figure out how to explain this. The food that you are describing is a thing of the past. Literally. Think, James. If humans can't survive the atmosphere, how could a cow? We have meat substitutes now that are so close to the real thing, from what I understand, I don't think you'd be able to tell the difference."

That's right. He should have made the connection at the dog park. At least imitation meat would be better than eating rice and noodles all the time. "Then can we get some of that?"

"REAL Steak and enviro-greens are premium products. Most people now can only afford to enjoy that on special occasions, like their birthday or Holiday. If I shifted some things around in my budget, we could probably afford them once a week. But . . ." Kate's Scientist Face slips back into place. "No, I don't think that would be wise, considering your lease. With the clothing, the extra food . . . I don't think we should splurge. You're going to have to get used to the food I provide. As far as nutrition goes, that's what the morning pick-me-UP nourishment packets and mealtime VitaShots are for."

It takes him a moment to process what she's saying, noting she didn't mention forgoing the expensive shoes as an option. He eyes the packages still sitting inside the door.

"This brings up something else I've been meaning to ask you about." He considers the best approach. There must be a financial services industry, even if there isn't a stock market exactly. People retire still, right? And there are still scientists. And cosmetic surgeons, or whatever the equivalent is during this time. Surely that means that there are still financial analysts and venture capitalists. Someone has to own all of these businesses and buildings.

He'll have to start from the bottom, but he's done it once before. He never touched a dime of his trust fund. It was like a rite of passage to him. This would be the same.

But here in this future world, he isn't supposed to be a real person. For all intents and purposes, he is a product. Solving his identity is a top priority. "Now that I'm here, there's no going back."

When he pauses to gauge her reaction, she urges, "Go on."

"I don't suppose we can take out a loan or open a credit account with GROW?" Surely, if that were an option, she'd have already mentioned it.

"No. Credit is a thing of the past. Loans in all forms are banned. If you can't pay with unicoin upfront, then you don't get it. And that includes loans from your friends," she explains. "NHOS set laws in place banning any of the pitfalls of prior societies, hoping to avoid those same outcomes. The current economy is a highly regulated system, which limits speculation."

He nods, processing. "Which would include extending credit."

"My friend Aurone can tell you more about it if you're interested. It's not really my field of expertise. He's a systems engineer, so it isn't his either, but he likes to dabble with his little side projects." She nonchalantly waves a hand through the air.

Side projects? That sparks James's interest. He definitely wants to meet the friend she's referring to. "Okay. That means I have a little under three months to figure out a way to make an income. Then I'll get my own place and pay you back, as we discussed. I assume I'll have to get some sort of identification to do this, correct?"

She gives him a reluctant nod.

"That's what I figured. People can't pop into existence out of nowhere. Is there a dark web still?"

Another nod. This time, her eyes narrow.

"Great. We'll need to purchase a fake ID. I'll add it to the tally, of course. I'll find a profession I'm suited for, get a job, then pay you back for everything. After that, we can part ways and you can get a real GROW so you can use him however you planned to use me."

Kate's cheeks flame as she stands.

Shit. "I didn't mean . . ."

But she walks away, muttering, "I guess you have it all worked out, then. You don't need me." She doesn't try to hide the hurt in her voice.

He watches her graceful form glide into the kitchen. When she eventually returns, he can't help but notice the resolved set of her jaw. "There's a bin for whatever you don't eat and another for the recyclables. Take care of your mess when you're done. I'm going to bed."

He didn't intend to upset her. But what did she think was going to happen now that she's discovered he's real and not some sex doll for her amusement? While he appreciates the help she's offering, a nagging thought enters his mind. Does she still think to benefit from him? For companionship or otherwise? Unease prickles the back of his neck. *Ground rules.* He is supposed to be setting ground rules.

Without thinking, James shoots up. His bare feet slap the cool concrete as he stomps across the room. "Wait!" he demands as she slips into her room.

She steps out, furtively closing the door. Does she not want him to see into her private space? "Yes, James?" She sighs, the hurt in her voice transforming into something more akin to exasperation.

"Listen, lady." She retreats a step, which he matches. "I don't know what's going on in that pretty little head of yours, but I do not belong to you. I am not your sex doll, and I am not your friend. I'm not the answer to your loneliness, and I don't plan to stay here a moment longer than I have to. You may not like that, and while I appreciate your help, I don't care if you don't like my boundaries. They are here to stay for the duration of our acquaintance."

"But . . ." she protests, her voice wobbling. Fuck. He shouldn't be such an ass. If she really is different—but that doesn't give her an excuse to have designs on him or his time just because she's helping him.

He leans in so they are eye to eye, attempting to soften his tone. "No buts. I get that this isn't what you planned, or that you have your reasons for never wanting a manupartner, and that makes you the odd man out in your fucked-up society. I get that it must be hard for you. Isolating even. We've both had some shitty luck, I get it. But we're going to have to figure out a way to cohabitate without adding to each other's problems. Once I can get my own place, I'm doing just that." When he finishes, his heart is beating heavily in his chest.

Kate's mouth falls open as she draws in a deep breath, like she can't believe what she's heard. His stare instinctively finds her full lips, then dips down to her chest, which rises rapidly. Only then does he notice his hands are flat against the door on either side of her head. When did he box her in?

He meets her gaze again. It's no longer sullen. There is such vulnerability in her deep brown eyes that his stomach dips without his permission. *Fuck*, he thinks, as the sudden wild urge to grind her into the door washes over him. To have her quivering beneath him. God, he's sick, but the thought of it has blood rushing south. No, she'd like that too much.

"Understand?" he gently urges.

"Got it." She clears her throat, eyeing his hands.

"Good." His voice is a little huskier than it was before. He pushes off her door and storms into his own room, shutting the door behind him.

He leans against the wall, willing his body into a calm state. Surely she didn't notice his rapidly stiffening cock. Goddamn his overactive male hormones.

He tries to recall the last time he was with a woman. There was that girl at the club before he started dating Blythe. But that was a quick fuck in a dark hallway. And he cut it out because Blythe was the first woman he'd dated that he considered wife material. She came from a good family and had a substantial trust fund of her own. And she'd finished her residency as a pediatric oncologist. She was equally driven and beautiful, in a demure sort of way. She would have been an excellent mother to his children. What happened to her?

Blythe was nothing like the Playboy Bunny he is currently living with. Who is also intelligent enough to be a highly specialized scientist, yet flippant and shallow enough to have ordered a manupartner kit and have an apparent shopping addiction. Who has the most perfect, luscious body he's ever seen. This is not the direction his thoughts should be taking. He glances down at the protrusion tenting his pajama pants. "Fuck," he mutters, grabbing hold of it through the soft material and squeezing as if that will help.

He eyes the bathroom. A cold shower is exactly what he needs. The last thing he should do is jerk off to thoughts of the crazy woman on the other side of the wall. He quickly makes his way to the bathroom and turns on the shower. In front of him, a timer displays a countdown in red numbers. 5:00. 4:59. 4:58.

He groans, tearing off his clothes. How do you make it cold? He steps into the perfectly warm water, pushing buttons, which only change the flow from the shower head. This either adds to or reduces the time left on the timer. The perfect, delicious heat only makes him throb harder. 3:47. 3:46. 3:45.

He braces his left hand on the wall as he dips his head beneath the stream. *Just this once*, he promises himself. Then his other hand makes a fist around his cock.

11 – An Unfortunate Notification

K8

K8 has never encountered someone so brazen. *Boundaries*, he said. Now that she's gathered her wits, she has more than a few retorts. Boundaries of her own to set. The man has a few things to get straight himself. But if that energy could be channeled, perhaps his overbearing temperament could benefit her. A delightful flutter erupted low in her belly as James loomed over her, telling her how their relationship would be. His domineering manner swept over her, catching her off guard. The way he stood over her was, dare she say, sexy.

She can only imagine how pleasurable that demeanor of his would be in the bedroom. Taking charge, leading her for a change. It ~~might be~~ would be refreshing. Her last several sexual experiences felt overly orchestrated. As if she and her partner were players in the live production *Kinky Sex*. Sure, they were adventurous. And physically and momentarily satiating. But passionate, not at all. Not spontaneous, not heart-stopping. Not this reckless feeling that now has her in its clutches as she crawls into bed.

James offered her a mighty protest, but she didn't miss how his eyes dipped to her mouth, then her chest. She thought for a moment that he was going to betray every word he'd uttered and take her against the wall. The thought makes gooseflesh erupt across her skin.

She turns over, seeking the warmth of her FauxSilk sheets, and they tauntingly scrape across her nipples. A whimper escapes her lips. She can feel her desire pooling between her legs. Would it make her as bad as he claimed if she were to reach down with her fingers? Or better yet . . . She mentally searches the room for where she stashed the PUSSYzapper3000.

No, she chides herself. She can't do it. Especially to the fantasy of a man who wants nothing to do with her. Sure, he finds her sexually attractive, but he simultaneously feels disgusted by her. He thinks she's a lonely woman.

But isn't she?

Her loneliness was the reason she finally broke down and ordered the GROW kit in the first place. She sighs as she turns over again, resolving to ignore the ache between her thighs. They have bigger problems to tackle; for example, his three-month countdown.

Getting a fake ID is a good idea, but James finding work enough to pay for his lease feels like a near impossibility. Does he have some skill that translates to the modern world? And will he be able to learn enough about the current time to pass as someone born in this century? At least she can cover month four while they figure it out.

After how bewildered he'd been throughout the day, she knows his learning curve will be steep. K8 falls asleep with thoughts of her unexpected plight still swirling in her mind.

October 7, 2390, Day 81.

"Good morning!" she chirps as James emerges from the bedroom. The lines etching his face seem a little less deep. As if he is more relaxed. "How did you sleep?"

He makes his way to the kitchen, avoiding her gaze, which strikes her as odd considering the lion she encountered last night. "Fine, thanks," he mumbles.

She follows him, finding him rifling around in the cold storage. He pulls out a pick-me-UP nourishment packet and downs it in one quick gulp. Perhaps he is learning more quickly than she anticipated.

Her stomach flutters, but she spent all morning gearing herself up for setting her boundary. She clears her throat. "About last night." His shoulders stiffen, but she bravely presses forward, determined to tackle the issue head-on. "I appreciate that what you're going through is overwhelming, but you must learn to control your temper. Speaking to me that way is inappropriate." Zephyr, she hates confrontation.

"You're right. I was rude, so I apologize. I'll do better." His words surprise her. Again, without eye contact, he brushes past her, out of the room.

She didn't expect his acquiescence so quickly. So again, she follows him, now more confused than ever. "That's it?"

He glances up, letting his gaze dart over her outfit before meeting her stare with a pained expression. "Yes. I was wrong. While I meant what I said, I shouldn't have approached the situation in anger. I apologize. I won't speak to you that way again. There is nothing more to say. Unless there is something else bothering you?"

She twirls a lock of hair as she considers his apology, determining that she is satisfied with it and more than a little happy her confrontation was successful, and she can move onto more pleasant things. "Nothing else."

"Good." He rummages around her desk, looking for what, she doesn't know. "Do you have any paper? Like a notebook or something. Or maybe the tablet you mentioned. I'd like to do some research," he says, still not looking at her.

Maybe he feels shame for the way he spoke to her? Well, that's understandable. "Sure. Let me go get it." She collects a spare tablet from her bedroom, handing it to him. "No paper, but"—she points to the stylus—"you can use that, and there's an app called Scrawl you can take notes in." She picks up the crystal VR headset from her desk. "You can link these to the tablet if you want. I have some work to do."

He takes the items offered to him. Despite the fact that he can hardly make eye contact with her, she thinks the morning is going rather well. She sits down at her desk and logs on to her system. Out of the corner of her eye, she sees James go to the kitchen and come back with a bottle of water. He arranges himself in the corner of the couch. Once the tablet's retina scanner recognizes his GROW DNA signature that she programmed that morning, it unlocks.

About fifteen minutes later, the glow from the particle panes transforms from a serene pink sunrise to a lush green. She glances up from her work to see James operating the remote with the tablet perched on his knee. An image of a dense jungle surrounds them.

He taps the remote again and the scene changes to a busy skyline. A clear night sky frames clunky, block-shaped buildings. The white and yellow lights that illuminate their windows are clearly visible from the vantage point of the photographer lending a glittery feel to the scene. There's no air pollution. No SATs or MagTrack lines. A boyish grin creeps across his face.

"Is that from your time?" she calls across the room.

He sets the remote down as he surveys the image, clearly pleased with himself. "New York City. Home." After an extended pause, he continues. "Well, it used to be, I guess." Then he shakes his head like he's throwing off a memory. It's clear to her that he really loved his world—or maybe the place he'd made for himself in it.

She can't help but ask, "What do you see when you look at it?"

His brows furrow—something she'll have to book an appointment for—and he turns to her. "I suppose I see progress. Forward momentum and limitless possibilities. I think that's what New York City has always represented to people. I guess not anymore."

"No, not anymore," she agrees.

"Well, we're making the most of it, aren't we?" He looks away. "No use dwelling on the past and things we can't change."

Her stomach lurches in the same funny way it did the night before, even as something in her chest expands. Pride? Or something more nefarious, like a craving? It almost hurts. Seeing James figure out what she thinks is an irritating bit of technology so quickly gives her hope. That's what it is. This man elicits so many confusing emotions in her. His hope about the future gives her an unexpected affinity for him. As if his inexperience in her world and his willingness to meet it head-on is drawing her to him. She's intensely curious to know more about him, yet she's wary to push.

Curiosity. Well, that's harmless. Probably. As she carries on with her daily routine, she resolves to respect his boundaries. The truth is, he guessed correctly about hoping he might be the answer to her loneliness problem, and that's why it stung so much. Or maybe he didn't guess. He saw her like no one from her time has.

It's beyond her how modern society became so disconnected. Every time she even tries to scratch the surface and discuss something deeper than the latest cosmetic treatment or exercise simulation with her FRIENDS, their eyes glaze over. Or they become overly cynical about it, like her conversation with Jett the other day. At least he didn't shut her down outright. It's only that the same question continues to gnaw at her. How has she not met anyone with similar desires? It's as if true vulnerability is the plague of her time.

Since James has positioned himself as off-limits, a lottery win from the Birthing Agency is still her only hope. It was stupid to think he might be an opportunity. Surely having a baby with someone from her time would foster some sort of connection. There would be companionship as they brought the child through its early years together. And that is *if* she could find someone willing to give it a chance with her. The lottery win would give her the leverage she needs. Something valuable to offer.

Instead, the universe has gifted her with this man. A man who has no interest in her—not a gift so much as a taunt. *I'm not your friend*, he said. And they didn't have manupartners during his time. Marriages, partners, and what they called "friends with benefits" were commonplace. Why couldn't they be that? She woke up early that morning and did her research in an effort to better understand him. What she learned only confounds her more. He still doesn't want her.

That only reinforces the notion that there is something wrong with her. She's been clinging to this overripe longing for so many years that it's started to taste stale. The scientist in her refuses to review the evidence. Time passes by with no hope of change. No matter what she does, she still comes up wanting. Does that make her a fool? She can feel the sob welling up inside her throat at the gut-wrenching thought. No, she can't do this. If she breaks down in front of him, he will think she's even more pitiable than he already does.

She really should focus on the pile of task orders in her inbox, but it's time to look at this logically. He's right. She's been a lonely, pathetic woman wishing for something that doesn't exist. It's time to move on.

If the wall James is determined to put between them isn't the proof she needs, then what is? She'll do as he asks and help him get on his feet. They'll part ways. Then she'll get a real manupartner and try to enjoy life as best she can. ~~Then she won't be alone.~~ And that will be good enough.

Her eyes flick back to James and that stupid grin he's wearing. He's put on the VR headset and become amused with whatever he sees. The nasty P word floats around her mind: Potential. So much potential. But how can you be so near another person yet feel a million miles away? K8 clutches her chest. Is she dying? Logically, she knows that is impossible. At eighty-six, she is the definition of health. Fourteen years from entering her prime. But this horrible sensation threatens to split her breastbone in half.

Two pings sound in unison, drawing her from her spiraling thoughts. One from the tablet James holds and the other from her workstation. An email pops up on her middle screen. The subject reads:

URGENT: GROW RECALL NOTICE.

That awful feeling that was seizing her chest moves to her stomach. She scans the notice.

Dear Valued Customer C-K8lyn-MSP-00023468,

The team members at GROW appreciate you taking the time to submit the recall notice survey. We are pleased to learn your GROW: Unit 2899-MSP-James-00023468 is functioning as designed.

Because of our commitment to the quality and safety of you and your product, GROW is conducting a series of random field reviews to assess the stability of your manupartner. Please be available with your manupartner at the location you registered the unit for the following time slot:

Seventhday, October 14, 2390, 14:00-16:00.

The review will only require a small amount of your time and will ensure the continued efficacy of our product. Should the inspectors discover anything faulty with your unit, they may repossess your unit for recycling. In this case, you will receive credit for a new unit at no additional cost to you, along with three complimentary months added to your lease.

We thank you for your patience and cooperation during this process.

In service,

Your GROW Team

K8 rereads the notice three more times before allowing her gaze to drift up to James. He's taken off the VR headset and sits, staring at the tablet. She clears her throat. For the first time that morning, his eye contact isn't forced. He's read the synced email too.

His voice comes out gruff as he asks, "What does this mean?"

Her first instinct is to reassure him. Faulty manupartners, like Purpl, happen from time to time. Especially as they age, but it's usually a much simpler problem identified during the activation process. For example, a unit won't wake up, or it develops a deformity, like freckles or James's crooked nose. It is uncommon, but the more premium brands have a reputation for dealing with any issues that arise promptly by replacing the unit. No questions asked.

What could the inspectors possibly be looking for now other than to assess if James has retained his identity, though? If they find out, they might take him and either study him as James suggested or ~~kill~~ recycle him.

"They want to know if you've retained your identity," K8 says.

"No shit. What do we do about it?" He looks at her as if she's an idiot.

She knows she isn't the subject of his ire. Patiently, she rises and moves to sit beside him, placing her hands on her knees. The urge to take his hands in hers to comfort him overwhelms her. The tension that melted away overnight has come back in full force.

"We will figure it out," she assures him.

"Is there somewhere I can go—I could hide. And, they can't—we can't meet them. They'll find out. Then they'll take me—"

"James, look at me," she says, interrupting his panic. She imagines the proximity to one's own death again in such a short sequence must be unsettling. He comes across so utterly human as his vulnerability unfurls before her. This only increases her growing ~~affinity affection feelings~~. Zephyr, she does not need this. <u>Sympathy</u>.

"If we try to hide you, I will be questioned and possibly penalized. And it isn't sustainable. We have to meet with them. You're going to have to figure out a way to be a believable manupartner. We probably better start practicing. I'll take the next few days off work, and I think we could get Jett and his CHOICElover to help us."

"No!" James blurts. "No one can know."

This time, K8 doesn't resist the urge to reach out and clasp his hands. They feel firm and rough compared to her own, invoking the need to summon her resolve to the forefront of her mind. "Jett would never share our secret."

"Shouldn't this be my choice? It's my life we're talking about," James pleads.

His earnestness makes her want to run soothing hands through his dark hair and make promises she isn't sure she can keep. K8 sighs. "I'm too close to the situation. We will practice for a couple of days and then loop Jett and maybe Lessa in. They've been my FRIENDS forever. Oh, they are going to die when they find out you're real. It's peak irony. But I think having a third party test you will be beneficial."

"I don't know . . ." James argues.

The next week is certainly going to be entertaining. And she must have utter confidence that they'll succeed. Otherwise, the consequences are too . . . never mind. No need to think of that. K8 gives James an assuring grin. "You're going to have to trust me about this."

12 – Bombs Are Dropped

James

October 11, 2390, Day 77.

Lessa and Jett sit on the couch, diagonal to James. Their mouths hang open as they stare, blinking at him. He really wishes one of them would say something so this nervous flutter in his stomach would abate.

Moments earlier, Kate dropped the bomb of his retained memories on them. Before that, due to his heightened paranoia, James had requested that Decci get locked in Kate's bedroom. The manupartner was all too happy to please.

"Hello?!" he demands as her friends continue to wordlessly stare at him.

Lessa opens their mouth as if they are going to speak, but then closes it.

Jett steps in. "So what you mean to say is you have some of this James fellow's memories?"

"What I'm saying is I am James Fletcher. I am him. I have all of his memories. Well," he backtracks. "At least the ones I've always remembered."

"It seems there was a glitch in the DNA processing," Kate says. "Researchers have known for a while now that DNA carries memory. Particularly in the cells that make up certain areas of the brain. When James died, they pulled him from a plane crash. He had severe brain trauma and died before they got him to the hospital. I'm wondering if that trauma somehow caused his memories to imprint more deeply in the cells that got collected for research purposes. James donated his body to science." Kate proudly pats him on the knee.

Listening to people talk about his death so nonchalantly in front of him is unsettling. James ignores the discomfort. "But how would my DNA have ended up in a GROW database?"

"Over the years, batches of DNA have been traded. Acquired by different companies, to study or formulate products, like the manu-partners. Yours must have got swept into one of the batches." Kate's explanation makes him shiver. What else has his DNA been used for?

Jett leans forward, grinning. "This is fantastic. I *knew* there was something off about you!"

Kate perks up. "Exactly! That's why we need you two to help us prepare for the inspection."

God, she is positive. Almost annoyingly so, if she wasn't using her perky energy to keep him from being recycled.

"If we fail, they will recycle me." He hopes her friends understand the urgency. "That means death number two, and this time I'll see it coming." Not to mention he'll lose the chance to test himself in this future world. They don't need to know that, though. Keeping him breathing should be enough, but who knows with these future people—had he not seen the woman commit suicide on his first day, he would feel comfortable relying on human instinct when it came to his life.

Lessa sighs, leaning back in their chair. "I'm going to need a cocktail for this." They keep fidgeting with an invisible speck of lint on their pant leg.

The tic is familiar. Someone he knew from before did that.

"Wait, so who were you?" Jett asks as he scrolls through his device. "There are a lot of articles about you from your time. Did you know that?"

Even though Jett is doing his own research, James tries to explain, as it is unlikely the articles accurately represent him. "I was an entrepreneur. A job creator. I had a business and made investments," he says, thinking that about sums it up. Before, those words would have felt like enough. They feel brittle now as he speaks them to these future people. But surely there are still people like him?

Jett continues scrolling as Lessa leans over to look at his screen. "You were a billionaire," they say. "That was a lot of money then, right?"

James rakes his fingers into his hair as he buries his face in his hands. The heels of his palms press into his closed eyes as if the action might soothe the sting of the memory. "Yes, that was a lot of money." And he can do it again. He will do it again.

"Did you have a will?" Lessa asks.

"It wouldn't matter if he did. A manupartner couldn't claim it even if The Great Equalizer hadn't wiped out all personal wealth from his time." From Jett's tone, he doesn't realize he's delivered a crushing blow. James makes a mental note to research the ominous-sounding event.

He must appear crestfallen, because Lessa frowns, seeming genuinely concerned. "I didn't mean to upset you."

"It's only money." Jett waves a pale hand through the air as if it's no big deal for James to learn some historical event would have wiped out any legacy he might have passed down because, of course, he had a will.

Lessa smacks Jett's arm. "Don't be insensitive. Clearly, James isn't upset about the money. Speaking about the past probably reminds him of the family he's left behind. Right, James?"

Jett gasps. "Wait, were you *married*?" He says the word like it tastes funny.

James looks at Kate, hoping she'll interject so he doesn't have to answer, but she only stares at him like this question intrigues her, too. Her brows edge together, creating the slightest line between them, as if this question is a hypothesis in need of study. She's watching him as he says, "I wasn't married, but yes, I had a family. My parents were alive, and I had a sister."

Abby's face pops into his mind. It's his sister who Lessa's nervous perfectionism reminds him of. But he hasn't spared his sister a single thought this entire time. Does he have any living ancestors? Abby had children. He makes a mental note to look into it. But what would be the point if some event wiped out all personal wealth?

Kate is staring at him as if she can see right through him. Like she knows he isn't being forthcoming. Jett, with his sharp, appraising scrutiny makes James want to take charge and redirect the conversation. That's what he would have done in the past, but at the moment he feels a little off-center.

Lessa seems to be the only one he's managed to convince. Probably because they only appear to be half-paying attention. They say, "Poor thing. I can't imagine what you must be going through, wondering what happened to them all those years ago."

They're all dead now is implied. It doesn't hurt as much as one might think. For all James knows, they lived long and fulfilling lives. Is that a consolation, or is James really that callous? Never mind.

Lessa pats Jett on the knee, which is apparently a signal to put away his device because he tucks it into his pocket. Then they say, "How can we help?"

Kate claps her hands in front of her chest, content to put away the prior conversation. James is too. "I think we need to practice. Then, drinks on me," she says.

Jett stands to pace in front of the particle panes. "Okay, from now until you pass the inspection, you must remain one hundred percent *in character*." James can't help but notice the sly look he shoots Kate.

Kate, to her credit, only shakes her head.

James scoffs. "And what exactly does that entail?"

"Well, to start, you should at least act like you like your *owner*," Jett says, pointedly emphasizing the word *owner* as though he knows it will needle him.

James raises an eyebrow at the irritating man.

"You're meant to be ultra masculine, so you can get away with being a little gruff, but you need to let your body language speak for itself. Like this." Jett sits back down next to Lessa and slips a casual arm on the couch behind them. Then his fingers absently pick up a strand of their shiny silver hair. As he keeps his attention focused on James, his body gravitates toward Lessa. "See?" Jett asks, reverting to his former position.

Lessa gives him an exaggerated shiver, fanning themself. "That was quite effective, Jett. I didn't know you had such skills."

James rolls his eyes. "I know how to flirt."

Jett's smirk taunts him. "Are you sure?"

He stares at Kate for a moment. Something about fake flirting with her feels different. Whether it feels like betrayal to his resolve or opening Pandora's box, he isn't sure. But this is *his life* that hangs in the balance. He needs to treat this as any other job and do it.

James takes another look at Kate, then a deep breath as he steels himself to take on the character of fake lover. He can do this.

Right as he leans sideways, Kate jumps to her feet. Out of nowhere, tears burst from her eyes. Between sobs, she bites out, "I can't be that bad. I can't." She dashes to her room, leaving James dumbfounded.

"Kate, honey," Lessa calls after her, only a few steps behind.

"There's something wrong with me," Kate cries. Lessa makes it into the room before Kate slams the door.

James sits frozen on the couch, staring across the room at the closed door. "What just happened?"

Jett's voice draws him back to reality. "You fucked that up, didn't you?"

James whips his head in Jett's direction. "You're an asshole, you know that?"

Jett only laughs. "If you get recycled, it's on you. Kate is putting herself out there by trying to help you, and you act as if you're loath to touch her. Do you have any idea the trouble she could get in by violating the terms and conditions of the GROW agreement?"

James shakes his head, a little ashamed that he didn't give it a second thought when Kate mentioned it after he submitted the GROW survey for her.

Jett continues. "Did you even think to ask, or were you only thinking of yourself?"

Guilt nips at James's conscience. "I know she's trying to help, and I appreciate it, but I'm not used to accepting help unless it's from the people I've hired. Otherwise, I like to figure things out myself."

As if reading James's thoughts, Jett says, "So you're hyperindependent. You realize that isn't an admirable quality, right?" When James doesn't respond, he says, "I think maybe *you're* the asshole."

"You're right," he admits. "I've been selfish." He's always seen himself as self-reliant, but is that only a clever way to excuse his selfishness? God, why is the future so intent on highlighting his flaws?

"Don't be a Z-quad," Jett says.

"I'm not," he says, instinctively rebuffing what he assumes is an insult. "You're right. She's been nothing but kind and positive. I've been an asshole."

"So then, what's your problem?" Jett leans forward, lowering his voice. "We both know you've barely thought of your family, and you're not pining over some lost lover. I would imagine self-preservation should be no problem for you. What's holding you back? Don't you find Kate attractive?"

Of course he finds her attractive. The woman is a fantasy. Not that he will ever admit that, and it isn't that simple. James shakes his head, ignoring Jett's question. Damn him for being so perceptive. Should he go to Kate and clean up his own mess? Surely Lessa can handle it.

He needs to talk through this, and he can hardly do that with the subject of his conflicted thoughts. "The thing is, when I woke up, I thought someone abducted me. Like a sex trafficking thing. Then I found out I died and it was the future. Ironically, the woman who purchased me intended for me to be some sort of in-the-flesh sex doll. It's repulsive."

"So what you're saying is you're a prude?" Jett shoots him a challenging look.

James chokes back an agitated laugh. "Hardly. How would you feel if someone brought you back to life only to fulfill their sexual fantasy? Even if it was a beautiful woman. Well, man, in your case."

"With lovers, I don't discriminate. And to answer your question, I suppose a part of me would be flattered while another part of me would feel . . ." Jett takes a long moment, as if the word *feel* is a foreign thought. Then his eyes widen. "I would feel like I was being used."

James jumps to his feet. "Exactly! I know she never wanted one of those things, but it doesn't change the reality I found myself in."

"Despite what you must be going through, you should know that Kate is one of the best people I know. She's honest and earnest and hopeful. And she would never take advantage of you. Even if she wanted to, which I imagine"—Jett's gaze swipes him up and down—"she does. I think maybe you need to be open to life's possibilities."

"What does that mean?" *Life's possibilities.* James scoffs. Does Jett honestly think he's going to sleep with Kate to save his own ass? Well, he would if it came to that. And if it wasn't for this weird situation, he'd gladly take her to bed.

Jett only replies with a shrug.

"Kate told me she was the last of her friends to get one of these manupartners." He isn't sure why he says it, but he's been mulling it over in his mind.

Jett laughs. "That's our Kate, and what makes her so unique. You should know that relationships that were typical during your time are not common now. People come together to procreate based on the lottery system, or they might find a partner for a night or two, but long-term couplings don't happen anymore. With the manupartners, people can get whatever they want out of a relationship. And when it no longer meets their needs, they take them to the recycle station. The organic material gets reprocessed for the next person's short-term affair, and the cycle repeats."

"That sounds awful." James has never put a high value on human connection, but he's always assumed he'll come to a mutually beneficial agreement with a woman. They would share their lives and build a family together. And maybe one day an affection between them would develop. And if not, they both would carry out their duty and find enjoyment on the side like so many people in their circle did. But the point is, there would be companionship at a minimum. A loyalty not so easily disposed of.

Is this what Kate wanted? Why she held out for so long? And he's treated her so poorly. He feels sick at his own behavior, a sentiment entirely foreign to him. He's had it all wrong—she didn't see an opportunity to use him. She wants a real relationship. As smart as she is, she probably made a connection with how things were during his time and thought there was a chance. As James walks past the other man, he puts a hand on his shoulder. "Thanks, Jett. I get it now."

"Do you?" Jett turns to look at him. "Kate isn't like the rest of us. She hopes to find something I'm not sure exists anymore. She's special, and if you hurt her, I'll turn you in." Jett's smile, in combination with the black snake scale tattoo wrapping his neck, is a little disturbing. The threat serves its purpose, and Jett's protection of his friend reassures James to know the future isn't completely devoid of connection.

He doesn't answer. Instead, he knocks on Kate's door. "Kate, can I come in?"

"NO!" she shouts from the other side.

"Please, Kate. We need to talk. I'm an asshole," he admits.

He stands there waiting for her reply. Eventually the door swings open and Lessa exits the room, followed by Decci. Kate sits on the corner of the bed, ringing a handkerchief in her hands. She looks up at him with the loveliest tearstained eyes. "You are an asshole. Did anyone in your time even like you? I can't possibly see how you would have been successful, acting like that all the time."

Her words hit him like lashes from a whip. But he swallows them down. He deserves them, after all.

Stepping inside, he closes the door behind him, then crouches at her knees. He needs to be very careful with what he says. "There is nothing wrong with you, Kate. And I don't think you're pathetic. I think you are a very kind, intelligent, and beautiful woman, and we are both in a very fucked-up situation, trying to do our best."

She sniffles. "Then why did you act so repulsed by me?"

"It took me a few days to understand your culture. A manupartner is a foreign concept to me. I didn't understand why you would want one. Especially with how appealing you are. I thought you could have anyone you wanted. That's how it would have been during my time."

She brushes away the residual tears. "Really?"

"Yes. And you're successful. And quick-witted." This is where he knew the conversation would inevitably lead. To the admission he still feels uncomfortable about and would prefer to not admit to either of them. "And I'm afraid if I fake flirt with you, I might end up real flirting with you."

Her wet lashes cling to each other as she blinks. "Would that be so bad?"

He glances away. "It's just…" He hesitates long enough for her bright mind to solve the problem.

"It's just that I intended you to be a manupartner and that disgusts you, so now that clouds how you see me." She buries her face in her hands. "I knew it was a bad idea. That's why I never… I never wanted …" Her sobs overshadow whatever she is trying to say.

James gets up from his crouch and sits down on the bed next to her, pulling her into his arms. "Hey, don't cry. I didn't mean it like that. I understand now. Jett told me about how things are now. I know it's not what you wanted and how awful this must be for you."

She jerks back enough to crane her neck to look at him. "You do?"

He nods, unable to keep his hand from wiping the tears off her pink cheeks. "I do."

There it is again. God, she's so fucking sweet. And vulnerable. That urge to get her beneath him bubbles up inside him. But this time it's to protect her from the world and give her whatever she desires. Whether it's pleasure or friendship. *Fuck.* He goes stiff as the thoughts rattle him to his core.

He's never held a crying woman before. Perhaps this is a normal reaction that will pass once she fixes her makeup. That must be it. He never saw his mother or sister shed a tear. He assumes it happened in private, but they just raised their chins and pressed on.

If that isn't it, he's totally screwed. Because he can't handle her like this. Handle himself being the one who caused it.

They sit there, searching each other's expressions for long moments. This is why he tried to keep the distance between them. A draw like this is unnatural.

"We should probably go back in there." Her whispered words are reluctant, as if she senses the charged pull between them and is awed by it, instead of mildly horrified like he is.

Kate pulls out of his arms, standing, but he grabs her wrist before she moves too far away. "I'm going to do it, okay?"

"Do what?" she asks, like she doesn't already know.

Like he isn't being vague because he doesn't want to say it. To spell it out. Because it still feels like a surrender, even with his new understanding. "Flirt with you. And if it becomes real, and I do anything you don't like or that makes you uncomfortable, tell me. Okay?"

She studies him for a moment. "Okay." She walks away, keeping her back to him as she says, "Don't worry. I understand that nothing between us will be real. I won't get confused."

13 – An Electrical Charge

James

An hour and a half later, Lessa finally convinces Kate to end the practice session. "It will be so much easier in a real-life scenario," they say. The others all know they've been gunning for the promised cocktails. It doesn't take much arm-twisting.

At the bar on the ground level of Tower CA26, James sits to Kate's right, arm lazily lying across the back of her chair. She angles her body toward him, giggling at something Jett says. James isn't listening. He is too focused on the knee that keeps brushing against his under the table. At the little jolts of electricity that make him want to angle his body away from her. To run screaming in the other direction. But he can't, for his own sake. And he now knows if he does, Kate will think it means the exact opposite of what it actually means. Then the waterworks will start again. Then he'll get that sick feeling again at having caused it. Really, every action he takes revolves around self-preservation.

Kate's delicate hand waves through the air as she conveys the details of his awakening. Then it lands on his thigh. He glances around the bar, grateful to be in a corner booth, out of earshot of the other patrons. Once he feels secure, his focus goes back to her hand. Her fingers are now drawing ovals up and down the inside of his thigh.

As they trace dangerously upward, he covers her hand with his own before it can roam any further. She starts, turning her attention to him. He lets his eyes smile as he brings her hand to his lips for a kiss. Then he sets their clasped hands on the table.

"Out of character!" Jett announces from across the table.

James groans. This has become a game for them.

"A manupartner would gladly allow Kate's hands to wander freely," Lessa interjects.

Kate squeezes his hand, speaking low so only he can hear. "Sorry. I didn't realize that would make you uncomfortable."

He looks at her. Really looks at her. The concern in her shining eyes causes him physical pain. He takes her hand and places it back on his thigh, then brushes a lock of hair away from her temple. He really, really wishes her friends weren't sitting across from them, gleefully observing the spectacle. What feels like such an intimate moment isn't for their eyes. Still, he cups the corner of her jaw, capturing her attention. "You are perfect and have nothing to apologize for. Act natural. I'll adjust."

"But . . . I don't want to make you uncomfortable."

Sweet, sweet Kate. Jett's assessment was correct. He was so blinded by the shock of waking up in the future, he hasn't been assessing her accurately. She'd never intentionally do anything to harm him. That only makes this harder. And if she pulls back because of something he does and the inspector gets suspicious, it's his life. He shouldn't have moved her hand. There is only one way to convey this to her. So he looks into her eyes and tells her the truth.

"Kate, when you touch my leg like that, I promise, *uncomfortable* isn't what I'm feeling." Why did his voice get low like that? And gravelly. What is he doing?

Kate's mouth falls open, exposing her rosy tongue. He wants to slide his thumb into her mouth and see if she'll lick it. Suck it.

Fuck. What is wrong with him? Why do his thoughts always turn sexual with her?

He drops his hand, adjusting in his seat to shift the straining fabric of his pants. Kate's nails are digging into his thigh now. He leans and whispers into her ear, "Easy," as he encloses her hand with his. The moment their skin touches, her fingers relax.

As the heat of the moment dissipates, Decci appears with a tray of drinks. He surveys the four of them. His voice comes out singsong as he asks, "Did I miss something?" The manupartner passes out the drinks as if he wouldn't register the answer to his question if someone supplied it.

Lessa leans back against the seat, fanning themself with a menu.

Jett, whose cool skin is now a pale pink, leans forward. "It seems I was wrong about your ability to flirt. Do you feel that electrical charge, Lessa, or is it just me?"

"Mmmhmm," Lessa mutters.

Jett picks up his cocktail and downs it in a few gulps. "I hate to run, but . . ." He gets to his feet. "Decci, shall we?"

Lessa excuses themself a few minutes later, then Kate and James are alone. They finish their drinks, and as James escorts her back to the elevator, he can't help but sense disappointment hanging like a cloud around the beautiful woman. It follows them into her unit.

She pulls her device out of her fluffy bunny-shaped handbag. "I'll order you something for dinner." Different colors light up the screen as she places the order.

Dinner for him. And not her. She is shrinking away from him. A knot of dread twists his stomach. Before she can retreat, he comes to stand beside her, brushing the backs of his fingers down her arm. "Is everything okay?"

Kate flinches so subtly he barely catches it. Then she turns to him and plasters on the first fake smile she's given him. "I'm tired. I think I'll go to bed." She points to the smartwaiter. "It will be ready in about fifteen minutes. Goodnight."

Without another word, Kate slips into her bedroom and closes the door, leaving him alone.

14 – Let the Yearning Begin

K8

I am the flesh robot going through my nightly routine. The thought strikes K8 as ironic as she removes her makeup with a Vanish Me water-saving pad. Rubbing serums and creams onto her face. Changing into her night slip. Crawling into bed. Clinging to the numbness, lest she feel.

She lays in bed, willing her tears to remain at bay. They would, after all, age her. And she can't have that. As it stands, she'll already need a trip to the MediSpa. With all this added stress and the crying earlier, a Refresh session is in order. Absently, she wonders when her medi-artist's next opening is.

Not that she cares, but her beauty is the one thing the man, James, appreciates about her. Because she sees the way he looks at her. He wants her. Physically. But she disgusts him, too. He said as much. Though he told her he understands now, she can't expect his opinion of her to change overnight. All because of one stupid decision, one drunken evening. But her stupid decision led to his second chance. Is he grateful? No. He isn't. Not really.

She's coming to understand his character. He isn't a nice person.

Granted, he apologizes when he's wrong—which is all too often. He's selfish. Aggressive, disagreeable, idealistic, too independent, stubborn, arrogant, thoughtless, domineering, rude, aggressive . . . did she say that already? The point is, she doesn't much like him. What an awful collection of traits. Ones she'd never have selected for him. She meant what she said when she asked if anyone during his time liked him. He doesn't make himself available to be liked.

So why then does she feel this inexplicable draw toward him? That was the second time she thought he might kiss her, and he didn't. It stung like rejection. It's like Holy Mother Zephyr gave her this man only to taunt her with him. Because he is achingly handsome. And that stubble. He shaves only for it to appear a few hours later. ~~It would be so nice against her~~—No. She needs to put those thoughts out of her mind.

But it's the side of him that seems so utterly human, too. Watching him faced with the reality of his situation—she imagines she's seen a version of him no one before her ever has. Not that he's chosen to share it. She's only seeing it by circumstance. She's been watching and hasn't missed his little reactions. The way his eyes widen when he sees something that shocks him and tries to hide it. Or how when he apologized earlier, he leaned toward her like he couldn't help himself. It's the way his flaws mix with his . . . hope or drive? She pauses, considering the word. Well, the right word isn't important. The point is, she's witnessing his humanity emerge, like a flower blossoming. She just isn't certain if the flower is going to be poisonous. Based on what she's seen, it probably is.

He's made it perfectly clear where he stands. She doesn't like him, anyway. And she's promised not to get confused, despite the electrical charge between them. The only path forward is to look at this logically. From now on, James will deal with Scientist K8. Coolly logical K8. The K8 that kept her head down during her schooling and made it to the top of her class, then landed her job right out of training. Who became the top paid member of her division. That K8 can do anything she sets her mind to. Now she has her mind trained on getting through the inspection. She owes it to him to take this seriously. If it weren't for her foolish decision and the moral obligation that came with it, he wouldn't be in this situation. ~~He would still be dead~~. He would be blissfully unaware.

She'll fake it—the horror—and when they pass, she'll put some distance between them. Then move on with her life. Maybe she'll even go to the club she's been avoiding where she met Viper to prove she's well and truly over him. She'll find a lover. Someone willing to engage in a nightly meetup for a week or two. Surely she can manage at least that.

K8 rolls over, adjusting the setting on her Ageless Body Pillow for side sleeping. A moment later, the pillow shifts, folding into the curves of her body to support her in a way that will prevent cricks and creases.

A lover is precisely what she needs. She refuses to take care of her needs herself. That would only give her thoughts unrestricted liberty to settle on the man a room away. Tomorrow, she'll sneak her new sex toy into a kitchen cabinet so she isn't tempted. She suspects she only feels this drawn toward him because of proximity. He is attractive and available. Couplings were common during his time, so that fed her misguided thoughts. But if she looks at it objectively, besides being good-looking, there isn't much to like. K8 does not like James. There.

With that settled, K8 closes her eyes. Never mind that yearning feeling burrowing deep inside her.

15 – The Inspection

James

October 14, 2390, Day 74.

James holds a tablet in his hand with the World Clock app pulled up. He stares at the glowing red digital numbers. They flick from 14:59 to 15:00. He's done this for an entire hour now, watching every minute tick by. He counts the seconds. This is ridiculous. He's handled immensely stressful situations with such ease in the past.

If only he could face another economic downturn. At the first signs of the last financial crisis Tiger Capital handled, he made the risky decision to offload a portion of their portfolio at a loss. He convinced investors to hold tight. They sat on the capital for over a year. Then, when the market took a nosedive, he made some very strategic acquisitions, which amounted to the most substantial portfolio growth his group had seen since he founded his company. Managing the investor emotions during that period, however, was tenuous at best. Who wanted to listen to a twenty-five-year-old—even if he had his family name to back him up? He only lost one client that year. He'd much rather live through all those late nights and anxious phone calls than meet the impending inspectors. This was another thing his death stole from him.

15:01.

A series of chimes intersect the silence that spans the distance between James and his roommate. Kate pops up from her seat, giving him the eleventh fake smile since that first one, making it an even dozen.

James isn't one hundred percent sure what he's done to cause her distance, but he is one hundred percent sure he's done something. She seemed fine at dinner after he apologized, but something had changed, and he wasn't sure he liked it. After a day of placating smiles, he tried to confront her. To get her to tell him what's going on. Instead of sharing her feelings with him, she brushed his questions off entirely. Like he demanded, it appears she's entirely given up on the notion that something might develop between them. His bold little speech backfired on him.

He can hear Jett's voice crystal clear in his mind. *If you get recycled, it's on you.*

Not that he wants to use her—he feels like he made that clear. It's only that he may have misjudged that he had no lifelines. Because maybe Kate was offering to be that lifeline, and he rejected her outright. That only makes him more terrified of whoever stands on the other side of the door.

Led by his dread, James comes to stand behind Kate before she can open the door to his fate. He places his hands on her hips and leans down to whisper in her ear, "I'm feeling a little desperate, sweetheart.

You going to throw me a lifeline before you let them in?" *Please be the chipper, positive Kate I so desperately need right now. I'm sorry. I take back everything I said.*

A combination of factors beyond his control has awakened him to a previously uncharted and sprawling emotional landscape within himself. Strange new people and technologies bombard him constantly. He has no means to exercise any of his significant and finely honed willpower over his fate. He's faced with the knowledge—thankfully not the memory—of his violent first death every time he closes his eyes, and now the potential for his second looms right outside. Kate's withdrawn state is the icing on the cake. If she would only offer her friendship like she did before he screwed things up. He'd gladly take it now.

It's easy to find someone to blame for why this is so difficult and unfamiliar. The people who raised him were emotionally repressed. Based on his experience this last week, he can see that. *Stoic* was never the right word for his father. Inhibited, stifled. Emotionally constipated. His mother wasn't any warmer. She only embodied a different brand of aloofness. He remembers thinking they were calm, cool, and together. Competent and consummate adults. Figures to emulate. He's slowly coming to terms with how, in this new time, his emotions roam unbridled. He has too much time to think. He hates it. *What would my parents think of me now?*

Perhaps what he's experiencing is a bursting floodgates sort of situation that will soon ebb. He ought to bank on that. He's almost convinced himself when his stomach gives a nervous flutter. Kate hasn't responded to his plea, so he gives her hips a squeeze. "Baby, please." He isn't in control when his lips brush the skin of her neck.

She stiffens. Shit. Why did he do that? The more she pulls away, the more he wants to . . . what does he want? To win her to his side? Gain back the ally he lost in her? Make her smile? His stomach dips as he imagines her smile. Has he somehow become addicted to it in only a week? No, that can't be right. She's an incredibly beautiful woman who's giving him the cold shoulder. It's only his male instincts firing to rectify the situation because he definitely wants to do something with her. Where is his self-possession when he needs it?

Kate turns in his arms, inspecting him with a clinical expression. Her countenance is so frigid, it threatens to give him frostbite. He loosens his grip on her.

"Kate?" Why is she doing this now? His lungs seize like he's been sucker punched. She's going to turn him in. Oh God. He has to run. They are going to open the door and instantly know. And if they don't, she'll tell them. He upset her, and now she's eager to rid herself of him. He should have given more consideration to what Jett told him about the potential consequences for her. He should have said something. Thanked her. Now she isn't willing to risk it. She doesn't consider him worth it. And it's his fault.

But maybe she's right to turn him in. James is an asshole.

As if sensing his fraying mental state, she reaches up to pat his cheek. "You're freaking out for nothing. We'll be fine."

There isn't any feeling in what she says. Only the cool confidence of Scientist Kate.

"Listen, Kate. I'm sorry—"

"It's a little late for that," she says.

The door pings again, and without warning, she reaches out and quickly undoes a few of his buttons. She musses his hair, then hers. Then she slides the strap of her tank off her shoulder. She grabs his head, yanks it toward her, and rakes his stubble against the fine skin of her neck. The effort leaves her flushed and him breathless. Her sweet floral scent lingers in his nostrils, momentarily causing him to forget the gravity of his situation. God, she smells so good.

Then Kate sets a smile on her face and opens the door.

As the two men take in their appearance, reality comes rushing back. The taller of the two, with a perfectly Roman nose and cropped green hair, speaks first. "You're aware of your appointment time." It isn't so much a question as it is a statement.

"Oh, yes," Kate says, blushing. "We got a little distracted while we were waiting. Please come in."

The men eye James as they follow Kate into the living room. After they take their seats, she sits adjacent to them. James comes to stand beside her, keeping his expression carefully blank as he awaits her instruction.

The second, more physically robust man introduces them. "I'm GROW Inspector B-Corgi-MSP-00023599. This is my partner, B-Tepin-MSP-00024126."

"James, darling. Go fetch Inspector Corgi and Inspector Tepin a bottle of water."

Corgi, like the dog? James remembers the expression Decci made when Jett ordered him around. He tries to mimic it as best as he can.

When he comes back with two waters, he hands them to the men before taking a seat next to Kate. Inspector Tepin is speaking. "We'll need to take a blood sample from him before we begin our evaluation."

"Of course," Kate says, holding out her hand for Tepin's contraption. He eyes her warily. "I'll do it. See, I'm a scientist," she urges.

The one with the green hair can't seem to tear his eyes away from her chest and the strap that is now dipping precariously low.

A bolt of possessiveness shoots through James, but before he does something stupid like put the strap back in place, he remembers what she told him. A manupartner wouldn't care if their owner took a dozen different people to bed.

Kate, noticing the inspector's wandering eyes, plays to it. "Oh," she giggles, tugging the strap back into place. "I was getting a little frisky."

She flirts so easily, offering them the warmth she withholds from him. James refuses to get jealous.

The green-haired man, *Corgi*, swallows, taking the contraption from Tepin, and hands it to Kate. She sets it on the table and detaches a little cylindrical silver stylus from its side. She turns to him. "James, give me your hand."

James does as she bids, placing his hand in hers. He trusts her, he realizes. She presses the device that reminds him of a blood sugar monitor on his pointer finger. A sharp prick lances his skin. As blood wells, she holds his finger over the receptacle until he counts five drops. Neon colored lights illuminate the tablet.

Across the screen, words flash: *GROW: Unit 2899-MSP-James-00023468 Identity Confirmed.*

James withholds a sigh of relief. One test passed.

The attendant nods, collecting the tablet and stylus. He tucks the stylus into a bag and retrieves a new one from his shirt pocket. This one appears to be for operating the tablet.

"Let's see," Inspector Corgi says, scrolling through a list James can't see. Finally he stops, his eyes scanning. Then he looks up. "James, can you tell me what year you were born?"

Suddenly, James feels grateful for the line of questioning he put Decci through that first day. He wrinkles his brow, hoping he's a decent enough actor. Then he looks to Kate like he's confused. He tries to sound dumb as he answers, "I don't understand."

She gives him a gentle smile. "Do your best, sweetie. There is no wrong answer."

He figures this would relieve a manupartner, so he releases some of the tension he's been carrying. "Twenty-three ninety?"

"Perfect!" Kate announces. Like Decci, James grins, pleased that he's pleased her.

This is insane. If James survives this, he's getting drunk tonight.

"And what about your memories? What is the first thing you can recall?"

This one's easy. James keeps the serene grin. "Kate's beautiful eyes."

Beside him, Kate, who's watching closely, blushes. He reaches out and strokes her cheek in awe.

She glances at the robust inspector. "He's sweeter than he looks, isn't he?"

"What happened to his nose?" Tepin, the more skeptical of the two, asks in response.

Kate only shrugs. "I assumed that's what your inspection was about. I kind of like it. Makes him more rugged, don't you think?"

Tepin grumbles as he looks over at his partner's tablet, probably ensuring he's recording the information properly. "Looks like a broken nose. James, how did you get that injury?"

Momentary panic lights him up from the inside. He hopes he conceals it well enough as he says, "It was Kate's wish for me to be authentic, right, Kate?" He reaches up and touches his nose as if he doesn't quite understand what the inspector means. He's never been asked to play dumb before. But he does exactly what Jett told him to do. Act clueless and lead every answer back to Kate. He looks at her for confirmation.

"Yes. I was a bit shocked at first, but I've come to enjoy the little defect. He has little calluses on his fingertips, too." She takes his hand, turning it over for the inspectors. "He is my first GROW, and I'm very impressed with the authenticity of your product."

He sits blankly as both men touch his fingertips. A beaming Corgi says, "How odd. This isn't something our DNA manipulator technicians would have programmed, though. We might need to take him—"

Panic grips James and he can only hope sweat isn't beading across his forehead.

"What a happy accident! They feel glorious against my skin," Kate gushes, cutting the inspector off. "You should consider adding that as an optional feature."

It takes all of James's focus not to stiffen. She thinks of him touching her?

"And look at his eyes. I ordered blue, but they're more of a gray, don't you think?"

Tepin gets up from his seat and comes around to inspect him. "Yes, we'll need to take some images of that before we leave."

Corgi seems to have forgotten his suggestion of taking James somewhere, presumably to study, so he'll let them take as many pictures as needed. As long as he doesn't have to leave Kate, whose knee is vibrating subtly beside his. He reaches out, placing his hand on her thigh. Squeezing reassuringly.

James plasters a dumb grin on his face as the man prods at his eyes, opening the lids wider one at a time.

"That is interesting." Tepin goes back to his seat, saying to Corgi, "Did you make a note of that? Our quality control department will want to know."

"I assume you'll offer me some sort of discount?" she presses. Smart, smart Kate. Putting them on defense.

"Uhh . . ." The inspectors share a glance. "We'll see what we can do."

"I'm sure GROW would be happy to offer you a replacement if you aren't satisfied," Tepin says, narrowing his eyes at her.

Kate stands, cocking her head as she studies the man. "I told you I liked the defect and the calluses. Why would you offer me a replacement? Do you think I don't know my own mind?"

"Well, we weren't trying to insinuate any such thing . . ." Tepin sputters.

Corgi glances toward the door.

They both stand and James remains seated, awaiting Kate's instruction. He can only assume that Kate is playing it this way because she's trying to end the meeting. She knows the people in her world far better than he would, so he trusts that she knows what she's doing.

Corgi seems just as eager to end the meeting. He gives James a last glance, seeming satisfied with his robotic happiness. "Of course, Tepin is right. We didn't mean to imply that. We only wish you to know that GROW is committed to delivering you the premier manupartner experience you deserve."

To this, Kate reaches up and twirls a lock of hair. She looks away like she's become bashful. "That pleases me. A discount will be fine."

Corgi swallows, his gaze again dipping to Kate's neckline and lower. "Sure. We better get out of your hair. I'm sure you're eager to resume your *activities*. There are a few positions I could recommend if you were interested," he offers.

Kate gives a shaky laugh. "That won't be necessary. I'm plenty creative on my own."

Corgi smirks. "Are you sure? There's one that requires two males—I could stay and show you."

James can feel the waves of discomfort rolling off her. His every instinct is firing to shield her from this man and his leering eyes. If his skin is crawling, he can't imagine what hers feels like. He subtly reaches a hand in her direction, offering himself if she needs it. The moment she notices, she slips into his awaiting arm, pressing herself against him. She's using him as a shield. As he wraps his arm around her, a little of her tension eases. It feels fantastic, like she trusts him. His chest expands with something like . . . pride? It doesn't matter. Whatever this addicting feeling is, he's greedy for more of it.

He's about to reply for her, consequences be damned, when she says, "You're so kind to offer. I'm afraid I'm not that adventurous, however."

James tries to disguise the mixture of anger and elation swirling in his mind behind a mask of indifference, but as a disappointed Corgi packs away the tablet, Tepin studies him. James is sure he can see right through him because he is barely restraining the urge to throw them out.

Kate, noticing, says, "I selected protective. Well done!"

But it's too late. Whatever Tepin sees causes him to ask, "If we wanted to run a few more tests this afternoon, would you be opposed to sparing your unit for a few hours? We can do the pictures then."

James's heartbeat stumbles. They're going to kill him. He's going to go with them, they're going to discover he's from the past, and they're going to study him, then kill him. Logically, they can hardly have people from the past running around. He doesn't know much about the government or regulatory boards now, but he can't imagine they'd let GROW off lightly if they knew they were bringing back people from the past. He will most certainly be eliminated.

He glances down at Kate, who he's now clinging to. Her brows are twitching like they want to pinch together but can't. "I suppose not. You'll have him back by dinner, though? I was planning to take him out to show him off to my friends. I'll be so disappointed if he misses it."

James reminds himself that to these men, that story is plausible. Someone from this time would do something like that.

"We'll make sure he's back in plenty of time." Tepin steps toward James like he might offer a challenge.

"Unit, would you mind coming with us?"

James only looks at Kate, his grin frozen in place. He awaits her permission. Instruction. Salvation. *Don't let me go with these men*, he wants to beg. But he doesn't. Still, since he woke up in the future, as awful as it has been, he's had a glimmer of hope. A chance to prove something—but suddenly that doesn't seem like the most important thing. Maybe it's his survival instincts sounding the alarm. *I don't want to die.* It's almost like he's said that before. Was he awake during the plane crash? Did he say those very same words? He can't repress a shudder at the thought.

"James, sweetie, please follow the young men," she says, drawing him to the present. "Do as they ask, for me?"

James's heart hammers in his chest as he stands. Thankfully, to his ear, his voice remains bright and untethered as he says, "Of course. I'll be back soon. I can't wait to meet your friends."

It seems like the asinine thing a manupartner would say. He follows the inspectors to the door, hoping this is a bad dream.

Corgi turns, eyeing James. "Aren't you going to give your owner a goodbye kiss? Something to hold her over until you return. We don't want her disappointed with our premium product, do we?" His tone is chiding.

Fuck, he doesn't want to kiss her without her permission, but what else is he supposed to do? Essentially, his boss has given him an order.

He turns slowly, trying to figure out an excuse to forgo the kiss, but his mind is so scrambled, it's gone blank.

He strides across the room to where Kate stands, hoping his eyes convey the apology he feels. He shields her body from their view. She's trembling, and he feels awful for putting her through this. Taking her delicate jaw in his hands, he draws her face toward his as he leans down.

His lips hover before hers for a moment and she must sense he's hesitating because she demands, "Kiss me."

"I'm sorry," he whispers. Not because he doesn't want to kiss her, he realizes—just not like this. Not here in front of these men. But fuck, being this close, there's no sense in denying he wants to kiss her.

Right as their lips are about to brush, she whispers, "If they don't send you back, I'll find a way to get you out. I promise."

He believes her.

Gone is the cold scientist. In her place is the woman he took for granted. Warm and tender. And open.

Sparks ignite as James closes his mouth over hers. She must feel it too, because her mouth opens to let a sound escape. James swallows the half whimper-half sigh and takes advantage, gently dipping his tongue inside. He finds her rosy tongue. She tastes like mint and honey. Her lips are so unbearably soft. He needs to let her pull away. They have an audience, and he wants to do so much more than kiss this woman. Instincts have him snaking an arm around her waist, pulling her into his body. *Shit*.

He relaxes his hold, hoping she'll understand. She does, pressing gently against his chest. Their bodies part, and it's a painful separation. Her eyes are glazed as she says, "Oh, James. That was quite the goodbye. Run along now. Don't be late!"

She gives him a playful smack on the ass as he walks away.

Corgi's brows lift as his gaze sweeps over James. "That was quite the show."

Corgi isn't wrong, though James hates the thought of them watching. Still, his heart is fluttering wildly. He doesn't even have to fake his elated smile as he says, "I'm ready now."

Because something about that kiss has given him another reason to survive this inspection. He needs to step up and play the part in order to get back to her. Because more than he cares to admit, he wants another kiss.

16 – They Took Him

K8

K8 sits at her desk, furiously punching away at her 3key. In seconds, she pulls up the GROW Unit Contract, Warranty, and Terms of Service. Her fingers leave clammy prints on the keys. Then she taps up her device, which activates her m-volt. She thinks the command: Call Lessa.

Thank Zorg they answer on the first ring. "How'd it go?" Her m-volt delivers Lessa's voice into her mind as if they spoke the question aloud while in the same room.

"They took him!" she shrieks, both mentally and audibly, because sometimes thinking the words alone isn't enough.

Lessa sighs. "Calm down, K8. I'm sure there's a reasonable explanation. Now tell me what the inspector said."

"I need your help," she says, ignoring their question. "We have to read the documents. I sent them to you."

"When?" they ask.

"Just now!" K8 winces at her own electrified tone. "Sorry. I shouldn't have raised my voice at you. Please help me."

As K8 waits for Lessa to get the email, she tries to scan the text of the contract through glassy eyes. The words become too blurry before she even gets through the first paragraph. Why is the urge to cry her immediate irrational reaction to adversity? Stupid hormones. She can't even remember the last time she took a BalanceMe tablet.

"Did you get it?" She needs them to get it, open it, and tell her what it says. She needs them to find a loophole. Lessa is an expert at interpreting modern legalese, which incorporates the six major languages, so agreements only require one contract. It's complicated, but Lessa is a genius.

"I'm reading it now. Calm down and tell me what happened," they say.

So K8 does. She takes a deep breath, then tells Lessa every horrifying detail. With each word, her guilt weighs her down a little more, like it has decided to make her shoulders its perch. "It's my fault. If I didn't point out his eye color, they wouldn't have taken him. But I thought it would help because they would have figured it out, eventually. I thought it made it seem like I knew about his quirky defects, but that didn't mean he had any memories. I was trying to distract them, but I doomed him. And when they recycle him, it'll be my fault. Oh Zorg, Les, does this make me a murderer? Do you think it hurts?"

Lessa is quiet for a moment. "K8, seriously. I understand your reasoning. I think you did the right thing. They probably want to run a few lab tests to be safe. Since you didn't turn him in and he isn't malfunctioning according to the contract's definitions, it appears you still have rights to him."

"Okay, good. I only need to be patient and wait it out." K8 leans back in her chair, trying to feel relieved.

"Precisely. James won't do anything to get himself killed. Jett says your man is too self-important to do that."

"He's not my man." Still, K8 considers what they said. Jett is right. James is one of the most self-important people she's ever met. And as he would be quick to point out, she lives in *the future* where one's every whim is catered to.

But when he pleaded with her and kissed her neck while the inspectors were on the other side of the door, he was different. And when he tried to get her to talk about her feelings and she brushed him off. Again, different. "He's more than one thing."

"Uh oh . . ." Lessa's tone is skeptical, like they already suspect where this conversation is heading.

But K8 breezes right by. "I got eager to end the inspection. I tried to get them out the door, then one of them propositioned me—while he was working. It was so uncomfortable. Can you imagine?"

Lessa scoffs. "Sounds like he's due for a Respectful and Considerate Conduct Course."

"Agreed. James could tell I felt uncomfortable, and he got defensive. He let me hide against his side. It surprised me, but it felt good. Is that weird?"

"I don't know. Ten percent decent person does not make him a suitable man, if that's what you're thinking. He made you cry, remember?" Lessa's tone is enough to convey their disapproval, even without their forthright words.

K8 groans. "I know. But I think acting so protective of me is what ultimately made them ask to take him. Maybe it wasn't my fault?"

"It wasn't," Lessa says definitively. "What'd you say when they asked?"

"I said, 'Of course,' then prayed to Zorg that James didn't do anything stupid. He didn't, though. He cheerfully played along. Les, I was freaking out. When he followed them to the door, the creepy inspector made up this stupid thing about how a good manupartner would kiss me before he left."

"And?" Lessa prods.

"And . . . It's kind of a blur. He seemed like he didn't want to, which made me think he was still being protective. Like he didn't want to kiss me without asking if I was okay with it, because he whispered, 'I'm sorry.' But now that I've had time to think about it, he kissed my neck before the inspectors got there, without asking."

"Sounds like he was trying to save his own skin," Lessa observes.

"I know. But I was so caught up in the moment, I promised him I'd find a way to save him." K8 sits there for a moment, contemplating her options, as a numb sensation crawls up from her fingers and toes to take root in her chest. Finally, she says, "Then he kissed me."

"Yes, that was the ruse," Lessa agrees.

"No, Les. He really kissed me. It wasn't performative or quick or cold. It was . . . well, I don't really know what it was, but it wasn't nothing. And now he's gone. And I don't know how to keep my promise to save him."

"Wait, I know you want to help him survive from an ethical standpoint, but it doesn't sound as if you actually like him."

K8's stiff forehead is trying its hardest to wrinkle. "I don't." And she doesn't. She decided that two days ago. But the thing is, she's attracted to him. Now that he's kissed her and ~~her heart~~ her mind is fabricating its own ideas about ~~how she feels~~ what she thinks about him. Despite her brain telling her she doesn't like him. It's highly illogical—what a conundrum for a scientist. "I know he only kissed me because the situation forced him. But I still have to help him. What do I do?"

In her receiver she hears Lessa click, click, clicking. "Hold on," they say.

As she holds on, she paces, trying to work out the frozen feeling in her limbs. "Lessa?" she prompts. "I'm still holding on."

"I sent you something." The gravity in their voice makes her stomach clench.

She rushes over to the living room table, collecting the VR headset. Once it's on, she thinks the command: Open message. It's a Flash News article. The headline reads:

BREAKING: GROW SEARCHES FOR MISSING MANUPARTNER.

K8's throat clenches tight. This can't be good.

Missing manupartner reported at 15:30.

K8 thinks the command: Time check. The system speaks into her ear: 15:47. How much time has elapsed since James left? When did the inspectors arrive? They were late, she remembers, but James was watching the time so intently for both of them that she didn't bother. She reads on.

The unit is considered unstable and may be dangerous. Do not approach suspicious persons claiming to be from the past under any circumstances. Report any unusual encounters to the authorities immediately.

This report comes after GROW issued a Recall Notice claiming that some manupartners may retain embedded memories from their DNA origin vectors. NHOS citizens should report any unusual activity to authorities immediately.

GROW spokesperson states, "Leadership at GROW is working around the clock to swiftly resolve this minor incident. Citizens have no reason to fear their manupartner. If you have not received a notice, your unit is not at risk. This recall only impacts a minuscule batch of units, and inspectors are already in the field assessing units affected. Please cooperate with authorities if your unit is assessed to be faulty. GROW places the best interests of NHOS citizens at the forefront of every decision we make.

We will continue to provide you with the most realistic manupartner experience for years to come."

We reached out to several other manupartner producers for comment, and only CHOICElover owner Res6 provided a statement: "To my knowledge, this serious problem is isolated to GROW as a result of the release of their Realer Than Real production line. Often, a business may look to gain an edge over their competition with a product advancement, but it seems the leadership at GROW put this line out before they properly tested it. If consumers are concerned about the safety of selecting a GROW manupartner, CHOICElover will be here to provide the most premium original manupartner experience their unicoin can buy."

Clearly, Res6 saw an opportunity to gain market share. James isn't dangerous. Is he? *Did he kill the inspectors to escape?* She figures he could. And does that mean she's on the run now too? She watches too many thrillers. No, surely, he isn't that reckless. They'd be caught by nightfall. She isn't built for a life of crime, for Zorg's sake!

"Did you read it?" Lessa asks. When she doesn't say a word, they press, "K8?" Then, "I'm coming over."

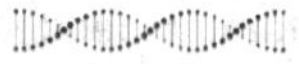

Lessa and K8 rush to the elevator, which opens to reveal Jett. They must have called him on their way over.

"Negative-K8!" he says, consolingly, and she can't help but chuckle at his clever yet poorly timed nickname. "Lessa told me what happened. Where do you think he went?"

"I have no idea. But we need to search for him. If they find him before we do, they'll . . ." K8 can't say it.

"They wouldn't," Jett says.

Lessa is shaking their head. "I'm afraid she's right. Stupid man. Before she had rights to him, but now, especially if he's assaulted an inspector—"

"K8's right. We need to start searching," Jett suggests, cutting Lessa off before they can say any more damning words. K8 and Lessa nod their agreement. "This'll be fun. We're like detectives. Lessa, you start on the top floor. K8, you take the floors with public areas. I'll start at two." Jett squeezes her hand reassuringly. "We'll find him."

Lessa pulls her into an embrace. "Worrying is going to give you wrinkles."

K8 tries not to giggle, but they are so ridiculous it's impossible.

Then they separate. K8 tackles the ground floor first, pacing the expansive space, trying not to look as if she's searching for anyone. An hour later, when she makes it to the twenty-fifth-floor fitness park, she's surprised no one has reported that she's the suspicious person. Because with her increasing panic, the way she's wandering around with her darting stare, she's certain she looks suspicious. She should have put on her black air control officer uniform. At least then she might appear official.

Perhaps a drink would help with her rising anxiety. And it would be rude not to offer her FRIENDS one after they've been searching so diligently on her behalf. She taps her m-volt to activate it, then thinks the command: Message Lessa and Jett, *Meet me at Tower Bar.*

A quick elevator ride takes her to the top floor. The doors open to the expansive lobby. To her right, penthouse units hover over the congested city. The left side hosts the bar and a sad excuse for a nightclub. Lessa is already there and halfway through a Bizzy-bee when she slides into the chair beside them. Jett is only a moment behind her.

"Great idea," he says as Lessa slides them both a preordered drink.

K8 stirs the cocktail with the little metal stick. "I'm surprised we didn't find him yet."

"I know. I spoke with the section manager in the lobby on the first floor and she said it's been quiet all afternoon. Do you think they took him to another tower before he escaped?" Jett rattles the ice in his glass as he looks over the rim.

"They must have. I made it through each shop and restaurant in my search." K8's eyes go wide as her stomach grumbles.

Then Lessa's hand is in the air to flag down the bartender. "Some peppered pastry twists and the dressy eggs, please." They turn to K8. "Can't focus on searching if you're hungry."

What's a man's life when compared to dinner? They're right, though. She is hungry.

The bartender delivers the food and another Bizzy-bee each. K8 is about to suggest they recommence the search, when Lessa gives a weary sigh. As if he knows what she's going to say, Jett averts his gaze before he finally asks, "Won't he try to go back to your unit?"

K8 pauses mid-sip. "I hadn't thought of that."

Jett's device pings. He lifts it, scanning the message. "I know someone who works for the Information Distribution System. I asked them to message if anything comes through."

K8 and Lessa lean closer.

Jett lowers his voice to a whisper. "They found *her*."

What? It was a *her*? As in a woman. So, not James? Not James. *Not James*. This is good, right? Or bad. If they returned him like they promised, he would have been back to her unit hours ago. Oh Zephyr, what was she doing running around like an unhinged person? Sitting at the bar worrying the night away. She always knew a manupartner would be nothing but trouble.

"The runaway was a woman?" Lessa asks.

"The initial report didn't say. What a strange and misleading coincidence," Jett says, then taps his device, presumably responding to his IDS contact.

"That might have been helpful to know earlier," Lessa complains.

"I don't think they knew, Stress-Les. GROW seems to be trying to make light of this," Jett says.

And it's true. The casual pretense of the press release surprised her. Retained memories is a gross understatement. GROW is bringing people from the past back to life. It's unprecedented.

Lessa sighs, slinging an arm around K8's shoulders. "What are you going to do now?"

What is she going to do? "I guess go back to my unit and hope James shows up."

As the trio separate, Jett gives her a hug, saying he's going to get more food at a higher quality establishment, but then he'll be available afterward if she needs to talk.

Then K8 goes back downstairs to her unit, a little buzzed and, of course, alone.

17 – Kate Will Be So Pleased

James

With each step they take down the hall, James's elation at the kiss transforms into something darker—like panic. He's practically vibrating with it. They're going to find out. They're going to kill him. He's going to die again. Never have a chance to test his mettle in this future world. Never again see the strange woman whose face he can't seem to get out of his head. Whose lips he now knows are as soft as they look. He can't die. Again.

What was it like the first time? He can't remember the plane crash. He's thought about it a dozen times since waking up in the future. Will the procedure to recycle him hurt? Or whatever tests they put him through after they discover he's real?

They pass the stairwell, and James considers making a break for it. No. Surely they're only going to run a few simple tests that he can bluff his way through. Act dumb and, when in doubt, say, *I don't know.*

The elevator doors open and Tepin motions for him to enter. He complies, turning to face the doors as they enter after him. He stares blankly ahead, trying to blink at his reflection in the shiny doors at regular intervals. As the elevator descends, he watches Tepin reach into his pocket. He raises the clear device so he can read whatever is on the screen.

"Did you get the notification?" he asks Corgi.

"No, what is it?" Corgi asks.

The elevator stops on the next floor, and a few other future people enter. James and the inspectors make room. When the door closes, Tepin insistently punches the SAT B button, reminding James of how he did the same that first day.

James can barely hear Tepin's voice as he leans toward Corgi and whispers, "A manupartner with retained memories escaped the inspectors trying to bring them in. They're on the run in Sector B. We're the closest. The team there is calling for backup."

James's blood goes cold. Does that mean what he thinks it does? That they've caught someone from the past—someone like him—and they're going to hunt them down. On the one hand, it isn't him, so that is good. On the other hand . . . he doesn't want to consider what the other hand holds. All he can do is hope the person gets away and enjoys their do-over as much as he will his. If he gets out of this.

The elevator stops and the button for SAT B lights up. He compliantly follows the men off into what looks like an oversize single-car garage. In front of them, through the glass chamber they stand in, is a SAT.

"What are we going to do about this one?" Corgi asks, nodding behind him toward James.

Tepin glances at him as if the inspector's forgotten James is following them. James gives him a dazed grin, like they have addressed him and he's waiting for instructions.

Tepin waves a hand. "His programming is malfunctioning. Did you see the way he glared at you when you offered to show that woman a few things?"

"She said she selected protective." Corgi turns around to look at James. "You wouldn't care if your owner took me up on my offer, would you?"

Absolutely, he would care. Still, he clears the emotion from his face and steals a line from Decci, Jett's manupartner. "If Kate is happy, then I'm happy." He hopes it and his stupid smile is enough.

Tepin shakes his head. "He doesn't appear to hold any stored memories, and that is what we're supposed to be searching for. Something so minor probably isn't worth reporting."

Relief hits James like an avalanche. Keep grinning and this will all be over soon.

"The lady seems to like him. And she's right about the calluses. 'Realer Than Real,' after all. Do you think if I proposed that to Finx, he'd add it to the specification list? I bet they'd catch on. Maybe flawed will be the new trend and they'll call it the Corgi Adaptation."

The air in the room shifts and Tepin addresses James again. "Go back to your owner. Tell her you've passed inspection and we will send a confirmation report before the day is over."

James doesn't need to be told twice. A lightheaded sensation sweeps over him and he's sure he's the one going mad when he says, "Kate will be so pleased."

18 – A Far Cry from Mr. Darcy

K8

Back in her unit, K8 thinks the command: Time check. Her m-volt responds: 23:15. Her delightful buzz has worn off, and she's spent the last hour and a half fixating on the still missing man: James Alexander Fletcher. Her initial search was rather innocent, driven by curiosity, like all the other times she's sifted through the Old News app in search of something amusing. That is, until she stumbled on the first damning article. The man had more than a dozen articles written about him postmortem. So many that they fill five of her six screens. None of them are remotely amusing.

Her anxiety about his whereabouts has converted into agitation since they quit searching for him. The articles didn't do him any favors. There is only so much a searing kiss can do.

Finally, she gives in and thinks the command: Call Jett. While she waits for him to answer, she rereads a particularly disturbing one:

Development Group Evicts Elderly Tenants.

"Hello K8ie Pretty Lady?" Jett answers. She can hear sleep in his voice.

"Not your best work," she says, almost feeling guilty for waking him up. Almost. But the number of times she's supported her FRIENDS as they've wallowed over a manupartner dissuades her.

"I've been reading the articles about him from his time," she confesses.

"He hasn't made it back, then?" Jett asks.

K8 sighs. "No." She doesn't want to put the thoughts to words, but she feels she must ask, "Do you think they've decommissioned him?"

"It is a little concerning that you haven't heard anything from GROW. If they were holding him, I would think they'd be obliged to communicate that to you."

This is why K8 likes Jett. Of their FRIENDS group, he matches her ability to be ~~cynical~~ logical the best. If she called Lessa, they would only assure her about how everything would be fine and tell her to go to bed and worry about her nonexistent wrinkles.

"I feel so useless. If something happens to him . . . if he's gone, all I've done is drag my FRIENDS around on a fruitless manhunt." Unable to tolerate the silence, she breaks it after a few stagnant moments. "He has to be alive. I'll go to GROW when they open. They'll have to give me answers. Lessa said I still have rights to him."

The consumer rights board is one of the more powerful NHOS divisions. She'll bring Lessa so they can speak some legalese at them and get them to return James to her. Who cares if he is from the past—he's hers. That's not right exactly, but technically, if she still owns him, they can't take him. That's the point.

"Lessa's right," Jett says. "I don't see why you care so much, either. Let the people at GROW deal with him. I read that article you sent. He wasn't a good man."

K8 knows this, but she isn't sure it's fair to judge the past by the standards of the present. Clearly, some people had a problem with James, but nothing he did appeared to be illegal. And people seemed willing to work with him, so that suggests trust, or ironclad contracts. It's just that everything she's read seems to point to the same character flaws. "But he's still a human being. How can you not see the ethical dilemma I'm facing? I'm morally obligated to help him. Besides, I promised."

"K8, darling. It is not your ethical dilemma. GROW should shoulder that weight. Not you." Jett is only a decade older than her, but he affects a fatherly tone so well when he's trying to impress a point.

K8 appreciates the sentiment. But he doesn't understand. Even if it was her ethical dilemma, she imagines he'd dismiss it the same way. Such is the way of her FRIENDS. She must make him see.

"If they try to recycle him, he'll admit he's real. Then they'll have questions for me, and who knows what they'll do with him? He'll become their experiment. Look at how they handled the runaway unit earlier. They told the public it may be dangerous. Do you think they're going to let their mistakes live? I imagine there's a massive coverup being planned as we speak." She feels her argument is quite stable. "I'm the only one who can do anything to save him. I have to try."

As if Jett summoned it, her device, which has been sitting idly on her desk, flashes at the edge of her vision. "Oh!" she exclaims. "An email from GROW."

"What does it say?!" Jett barks into her ear.

She snatches the glowing glass gadget and thinks the command: Open email. When the message pops up, she furiously scans it. Impossible! "It says my unit has passed the inspection and that nothing further is required. They released him hours ago." Technically, the report says more than that, but that is the gist.

"Wait, he passed inspection? So where is he?"

"Great question," she says, more than a little irritated.

Right then, the door handle rattles, followed by a pounding fist. The series of automatic pings that alert the resident to visitors sounds. K8 turns, dropping the device to the desk with a thwack. The sound reverberates in her mind, and she imagines it does in Jett's too. "Sorry."

"What happened?" he asks.

She thinks the command: System, unlock door. The lock hisses as it clicks open, and whoever is on the other side will have heard.

"K8, what is it?" Jett presses.

She wants to answer, but what she sees as the door cracks open effectively silences her. James steps through, looking as whole as he did when the inspectors escorted him away. He's grinning like a madman.

"K8, what's happening?" Jett barks in her ear.

"He's back," she whispers. "I'll call you tomorrow."

She doesn't take her eyes off James as he saunters toward her. She turns her chair to face him, crossing her arms. "Where have you been?"

"Nice to see you too, beautiful. I thought you'd be happy to see me." His grin transforms into a lopsided smirk. In response, her heart catches in her throat despite her many misgivings. "Come here."

Her body launches itself out of her chair. He's so handsome, and she's so relieved. And angry, but mostly relieved. She isn't thinking as she throws her arms around him. He returns her embrace, holding her almost too tight. She doesn't care, burying her face in his chest. Breathing in his delicious scent. Feeling his firm body beneath her fingertips. She still isn't thinking as she runs her hands up the firm muscles of his back, tilting her head back to look at him.

"Oh, K8, you have no idea how happy I am you're here." He leans down to kiss her forehead. "I thought they were going to turn me into a lab rat and I'd never get to see you again. It made me panic. I just needed to see you."

He nuzzles her neck, and she lets every word he says burrow into her psyche. She's so dangerously close to getting lost in the moment. She could arch her neck in offer to him. What would he do? Kiss her slowly and draw out this first time, teasing her until she's overcome with desire, or would it be an explosive frenzy? The warm feelings make her dizzy.

James, however, is stroking her waist as if he's content to keep holding her.

"James," she prompts, curious about what he's thinking. What he was doing for those several hours . . .

"Yes?" He pulls back and takes her jaw in his hands, tilting her head so she's staring up at him. His eyes dip to her lips, causing her pulse to skip.

She steadies herself. Answers first, then kisses. "I got an email that said you were released hours ago. Where have you been?"

"Hmm?" he mutters, seeming more lost in the haze between them than she is.

But she's been worrying all evening for his safety. "Where were you?"

"Oh," he says, chuckling. "We only made it down to the SAT garage when they got called to hunt down some missing unit. They decided my defects weren't worth the trouble after all. I came back right after they released me. Your door was locked, and you didn't answer. I waited around for a while, then I figured your unit number would work to get me a drink."

K8 blinks, hardly able to process what she's hearing. His words confirm every article and everything she thinks of him. Of all the selfish people . . .

He must misinterpret her expression, because his eyes dip back and stay glued to her lips. "I've always been lucky." He leans forward.

He's going to kiss her. The part of her that craved another kiss moments before gives way to a chilling sensation. "Excuse me?"

He pauses. "Your unit number. I gave it to the bartender, and he gave me drinks." He grins like he's proud of his cleverness before leaning forward again.

She releases the back of his shirt, which she's been gripping. "Get off me, you monster. Zorg, I can't believe I almost let you kiss me again."

He steps back as if she's slapped him. Good. She might slap him if he doesn't start talking. With her hands planted firmly on her hips, she levels him with a glare.

"You weren't here. Did you want me to sit outside your door like a lost puppy? I figured after the day I've had, you wouldn't mind." He glowers down at her as if he's the one being slighted.

Her skull might actually crack. "You figured I wouldn't mind?!" The walls between units are thick enough that surely her neighbors can't hear her. Even if they can, it doesn't slow her down. "I thought the Flash News article about a runaway unit claiming to be from the past was you! While you were having a relaxing drink, Jett and Lessa spent hours helping me search for you. I thought you were dead!" Her voice rattles precariously, but she refuses to shed a single tear on his behalf. Her boiling anger is making her feel overheated and freezing at once. How could he be so stupid? And inconsiderate? How could she have even considered whatever ridiculous feelings that kiss tricked her into feeling?

James's face becomes serious as her words seem to sober him. Is he remorseful? Or at least questioning his actions? She looks away.

Back to the screens, where the articles remind her of who this man really is before sympathy can crowd out more appropriate emotions. He comes to stand behind her, taking her hair in his hands. He moves it to one side, exposing her bare shoulder.

She feels him lean down, feels his breath on her neck, and she thinks he's going to kiss her skin again. Like this is some move calculated to calm her down. She doesn't want him to, and she does because there is clearly something wrong with her. The conflict and anticipation prickle her skin. Didn't she read that hate sex used to be a thing? Before she can decide if she'll allow this or tell him to stop, he sucks in a sharp breath. She turns her head to the side. His face is so near she can feel the heat radiating off him. Smell his heady scent. See the individual hairs of his stubble.

But he isn't staring at her. He's staring at the screen. At the article she sent to Jett. The one with the damning headline:

The Folly of Mourning Monstrous Men.

Beneath it is a photograph labeled *James Alexander Fletcher*.

19 – All the Saints You Know are Dead

James

James recognizes the journalist's name immediately. Borne was a harsh and regular critic of his ever since he campaigned for the city to tear down that dilapidated property so his investment group could put up another tower. He doesn't remember if the project replaced an unregistered historic site or a community center. People got so uptight about those types of things.

He has to give it to Borne, though. It is a catchy headline. Too bad Borne, the saint, is long dead, along with anyone who might have read his disparaging take on James's life. Except Kate. She's clearly read it and is allowing Borne's claims to color her judgment of him. James, the sinner, has a future. It would almost be worth resurrecting Borne to see the look on the man's pasty face. But he has more pressing things to consider now.

Slowly, he rises to his full height, only beginning to understand how complex Kate's anger toward him really is. He thought when he returned, she'd be pleased to see him. The way she'd responded to his kiss . . . well, it had him backtracking on his previous stance of refusing to be this woman's lover in favor of kissing her again to see where it might lead. He was about to kiss her neck, like he did earlier, and try to make up for the easily forgivable mistake of not being at the right place at the right time. Now he knows it will not be that simple to earn her forgiveness. She called him a monster. It is incredibly unfortunate, since during his highly unpleasant day he came to the determination that he wants this one thing—this pleasure in a sea of challenge—to be simple.

He needs to read the full article to know what there is to smooth over to make it so. But first he needs to determine how bad she thinks it is. "What's that?" he asks.

"It seems I was right," she says, speaking to the screens.

"About?" he urges, wishing she'll get to the point so he can get to defending himself.

Her chair rolls backward, and he has to move so it doesn't knock into him. She walks to her bedroom door, not facing him as she says, "There's nothing about you to like. You're selfish, thoughtless, and, according to numerous articles, ruthless."

He can hear the conviction in her voice. She means it and it stings. He opens his mouth for a rebuttal, but she slips into her room. When she shuts the door behind her, she leaves a vacuum in her wake.

"Fuck," he grumbles, torn between knocking on her door and reading the article.

As the air returns to the room, he breathes. Then he turns and glares at the monitors. Time to retread the sins of his past.

The Folly of Mourning Monstrous Men: Editorial

If a wealthy man falls in the forest, does he make a sound? In our society, he does—when his plane slams into a Colorado cliffside. News outlets across the country are heralding the tragic loss of the newest member of the Forbes Real-Time Billionaires list: James Alexander Fletcher.

But I ask, why do we mourn such a man, and not shower more media attention on the sinking of a vessel carrying over 600 migrants in the Mediterranean?

I'll tell you why. Our society has a sick fascination with men like Fletcher. But what, besides his wealth, makes such a man worth our interest? Let's dive in.

James Alexander Fletcher was born the first and only son to modern shipping magnate Arthur Fletcher and his international trade brokerage heiress wife Cathy Pennington. After attending Dwight, a prestigious New York City preparatory school, Fletcher went on to Dartmouth, where he majored in industrial organization economics before dropping out in his junior year. At this point he had amassed a modest portfolio of 10 condo buildings, had founded an up-and-coming REIT, and was on the threshold of launching what would later become his flagship enterprise, an investment group called Tiger Capital.

But how did Fletcher get his start? There are dozens of podcasts where you can watch him prattle on about what a self-made man he is. But was he really? Are any of today's modern billionaires? Can they call themselves self-made considering the substantial impact of outside influences, such as their background, in-place social systems and public works, chance opportunities, or inherent privilege, that undoubtedly fast-tracked their success?

Case in point: Fletcher notoriously built his wealth from a luxury watch business he started as a ten-year-old, a story he reportedly told often. According to Fletcher, when his father challenged him to create a business plan and implement it, founding his first company, then refused poor Fletcher's request for a business loan, he struck out on his own, building capital little by little by selling luxury vintage watches, starting with those in his personal collection. Mind you, he was ten, which begs the question, how many ten-year-olds do you know that sport luxury watches?

Fletcher proudly described the shock on his father's face a few years later when he showed him his balance sheet, valued at well over five hundred thousand dollars. Displaying situational blindness to the privileged source of his original capital—the watch collection—he called attention to his self-made status. From there, Fletcher believed he had no limits.

Randal Carlyle, a peer of Fletcher's from his formative years, fondly recalled, "I still remember when Fletch offered me $10,000 for my first Rolex. Of course, I didn't want to part with the gift from my grandfather, but Fletch had a way of convincing people. I took the $10,000, which sounded like a lot of money to me at the time, but the kid had it sold for $34,000 two weeks later."

If that doesn't sound like a typical upbringing to you, we're on the same page. But after all he was blessed with, Fletcher wasn't satisfied. He developed a ruthless reputation as his private equity company purchased countless struggling businesses only to strip them of their property, a form of venture capitalism known as vulture capitalism.

Maria Rossi said of the Brooklyn apartment building Fletcher's group purchased last year, "He told me he wanted to do something really special with the place. He had a vision." Rossi shakes her head as she fights back tears, before continuing. "It has been in our family for generations. I never should have trusted him."

Of course, Fletcher did have a vision for the distressed property. At the height of the third modern pandemic, the Rossi's low-income tenants had struggled to pay rent, resulting in financial hardship for the landlords. Fletcher provided a quick and seemingly easy solution. With a proven track record of turning struggling real estate investments around, he convinced them to sell. But within months, longtime tenants received eviction notices. After six months of around-the-clock renovation, the new luxury units were being marketed for exorbitant rates.

At the time, we reached out to Fletcher for comment, but we never received a response.

These stories are not isolated incidents. If I had more page space, I could fill a catalogue with the misdeeds of Fletcher and his peers. And the sad thing is, you would read them.

I believe humanity is on a precipice, and we have a critical choice to make. A course correction of monolithic proportions may be the only thing we can do to save ourselves. Because with puppet governments controlled by the ultrawealthy, and our ongoing fascination with such larger-than-life figures as James Alexander Fletcher, will we be able to slow the decline of empathy and halt the rise of narcissism before it is too late?

Timothy Borne

Editor, New England Conservator

He remembers the building Maria Rossi referred to. The structure was a safety hazard, and they didn't have the funds to do the proper maintenance. As far as he was concerned, he'd done them a favor. It's not as if the existing tenants could've afforded the rents needed to justify the improvements. Government grants and rezoning might have been possible—other wealthy families exploited such means, pocketing the profits—but he firmly rejected the idea of taking such financial assistance. He didn't need anyone, much less the government, to help him get a project off the ground. So, he did what was needed and ignored the criticism. There would always be those who fought progress.

After the plans were approved by commissioning, it only took the leasing agency a month to have the entire building rented out. They even put together a package of special rates to help the minority-owned businesses that would occupy half the spaces on the ground floor. Not that they needed to advertise that shit. The name Fletcher was already engraved into enough plaques and founders' bricks throughout the city to justify his family's contribution to the community. To do more would have been bragging.

He's still sitting in her desk chair, tapping his fingers on the smooth surface, when she finally emerges. For the life of him, he can't figure out an angle to get Kate to see things his way. He's done a little research, though, and it seems Borne wasn't a complete saint either.

She breezes past him, heading to the kitchen.

"Listen, Kate. There are two sides to every story—"

Her shoulders tense. "I only came out to get some water. I'm not discussing this."

If he can show her that Borne's opinion should not be trusted, she might not take the articles so seriously. To some, Borne might even be viewed as more monstrous than him. "Did you know the journalist who wrote the article was one of the founding members of The Wealth Centralization Resistance? He literally helped bring about The Great Equalizer. By comparison, I'm not that ba—"

"Don't you dare say that. You evicted elderly tenants who didn't have near the resources you did," she says, cutting him off, as if it would put the matter to rest.

"You're not even listening to what I'm saying. Sure, some people may have disagreed with the way I conducted business, but you should direct your fury at men like Borne. He's the one who caused millions of people to lose everything. And what was it for?" He prays she'll see reason.

"Did it ever occur to you that I might agree with Borne in principle? And don't think I'm so naïve as to not realize that innocent people suffered too, but no one else was brave enough to do anything, and something had to be done." When she turns, her stare could cut glass.

"I don't have a problem with people in pay bracket A+ or wanting nice things." She gestures to her outfit. "But how could hoarding billions be ethical?"

"It's only one article," he says, scrambling to come up with a different argument.

"There are more articles, James," she says with finality.

He sorts through his catalogue of acquisitions. God, if his memory were crisper, this would be so much easier. "I think I know what project you were referring to a minute ago. That building we tore down was full of asbestos and mold. If I recall correctly, several of the tenants were having respiratory issues."

"That isn't the point. When you evicted them, did you think to make sure they had somewhere else to go?" she demands. "Or did you only see your bottom line?"

"They weren't my responsibility. That's just the way the world works," he says, repeating the line his father said to him throughout his childhood when he had similar questions.

He remembers the first time it really stuck in his mind. His nanny had taken him to a friend's birthday party held at the pool of one of the boutique hotels his family owned. He'd seen his mother get into the elevator with a man he didn't recognize, who drew her close before the door closed. James asked his father about it. He said he knew about her arrangement and explained that sometimes people like them had different types of relationships with different people. He and his mother went through life as partners, but other relational transactions that James would learn about when he was older might take place outside the marriage. Granted, as he got older and came to understand what precisely his father meant, he thought he may prefer not to share his wife when he got one. But at the time James pressed, still not understanding, until his father told him with finality, "That's just the way the world works." When that appeared to provide a sufficient explanation, the phrase gained traction in their father-son talks.

It doesn't seem to have the same effect on Kate. In fact, her cheeks have blossomed an ominous shade of pink. "Well, James Fletcher, that isn't how the world works anymore. If you can't figure that out quickly, you're going to get recycled." Her mouth snaps shut, but not before a gasp escapes. She slaps a hand over her mouth as though she's surprised herself with her biting words. It almost makes him grin, but he holds it in. Her hand falls limply to her side. "See, this is why I didn't want to discuss this."

He shakes his head. "It's fine. I deserved that."

Jett is right—Kate is special. A truly good person, which makes him look especially muddy. Would she have taken the time to find a solution for the elderly tenants? Undoubtedly, yes. She is helping him out of the goodness of her heart, for fuck's sake. He didn't even give the elderly tenants a second thought. He just assumed they'd figure it out, but what if they didn't have the resources, as she suggested? Shifting, he rubs a hand across the back of his neck. But wouldn't it have been worse to leave the elderly tenants in a problematic facility? Surely someone helped them.

It isn't as though he is monstrous, as Borne suggested. It's just that he isn't *not* monstrous. James falls somewhere in the middle. Some undefined gray area.

But if this is what she thinks of him . . . How is her opinion, more than that of any of his former critics, making him question things? Or is it everything that has happened in the past week since he awoke in the future?

During his time, he was a determined man marching toward a clear objective. Waking up in the future, he just assumed he'd carry on in the same vein. Double down. Make it twice. But now he isn't so sure. It's as if some cosmic force is presenting him with a different challenge. Only he's clueless about what it might be.

She turns to walk away, but he calls, "Kate."

She glances back, and the way she's looking at him, like her anger toward him has transformed into something more like pity, makes his chest clench.

She stares straight into his eyes and says, "You could choose to be better this time around if you wanted to."

Does progress have no value anymore? In the future, does building things not matter? Outside the window—*particle panes*, he corrects—several SATs zip by. When Kate got home from searching, she must not have bothered setting them to a scene like she normally would. The SATs and the smog-filled air serve as a reminder of how different the future is from his time. Look what progress has earned humanity. Even if he argued for it, she would never see what he spent his life doing in a positive light.

When he turns back to her, she's studying him again. Does she really believe he can become something more? Someone better? Does he want to? Does he need to change? Or will these realizations brought on by his shocking arrival in the future fade with the progression of time until he no longer remembers or cares? And what does the woman walking away from him have to do with it?

A part of him thinks the answer is *Everything*.

Before Kate steps inside her bedroom, she hesitates. Like she's waiting for him to tell her he'll try. Or say what she read was a lie. He's sure it's all true, but truths have different lenses. Different colors and shades depending on who you are and how you see the world. Yet to her, it doesn't excuse his selfishness, thoughtlessness, or ruthless drive. Traits the evidence suggests he has. Traits she clearly sees as faults. Enough to dislike him.

He hates these new and unwanted realizations and the feelings they bring up, but he hates that she doesn't like him more. It seems so silly, so juvenile. Likability wasn't ever his top priority, yet he's unknowingly given this woman some mystical power over him. He cares what she thinks. Wants her to like him. He hates that, too. But it can't be helped. It just is.

The James of the future is becoming a foreign creature to himself.

He approaches her slowly. Drawn to her. Unable to stop himself. Stupid kiss. He runs the calluses of his fingertips up her bare arms. Relishes her shiver. He won't lie to her and tell her he'll be better when he doesn't know if he can, but maybe he can convince her there are other things about him to like. With a confidence he doesn't feel, he asks, "Do you want me to be better?"

"There are so many articles about you. They can't all be wrong," she whispers, turning. Her gaze feels like a careful inspection. Like James is the particle under the microscope of her judgment.

His jaw hardens. *You can't believe them,* he wants to tell her. *I'm not that bad.* But he can't say the words because they feel too close to a lie. If only he could offer her some evidence.

By now, any residual alcohol in his body has dissipated enough that he feels in control of his own actions. His fingers continue to trace a path up and down her arms. Maybe he could be good for her in a different way. He knows what he wants, and he thinks she wants it too, despite herself. The day has been long, and they are both tired. His defenses are low, and he doesn't have the energy to ignore his desire to be near her. His need for her that's been there since the moment he opened his eyes.

He reaches up, brushing his knuckles across her flushed cheek. "Do you think I'm a bad man, Kate?"

Stepping closer, he waits for her answer. *Say no, and I'll kiss you. Say no, and I promise, I'll please you.* Maybe he can become a little less gray for her.

"I'm not sure what to think," she admits.

He considers it a half win. It's better than a yes, so he takes it. He'll kiss her anyway. Her gaze drops to his lips as her warm palms press against his chest. He knows what she's thinking because he's thinking it too. Placing a hand over hers, he braces his other on the wall next to her face.

"Let me give you a reason to like me." He allows the heat coursing through his body to fill his stare. Electricity crackles between them, intensifying as her hands fist in his shirt. She's perfectly still as he leans forward. Their lips brush, and she sucks in a sharp breath.

As her head tilts, giving him better access to her mouth, she whimpers, "James." It's the prettiest sound he's ever heard. "This isn't going to make me like you."

He grins at the weak protest. He'll get her to like him, eventually. A challenge for another day. She's given him hope.

Their first kiss, like the gentle one now, was a cosmic shift. With every brush of their lips, something awful is happening in his chest. He ignores the wild thumping. His heart isn't going to fail. He wills it to beat rationally. It's only another kiss.

"Kate," he returns on a rough breath. "I don't need you to like me right now. We'll get to that. Just focus on kissing me." She moans into his mouth, melting into him.

God, he's going to take this excruciatingly slowly and draw out every delicious second. The air seems to vibrate between them as their noses brush, and he delivers a whisper-soft peck to the corner of her full lips. Another to her jaw. She squeaks and, fuck, he wants her. His cock is painfully hard now. And from barely a kiss.

But as they breathe each other's air, he can feel her scarcely perceptible hesitation, her uncertainty, even as her lips chase his. As if she is waging a small yet significant inner battle in her mind. He catches her cheeks, and this time as their lips touch, he forces the kiss to turn sweet because his alarm bells are going off. He doesn't know why, but he can't let her do this. That protective urge he's felt toward her is firing. Trying to alert him to danger. *Protect her.* But there's no one around. It doesn't make sense. At once, he realizes what he's meant to be protecting her from.

Himself.

The shock of it steals his breath. He stays like that for long moments, keeping his lips pressed to hers. Then James does the first truly unselfish thing he's done in his entire life. He steps away.

Kate gasps. "What are you doing?"

He has no fucking clue. He's way out of his depth. James runs a hand through his hair, cursing himself for his honorable decision. His groin throbs in protest. Ignoring it, he says, "Your mind and your body are at odds. You don't want this. With me. I don't want to manipulate you or coax you into giving me something you'll regret in the morning. I respect you far too much to put you in that position."

James points to the monitors, which still display the damning articles, because the gesture says enough. *You are white and I am gray, and I'll only make you muddy. I am not worthy of your goodness.* The realization is more painful than a perfectly landed right hook.

Still, it doesn't stop the way he aches for her. Tomorrow, when her head is clear, if she decides to muddy herself, then who is he to stop her? Because no matter how much better James becomes, he'll always be a sinner. But that doesn't feel right. The harsh reality is that she doesn't want *him.* She wants a warm body, someone to make her forget she's alone in this strange world. With how good she is, he isn't sure he can ever be the "better" she deserves. Even if he figures out how to make it in this world and has something to offer her.

Kate lifts her fingers to touch her lips. "How is this possible?" she asks, more to herself than to him. They stare at each other as time drifts past. Finally, she says, "Fine."

He's been so focused on his own thoughts that he isn't sure what she's thinking. But right now, he's dangerously close to changing his mind. He lets her slip into her room and shut the door. Being a decent guy sucks.

20 – Capital F, Frustrating

K8

"You've got to be kidding me?!" K8 shouts. She doesn't care if he hears her through the door. Who does he think he is, trying to tell her how and what she feels? Arrogant ass.

Does she like him? No.

Does she want to sleep with him? Yes.

See, she knows her own mind. Sure, it's kind of sweet that he thinks he's protecting her from himself, but she doesn't need him to. She's a grown woman. And it's rather offensive. *Frustrating.* It's really, *really* frustrating. She was hardly going to throw herself at him. She needs . . . K8 opens the drawers of her nightstand, searching for her newest toy. She rifles around in her dresser and the bathroom vanity, then the closet, coming up empty-handed.

She groans as she remembers she stashed the thing under the kitchen sink in an effort to keep herself from thinking about James sexually. To *not get confused*, as she put it. But she is far past denying the fire he stokes in her. The last thing she intends to do, however, is go into the kitchen and retrieve a contraption labeled "PUSSYzapper3000" in front of him. That would be worse than the rejection and the incessant ache pulsing between her legs. The thought is worse than a trip to the Cold Compression Chamber.

K8 tilts her head to the side. That's actually not a bad thought. She is feeling a little inflamed. Pulling up her wellness app, BodyLock, she makes the earliest available appointment at C^3, which is next week.

Her thoughts inevitably drift back to him. A few minutes ago, she was ready and willing to enjoy the chemistry between them, consequences be damned. It's not like her heart would have been involved in the transaction. He could have her body, but she's smart enough to know he isn't the type of man to give more to. That kiss, though . . . how did he do that? With such seemingly little effort, he set her ablaze. And then he rejected her.

She goes on readying herself for bed. As she catches her reflection in her bathroom mirror, she studies the puffy skin around her eyes. She's cried too much for him. Logically, if her heart isn't at least a little involved, then what's with the tears? No, it's only the shock of it all.

With her nightly routine complete, she tucks herself into bed. Then she snatches her device off the nightstand and promptly makes a Refresh appointment for half past ten tomorrow. She should probably hit the Sports Simulation Center for some exercise, too. If she wakes up an hour earlier, she can squeeze in a full match. She messages Oro1, who she hasn't seen since her birthday, then books a court.

Then she needs to get some work done. Hopefully, James will want to continue learning about her world, because there are dozens of climate reports and open task orders in her inbox to sort through. And this time of year, the atmosphere always gets shifty. The predictions are harder, and getting the exact calculations correct, especially for the big air interchanges like the SAT garages, is critical. Lives depend on the accuracy of her work.

That's what she will do. Focus on her self-care, her FRIENDS, and the important contribution she makes to the safety and well-being of the people in her sector. That leaves no space for the man in the other room.

As her worries melt away, she feels better. Lighter. She drifts off running soothing air volume transfer calculations over in her mind.

21 – Virtual Tennis Ball

James

October 15, 2390, Day 73.

Kate flounces out of her room the next morning, wearing what James thinks must be what workout clothes are now, but might have been worn to the club in his time. They are futuristic but have a throwback quality to them. She's tucked a—because why would she spare him—*sheer* collared shirt into a short, subtly metallic pleated white skirt. She's cinched her long auburn hair in a high ponytail and wears what appear to be extra bouncy sneakers. Kill him now. The look is equal parts naughty schoolgirl Halloween costume and Tennis Player Barbie. He can't peel his eyes away from his roommate.

She's nothing like Blythe, or any of the elite pool of women he and his family would consider wife material. Kate was certainly polished, but not in a demure, understated, pearls on Sunday and a house in the Hamptons sort of way. It seems he's stopped caring. He thinks she's perfect—loud and revealing outfits, dragon scale tattoos, ridiculous virtual dogs, and all.

"Where are you off to?" he asks.

She shows very little interest in him as she breezes into the kitchen. At least she seems to be in a good mood. All sins from the night before are forgotten, or at least are being ignored. Over her shoulder she says, "Tennis. Then the spa."

He huffs, giving her an indignant glare as she comes to stand before him. He watches her down her morning pick-me-UP packet before taking a few sips of water.

"You didn't think I might like to go?" he asks.

Her eyebrows lift slightly.

"Never mind," he says. He shouldn't have said anything. He should leave her to do her thing and be happy with copious amounts of research time, hoping to discover some employment he's qualified for. It isn't as if he's feeling bored or purposeless. He only wishes he had some agency or some actionable task to focus his mounting energy on instead of research. At this point, he'd take nearly anything.

"Oh, James. I'm sorry. I didn't think," she says. Her head quirks to the side. Then she's on her device. A minute later, she looks up. "Got you added. Go change. Hurry, or we'll be late."

Despite himself, James is glad for the opportunity to get some movement in, and possibly spend more time with Kate, so he goes to his room to put on a pair of jogger-like pants and a T-shirt. Maybe they have a pill in the future to help people to get over weird crushes. He should look into that, because his little *Kate is off-limits* problem is already becoming difficult.

When he comes out, Kate gives him a once-over, landing on the joggers. "Don't you think you'll get hot in those?"

"I'm fine. Let's go." He frets to think of what the men in this time consider appropriate gym attire.

The Sports Center is on level CA25-100. They enter and get checked in. James follows as Kate shows him the locker room. Before he goes in, she tells him to put his things away and meet her at Court 16. This is easy because he has no things to store. Instead, he noses around, curious what other amenities the Sports Center offers. Does she have a membership? Can he get one too, or does he always have to be with her?

Figuring out how to get an ID will solve that issue. Aside from learning everything he can about the future—the *present*, he corrects himself—including but not limited to the financial systems, he will make getting the ID a priority. Then unicoin.

The locker room holds a compression chamber, which looks to him like a steam room with an airlock. Plus an infrared sauna, showers with the same little timers as his at Kate's unit, sinks, toilets, recycling bins, towel racks, and lockers. Nothing out of the ordinary. He always thought the future would be more *futuristic*. Like Mars trips and robot assistants. Mostly, it's just weird.

Outside the locker room, he finds a section called Classic Country Sports. The placard below has a long list written in several languages, like the police station. It lists baseball, golf, archery, tennis, track and field, horseback riding—which elicits a shudder considering the dog park thing—and beach volleyball.

He enters, first coming upon archery. A slim woman outfitted in neon pink army fatigues stands facing the inside of the small cube she's in. She wears an elaborate VR headset and holds what he can only compare to a bicycle pump in her hands. Her fingers wrap around the handle, and she pulls it back. Her knuckles go white as her arm trembles. Clearly there is tension in the tube. Then she lets it go.

Whatever she sees must be climactic because her mouth falls open and she emits a shriek that is muffled by the glass.

James shakes his head. He passes golf next, which holds a similar spectacle, except the clubs are full length. And there is a ball attached to a tee. When the man swings, he somehow hits the ball perfectly even though he has the VR set on. Upon impact, the ball spins down under the floor before popping back up, ready to be struck again.

Finally, he gets to tennis. He passes several cubes labeled Court 1, 2, 3, and so on, until he gets to 16. Inside, Kate is bouncing around, reacting to whatever she sees in her VR headset. He pushes the door open, and she turns around. Something must have sounded in her ear.

Her warm-up has already created a slight sheen of sweat on her skin and the dragon scales peeking out of the neckline almost shimmer. Now that he's used to them, he thinks he might like them. He wants to touch them, anyway. He can make them out curving around her sides through her shirt, which the bright lights of the cube have made ineffective. Her sports bra is minimal and—Heavenly Father—the top clings in ways he should not be considering. He's definitely not here for the exercise.

"Hi," he says stupidly as she comes to his side, clicking a setting on the crystal VR set so he can see her eyes instead of the usual reflective surface.

"James is here," she says to someone he cannot see. Then to him, "I switched us to doubles. We're playing with Lessa and the third member of my friends group, Aurone, who you haven't met. Here."

She hands him a VR headset that she plucks from the wall. Then she passes him a tennis handle minus the racket head. Once she gets him set up, she goes to the cube across the hall. This is so overwhelmingly foreign that he can't help but go along with it. There are no questions or protests. And he's curious, which feels so much better than being afraid.

Jett's voice rings in his head as a reminder. *Be open to possibilities.* He hardly has a choice, but this seems to make Kate happy, which is enough to melt away any misgivings he may have.

Through the glass walls, he watches Kate put her headset into place before he mimics her position, flipping his down. Unlike the set in her unit, the one he wears now surrounds him with an image of him and Kate standing side by side. Across the net stand Lessa and a tall, fit man with a physique that almost reminds him of himself but with dark bronze skin and hair nearly the same shade. On second thought, the man looks eerily similar to an eighteenth-century Apollo statue his mother had been rather proud of. The man is possibly better looking too, if one were to line up their flaws for comparison. It's not James's fault his parents couldn't select his traits so he resembled a Greek god.

James is not jealous. He does not care how close a friend this man is to Kate.

"You know the rules?" she asks, walking to the net. He nods, following her, only slightly worried he's about to walk into a wall inside the tiny cube.

The team on the other side does the same, and Lessa spins the grip in their hand. "Up or down?" they ask.

They play "tennis" for the next two hours. The handle, James discovers, is more than a piece of graphite. It's an electronic device that vibrates and creates the simulation of weight and impact as he swings it and strikes the ball. If he didn't know better, he would think what he's experiencing is real. The sounds, the smells. Even a breeze in the room is simulated, as if they're playing outside on a sunny day. Then he realizes the floor must be somehow moving beneath his feet as he sprints to the net, because he hasn't crashed into the wall once. The only thing that is off is when it's his turn to serve. The ball appears before him, and he takes it from the air. But his fingers close around nothing. He has to adjust, and he takes several tries to get the fake toss right.

James and Kate lose 3–6, 6–4, 5–7. He thinks if he got the serve down quicker, they would have won. They meet Lessa and Aurone in the break room once the match is finished.

Aurone steps up beside him and claps him on the shoulder. "James, right? I might have to steal you for my Sixthday league, if you're open to it?"

"Or get your own," Lessa says, biting their lip. "I may have filled Aurone in . . ." They nod in James's direction.

Kate puts a hand on his arm. "Don't worry. Your secret is safe between the four of us. We've been a friends group forever."

Then Kate gives Aurone a sweaty side hug. "Sorry I haven't told you sooner."

James's jealousy flares when Aurone doesn't immediately release her. "Kate mentioned you," he pauses for dramatic effect, "at breakfast one morning. Or was it before bed? You're a systems engineer? That's basically a fancy way to say IT guy, right?" Aurone's eyes narrow as if he's picked up on the subtext: *I live with her, not you.*

"Yes, I manage complex network monitoring systems, so an *IT guy,*" Aurone says, parroting James's description like it was a dirty word.

Aurone is gawking at him like he's trying to figure him out. James stares back. Not to be an asshole, necessarily, as Kate is probably assuming. Only because he doesn't know what else to do.

In a muffled tone, Aurone asks, "So, you're real? And you remember your life from the past?"

Aurone doesn't seem too shocked, so he must have heard of this happening in GROW's recent batch. "Yeah, man," James says. "I'm real." He doesn't feel compelled to share the status of his memories with the man.

"Fuck. That must be strange for you," he says, and it almost makes James like the guy. But as Kate's arm slides around Aurone's trim waist, James decides it's impossible.

She glances around the room to make sure no one is in earshot. "James needs a device of his own. Can you get me one?" It's a good idea. And thoughtful—a trait that he lacks, which she demonstrates consistently. A trait she values.

Over the last week, she's done little things here and there to make his life more comfortable. Like the day he crawled into bed and noticed it felt softer than it was the night before. Upon inspection, he found a new foam pad over the mattress. He'd complained once about the flavor of his tooth cleaning kit. She swapped it for a different flavor the next day. And she drew attention to none of these things. She just did them. It's another of the many reasons he shouldn't, no, *wouldn't*, manipulate her into giving him something of herself, her body or otherwise.

"It will take me a day or two, but I'll send one once I get my hands on it," Aurone says. Then he leans down to Kate and says, "I've got to run, darling." He kisses her cheek, which she angles up for him. It's a little too close to the corner of her lips and James's head almost explodes, instantly contradicting his previous line of thought.

Not that his head has any right to explode. In fact, his head has no rights at all. If only he'd known he'd develop this strange affinity toward this woman, he wouldn't have been such an ass to begin with. Fucking fuck.

"Call me later," she says to Aurone.

Pointedly ignoring that.

Apparently, this guy has some connection to the underground of this time, or at least a way to get things one might need. He should probably bite back his ridiculous jealousy and befriend him. This is what James has spent a career excelling at. Building resources, cultivating contacts, regardless of his personal feelings about the individuals. This guy might be his first contact. Wouldn't hurt to have a good IT guy on the team. Especially now, when nearly everything has a digital component.

Never mind that this is a *real man* who might have an interest in Kate. Unlike him, who's a fake, manufactured person. At least he isn't a *flesh robot*. He isn't sure why this bothers him. But somehow it makes him feel that this Aurone character might have the advantage if it came to it. Kate wants real, and Aurone is definitely that. But if they've been friends forever, as she said, maybe there was nothing to worry about.

James forces himself to hold out his hand to the man and give him an amiable smile. "Good to meet you. And for the record, I'd be happy to sub in for your league anytime. Kate speaks highly of you. Why don't we grab a drink sometime? You can let me pick your brain about how to do business in this future world."

Aurone grins at his blatant about-face. "You're interesting, so I think I'd enjoy that. I'll reach out when I send your new device."

As Aurone steps away from Kate to take his hand, her fingers slide across his ribs. James's eyes zero in on the movement. It isn't quite sexual, just familiar in a way that James wants to be familiar to her.

Aurone catches him noticing. He gives James an *I saw that* grin before taking his hand and squeezing tight. Aurone doesn't say anything, thank God. He says goodbye to Lessa, who's been intently focused on their device.

As James and Kate leave, he congratulates himself for not punching Aurone in the mouth. Did she notice him being the bigger man and making the connection? Does she care?

Kate is oblivious and chipper as ever as she leads him to the MediSpa for the Refresh she's booked them. An hour after the treatment, he's feeling better than he has since before waking up in the future.

She suggests they pick up to-go noodles, but when they walk by a café that serves pizza, he suggests they stop in for a slice. The thought of cheese makes James's mouth water, but eating isn't his primary intention. If they go back to her apartment, she'll start on task orders and he'll end up doing research, and he isn't ready to lose her attention just yet.

"This is actually good," he says, and takes another huge bite. "Let me guess. The cheese isn't real?" *Pay attention to me.*

She doesn't look up from her device as she says, "No. Are you dissatisfied?"

Is she baiting him to see if he'll complain? He won't fall for it. "I said it's good, and I meant it. I promise, I'll never lie to you. If I say something, I mean it. You can trust that."

Her gaze flicks up to meet his. Good, he's got her attention. Now to keep it. "Tell me about being an air control officer."

She huffs. "You don't actually care, James. And I'm trying to read this article."

It's bold, but he reaches forward, takes her phone, and sets it on the table. "I'm truly interested in the job you've dedicated your life to, Kate. It sounds important. Please tell me about it."

She glances between the phone and him like he's tipped her off balance. Then she seems to come to a decision. "Okay, James. What do you want to know?"

James grins. He's been thinking about ways to reciprocate her thoughtfulness and prove to her he's capable of it, but since he doesn't have any funds, he can hardly gift her things. That means until he can, he needs to be more creative. This plays to his strengths. He's come up with a dozen questions, and he wasn't lying. "What type of scientist do you have to be for your job?"

At first, she looks at him like he might be toying with her, but when he leans forward, genuinely imploring, the corner of her mouth quirks up. She quickly forces it back down, replacing it with the cool demeanor of Scientist Kate as if she doesn't want him to see that his interest pleases her. Finally, she says, "A particulate pollution scientist."

"Did they have those during my time?" he asks. Then their conversation is off and running. Brick by brick, he will build back what he so carelessly brushed aside. Then she'll see—well, maybe they both will see—that he can be a little less gray. He isn't foolish enough to think it will make him deserving of her. But maybe it will make this uncomfortable feeling now lingering around his conscience go away. A feeling she seems to be at the root of.

22 – BLACKOUT

James

October 21, 2390, Day 67.

James's stare tracks Kate, who's changed from her daywear into a pair of high-cut shorts and a slinky oversize top, as she saunters over to the smartwaiter to collect a package. She flips it in her hand, cocking her head, which makes the knot of hair on top of her head tilt precariously as she studies it. She looks so fucking sexy he has to bite his knuckle so as not to groan. He isn't egotistical enough to think she chose the outfit as a punishment to him, but it serves as one all the same. She doesn't seem to notice his anguish as she walks over and hands him the box. Their fingers brush as he takes it, and his heartbeat stumbles.

"It's for you," she says, glancing at his hand, which now feels as if it's on fire. She doesn't seem remotely affected as she goes back to her computers and back to ignoring him.

That's the worst part since he decided to be a good guy a week ago. Kate is pleasant to him. Detached. Platonic. James hates it. Hates how warm she is to Jett and Lessa. And especially to Aurone. It's like she's created an impenetrable wall against him. It grates on him, getting worse by the day. Like an itch under his skin that he can't scratch. And James is dying to scratch this particular itch. He's about to get up and head to his room to scratch it solo when the box in his hand vibrates.

James excitedly opens the package. Aurone came through! Inside is a clear device like Kate's. Its screen is lit up. It responds to his face by opening to display a message that reads: *Tell our girl this one's on me. —Oro1*

Of course, that's how you spell it. Stupid futuristic names.

He types out *Fuck off*, hovering his thumb right over the send symbol before deleting it. Instead, he sends: *Thanks, buddy.* No one, future, past, or present, likes to be called "buddy" unless they're seven, they just hit a home run, and it's preceded by "good job." Or they're an Irish Setter. James grins as he imagines *Oro1* grimacing as he reads it.

A second later he gets another message: *Sure thing, champ.*

James laughs, earning a glance from Kate. Maybe he and Oro1 can be friends after all.

A third message quickly follows: *Thought you might find this useful.*

A link to something called BLACKOUT follows, along with a series of codes.

Intrigued, James clicks. The link takes him to a portal that seems to be an access point to the dark web of the future. The platform requires each user to create an ID, which he does using the codes Oro1 sent. Fortunately, the platform doesn't ask for Kate's NHOS identification number.

James' skin prickles with anticipation. Despite the man's excessive familiarity with Kate, they were definitely going to be friends. He replies: *Very useful. Thank you.*

The first index he comes across seems rather harmless: an odd jobs auction that lists non-NHOS positions. One ad requests an individual who excels at "texture sampling." A discerning tactile feel, along with very long fingers, are the main requirements. "Strange," he says, which earns him an interested glance from Kate.

Since she's been shunning him, he's a bit of a glutton for her attention. "Listen to this ad," he says. " 'Looking for two individuals, preferably twins, able to hold perfectly still for long periods of time. Candidates must provide their own body paint and be ready to start immediately.'"

Kate is now eyeing him with a wry grin on her face. Maybe amusing her is a way back into her good graces. It's worth a shot. None of the listings appear to be illegal, but he can see why none of them are advertised through the Jobs Exchange on the NHOS government website and paid with unicoin. Most of the classifieds that aren't strange seem more highly specialized and advanced than anything he's qualified for, momentarily making him question how far out of reach his ambitions are. No, he can do this. Even if he has to take on a menial role at first. He'll find something he's capable of, then start there. He skims through a few more listings.

"What about this one? 'The Holiday committee of tower A10 is looking for a group of petite persons to present as 'water fish'—as if there's a different kind of fish—to splash holiday joy around the atrium tower pond during this year's annual celebration. Costumes will be provided.'" James squints as he scrolls down to see a picture of several people in shiny orange and white, bright blue, and brown spotted fish costumes lying on a particle pane floor set to a pond scene. *Is that a lily pad?* "What on earth type of holiday is this?"

Kate covers her mouth, suppressing a giggle. "It's the only one we have called *Holiday*." She's glowing with mirth, and the feeling James had earlier surges forward. It's a fine line to walk. Already, he's beginning to question if he's even capable of enduring her presence without trying to seduce her. "From what I gather, several holidays merged over the centuries into one. The fish costumes have pouches you can reach inside and fish out sweet treats. The sticky ones that taste like sweet mint are my favorite."

"I'll pass." James's nose wrinkles at the thought of eating something sticky from someone's pouch. It only takes a second, but he watches her mask of indifference slip back into place. *Damn it*. As her focus returns to her work, he retreats to his research. He needs to find something he can do to earn a little capital. At least enough to cover his lease in the interim until he can build something more substantial. It's just like when he was ten—except he doesn't have a Rolex to sell. The thought causes a swell of pride. If he can build something big this time, it'll really count.

James uses the tablet to lay out a calendar, creating a rough timeline and a task list, putting Solve Identification at the top. Then he creates a tally labeled Blackmarks, the digital currency used to trade in illegal or off-market wares, like the various digital currencies during his time. In the first cell, labeled Balance, he types a sinister zero. He goes back to BLACKOUT, determined to find some task he is capable of completing.

After searching for an hour, he comes across an underground sports site where he guesses most of MSP's illegal betting takes place. While he's not generally a fan of gambling, one group catches his attention: Off-the-Books Boxing. The notice on BLACKOUT calls for "experienced fighters only" for a "discerning crowd." The figure representing prize money seems significant enough. Especially considering the other available *and ridiculous* jobs that there isn't enough money in the world for him to take—every man has his limits.

But he knows how to box. If he could win a few matches, build up a reserve of Blackmarks that could later be converted to unicoin, that would be a start. Especially if he could accumulate a small surplus this soon in the timeline he created. The thought of his options opening up makes the tightness he didn't realize he'd been carrying ease a little.

He shoots a quick message, including a link, to Oro1: *What do you know about this place?*

Oro1 responds immediately. *Perfect way to spend a Fifthday night. Busy?*

An hour later, Kate is still working on task orders when the door chimes to alert him to Oro1's arrival. He steps out of his room, dressed in athletic clothing, to find Kate staring quizzically at the door.

"Were you expecting someone?" she asks.

Interested to gauge her reaction, he says, "Oro1 and I are going to watch some illegal boxing."

Her eyes narrow.

"Guys' night," he says.

She shrugs, turning her attention to the screen. "Have fun."

She doesn't seem angry or disapproving. Excitement trickles over him as he slips out the door.

A SAT takes James and Oro1 to a small arena built out in a warehouse in Y Quadrant, which is home to unregulated gaming. It's on the same floor as the fitness center in Kate's tower in C Quadrant, making him think it used to host a fully legal fitness facility before it became a fighting ring. They take a seat in the stands to watch as two gloved women enter the center ring. The two rings that flank it are empty.

Orol leans over. "As the night goes on and more people sign up, those two will have fights too. All the betting is in Blackmarks that can be washed into unicoin. I have an account."

James watches with interest as Orol opens a betting session, wagering on a woman with stark white spiky hair. *God, that is a lot of zeros.* "How is that possible if NHOS monitors the financial systems so closely?"

Orol grins. "Government officials still take bribes to look the other way. Sometimes a coin washer has to shut down and wipe out all their records, but they just open up again under a new name with a different BLACKOUT address."

"So I guess a fake identity is similarly easy to manage?" James asks, thinking this might be a good time to broach the next item on his list.

"Oh no. They monitor IDs much more stringently. Blackmarks turning to uncoin just means people can spend more. Fictitious identities can be used for far more nefarious purposes."

James is about to ask him how he might get around the identification issue when the ringmaster steps onto the floor, drawing their attention back to the center ring. The crowd is electric as the bell sounds. Then the white-haired woman throws the first punch. The red-haired woman narrowly dodges.

"Once you've registered an initial bet, you can just start calling them out. The organizers do it for the frenzy it creates," Orol explains, before getting to his feet along with the crowd.

As the fighters circle each other, the crowd starts calling out bets. Orol shouts what sounds like an obscene number. Above the ring, a screen displays the odds and appears to be recording the wagers as they're entered. He glances around for who might be doing this when he realizes the betting system must recognize their voices and somehow connect it to their account. Fascinating.

James senses his own adrenaline rising to match the energy of the room. In the ring, the red-haired woman cries out. Her blood sprays across the mat as the other contestant's left fist connects with her jaw. The displayed prize money figure doubles. As he scans the crowd, he can pick out the signature of wealth. If he had to guess, the majority of these people live in A or B Quadrant.

A thud draws his attention back to the ring. The red-haired woman apparently rallied. She stands over the other unconscious woman with her fists raised high. Once the white-haired woman comes to, they are escorted out of the ring.

James pats Orol on the shoulder. "You'll win the next one."

Up next is a man wearing a minuscule pair of lime green shorts and a full body tattoo that makes him resemble a giant gray lizard. When the close-up of his face appears on a particle pane, James can make out little slitted pupils. Another man steps into the ring and with the asinine way he's grinning, James is certain he's a manupartner. Once the announcer finishes, the fight begins.

"I have an idea," he says to Orol. "Just go with it."

"Wait, where are you going?" Orol asks.

"I took boxing lessons as a teenager." When Orol's brow quirks incredulously, he says, "It's excellent exercise and, unfortunately for me, it's the only transferable skill I've discovered. I've got to start making money somehow."

Orol groans. "You sure you want to do this?" When James continues making his way down the aisle, he hears the other man grumble, "Kate is going to kill me."

James makes his way down to the pit, where the ringmaster has taken a seat to watch the fight. As he approaches, the man's attention moves from his tablet, which displays a ledger of participants, to James.

The man's gaze sweeps over his physique, then his dumb manupartner expression. He rewards James with a huge, greedy grin. "May I help you?"

James leans in. "My owner wants to watch me fight. That's him right there." He points to Oro1 and blows him a kiss. In response, Oro1 catches it out of the air and brings it to his chest. James bites back a laugh. "How do I sign up?"

The ringmaster gives a knowing chuckle as he taps at his screen. "Let me see what I can do to move you up the list."

Half an hour later, a club escort kindly helps James sign up for an Off-the-Books Boxing account, and even shows him several reputable platforms for a Blackmarks account and how to link it when he asks. Thankfully, they're not paying enough attention to know or care if he's a manupartner.

Once official, James changes into an outfit from the costume closet, which amounts to a pair of traditional silk black shorts that almost hang to his knees and a pair of matching lace-up boxing boots. He assesses himself in the mirror. It is so surreal he considers backing out for a moment. But he can't let himself. Focusing on the money he's earning, he steps into the ring. The overhead cameras zoom in on his face, focusing on his nose. He gives the crowd a winning smile before turning to assess his opponent. If only his old coach, Jimmy, could see him now.

Across the ring, a man with long blond hair tied at his neck sits, seeming to have raided the costume closet in favor of a fitted leop-ard-printed wrestling-style singlet. He's got whiskers either drawn or tattooed on his cheeks. If James can't beat this guy, he deserves to lose.

The ringmaster calls them to step to the center of the ring. When the bell for round one rings, James springs into action, assessing his opponent with a quick jab-jab-cross combination. The man dodges the first punch, but James's fist catches his jaw.

They break apart for a second, but this time the man comes back with a combo of his own, landing a hit that splits the corner of James's lip. As the metallic taste of blood fills his mouth, his adrenaline spikes. For the first time since being in this world, he feels like he has a little control. Like he stepped into a boardroom where he knows the outcome before he opens his mouth. The deal is already sealed. He only needs to execute his plan.

It only takes him three rounds for the blond man's guard to slip enough to get the knockout. He finds Oro1 in the stands, who is cheering loudly along with the rest of the crowd. Oro1 returns the blown kiss from earlier, which the cameras love. When James smiles, his amusement is genuine. The future is fucking weird, but at least he's having fun. *And making money.*

After he leaves the ring, he's escorted to the medical room. While he's waiting on the physician to treat his opponent, they schedule him for two more fights and tell him he's welcome back the following week.

Finally, he's called into the room. A woman wearing an iridescent blue lab coat that looks like it came from the adult section of a Halloween shop directs him to an exam table. "Sit," she says.

Her face is open, set off with deep, discerning eyes. Her mid-tone olive skin contrasts nicely with her straight, presumably box-dyed blonde hair that is cropped so close to her head it's almost a buzz cut. Like everyone in the future, the woman paints a striking image.

She pulls out a light from her pocket, then unceremoniously uses her other hand to hold open his eyelid, preventing him from wincing, as she shines the light into his eye. She quickly does the other eye and when she's finished, he shakes his head, forgetting himself for a moment. "Fuck."

The word draws her attention. They stare at each other for a moment before he remembers to put on a dumb grin. She goes about patching up the minor cut on his lip, and he tries not to react to the discomfort.

"I'll fix this and any other cuts you have more permanently after you're done for the night. Unless your owner prefers you to keep them?" she asks.

"He prefers them mended," James replies, curious about the technology she's using.

When she finishes his lip, she taps his nose. "And this? Is it from fighting?"

He represses a wince. Maybe if he kept his cut, his crooked nose would make more sense, but he was concerned about what Kate would think. "Yes," he says, since it seems like the only reasonable explanation. He figures the less he speaks, the better.

"Funny, because they would have sent you to me for a fracture like this, even if it wasn't my night. I don't remember treating you, and if I had, I certainly wouldn't have done such shoddy work." She retrieves a tablet and before he can protest, she has it pointed at his face. "I'm just going to take an image to verify it was like that before I treated you."

"But you already fixed my lip," he protests.

"There would be residual bruises and swelling for a break like that," she says matter-of-factly. The way she's studying him makes his arm hairs prickle.

James scrambles for a way to explain why a manupartner like him has an old injury like his. Maybe the boxing club wasn't such a good idea.

But then one of the escorts pops her head in the door. "The last fight just ended, and one contestant is bleeding pretty bad." She inclines her head to James, meaning to clear the room.

The physician stands. "We're done here." She motions for him to leave, which he does. Quickly.

James beats his next opponent in four full three-minute rounds with a unanimous decision by Judge Master, a boxing analyzation software which he learns has replaced the human judges. Apparently, the point of the shorter matches is to provide the crowd with plenty of matches to bet on. Plus, it means fighters can enter up to three fights each night. Probably has something to do with the crowd's limited attention spans, too.

James's escort helps him under the ropes and to his corner. The crowd goes wild, and he turns to see what the commotion is about right as his opponent steps into the ring.

Fuck, it's the Lizard Man.

The fight, which he loses, goes by in a blur. At least the Lizard Man didn't get the knockout.

"Back again so soon?" the physician asks. Her name, he's overhead, is Sable.

"I fought the Lizard Man," James replies, remembering to put on a placid grin. His head is still spinning from the loss, and he's being careless, but he can already feel his eye swelling.

Sable walks over and closes the outside door, which makes his stomach pitch. When she turns back to him, she cocks her head and studies him for a long moment. "You can cut the manupartner shit."

She holds up the tablet, which displays side-by-side images of him. One is the picture she just took. The other is the shot from an interview he did a few years before he died. It's like she's dumped a bucket of ice over his head. His mouth opens, but he can't seem to find the words.

"Facial recognition software. Plus, I'm one of GROW's lead technicians. I'm around manupartners all day long, and it is quite obvious you aren't one," she calmly explains, as if she hadn't dropped the most terrifying and threatening piece of information he's heard since waking up.

James rubs his clammy palms on his shorts. "I'm here because my owner—"

Sable laughs, which cuts him short. When she recovers, she says, "Don't worry. I have no interest in turning you in. I only caught the whiff of an opportunity when I looked you up and read a little about what you did in your time."

"An opportunity?" His blood hums.

"You were an entrepreneur." Her tone is matter of fact and he isn't sure what level of alarm he should be feeling. James never had to do anything illegal before, but now he's not even legal, so he has no choice.

"I won't be manipulated," he bluffs. But clearly, he's in no position to haggle with this woman if she decides to extort him. His nerves fire as he eyes the door, briefly considering running. That didn't go well last time he tried it, so his best bet is to talk his way out of this. Reason with her.

Seeming to sense his wheels turning, she says, "You're worrying over nothing. I just work there. I haven't decided how I feel about our current batch of errors yet. I'll have to think about how we can use this to our advantage." Her presumptuous words and calculating grin make his stomach twist.

"*Our* advantage?" he asks, equally intrigued and terrified.

She shrugs as she holds a little medical device up to his banged-up face. His face heats under the light it emits, and he has the urge to jerk away, but he holds still.

"Yes, *our.* Unless the several articles I skimmed about you incorrectly depicted your capacity?" She raises a brow, smirking in challenge.

His pride makes it impossible to resist defending himself. "They weren't wrong."

"Good. I only do this once a week for the Blackmarks. I should be running my department, at minimum," she grumbles. "At least until

I can invent something." Then she narrows her eyes at him. "You're here for the same reason, are you not?" When he doesn't disagree, she continues. "It's easy enough to surmise. You'll soon discover that the payout for the fighters doesn't go as far as you're probably imagining."

She hands him a mirror, letting him survey his nearly unblemished face. "Those bruises will fade in a day or two. Otherwise you should be good as new. Next time, avoid the Lizard Man. He never loses."

"I'll try," he says, as if he'll have a choice who they pair him against.

There's a knock at the door. His signal that his time with the physician is up.

"If I come up with any ideas of how we can capitalize on our unique opportunity," she says, waving a hand at his general person, "I'll message you."

James paces to the door, feeling a little untethered by this strange, somewhat cold woman. "But you don't have my contact information."

They size each other up while his hand rests upon the doorknob. He senses they share a common trait: drive. But he has no idea what her motivations are besides running her department at GROW. Even if she is a threat, there really isn't anything he can do about it now. She knows that he's been, in a way, reincarnated. But if they are similar—even a little—then maybe there's an opportunity, like she suggested. In that case, he'll think about it too. And try not to get a crick in his neck from looking over his shoulder.

There's a catlike cunning about her as she says, "I'll have your contact information before you know it. See you next week."

"You're kind of terrifying," he says.

Her grin widens. "I've been told that before."

23– The Thing About Luck

K8

October 28, 2390, Day 60.

K8 glances up from another long day at her workstation and notices James has sent her a message: *Headed out. Be back in a bit.* He has spent an inordinate amount of time at the boxing club over the last week. At least it gives him something to do so she can work. Having him sit there on his device, becoming increasingly frustrated, isn't fun for either of them. His antsy energy alone is enough of a distraction. It seems, in his past life, he was a man of action.

K8 debates for a moment before deciding to include him in her dinner plans. She sends a message to his new off-market device: *Going out in an hour to meet everyone for our weekly dinner and drinks. Lessa has BIG NEWS to share. You coming?*

Out of nothing but her inherent kindness, she's about to tell him that there's a chance to get Lessa to buy him REAL Steak, when his response comes through. *Yes. I'll be back to collect you shortly.*

K8 can't help but let out an undignified snort. This man. Honestly.

Half an hour later, he breezes into the room. *Is that blood?* "James!" she cries. She's on her feet before him in an instant. Her heart is thundering, and she's becoming lightheaded. "What happened?"

His hand catches her hip, steering her out of his way. "I'm assuming you aren't asking for the play-by-play?" He pauses long enough for her to scowl at him. "I won the first two rounds before I had to fight the Lizard Man—again. If he hadn't distracted me by flicking out that freaky tongue, I'd have had him, but I can't figure out how to beat that guy."

"You're fighting?!" she hears herself shriek.

He points to the slight misalignment of his nose. "Remember, this came from boxing."

"Yes, I remember," she says, sighing. "But I thought you were going because you enjoyed watching. I didn't know you were taking part." She tries and fails to tamp down the panic. "It's illegal!"

"My very existence is illegal, K8. How else am I going to build a surplus of funds? I have no skills that transfer to typical jobs now, and it's not like I can get an NHOS-approved job anyway. I'm certainly not dressing up as Holiday fish."

When it doesn't seem to placate her, he rubs his hands up her bare arms. "It's going to be fine. My BLACKOUT account isn't traceable to either of our identities."

Well, that's a relief. Though she knew Oro1 dabbled on BLACKOUT for his side projects, she's never been on the illegal network herself. She isn't only thinking about the legal ramifications. She reaches up and traces the blooming bruise on his jaw with trembling fingers.

"Boxing doesn't seem like the type of thing a boy like you would have taken part in." In her Old News app, she's read plenty of articles from his time about rich families and their lifestyles. She imagines the type of teenager who had a trust fund, probably wore suits, and owned a pony would not likely voluntarily get roughed up at a boxing gym.

"That's precisely why I did it," he explains.

James Fletcher, a boy who grew up with wealth and privilege, was also James Fletcher, a boy who took up boxing to rebel against something. His parents, who he said forbade it, perhaps? It isn't enough to shift her view of him, but it adds another dimension.

Dried blood stains his chin, likely from a split in his lip that is now healed. His beautiful, full lip. She realizes she's inconveniently concerned about him as she takes hold of his hands, studying the angry red marks on them. "Your poor knuckles."

"Barely hurts, and when I make enough to cover the next month's lease, you'll agree it's worth it," he says.

She willfully ignores his cocky smirk. "Don't worry. I have the next month covered," she says, fairly certain that's true. "But how much are we talking?"

He proudly takes out his phone to show her his Blackmarks account. The prize funds are there, but . . .

"This is all of it?" she asks as a sinking feeling blooms in the pit of her stomach. He nods. "Oh, James. This is barely what I make for one task order. You'd have to fight dozens of times to cover your lease. I'm not sure this is worth the risk. If someone were to see you . . ."

She takes a deep breath, considering. He's trying to contribute, which is nice, but her panic is transforming into something more troubling. Her fingers, all on their own, make their way to his lapels, twisting them in her fists. "Do you know how bad it would be if you were caught? They'll decommission you and jail me. I wouldn't be able to get MediSpa treatments. I'll age!" she exclaims, her knuckles turning white.

His shoulders tighten as the reality of what she's said washes over him. "K8, it's fine. No one is going to turn me in, considering we're all there doing something illegal." He pries her hands away, pressing them flat against his firm, warm chest.

"How do you know?" she asks.

He sighs. "Trust me. I do. I'll fill you in later. For now, I need to get ready for this dinner, okay?"

She reluctantly nods, eager for the "fill-in" he's promised.

When he releases her, he casually saunters toward his bedroom.

Speaking of his lease, she should probably check the balance of her Worldbank account. She's been avoiding that since before she ordered him. She goes to her system and logs in. Her focus zeroes in on the available balance. That number seems low. Low enough to make a chorus of nervous bees swarm around her belly. Not to worry. She's probably getting paid soon. Sure, since she's had James, she hasn't been able to pick up as many task orders as normal, but it will be enough.

Nothing to fret about now—checking was ill-advised. She should have put it off till tomorrow. Not give herself another thing to stress about when she has an announcement dinner to get ready for.

Deciding to put off worrying until later, K8 retreats to her bedroom. The hour flies as she meticulously performs her makeup ritual. Once she has on a smart skirt and jacket set and applies a final dusting of powder finish to every inch of exposed skin, she's ready. The breath leaves her lungs as she steps out of her bedroom and is confronted with what her roommate is wearing. Particularly the interesting fabric that pulls nicely over his backside as he leans over her desk chair to click on the 3key. Her heel strikes alert him to her presence. Rising to his full height, he turns around. As his eyes make an elaborate sweep of her person, hers does the same to him.

"What on earth are you wearing?" she asks. Not that she minds the look. The simple fitted long-sleeved black T-shirt hugs his broad shoulders and chest delightfully. Not to mention how he has the sleeves pushed up, displaying his forearms. And the way those strange pants sit low on his hips—she's staring at his crotch now. K8 clears her throat, bringing her eyes back to his. Zorg, that bruise makes him look more rugged than he did before.

"They're called jeans, sweetheart. I gather you like them?" he asks, crossing his arms over his chest, looking excessively smug.

They must have been a part of his order from the vintage section. "They're fine. Let's go." She doesn't spare him any additional energy as she breezes past him and out the door.

"So, you mentioned my Blackmark balance isn't enough to cover even a small part of a month's lease," he says.

"No, it's not. And that's what you got after two weeks' worth of fighting?" she asks, trying to estimate how long he'd have to fight to earn even a month.

"Correct. So how much is my lease per month?" he asks tentatively.

As they step into the elevator, she pulls up GROW's latest email offer to show him. His eyes widen at the figure. "Do you understand now?" she asks. "I don't know what the point of signing up to fight is anyway."

"Winning is fun," he says defensively. But then he pauses in a way that makes her slightly nervous. "If the money isn't in the fighting, it has to be somewhere."

"The betting, I'd imagine," she says before she can consider of the consequences of mentioning it.

"Exactly," he says, seeming to have gotten there as quickly as she did. His face brightens. Oh Zorg, he has an idea.

She grabs his arm, making a mental note to keep better tabs on his whereabouts. She is responsible for him, after all. If he's willing to fight another person in an unregulated venue, what else would he be willing to do for funds? In her sternest voice, she says, "James, I forbid you from doing anything stupid."

The defiant tilt of his chin makes her think he'll refuse to agree to such terms. She's even more eager for the promised fill-in later, if only for the opportunity to drive her point home. For now, she decides to leave it.

A tense forty-minute SAT ride later and they are across town in B Quadrant at the swanky eatery Sear. K8 hasn't been to the establishment since her birthday, the fateful night she ordered James. The same opulent black chandeliers hang from the ceiling, and the faux candlelight in them flickers throughout the space. Particle panes line the wall, displaying various cuts of meat hitting grill grates and sizzling. The hissing sound reverberates through the room, timed with the videos. James takes in the decadent space with an expression of awe that softens his features. Of course he would like this place.

He rushes around the table to pull out K8's chair. She decides she likes the custom and wonders why it fell away. Then she tunes in to her FRIENDS. Lessa is intently focused on a conversation with Oro1 about the merits of some outdated cosmetic procedure called *breast implants* that only off-market physicians will perform.

"But the implant procedure gives you results immediately," Lessa is saying. "And from what I understand, they've eliminated the scarring the procedure used to cause."

"The growth period for breast tissue after the first round of injections is only three days. The customer has their new breasts to their size requirement within two weeks," Oro1 argues.

"Yes, but then the customer must get a monthly injection to keep them, otherwise they dissolve and you're back to where you started. And the insert, by contrast—"

Their argument only seems like a mental exercise, because she's fairly certain neither of them actually cares about the topic. K8 interrupts. "Your big news isn't that you're getting breast implants, is it, Les?"

Lessa spins to K8, only then noticing her presence. "Hello, K8, my lovely girl! Of course not. That would be absurd. I'm only suggesting with how fast trends change, more physicians should perform the procedure." Lessa leans forward, staring at James. "What on earth happened to his face?"

"Appears to be a nice bruise. Did K8 give you that?" Jett asks.

Beside her, James chuckles. "I entered a contest in Y Quadrant. I used to box. You're welcome to join us." He nods to Oro1, who K8 plans to have a stern conversation with later. James leans back, sliding an arm around the back of K8's chair like Jett did with Lessa the day she told them James was real. Ridiculous man.

"No more fighting, James. We agreed it isn't worth the funds."

"Sounds like you better do as she tells you," Oro1 says, inclining his head toward her.

She considers bringing up what a bad influence he is on James right now, but Lessa clears their throat, redirecting the conversation. "Now that everyone is gathered . . ." They clap their hands excitedly, bouncing in their seat. K8 can't fathom what news Lessa has to share. She's drawn forward with anxious curiosity.

A slim man in a dark jumpsuit comes to stand beside her. "Have you had a chance to review the menu?"

K8's first instinct is to snap at him to go away so she can hear Lessa's news. James must be rubbing off on her. Taking a deep breath, she places her order, then James's. "He'll have the REAL Steak, enviro-greens, and the roasted vegetable medley, and we'll both take a Spiral Apple."

"Actually," he cuts in. "I was thinking I'd have this Whisky Twist."

Since the server likely doesn't know James is supposed to be a manupartner, she lets his interjection slide.

"Excellent choice, sir," the server says. The rest of the group rattles off their orders.

When the man finally leaves, K8 leans forward. "So! What is it? Don't tell me you finally got that promotion you put in for."

"Even better," Lessa says.

Beneath the table, James moves his leg so it is pressed against K8's vibrating knee, putting pressure until she stills. She doesn't push it away because it feels ~~nice~~ helpful.

"The suspense is killing us, Les," Oro1 says, glancing pointedly at K8.

Lessa's chartreuse eyes are bright, bursting with joy as they say, "I won the lottery!"

K8 chokes on her sip of water. "The what?"

"The lottery! The Birthing Agency identified me as a candidate. I'm going to be a parent!" Across the table, Lessa beams.

K8 feels herself blanch, but forces a brilliant smile. She opens her mouth. Words get stuck in her throat. The lottery has always been her dream. Lessa never mentioned wanting to win the opportunity to have a child.

Thankfully, the others' exuberance is enough to distract Lessa momentarily. But when their chartreuse eyes land on her, expecting a response, she's still inert.

She's trembling when James, somehow knowing exactly what to do, pulls her into an embrace. Relief floods through her as her panic, which is sure to be staining her features, is concealed by the safety of his chest. She soaks in his warmth and the momentary reprieve. But as her jealously spirals, tears prick in her eyes.

It was supposed to be me. I was supposed to win it.

The sob that shakes her shoulders is followed by another until she's freely crying into James's chest. She's a terrible friend. Truly awful, but she can't help the overwhelming emotions raging through her.

James holds her close as he says, "Lessa, we're so excited for you. Look at sweet K8. She's so excited, she's a mess."

The conversation buzzes in her periphery like flies swarming a dying animal.

"That's our K8. She always feels everything so deeply. It's touching." K8 is grateful that Lessa seems to take her outburst as a positive sign. At least this is one time having FRIENDS that lack emotional intelligence is a benefit.

Slowly, her tears dry up. Her breathing evens out, yet her mind continues to spin. The odds of getting selected are staggeringly low. And if they selected Lessa, what are the odds of someone in the same FRIENDS group getting selected too? They must be even less likely now.

But she has James now. Wasn't that the goal? Well, she doesn't actually have him either. Maybe one day. K8 clenches her jaw. Her teeth grind together as she wills herself to calm down. Maybe James isn't the only awful person sitting at the table. Maybe they're suited after all.

Jett is saying, "You'll make an excellent parent, Les. What a lucky baby!"

"I know, right?! I feel so lucky," Lessa says. "I've already picked a suitable contact-free donor. His IQ rated off the charts. He's got the most shocking natural yellow eyes. And the good news is he wants nothing to do with me or the baby!"

It's as if Lessa has unwittingly plunged the knife into K8's chest and twisted. The sensation steals her breath. "Breathe," James whispers as he strokes her hair. She does as he says and slowly, her panic eases.

Resolved to be a better friend in this special moment, she pushes at James's chest so he'll release her. She can wallow about it later. Finally, she faces Lessa, plastering an unshakable smile on her face. "That's so great. I can't believe it. I'm so, so very happy for you."

Lessa beams, placing their hands over their heart. "I can see that. It means so much to me."

K8 only feels a little guilty as she nods. Then she has a thought that might be all the consolation she gets. She sucks in a sharp breath and exclaims, "Does this mean I'm going to be an auntie?!"

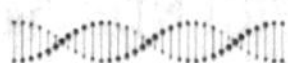

Once she and James are safely back in her unit, she asks, "How did you like the REAL Steak?"

"It was fine." He follows her as she quickly makes her way to her bedroom. As if he can sense her feeble control over her emotions, he catches up to her, taking hold of her elbow before she can secure her retreat. A cheery yellow light undulates in the room, and all she wants to do is escape to the darkness beneath her blankets. Or change it to a moonless night scene that is as black as her mood. She tugs at her elbow, trying to get him to release her, but he holds firm. "K8, sweetheart, what's wrong?"

"What about the enviro-greens? Did you like them?" she asks, though she senses he'll keep pressing until she gives him some sort of explanation for her odd behavior. Crying in public? A fate worse than age spots! Yet, what would she do if she looked in the mirror one morning and noticed a dark brown blob on her flawless cheek? She shivers. Perhaps her public display of misery wasn't so bad.

"They were fine. K8, what happened at the restaurant?" James guides her into the room, gesturing for her to sit on the foot of her bed. He sits beside her, and she can feel the weight of his attention as she stares resolutely at the blank wall in front of her. "You're upset. Talk to me."

"How do you know I'm upset?" she asks, even as tears well in her eyes.

His fingertips slowly guide her chin so she is facing him. He's so gentle it surprises her. She only saw this side of him the day he confessed that he was afraid he'd accidentally "real flirt" with her, a fear he's apparently recovered from—confusing man. "Do you think I haven't been paying attention? I see you trying to keep a brave face even though you feel you're missing out on something. But, K8, at the restaurant, I saw your brave face slip, and holding you was all I could think to do."

K8 shakes her head as he releases her. For such a selfish man, how is he so perceptive? Probably a business technique from his time, though she can't picture the man before her hugging it out with the competition. "I don't know. It was so shocking. Since every NHOS citizen is in the lottery, the odds of getting selected are slim. Many people never get a chance to have a child. And . . ." She considers how much of a confession is necessary. Considers what he'll think of her. How what she really feels about Lessa's boon might change James's opinion of her. Then she almost laughs. This is James. If anyone will understand her selfish motivations, it will be him. "I felt jealous."

His eyes widen, but she can't see any judgment in them, so she goes on. "Lessa never mentioned wanting to give birth or have a child. That was always my wish."

James's eyes are wider now. "You want a baby?"

K8 can't suppress an eye roll. "No, not a baby, exactly. I only thought . . ."

Zorg, if she tells him why, he'll think she's even more pathetic than he did before.

"You thought what?" he urges.

She releases a forceful breath. Oh, who cares? It's not like it matters. Not like there's anything between them to preserve. "I thought if I were to win the lotto, then I could select a partner to procreate with. Some people choose to select from the DNA database and get inseminated, like Lessa. But candidates can also select from a catalogue of applicants who also wish to procreate and be a part of the child's life."

James nods, seeming to understand where this is leading, but he doesn't speak. He's giving her space to work out her thoughts, which is nice, she supposes. That and the gentle circles he's rubbing on her arm lessen the sting of how vulnerable she feels.

"I thought if I could interview candidates, I might be able to select someone who might be open to a relationship. That through having a child together, a bond might form. Lessa knew how much I'd hoped to get selected. They never once mentioned they did, too. Zephyr, now that I've said that aloud, it sounds awful, doesn't it? It seems I'm just as selfish as you."

He chuckles, and she wonders if he'll call her a hypocrite or refrain like Jett. Considering she went back on her personal vow and ordered a manupartner, she's earned the insult.

K8 stares down at her hands, feeling even guiltier after her confession. James will see her as an entitled brat now. Not the usually mature scientist she is most of the time. Sharing such an ugly, vulnerable feeling makes her twitchy. Will he judge her? He's going to judge her. A manupartner wouldn't judge her . . .

To her relief, he says, "K8, you are one of the least selfish people I've ever met. You're kind and considerate. You even tried to hide your own pain so Lessa would have a good time. They are the one who acted selfishly, blurting out their news, not even thinking of how it might affect you."

That makes her feel a little less guilty. Makes her lean a little closer.

"There's one thing I don't understand," he says, and she nods, urging him to continue. "Most people now are happy with the companionship provided by a manupartner. From my vantage point, I can see why one would think they're repulsive, but why do you?"

She turns away, thinking of her parents. If she were to share this deep vulnerability, maybe they—no. She only told Jett during one of their arguments to justify her position, and Jett probably didn't think of it again until the next time they got into a manupartner conversation. If she told James, he would think her even more pathetic. Assessment made: not worth the risk. "Like you said, I'm just the odd man out."

He looks at her like he isn't quite buying it.

Eager to keep him from pressing, she says, "How is it fair that Lessa got selected, and I didn't?"

James brushes a strand of hair behind her ear. "That's the thing about luck. You can't count on it to do you any favors. Sometimes you have to make your own."

The warm feelings blossoming between them come to a frosty halt. Why does he always do that? *That isn't how things work now*, she wants to scream. The irony of her situation strikes her like a slap. As if she has any control over it. What he is suggesting is laughable. Her head whips up, and she glares at him. Then she gets to her feet, making her way to her bathroom. Standing in the doorway, she says, "You know, I thought I'd gotten lucky when I discovered you were real. Then I thought maybe this was the non-deities' way of gifting me with the companionship I've always dreamed of. But then you turned out to be you." James flinches, but she carries on. "And now Lessa's won the birthing lottery. And here I sit, as pathetic and alone as where I started."

Then she closes the door, leaving him perched at the foot of her bed. When she emerges half an hour later, thankfully, James is gone.

24 – You Weren't Invited

K8

October 29, 2390, Day 59.

In the morning, K8 has recovered enough from her emotional implosion to meet Lessa for a follow-up lunch. They spend the entire two hours discussing baby names and speculating how often one is required to change diapers. "At least once a week!" Lessa guesses.

The mood is light, and K8 is grateful Lessa was so wrapped up in their own *GOOD NEWS* that they didn't give a second thought to K8's unacceptable behavior. K8 leaves lunch vowing to herself to do better.

She makes it back to her unit on an emotional high, determined to put the positive energy into the task orders that have been piling up in her inbox.

Right as she's about to get started on the first one, two strong hands clamp down on her shoulders. Then they squeeze, and it takes all her willpower not to purr and arch back into them as his scent engulfs her. No. Absolutely not. *That's the thing about luck . . .* His words have been tumbling around in her mind since he said them.

Why couldn't things be simpler? Why couldn't he be a different, less *him* man, gifted to her by Zorg and Zephyr?

She jerks her shoulder, brushing his hands away without a word.

"K8," he says. His low tone kneads her, almost as nicely as his hands did. "How did your lunch with Lessa go?"

Does he actually care? It feels a little too much like companionship. But he doesn't get it. He's a selfish man, motivated by selfish things. It's not possible for him to change enough to become what she needs emotionally. Nor is he willing to provide her with what she needs physically. It will not happen.

"It was fine. I have work to do." She doesn't spare him a glance as she activates her system. She grits her teeth and gets to work. She has to support them both, after all.

But she can feel him still standing there, staring, as if she's the most pressing item on his task list. She refocuses, but the weight of his gaze is too heavy. If he wanted to cross her off his list, he would have when he had the chance. So what is he doing now?

"I said I'd tell you more about the boxing. Do you have a minute?" he asks.

Oh, that's all. He's not captivated trying to solve the puzzle of her, he's just trying to keep his word. It's a silly thought—she hadn't really hoped he spent all night dissecting questions about her that wouldn't let him rest. *Why did she never want a manupartner? Why does she desire companionship? Why hasn't she given up and turned him into GROW? Is she really that much of a good person to be so altruistic?* K8 isn't so sure, because aside from her moral obligation, there might have been a tiny part of her that had hung an even tinier bit of hope on him.

"Sure." She tries to remember what she wanted him to expand on as she makes her way to the couch. "You were trying to convince me that it wasn't as risky as I'm imagining."

"Right," he says hesitantly, sitting beside her. Angling his body so he's twisted toward her. She stays facing straight. "Naturally, there's risk with everything, so I won't lie to you and say there isn't. But there may be an opportunity for me to start building a surplus of funds. I've been messaging with this woman I met—"

K8 chokes. "A woman?" Her body pivots toward him without her permission.

"Yes, one of the physicians. Her name is Sable, and"—his pause is longer this time—"she works as a lab technician for GROW."

Her heartbeat skips once. Twice. How does he seem so calm about this? Unless he and this woman—

"K8, I can see your mind working. It isn't nearly as alarming as you're thinking. She just works there, and I'm only telling you that so you'll understand how she knew I was one of the reincarnates."

"Reincarnates?" she asks.

"Yes. It's the term I came up with for people from the past meant to be manupartners, like me. Anyway, I tried to hide it, but it was clear that she knew. She swore she wouldn't turn me in because she thought there might be an opportunity for us to work together. She's there to make extra money, too."

The swirling sensations in her gut harden into something like . . . anger? Jealousy? Worry? Doesn't matter. It's unpleasant and making her stomach feel heavy. "So you've been messaging her?"

"Well, she messaged me first, with a bad idea, but you already gave me a better one." He grins.

"The betting?" she asks sheepishly, wishing she'd kept her mouth shut.

"Exactly. I did a little research after we parted ways last night and put a plan together." At her disgruntled expression, he says, "If you don't want to know, I can keep it to myself."

Great, so definitely not pining over her all night ~~like she was~~ like she definitely wasn't over him. "How can you bank your life on gambling, James? I thought you were a successful businessperson. Shouldn't there be a few variables under your control?" Is he grinning proudly at her cleverness? Does it feel . . . good? No, that's stupid. She wishes he would get to the point. "Go on."

"The variable would be the fighter. Since Sable has access to manupartners before they're recycled, we could borrow them for a few days," he explains.

Realization dawns. If she's right, not only is his plan illegal, it might be dangerous. "You're going to use the manupartners to throw the fight."

"Bingo. And this way, I won't be risking myself in the ring." When she only glares at him, hating the idea, he says, "I thought you would be happy. I won't come back with bruises anymore."

"It wasn't your face I was worried about." Technically, it was her face she was the most worried about, if they were to get caught. But admittedly, seeing him bruised was alarming.

He leans closer. "You were worried about my face. I could see it in your eyes. Why don't you want to be friends with me, K8?"

She scoffs. "We are *friends*, you ridiculous man." Just like her FRIENDS, who are sometimes so emotionally vacant and superficial, they might as well be banned cyborgs. Wait—this means she has four friends—the optimal balance is off. Sound the alarm. The people at Project: LEN would probably freak out if they knew.

His eyes are scanning her again, making her itchy. She stands abruptly and stomps over to her desk. Time for more task orders. Before she sits, she turns, already knowing his eyes are going to be on her. "Whatever scheme you and this woman are planning . . . I expressly forbid it."

November 5, 2390, Day 52.

It takes K8 a week to catch up on her normal work, plus the extra task orders she picked up to offset some of the unexpected purchases she needed. Namely, that one-of-a-kind silver designer bag. Just a little something to curb the stress her roommate is causing by the illegal activities he's engaged in. No matter. He showed her the winnings from his and the woman's first experiment . . . and it might be worth it. If he can manage his lease himself, then Incredible Bill's upcoming line won't be so out of reach. Therefore, she's chosen to ignore it and him.

Things are going smoothly. Finally, *finally*, she's fallen into a routine since waking up her manupartner, now her new roommate, James. Fortunately, they have interacted very little. They get along as well as expected, knowing when to stay out of each other's spaces. Respectfully offering to include each other's food orders, etcetera.

He's really become the perfect roommate. He'd be ~~the perfect~~ a sufficient partner, too, if only they could come to some type of understanding. Not that she's been thinking of that. Especially since the night of Lessa's BIG NEWS. But who knows? Lightning might strike twice. Or she could figure out a way to *make her own luck*.

Never mind that. Everything is going well.

It's only that her roommate started walking around the unit in a pair of indecently low hanging pajama pants and nothing else, claiming it's hot in her unit. His torso is an unwelcome affront, like he's systematically assaulting her hormones with his perfect physique, most likely honed by his boxing hobby.

The point is, the temperature is perfectly comfortable, and it is her unit, so she refuses to change it. And he wasn't complaining, exactly. Only informing her of why he insisted on wearing only those pants when she demanded to know. He was wearing them, the navy ones, when she locked herself in her room to get ready for a night out.

Her MediSpa appointment that morning was exactly what she needed. She looks and feels great. And if it is his prerogative to taunt her with his forbidden fruit, so to speak, it's fine. Just because he's off-limits as a candidate to fulfill her needs doesn't mean she can't get them fulfilled elsewhere. What's the harm in a meaningless encounter? She used to have them all the time before she became so intent on the ridiculous notion of companionship. It's absurd now that she thinks about it.

Surely there is an attractive man in X Quadrant who will have no qualms about satisfying her. A man who understands that a woman like her knows her own desires, and who has no intention of making decisions for her. A man who wouldn't do such an aggravating thing as protect her from himself. A man who wasn't spoiled and rotten on the inside. Or a man who sees when she needs comfort, gently offers it, then doesn't ruin it all by espousing some ridiculous notion about luck that makes her vision darken. The thought still grates on the last dregs of her patience. A man who isn't so complicated—that's what she needs.

Applying a layer of gloss to her naturally rosy lips, she breezes into the living room wearing her new favorite silver heels and the matching bag she ordered a few days ago. The tastefully slinky, ridiculously expensive dress she bought before she had James's lease to consider glides and clings to her curves as she moves. It stops mid-thigh.

Retrospectively, she might have spent less of her funds on purchases if she knew she was taking on a manupartner. But she figures Drunk K8 only planned to have him for the initial three-month lease period. A sort of trial run.

As it stands, she has a little over seven weeks left to figure out how she's going to gather the unicoin to extend his lease, which she plans to have as a backup to his boxing scheme. That morning, she finally forced herself to study her Worldbank account. It was more startling than she expected. Before, when she noticed the low balance, she overlooked that she had gotten paid days earlier. That's why her usually precise calculations were off. But if she were to sell some of her designer collection—obviously not any of the new stuff—she'd probably be able to put together the fourth month she promised him she had covered. Maybe the fifth too, depending on ~~what she's willing to part with~~ the market and how well his plan worked.

James is convinced that if he can build up enough funds, he'll be able to start something more substantial, too. He has admirable confidence and tenacity, which she might find appealing if it weren't for all his other less attractive qualities. At least he hasn't come home with any more bruises.

In the kitchen, James is leaning on the counter, wearing the crystal VR set like he does every day. He's quickly scribbling notes onto the tablet.

"James," she says, trying to get his attention. But he's been so focused on his own tasks, she isn't sure he'll notice she's left. She doesn't know why she's even bothering to tell him. They've hardly spoken since she insulted him. Well, they have, but their conversations mostly revolve around his curiosity about the world now. They certainly haven't confronted the kiss on inspection day or what she told him the day

Lessa received their BIG NEWS. Nor have they kissed again. And she managed to sneak the PUSSYzapper3000 into her bedroom. It's quite the device.

Right as she's about to walk out the door, he removes the headset and places it on the table. Then his eyes make a sweep of her. Instantly she's nervous, like she's in trouble, though she doesn't know why.

He asks, "Where are you going?" *Dressed like that* is implied.

"Out," she says. *Because you have no claim on my time* is implied.

He looks startled for a moment before he leaves the kitchen. "Oh, you didn't tell me we were going out. I'll change." His muscles stretch and flex as he stalks past, and she holds her breath so as not to draw in a lungful of his scent. That doesn't stop their arms from brushing, or the heat of his nearness from permeating the wall she's built between them. At least she's able to preserve her dignity and stifle a gasp.

"I'm going alone," she says, refusing to let her stare follow him.

His steps halt. They both turn, drawn like magnets, as his eyes narrow. "Why?" he asks. But she can see he knows why. Perhaps he heard her using her toy, or perhaps he can feel her need vibrating between them.

She shrugs, trying not to look like a guilty child. She wants to yell, *You had your chance*, but she doesn't. Still, she thinks her frustration with him is entirely justified. As if luck has anything to do with her circumstances.

"K8," he presses. "Where are you going at this hour?"

"It's none of your business," she says. Why is she giving this conversation any energy? She could have lied and said she was meeting Jett or Lessa. She sighs. She isn't a liar. It goes against her nature as a *scientist*.

He gives her a disgruntled look until she can't take it anymore. He's repeatedly offered to bring her to the boxing matches, which she's declined. Was it fair not to return the invite? She should probably let him come.

"Fine, go change," she says, waving at hand at his bedroom.

When he enters it and closes the door, she hesitates, only for the briefest moment before convincing herself her trick doesn't qualify as a lie.

Then she slips out.

25 – The Slip

James

When James exits the bedroom, wearing the tailored black suit he now knows was a splurge, Kate is nowhere to be found. He checks her bedroom and the kitchen, then his device. Nothing. She gave him the slip. Clever, difficult woman.

Surely she didn't think he was oblivious enough to not recognize her intention. That dress and her sexy scent that still lingers in the air. And the come-fuck-me heels. He was right there.

But no, he's come to some ridiculous determination. He was thrown into the orbit of a woman who he's determined is the perfect package. Now he's attempting to be a good, *unselfish* guy. Trying to make himself a little less monstrous in her eyes and admittedly his own, which means for him, she is off-limits.

He became even more resolved after seeing her pure, unadulterated longing upon receiving Lessa's news. He was so close to giving in, well before her insult about him being *him*—an utter disappointment. But he would have easily gotten over that, because she wasn't entirely wrong, if her reaction didn't . . . what, scare him? Make him wonder if he could give that to her . . . if he wanted to. That is, if she wasn't off-limits to him. If he could somehow become exonerated enough to pursue her. It's possible that he wants the same things as her. Even the baby part one day, which she was clearly lying to herself about—he always expected to have children. Yet if this was the one thing he failed at, Kate would be collateral damage. The thought of disappointing her further makes him feel queasy. That is exactly why it is better to stay friends and grin and bear this lingering attraction between them. He is doing it for her sake.

But that fucking dress.

And it's not like she's stopped wanting him. He knows this because she's taken to staring. The temperature in her unit is slightly warm, but he wears the pants for her benefit, like he wishes to tempt fate. Or to get her to throw herself into the muck with him. His reasoning is not in control when it comes to her. And time has done nothing to dampen his interest. He thought maybe after they'd felt each other out—they were living together, after all—he'd develop some sort of immunity. Especially after that day she came out of her room with sleep still in her eyes and hair piled on top of her head. No makeup and a baggy sweatshirt that fell right below the curve of her ass. Her little *lounge around the house* outfits are a poison to his resolve.

Now he is practically a salivating animal. Hungry and struck stupid, while she's off to do things he refuses to think about. And he's stuck in an apartment he doesn't even own with nothing but his resolve.

I'm here, his device reminds him.

Oh God, not that again. This is going to be a long night.

He sits there staring blankly ahead, repeating all the reasons in his head that he pushed her away. His knee vibrates in time with the buzz of the particle panes. They say, *Even if you aren't a bad person, you have nothing to offer. You're broke. And our Kate likes pretty things.*

"Stupid electronics. What do you know?" he asks, taking the remote and turning the windows off. He may not have earned enough to contribute significantly, which weighs heavily on him. Since his conversation with Jett, he's considered his self-reliant streak that the future is trying to beat out of him. Left with no choice, he relies on Kate for everything. He hates it. At least he's earning something. It's not as if he is sitting on his ass, and soon he'll have enough to extend his lease. Pay her back with interest, then capitalize on it. Barely two more months, but he can do it. Sure, what they're doing is illegal, but what other choice does he have? It's not like it's hurting anyone. Well, maybe the losers, but it is gambling, after all. Had Kate never read those stupid articles about him, he probably wouldn't even be considering it.

The point is, he's well on his way. Fuck resolutions and restraint and all the meaningless drivel his guilty mind made up. If she wants a lover, he's the man for the job. That he can give her. And eventually, he'll be able to earn his keep. Then she can buy whatever her heart desires.

Then maybe you'll be worthy of her. He scans the room, searching for the inanimate object he's projecting onto. *Good luck*, the overhead light says.

Ignoring it, James picks his device up and dials Jett. He answers on the first ring. "James, is something wrong?"

He's never called Jett before, so his concern is understandable.

Jett gasps. There's a slurping sound in the background. "What did you need?" Jett's voice is a little high-pitched.

"God, Jett. I don't want to know what that sound is or what you're in the middle of."

Jett grunts, then must mute the device for a moment because the line goes silent. He comes back on, but not before James hears him say, "You can finish when I'm off the call."

James's stomach rolls. Not because of two men, but because of the sex clone thing. He'll never get used to the idea of manupartners.

"Jett," he says, letting his irritation bleed into his voice. "Kate went out without me. Where would she have gone?"

"What?" Jett asks. What James is telling him clearly confuses him. "Why didn't you go with her?"

James huffs. "I wanted to. She said she'd wait for me to change, then slipped out the door while I was getting ready."

Jett is quiet for a moment. "I see. Sounds like our Kate is off to make a new special kind of friend."

"I know," James growls.

"Oh my. You like her, don't you?" Jett taunts. "I thought you were above it all. That you were trying to keep your distance to protect dear sweet Kate from—what was it? The *monstrous man* you are?" Jett quotes the article that got him into this situation and he's loving it. Kate probably relayed the entire incident to him. Lessa and Oro1 too.

"What do you want me to say, Jett?"

"It's fun watching you squirm. Is that so wrong?" Jett's voice is amused now.

"Don't you think that's a little juvenile?" When Jett doesn't respond, he presses, "Where do you think she went?"

"Tell me why you want to know," Jett demands. Then, in a lower, conspiratorial voice, he says, "Tell me something juicy."

"Why?"

"Because at my age, I have to find entertainment however I can." Jett's tone is indulgent. He evidently sees nothing wrong with using James's predicament for his amusement.

"You're younger than me," James states, not wishing to feed into the sidebar.

It's Jett's turn to scoff. "Hardly. You're what, thirty-five? I'm three times your age, James."

"What the fuck?" James blurts. "You've got to be kidding me."

"Nope," Jett says. "I'm being straight with you." He's silent for an extended pause. Then he says, "Oh boy, you don't know how old your girlfriend is, do you?"

A strange dread blooms inside him. He knows future people live longer than in his time. Seem younger for longer. He knows all the routines and treatments they have must be doing something. Somehow, until now, he's always assumed Kate was in her mid-twenties because she looks like she's in her mid-twenties. Early thirties at the most, considering the treatments.

But she has a highly specialized job that puts her close to the top employee pay bracket. That must imply some sort of seniority. The kind earned with skill and time. The only way to earn more than the one above her would be to invent something and sell it, like a manupartner, since investing in the stock market or real estate isn't an option any longer.

He only catches the tail end of what Jett is saying. ". . . birthday was the week before she got you. She turned eighty-six."

"Eighty-six," he repeats. "That can't be possible. That means she's fifty years older than me."

"Welcome to the future, where medical technology has created the fountain of youth," Jett says.

"But I thought she was in her late twenties. Are you sure you didn't hear her say twenty-six," he says.

"I'm sure."

"Thirty-six?" James asks, because even that would be more plausible. Because, is it weird that he has a thing for a woman fifty years his senior? "She could be my grandparent. Great-grandparent, even," he says offhandedly.

Jett jumps on the comment he now regrets. "Oh, she's going to love that. Gran-Kate. No, that's boring. What about Kate-ma?"

"Damn it, Jett. Don't you dare." James sighs into his device, warring with his rational mind. "She's really eighty-six?"

"James, I've been friends with her for almost forty years and she was in her mid-forties when we met." When James doesn't reply that he's convinced, Jett adds, "We threw her a party and everything. That's when she got drunk, cracked, and ordered you. Tower Kate finally fell, proving she's just like the rest of us!"

Kate has her reasons he wants to defend, not that he knows them. Either way, he can't seem to muster a response.

"I always wondered how her parents made such a big impact on her in just twenty years," Jett muses, seemingly more to himself than James.

The comment perks his interest, however. "Her parents?"

"Yeah, their epic love is the reason for Kate's beliefs about companionship and why she never wanted a manupartner. They were a couple for almost two hundred years! She still thinks she can have what they did. She won't stop searching for it and just be happy. Imagine searching for something that is impossible for as long as she has. I'd get tired." Ice rattles in the background and Jett swallows. "I can see why she got excited when you turned out to be real, but then, the articles, you know?"

"Yeah, I know," James says. The whole conversation sobers him. Knowing Kate's reasons—unlike him, she'd had an example of a healthy relationship, so she wanted one. Simple enough, but hearing it from Jett and not her makes him uncomfortable. "I don't think you should have told me that."

"Why not?" Jett asks.

James groans. How can he explain that if she wants him to know, she would tell him? Maybe had been about to tell him the night of Lessa's BIG NEWS, but chose not to. Now he feels like he knows something he shouldn't about the woman who his affinity for is growing each time he sees her. Even if he is only watching. The future is giving him a headache. "You just shouldn't have."

Jett huffs. "Well, if it would make you feel better, we can pretend this conversation never happened."

James wants to laugh. It would make him feel better to close his eyes and wake up in a world where he didn't feel like a fish out of water. A world where he didn't have to resort to illegal activities to build something. Would that even count as making it? Well, it's his impossible standard, so he supposes he gets to choose.

If he only had one thing he could grasp onto. But Kate is eighty-six, which means she's had so much longer than him to develop into a secure person. To know who she is and what she wants. If he didn't feel so inadequate by comparison—like he has no hopes of understanding the woman he's been trying to see. God, he sucks at this. She wants and deserves more than he can give her. This is the simple proof.

It's humorous that he's been trying to protect her from himself. She must have experiences he isn't considering. She probably thinks he's absurd. Amusing, even. As if she needs protection from him. She can protect herself. He's such an idiot. No wonder she is elsewhere, probably with someone else.

This feeling of inadequacy has to be the worst in a long line of awful feelings he experienced since waking up. This future world is out to get him. Another thing on the list of things James hates. If only he'd had normal parents who didn't coordinate each other's extramarital affairs, he'd have some idea about how this works. No wonder he keeps saying the wrong things. At least his parents communicated honestly, which he's been trying to do with Kate, even if they'll only ever be friends. He runs his hands through his hair. How did he ever think, even briefly, that he might measure up to anything she could want?

"I'd rather not keep this conversation a secret, but thanks," he says. "And thanks for answering even though you were . . . busy." He doesn't want to think of the wet sounds on the other end of the line.

"Kate mentioned she might go to this club in X Quadrant she's been to before," Jett offers. "I can message you the address if you want?"

"Yeah, sure," James says, but he isn't sure he plans to go anymore. He hates the idea of her being with another man, but he feels even less justified in tearing her out of someone else's arms than before the call.

Where has his normal confidence gone? That's right—the future is slowly trying to snuff it out. He'll find it again in the morning. Tonight isn't the night.

He hangs up with Jett, then slumps onto the couch. From its prone position on the coffee table, the VR headset confronts him, saying, *Use me to distract yourself while the girl you like, who's eighty-six, is out getting fucked by some random stranger.*

His device chimes in, *If you weren't such a fucking idiot, you'd be the one cock deep in her right now.*

Her computer with its dormant screen bar things says, *You think that shit I showed her about you was damning? Think again. I've got way more material on you, buddy. Want to take a look?*

James realizes that he's anthropomorphizing electronics and allowing them to antagonize him, but he can't stop it. While it seems to be another fucked-up result of his death, at least it's entertaining, in a dark sort of way. What will the refrigerator have to say? Maybe it will be kind enough to offer him a drink.

He makes his way to the kitchen only to find it silent. He opens it and grabs a bottle of Vine, not bothering to get a glass. *Asshole*, the refrigerator says as he walks out of the kitchen.

"You'll find no rebuttal here," he says aloud, agreeing with the appliance. "Maybe I'll wake up a different man tomorrow." *Tonight, Vine.* He lifts the bottle to his lips.

Under normal circumstances, he isn't a heavy drinker. But his current circumstances are anything but normal. He's finishing the second bottle when Kate walks in.

26 – The Nasty P Word

K8

"Hey, beautiful," James slurs from his languid position on the couch.

K8 eyes the two empty bottles of Vine sitting on the coffee table, then raises a brow at the inebriated man. What exactly happened since she left three hours ago? "James?" she hesitantly asks.

"Did you have a good time? Get what you were looking for?" he returns. His eyes drift over her, giving her chills.

In fact, she did not get what she was looking for. But she isn't about to tell him that. There wasn't anyone suitable. She'll have to try again tomorrow night.

K8 crosses her arms over her chest. What exactly is with this behavior? She'd yet to see him drunk and . . . well, now his eyes loll. He leans forward. Is he drooling? "What is wrong with you?" she asks.

He stands from the couch and walks over to her, swaying. His hand threads into her loose hair, causing her internal alarms to scream,

Invader! while simultaneously plucking at the unsatiated strings of tension vibrating beneath her skin. He leans in and she can smell the Vine on his breath. Her heartbeats quicken.

"Nothing," he says, and she can taste his words.

But as quickly as he entered her space, he evaporates. "I hope he was worth it," he says. His words ring with loss. Then he saunters into his room, shutting them on opposite sides of the door.

K8 stands there, stunned. *First of all*, she wants to tell him . . . and there are so many ways to end that sentence. Too many. Why does this man stoke her desire and ire at such a fevered pitch? He's impossible. This is impossible. And how dare he? And what is he implying?

Before she can think better of it, she throws his bedroom door open. James is sitting on the end of his bed with his shirt off and his head in his hands. He looks up, and the blade-sharp pain in his slate eyes spears through her. She steps back as if she's been struck. "James?" she asks him again.

He only shakes his head. "Bad choice. All my fault," he mutters, and her heart does a funny thing. It flips and splits at the same time.

"What's your fault?" she asks, and she can't help but twirl a lock of hair in her fingers. Because she thinks she knows, but she'd never be so bold as to presume.

"Doesn't matter. It's pointless," he groans.

What's pointless? she wants to scream, but she bites her tongue in favor of waiting.

"What are we going to do, K8?" James says.

She's not entirely sure what he is talking about. She, having had several drinks herself, sinks to the floor, tugging her heels off. They stare at each other for a long moment. "Have you found a source for an ID?"

The composure in his face breaks. "No. Oro1 says it's going to be more difficult, if not impossible. I may always be someone who has to operate on the fringes."

He looks so dejected. This must really be a blow for his ego. "You'll figure something out. You're James Alexander Fletcher, after all," she reminds him, earning a chuckle.

"What about the lease?" he asks, shaking his head. "I feel like I'm forcing you to put your life on hold to pay my way. I'd rather pay my own way. And we're running out of time." She opens her mouth to protest. "None of this is fair to you."

"I'm fine," she says. "And it's okay to accept help when you need it. That's what FRIENDS are for. Literally, as in I'm pretty sure it says that in the Project: LEN handbook." He's looking at her as if she's an alien. "You're making funds with the boxing scheme," she offers, trying to brighten his mood.

"I know, but it isn't sustainable. That figure you showed me is due every month from now until I die, since buying me outright isn't an option. Unless I can somehow detach myself from GROW, but I can't think of how." He leans over his knees, massaging his head like it might make his brain work more efficiently. "I'll be eternally your burden."

Had all this been about the lease? She thought he'd been upset that she might have connected with someone else. This sobers her immediately. She can sense her eye contact with him becoming crisper by the minute. "We have time to figure it out before the extension is due."

"A little under two months," he says. "Trust me, I'm keeping track."

The words echo between them.

"I have month four covered, so don't worry about that," she reassures him. Granted, she might have to pick up a few extra task orders. Maybe sell a few unused items in her closet.

"Listen, K8, I know this sucks right now. And I promise I will figure this out and pay you back for everything. I'll think of something." Under his breath, he says, "I always do."

Her lower lip quivers, but she doesn't allow him any access to what lies in the depths of her. He still doesn't get it, and it hurts. When she opened the door and saw him looking so dejected, that feeling in her chest ballooned. She thought he was jealous. Stupid, foolish hope. Though she wouldn't tolerate jealousy normally, seeing him like that felt rather nice. Like she was something he coveted. But he's gone down a dark spiral about being a burden again. Money—that's what he cares about. It's a good thing to remember. A reminder she really should heed.

When did she become like this? He said she could have anyone she wanted in his time. But she doesn't have anyone. Not like she wants to anyway.

She wants to scream, *Why are you making me feel this way?* Every time she lets her guard down around him, he—but she realizes this is her. Not him. Sudden clarity strikes her. K8 is invested in this man and it's making her terrified. She wanted this. Prayed to the non-deities, Zorg and Zephyr, for this. Even held out on the manupartner game, hoping against hope. And now a real human man sits staring at her, wanting her, she thinks. And she's paralyzed. The stakes are too high, and it's making her too vulnerable, so she keeps putting reasons it won't work between them. She glances at the exit. This is significantly harder than she imagined. She's never considered herself a coward. She could do this.

But even he, the fearless entrepreneur, the business mogul, is avoiding the question of what is between them. Making it about the lease instead. At least that's what she thinks he's doing. If she really weren't a coward, she'd do a better job of analyzing this.

Okay, time to do that. James thinks he's a burden. That's a demon from his past. He's focusing on his lease, which is probably a natural reaction for someone like him. He's also concerned that their situation isn't fair to her. He stares at her constantly, like he's trying to solve her. He was the only one who could see she was upset at Lessa's BIG NEWS dinner. He tried to comfort her, even though he said the wrong thing. He's trying to protect her from himself, which means that, to him, she is something worthy of protection. Does all that somehow mean he's trying? If so, does that mean he likes her?

She turns her head away from the blank wall and back to him like maybe she'll find the answers there. Of course, he's back to staring at her.

"K8, sweetheart." His expression is sympathetic, his stare piercing, as if he sees her. The real her.

It breaks her. Splits her in two. The nasty P word rears its ugly head again. Every ounce of dangerous Potential crystallizes before her eyes. James is beautiful and only starting to realize his humanity. He's trying to be a better man. She has a front-row seat to that. It's life-giving and humbling and everything she might have asked for.

K8 rubs the ache in her chest, allowing their gazes to connect.

She's ready to break. Ready to cave and open herself up to him. Give him something for the beauty of his earnestness. Open the door and see where things might lead. Maybe he isn't only what the articles claim. Or maybe learning to navigate her world is making him better. Giving her a reason to like him. The thought steals her breath.

What if she allows herself to like James? To feel *more*? Despite what she knows about his past. To her, well, *to her*, he's an evolving being. Someone with a flawed but breathtaking self-awareness. So much rawer than the men of her time.

This must be what real meat tastes like. Like an animal, she wants to sink her teeth into his flesh and have a taste. Metaphorically, of course.

Maybe a little nibble. She is quite tipsy, and she can imagine the salty masculine taste of his skin. K8 wipes the corner of her mouth.

The cool concrete wall against her back steadies her. This isn't only about sex. She feels things. Her heart sings with them. Emotions that are getting away from her now. She wants to act on these feelings. These desires. Carnal and hungry.

But the bed creaks as James rises to his feet, breaking the moment. "I think I'm gonna be sick."

Suddenly, there's a green tinge to his skin. The moment shatters with his abrupt rush to the bathroom. He slams the door in her face. "I'm fine," he says, but she can hear him retch.

She tries the handle. He's locked the door. "Go away," he barks.

She tries not to let it sting. She really does, but as she leaves him to clean up his own mess, she wonders, *What if I could like him?*

27 – A New Day, A New Precipice

James

November 6, 2390, Day 51.

The throbbing in James's head won't quit. Goddamn the auto-lights. *It's daytime!* they scream.

God, this is a weird new habit. Letting electronics speak to him as if they know anything. The future is affecting his sanity, which also explains this strange feeling in his chest every time Kate enters a room. She isn't remotely his type, but he supposes she must be to incite this reaction in him. Because if he had the chance to pick anyone from this time or even his own time, he thinks he'd choose her. It's all rather aggravating.

Wake up, wake up! the lights scream again. James throws a pillow at the spot by the door where, in a normal apartment, a light switch would be. There isn't one, and nothing happens.

A moment later, Kate pops her head inside the door. She sits next to him on the bed, lifting a hand. In it is a little squishy-looking maroon cube. "Chew this. It will make your head feel better."

He does as she says, because at this point, blind faith is his only viable option. A violent cherry flavor bursts in his mouth, but within seconds, the pounding eases to barely a whisper. "That's impressive," he says. A second later, as the whisper finally dies, a rush of memories from the night before floods in. He wants to roll over and pull the blankets over his head. The woman he's become endlessly fascinated with is eighty-six and doesn't need his protection. Told him not to worry about accepting her help. He should feel relieved that she's got another month covered, but he doesn't. His pride or some faulty wiring in his brain makes him anxious about letting her. He's such an idiot.

She grins. "I know. The woman who invented these makes a fortune." She hesitates.

Before she can get up, he snakes an arm around her waist and pulls her near, so his head is buried in her lap. She probably only lets him because she's so taken aback. Then her fingers tentatively stroke through his hair. God, the feel of her touching him, of her soft body in his arms. It's heaven. He takes an indulgent breath, drawing in her sweet floral scent. When he finally exhales, he says, "I'm so sorry for what a dick I've been. And last night, I should have never implied what I did. You have every right to do whatever you want. I'd be lucky to have a sliver of your affection."

She stiffens, and her hand pauses the delightful finger-combing. "James, I didn't sleep with anyone, if that's what this is about."

He hates how relieved that makes him, but he shakes his head. "No. This is about this future world putting me in my place. And I'm trying to learn, Kate. I'm never going to be perfect, probably not even close, but I can admit when I'm wrong."

At this, she grabs a handful of his hair, twisting his head so he's looking up at her. She's so beautiful it hurts.

"Since when?" Her tone is playful, thank God. She's so good humored, he doesn't deserve it.

"Please be nice to me," he begs, and she goes back to petting him.

"Not until you shower. Currently, you smell like vomit and yesterday's Vine. And you upset Jett, which is strange, but also reassuring. Maybe you waking up in the future is having a ripple effect and causing everyone to learn a little."

How would that even be possible, considering her friends, besides Oro1, think he's a bad person?

When he doesn't reply, she continues, "He's here and wants to check on you."

James presses his face into her thigh. "Noooo," he groans, replaying his pathetic conversation with Jett.

"If that upsets you, then you're going to be even less happy when I tell you he's brought Oro1 and they want to take you to a *real* breakfast."

He was about to continue moaning his discontent, but he'd just about kill for a piece of bacon—fake or not. And since Oro1 is going to be there, maybe they can have Sable bring by the manupartner she's secured for tonight's match.

"Think of it. Eggs, red berry salad, Fauxsage, like what you would have had during your time," she says, clearly very pleased with the offering she's brought him.

He's so undeserving of her thoughtfulness, but she continues despite that. Which is what makes her so special. Well, one of the many things. Tears prick his eyes from out of nowhere. And his chest. The squeeze is so crushing, he might be sick again. He rubs his face against the soft fabric of her skirt, hoping the evidence of these intense feelings stays hidden.

Finally, he forces himself to sit up. When he looks at her, the openness of her gaze hits him in the solar plexus. Her wall is gone. And he desperately wants to kiss her.

But she said he smells like . . . never mind. And her friends—dare he say, *his* friends—are on the other side of the door. When he gets home from breakfast, he is going to do more than kiss her. He's going to start earning her.

Something shifted between them last night, and she felt it too. He may not be worthy of her now, but he can't ignore the magnetic draw between them that isn't going away. His only choice is to attempt becoming someone a little better.

He's almost exuberant as he shoos her out of the room and steps into the shower.

"Of course I'm attracted to her. Who isn't?" Oro1 says, stuffing a bite of the fake bacon into his mouth. James is too stunned to say anything. He only asked in case there was anything between them he'd be getting in the middle of. Not that it would stop him. He only wanted to know, so he could navigate it fully aware.

Oro1 continues explaining, saying, "I guess I never considered pursuing something more. It's just not done anymore. We definitely click, but I had a manupartner when our friends group was assigned. I'd had Blue for a long time then. Kate and I became friends."

"But you knew she wanted a long-term thing," Jett points out, and James is glad one of them gets to the point. That Oro1 says he and Kate clicked makes James's teeth grind.

"True. And I suppose . . ." Oro1 trails off, then takes another bite. "Kate's just so special, you know?"

Uhh, yeah. James has learned this quite well.

Jett clears his throat, fake whispering, "I think James is getting jealous."

James almost chokes on a red berry, which gets the momentary attention of a passing server. He eyes the woman wearing a foam pancake costume. She fits in perfectly with the pieces of bacon and fried egg costumes walking around the cartoonish café. "I'm not jealous." Then he turns his head so he can lock eyes with Oro1 in challenge. "Kate can have who she wants. Or no one at all. It's her choice." He may not be the better choice now, but he would be. And he will ensure that when she chooses, it will be him.

But instead of the barb landing as James intended, Oro1 leans back in his chair and lets out a full belly laugh. When he finally calms down, James is glaring at him. Then his hand claps onto James's shoulder. "You're too much. I thought you were over your little jealousy thing. That we were friends?" He laughs some more before raising his napkin to dab his eyes. "Hold on," Oro1 says. "Do you think Kate is interested in pursuing something with me?"

They are friends, and Oro1 is obviously goading James, but it still makes him bristle. "Ha. Ha."

Oro1 can barely contain himself now. "This is the most fun I've had in a while. Well, besides watching you lose to the Lizard Man. Speaking of, did Sable ever respond to you?"

"Yes, she needs us to pick him up from her unit after breakfast. I'm not sure how Kate would feel about having a borrowed manupartner in her apartment. Can you keep him until the fight?"

Oro1 rubs his chin. "Of course. I know how important it is for you to stay in her good graces."

James rolls his eyes.

"Do you think there are other manupartners who've retained their memories?" Jett asks, steering the conversation in a different direction. "I mean, besides the one from the paper they caught."

"I've been asking around," Orol says. "There have been a few others identified besides the couple that Sable told us GROW caught." He leans toward James, lowering his voice. "I could arrange a meeting. Might be nice to meet someone from your time."

James clears his throat as he tries to process this information. "Yeah, maybe once I get a few things settled. Did Sable mention what they're doing with the manupartners that have been caught?"

"They're holding them for now. They have a team trying to figure out what went wrong. Not her department," Orol says.

It is exactly what James suspected they would do, but the knowledge still has his wheels turning, though. "I don't think the boxing thing is going to be sustainable long-term. I have to figure out a way to cover my lease at a minimum until I can get an identity and make a break from GROW."

Orol raises an eyebrow while Jett pretends to inspect a cuticle.

"She told me she has month four covered," James continues. "I haven't seen her budget, but she's repeatedly assured me she has it *taken care of.*" He makes air quotes. The woman makes an excellent salary from what he understands, which would be sufficient if it weren't for her spending habits.

After a tense moment in which Jett continues to avoid eye contact, Orol finally replies. "Kate's a brilliant scientist. But just because someone's good at one thing, doesn't mean they're good at everything."

"For example, managing their money," Jett supplies. "If she has month four, great. But I wouldn't count on more than that."

"That's fine. I'll come up with something before it becomes an issue. How strict are the collections people at GROW?" James can only hope they'll understand what he's asking. Their shared glance suggests they do.

Oro1 sighs. "They used to not be so bad, but I've heard they've become a bit more aggressive since their recent price hike."

"Shit," he says, raking a hand through his hair. Suddenly, those last few bites of eggs seem less appetizing, which is unfortunate since, to his surprise, they are the first actually *real* food he's eaten. Even though Jett politely explained that while they are *real eggs*, they're technically clone eggs grown in a lab environment as opposed to a shell. He was so glad for something familiar *enough*, he'd dug right in. But now they taste like chalk.

"I've been thinking about the dilemma of your identity," Oro1 says. "There might be a way for us to solve it, depending on what you were up for."

"I'm very interested, and I have a few ideas myself, but go on," he says.

"I know Kate told you I dabble on BLACKOUT, but did she tell you what I actually do?" Oro1 grins like he's about to enjoy dropping a bomb in James's lap.

James shakes his head, eager for whatever the other man is about to say.

"My official NHOS day job, as you know, is a systems engineer, but I pay someone else to do my work. With my unofficial business, *I help people solve their digital problems*. Does that make sense?" Oro1 says the words slowly, as if James is a child.

"You're a hacker," James says. "Hence your familiarity with BLACK-OUT."

The entire time they'd been going to the boxing club, Oro1 never mentioned it. Perhaps building trust, or perhaps he didn't see a reason to tell James. But it made sense considering his willingness to attempt a risky endeavor. He was all for it when James introduced him to Sable and explained their idea.

Oro1 narrows his gaze.

"That's what you would have been called during my time. So, what do you have in mind?" James asks. He can't help but be intrigued.

"You're not the only ethical dilemma someone's facing. I'm guessing there are dozens of humans like you, waking up in the future. Maybe more. Thousands of GROW get purchased every day. And that's just in our municipality. There must be some way to turn this into a business."

James is nodding now. "I've been thinking the same thing. Businesses are born from needs."

"Exactly," Oro1 exclaims.

"Should I get you two a room?" asks Jett, who's been quietly observing the conversation.

Oro1 only gives him a jovial laugh. "Nonsense. I think James and I might be onto something."

"Go on," James says. His skin is tingling with the familiar thrill of a new venture.

"What if we could create a business that solves your lease problem and makes us both a load of Blackmarks? It's somewhat questionable, ethically speaking, but based on what I've learned about you and your needs, I think it might be right up your alley."

It's a strange thing to get reassurance from, but relief floods through James nonetheless. "I'm listening," he says.

"I haven't yet sorted out all the details, but identity can pose a significant problem, and no one has been able to solve it sufficiently. You see how they take a blood sample or do a palm or retina scan for everything from SAT rides to MediSpa appointments?"

"Yes, I have a tag on my foot. I'm quite aware." James scoffs as his eggs notably become more appealing.

"I have some ideas for a prototype of a silicone palm pad that will redirect the scanners to a borrowed identity," Orol explains.

"Like identity theft?" James isn't necessarily opposed if it means not getting recycled or put in a holding cell for testing.

"Not exactly. It could be like an identity-for-hire program. Participants could earn money by putting their identity in the system for rent," Orol explains.

James nods as his wheels turn. Identity for hire is a place to good start, but there must be a better way to solve the problem. He can't imagine that many people would want to take the risk, but he doesn't want to dampen Orol's enthusiasm by rejecting the idea outright. He only needs to come up with and offer a better idea.

Then it comes to him. His fingers tingle and his pulse jitters as his adrenaline surges. James leans forward, savoring the oh-so-familiar sensations. This is what he used to live for. What he's good at. "We'll call it IdenTECH. We can have two branches. The Identity for Hire Division for less challenging cases, then a Full Identity Replacement Division for reincarnates from the past, like me, or those needing a legal makeover, so to speak. Not truly hardened criminals, obviously. We'll have to figure out a way to implant fictitious identities into the NHOS system, but you're a systems engineer. That falls under your area of expertise, right?"

"So instead of altering existing identities in the system, you want to create new ones and deposit them." Orol's eyes take on a faraway expression for a moment, like he's calculating. When he comes back to the present with a broad grin, James knows they're onto something. "We'll need to hire out for the palm pad prototypes immediately so we can start testing. I'll have to find some time to work on the fictitious identities, but I think it can be done."

Jett clears his throat. "How are you going to replace someone's entire identification without hacking into the NHOS system? Because it's not like people haven't tried and failed at that before," he points out.

"The system is set to search for alterations of code or false users. But people are born and inserted into the system all the time. If we were to approach the problem as if we were a user from the Birthing Agency, we might be able to get around that, but it will take some time to figure out the details. Meanwhile, your lease will keep needing to be paid." Orol inclines his head in James's direction. "You should come up with a Plan B in case we can't figure it out in time and the scheme at the boxing club falls through."

James chuckles, thinking back to his first day in this world. "I think I have an idea, but we'll have to bring Sable in on it."

Orol nods. "There is something about that woman that frightens me."

"Me too," James says, chuckling. "I like her, though, and I sense she's trustworthy."

"Agreed," Orol says. "Looping her in will be a benefit."

Jett listens quietly as they discuss their plan over the next few hours, only chiming in occasionally as he sees an obvious flaw, and to make it clear he has no interest in being a part of their schemes. James and Orol, however, are thinking in tandem. Orol has the resources and knows how this future world works, and James has the strategic ideas and business savvy to pull it off. Between the two of them, they outline a rough business plan and a list of obstacles they'll need to overcome before they launch.

"We should meet tomorrow to get started. I have a contact who runs a polymer lab. I'll see if she's available."

As James leaves brunch to retrieve the borrowed manupartner for tonight's fight from Sable, he feels a niggle of doubt despite the thrill of a new business venture. Namely, Kate's finances. Surely she has the first extension covered, which would give them almost three months.

The anxious flutter in the pit of his stomach, which some might refer to as intuition, makes him think he should cover his bases, just in case. If she's miscalculated, that would mean he has about seven weeks left. But no, she asked him to let her help. That's what friends are for. Depending on someone else like that is a bit of a stretch, to the point of extreme discomfort. But for her, he can do it. He needs to show her he can change. He needs to trust her.

Either way, every second is priceless. Not to be wasted. God, he wishes he had time to do the things he wanted to that woman waiting back in the unit. But if this new business venture is a success, he'll have all the time in the world.

The Plan:

1. Launch the business.

2. Fill Kate's Worldbank account, then his own.

3. Date her. Pursue her like the treasure she is. Like she deserves. Take it slow. Earn her affection. Show her he's worth it.

4. Fuck her senseless.

Time to step up his game and secure their future.

28 – It's a Baby!

K8

"So you're going to use the Birthing Agency to create fake identities, then sell them?" K8 asks incredulously.

"It's more complicated than that, but yes, that's the idea," James says.

Is he serious? It sounds risky at best. "And if you run into a problem?"

They were sitting on the couch as he told her about his lunch, but he has since begun pacing. "I'll have the funds in my Blackmarks account I can wash to unicoin to cover the next few months' lease."

"But you have to pay for the PalmPrint prototypes, too," she says, letting her eyes track his restless form.

He pulls his device from his pocket and shows her the already impressive balance. "I think we'll be fine. Besides, we're splitting the start-up costs."

"But what if they catch onto you at the boxing club?" she asks. "BLACKOUT accounts can get frozen or deleted." A part of her is glad he's so forthright with his plans. His willingness to share the details of what he's doing gives her some measure of reassurance. But knowing the illicit nature of what he's up to makes her stomach twist.

"I know it's a risk, so I'm moving a portion of the funds to the IdenTECH account. That leaves almost enough in my Blackmarks account to cover half another month's lease. By the time I need it, I'll be able to cover month five, if not more," he explains.

She shrugs, twirling a lock of hair on her finger nervously. All this illegal activity is so nerve-racking. At least he is confiding in her; he could choose to tell her nothing. And while there is a certain temptation to being kept blissfully unaware, she vaguely remembers reading an article from the past about communication being at the heart of a relationship. He's trying, she reminds herself. Which is anxiety producing, but also sweet. Because he's doing it for her.

What she needs is a distraction. Something nice to take her mind off what he's doing. "I wish you didn't have to operate on BLACKOUT, but if you're certain you'll have month five covered—"

He raises a brow so she'll continue.

"I thought I might step out and see if I could find an outfit for Lessa's conception celebration." That's exactly what she needs. Something that will make her feel good. Maybe something that will cause James to be unable to keep his hands off her.

He chuckles, which makes her feel immensely better. "Go on. Plan on me covering month five. You deserve to have all the nice things you desire, as long as you're certain you can afford them."

"Do you want to come?" she asks hopefully, appreciating his confidence and ignoring that last part. Of course she can afford them. At least, she could before she got James. But it wasn't like a single outfit is going to make or break her. And Holiday is right around the corner. He's right. She deserves a little something nice.

"No. I have plenty of work to do."

She takes a few minutes to get ready to venture out. But there's something nagging her. Before she steps out the door, she pauses. "James?"

He glances up, giving her a once-over before grinning. "Yes?"

"I don't suppose you have to tell me any of that, but you are. Why?" she asks, biting her lip.

James sighs, leaning back in his seat. Does he look guilty? No, he's forcing the eye contact. "Because Jett told me about your parents. I didn't ask him to, but he did. And now I know the standard I have to live up to."

She nods, a little surprised at his definitive tone. Also, that Jett shared something so personal that wasn't his story to share. She's going to have to have a conversation with Jett about how that makes her feel. Namely, angry. That's why her tone might come out a little snippy as she says, "You want to live up to that standard now?"

He spreads his arms across the sofa, like he can read her desire for him to say yes. Like his confidence has fully rebounded since this morning and he has a new lease on life. The corner of his lip quirks up. "I thought I'd give it a try."

She wants to grumble at him, but instead she narrows her eyes, because there is no way he's saying what her ~~foolish heart~~ analytical mind thinks he is.

He stands and saunters over to her. Takes her hair and moves it over her shoulder. "I'm sorry, K8."

"It's fine," she hears herself say. "At least you know."

"I know you weren't ready to share that with me. I haven't earned that yet, but I plan to," he says, leaning down so she can smell the cool mint of his mouth wash.

Her breath hitches. He plans to earn her? That certainly sounds like what she thinks it does. What happened in the last twenty-four hours to cause such a shift? But what if he tries and can't do it? What if she becomes invested and what if—

As though he can read every thought on her face, he says, "In case you are wondering, I rarely, if ever, fail." Then he kisses the corner of her mouth, so lightly she isn't sure it happened. She wants to reach out and grab hold of him, but she's frozen. In shock. He steps away, leaving her blinking.

A little later, as she walks into the first shop, thoughts of him fill her mind. She's almost in a daze as she selects a few necessary items. How is James, of all her FRIENDS with their Respectful and Considerate Conduct Courses, the only one who seems to get her? It's uncanny.

Yet somehow she knows it isn't some magical twist of fate. It's because he's the only one paying attention.

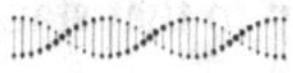

November 20, 2390, Day 37.

"I know your business needs your attention, but I appreciate you coming with me." K8 gives James a grateful grin. She thought when he got back from his brunch with Jett and Oro1 that she might be the recipient of that affection he'd been primed to give her *The Morning Everything Changed*. Zephyr, when he buried his head in her lap—well, it wasn't her fault that her mind wandered. But he was fully consumed with telling her about their idea, then working on it. It's all he's been doing for the last week. How irrational is it to be jealous of a business? One that he promises will be successful enough that they'll never have to worry about his lease again.

James only looks at his device, presumably for the time. "Sure. I can keep working when we get back."

K8 can't help but deflate, even though his hand feels delicious on her back as he escorts her out the door. Like a firework at the end of each fingertip is burning a suggestive promise into her skin. Like there's some unspoken understanding between them now.

As they step into the elevator, K8 gives him a reminder. "There will be lots of people who don't know you're real at the party, so you'll have to be on your best behavior." She runs a lacquered nail down his chest as the elevator takes them down to emphasize the point. James gives her a delicious smirk. "Do you like my outfit?" she asks, doing a turn for him.

His eyes rake up her form, catching on the way the flexible LED lighting embedded in the weave of the skirt changes with her movement. "That looks . . ." He hesitates as if he wants to say something like *expensive*, but settles on "interesting." Then his eyes trail up, snagging on her chest before meeting her eyes. He wraps an arm around her waist, drawing her near. "You look stunning, as always."

Flutters erupt in her stomach. Maybe tonight will be the night.

After a short SAT ride, they enter Tower CB49. "A lot of event spaces are in this area. Restaurants and things like that," she explains as they make their way through the air transfer chambers. James carries their gift as they enter the packed baby-themed room.

A screen across the room flashes between *It's a baby!* and *Congratulations, Lessa!*

Another screen depicts little rainbow-striped bouncy-bears swinging from cartoon trees, and yellow rubber unicats splashing in a candy-fluff pond. Another says, *Welcome to Lessa's Conception Party!* From the ceiling hang streamers in varying shades of blue, green, pink, and orange.

Now that K8 has gotten over the initial shock, she's thrilled for Lessa. She sees them across the room and promptly dances over to greet them.

"Lessa, you're glowing!" she squeals as she embraces the expectant parent.

Lessa fans themself. "Is it warm in here or do you think it's the baby?!"

It isn't warm, and K8 isn't sure if the baby is big enough to be causing Lessa to be overheated, but who is she to dampen their joy? And everyone knows white lies don't count. "Of course it's that little angel inside you." She makes grabby hands toward Lessa's belly. "May I?"

Lessa gleefully nods, and K8 places her hands on their nonexistent bump. "Oh," she exclaims, "I think I felt it move! James, you should feel."

She turns to see James's horrified expression as he stares at Lessa's perfectly still stomach. Sure, she's being a little fake, but Lessa shines under the attention. She inclines her head toward Lessa for James's benefit. *Please play along.* If only she could telepathically communicate that to him. Or if he had an m-volt, maybe she could call him before he did something very un-manupartner-like.

He clearly would rather do anything other than touch Lessa's stomach and pretend like he feels something. But because he's a manupartner in this setting, she's obligated him to do as she says. Several of Lessa's coworkers stare as James sets the gift on the table with the others. Right as he's about to reach out with a reluctant hand, Jett swoops in, spinning Lessa so their profile is visible to the group. People from their work or their former FRIENDS group drawn to the spectacle of someone they know becoming pregnant surround them. "I think I see a bump. What does everyone think?" Jett asks.

Murmurs of "Yes" and "Ooh, can I touch?" rumble throughout the crowd. K8 gives Jett a grateful nod before watching him drag James toward the bar, where they meet Oro1. She'll have to find him later. For now, she needs to hang around because she wants to be close to Lessa so she can get a seat near them when the games start.

Reusable confetti litters the floor from the last game. About half of the guests still linger, sipping on drinks and chatting. K8's setting her prize on a table by her handbag when hands slide over her hips from behind.

A deep voice whispers in her ear, "You're the one glowing now."

She giggles, glancing over her shoulder at James. "That's because winning the bottle toss took considerable effort, and what you're seeing is sweat."

"Are you sure you don't want a baby?" he asks.

She can tell his question was meant to be lighthearted, teasing, but it makes her chest squeeze. She shrugs. "I don't know. I told you I always hoped to win the lottery with the objective of companionship with the father." K8's explanation is clinical even to her ears. But it's not untrue, is it? His question rankles her. Why is he toying with her like this? So what if she is having fun with Lessa, planning for their baby? She thought James understood her, but maybe she was wrong.

"So no thoughts of starting a family one day, then?" he presses, making her stomach jump.

Is he serious, then? She can't for the life of her determine his motivation for asking and she can feel a furious blush rising on her cheeks. K8 glances over at her exuberant friend. Is this swirling feeling in her stomach *envy*? No, surely not. She only ever wanted to get selected for the aforementioned reason. No reason to be silly. She's only caught up in the moment. *Baby fever*, they say, which totally explains the dozen little outfits she's bought. Plus the baby name analyzation spreadsheet she's preparing for Lessa. Plus the fact that she's invited herself to every check-up appointment.

Still, James's question requires an answer. "I suppose I never really considered it like that. People who can bear children get implanted with a Prevention Implantation Chip when they reach sexual maturity, so a natural pregnancy isn't an option. Since getting selected is such a rarity, it is pretty much assured that if you get picked, you go through with it. The opportunity to give birth is coveted. Granted, some people don't take to parenting, so they either hire out for the bulk of it or release the child into the adoption pool."

"K8," James grumbles, as if he doesn't believe her. Then he nips at her ear, and she practically purrs, arching back into him.

"What about you?" she asks, trying to divert him.

"Yes, I always imagined myself with a wife and children. During my time, I was getting to the age and level of success where I'd begun considering the possibility. I don't know if I'd be a decent father, but I'm capable of learning."

As his warm breath caresses her ear, his hands snake around to her stomach as if he's imagining what it might be like to feel a child inside her. A dream she never once allowed herself to recall in the morning. She'd fallen for this once before.

He spins her in his arms. "Stop overthinking. I'm not trying to trick you. I may not be a perfect man, but I meant what I told you earlier. And there's no point in ignoring what is going on between us. But I want us to be on the same page about what we both want." He leans down and whispers, "Can you tell me what you need from me, K8?"

His attention washes over her, making her insides quiver, and suddenly that longing she always feels around him blooms. She knows exactly what she needs.

"James," she says on a breath, grabbing one of his hands. She pulls him into a dark hallway, determined to get this vengeful need relieved here and now.

He follows behind her, chuckling as if he can read her thoughts.

The moment they tuck into a dimly lit closet and the door clicks shut, he has her pressed against it. "Is this what you need, K8?"

She's nodding in the dark as his mouth meets hers in a searing kiss. His tongue sweeps into her mouth while roaming hands make their way down her hips, pulling them flush with him. Zorg, she can feel him already hard against her. Instinctively, she lifts her knee to the outside of his thigh, and he catches it, rolling his hips against her center. He repeats the promise of pleasure. Of connection.

She moans, narrowly biting back the chant in her mind: *Yes! This is it. Finally. Take me. End my suffering!*

Her hand grazes the cool metal of his belt. "Please," she whispers against his lips. Nothing wrong with pointing him in the right direction.

But he pulls away long enough to say, "The first time I feel you on my cock won't be in a broom closet, sweetheart."

K8 isn't above whining, so when she says his name this time, that's how it comes out. "James, don't make me beg. I need release from this perpetual torment." If he doesn't give her something, she might die. She can only imagine what the headlines would read.

NHOS Citizen C-K8lyn-MSP-00023468 Dies of Sexual Frustration.

Woman, known as K8, collapses after being denied orgasm.

Can withholding sex kill? Discover one woman's harrowing story.

When begging doesn't work. K8 — A Cautionary Tale.

James gives her a pained, muffled groan and says, "Keep quiet and spread your legs for me."

Then his hand snakes from the outside of her thigh to the inside. Then higher, until it grazes over the lacy material of her panties. She jumps, latching onto his shoulders as he leans in to claim her lips once again. In a deft flick of his fingers, he's inside the material, sliding through the wetness. He moans into the kiss as he teases her. He's barely dipped a finger inside and she's so close.

"Stop toying with me," she demands.

Just as she's about to thrust her hips forward to get more of his delectable digit, his other hand grabs her hip, bracing her against the door.

"No," he growls. "If you want me to do it, then let me."

When she stills, he rewards her, pressing in until two fingers are fully submerged in her heat. When the heel of his palm brushes her clit, she jerks, biting his lower lip. She can feel him grin against her lips as he repeats the motion. "You're so delicious, K8. So soft. So perfect. I've been dreaming of touching you like this."

After a few delicious minutes of his steady rhythm and the intoxicating words he's raining down on her, bliss pulses through her. He doesn't stop until her pleasure recedes, cupping her sex until she fully comes down. Finally, when she glances up at him in the dim light, he slips his hand from her panties.

He lowers her dress, and she's already reaching for the bulge in his pants.

As he pulls her hands away, he mutters, "K8."

She's so startled, she blurts out an undignified "What about you?"

"Not here," he says.

Her stomach drops. He still doesn't want her. Did he not like what he felt? Was she too eager? Her thoughts are a tumble. She might be sick.

James captures her jaw in his clean hand. "K8."

"Why?" Zephyr, she refuses to cry in front of him again.

He releases a breath, and she braces. "I'm afraid if I dive in, I won't be able to get out long enough to be useful."

That doesn't sound like he doesn't want her. But she doesn't understand. "Why do you need out?"

"Because I'll spend all my time drowning in you, and I have things I need to do before I can make that happen." He tips her chin up so he can stare into her eyes. "K8, believe me, there is nothing more I'd like to do."

"But—"

"But I must get this business off the ground. I know you have the next payment covered, but I need to secure our future if we're going to do this. Once it's established and we're out of the woods, then I promise you I'll get irrevocably lost. I plan to take the time to earn you. Make sure you have no reservations about me. Okay?"

K8 nods. He's thinking of a future that includes her. He wants to earn her. That sure sounds like what she thinks it does. Does he intend to give her companionship? It's too good to be true. His words almost make her feel safe enough to let hope swell. Now that she's chosen to explore liking him, she can barely control it. She feels lightheaded enough from his words and her very excellent orgasm that she has to grip his waist. Also, she should probably make a mental note to do something about her Worldbank account balance so she can make month four as promised. "Okay."

As they leave the broom closet, K8 smooths out her skirt, memorizing every word of James's promise. She's waited this long. Surely she can wait a little longer. Because if he's offering what she thinks he is, she plans to hold him to it.

29 – Identity for Hire

James

November 27, 2390, Day 30.

James glances across the food court to where Kate is making animated small talk with a woman in a striped and furry gray-and-black one-piece. The woman even has little cat whiskers painted or tattooed on her cheeks like his first boxing opponent.

Oro1 notices him staring. "Tattoos. She's the leader of a small cult that worships cats, like the ancient Egyptians."

James clears his throat as if that isn't the strangest thing he has ever heard. And he's pretty sure the Egyptians didn't actually worship their feline companions. "When do you want to finish the testing on the PalmPrint prototypes?" he asks.

It's been two weeks since they set their plan into motion, and they're both eager to make some tangible progress. The longer he relies on Kate, the worse his guilt is. She may be okay with it, but he can't seem to get his mind to accept the idea. Especially since the night of Lessa's conception party. The space between her thighs and the promises he made. The former, a memory he's caged and stuffed in a secure vault to be reopened once the business is launched. That is why he needs to stay focused.

"Since the PalmPrints are working in the SAT garages, we need to try somewhere with more stringent security measures," Oro1 says.

"Anywhere with a live person to accept the reading. We want to make sure they don't sense anything is off," James adds.

It only took them a few meetings at the polymers lab to develop two prototypes to test.

"I suggest we try this oxygen bar in W Quadrant that banned me for conducting 'business' there." Oro1 uses air quotes to frame the word business.

"Safe enough for our purposes?" James asks. The last thing he needs is a run-in with the authorities.

"They've never turned me in, if that's what you're asking. Establishments in the lower quadrants aren't known for strictly adhering to the regulations that govern them. They just don't want others bringing their business into their establishment, getting caught, and drawing the watchful eye of NHOS."

James nods. "I see."

They finish their plan to test out the Identity for Hire Division. James will wear Jett's print and Oro1 will use one from one of the technicians in the lab who's interested in renting out his identity after the launch. The key is that the renter must plan not to use their actual palm during the by-the-hour rental period. They'll sign a contract and confidentiality agreement to that effect, which will take care of the issue of the identity being used in two places at once. This will all be carried out on BLACKOUT through a secure portal Oro1 is setting up.

A successful trial at the oxygen bar will address Division 1. Now they need to assess the demand for the services of Division 2. How many people require a full identity?

"I put out a few feelers in a couple BLACKOUT chat rooms to see if there are any other reincarnates and I've gotten more than a few pings," James says. The chat rooms, he discovered, are a strange but useful resource.

"Have any of them agreed to meet?" Oro1 asks.

"There's one who has occasional access to an off-market device. They aren't sure when or if their owner will agree to meet. Messy situation from what I gather. Not everyone is taking the moral high road like Kate, it seems," James explains, earning a grimace from Oro1. "There are a handful of others represented by their owners, who have reluctantly agreed to meet. I've arranged meetings beginning later this week. We'll see if they show."

"That's discouraging. I thought there'd be more," Oro1 says.

In James's periphery, the cat woman pulls Kate into a quick embrace, nuzzling Kate's jaw with her nose like an actual cat might.

Kate rejoins him and Oro1 at their table, taking her seat as if that behavior didn't ruffle her one bit. "Sister Xelna told me she senses the emergence of an ancient presence in the energy fields. She thinks it means felines will be the first mammalian species to evolve with the ability to roam the earth freely once again. It's the psychic whiskers." When both James and Oro1 give her an incredulous look, Kate taps her nose to emphasize the point.

Oro1 leans forward. "Kate, darling, you don't actually believe that, do you?"

James chimes in. "They're tattoos."

Kate waves a hand through the air as if it goes without saying. "Yes, yes. I know. Still, it is rather interesting, don't you think?" She gives both him and Orol a pointed look. When neither of them is brave enough to respond, she says, "If you two are done here, I have a Japanese scalp treatment, and you have your appointment with *the physician* to collect tonight's boxing contestant."

James taps his device, noting that Kate hasn't warmed up to the idea of Sable being a part of their business yet. She's right about his appointment, though. Gone are the days when his personal assistant kept his appointments for him. Hell, back then, he would have had a team to take care of this all for him. It's energizing being on the ground level again, building something. Ironically, this time there's no trust fund to fall back on. Looking back, he was so naïve, thinking he made it on his own. This time it will be different. Harder. At least Kate has them covered for now.

As Orol's hand snakes around Kate's waist to hug goodbye, James only slightly grimaces. After her reaction to him at Lessa's party, he's confident that he's her pick. God, the way she begged for it. He could spend days making her legs quake the way they did. Thankfully, she's respecting the boundary he set, because he's pretty sure he isn't as strong as he's pretending to be. That doesn't stop him from putting a possessive arm around her waist as he guides them to the elevators.

November 30, 2390, Day 27.

James and Orol sit at a table in the back of a stark and dusty bar in Z Quadrant called Scraps. Compared to Kate's pristine apartment, the place is dingy, with dirty gray walls that might once have been black. The smell is dusky and a little acrid, like the few breaths of outside air he took before Kate saved him. It's apparent what she means when she claims her accommodations are high-end.

As they wait on the reincarnate, movement in the corner catches his attention. A small battle is being waged. He counts six, no, seven cockroaches fighting for the same crumb. The little piece suddenly breaks in two. The six still tussling for the larger scrap don't pay any mind as the victor scuttles away through a crack in the floor. A moment later, he sees the same creature emerge outside to scurry across the street and disappear into the adjacent building.

He lifts a brow in Orol's direction.

"Only a handful of lifeforms can exist outside still," he supplies.

"Of course," James says. "And the crack? Does that mean outside air is seeping in as we speak?"

Orol only shrugs, saying, "It's Z Quadrant, and it isn't like there's enough outside air seeping in to kill anyone."

James accepts the answer as he surveys the space again with a renewed perspective. The handful of patrons, like James and Orol, keep their heads down as if they're here for the same illicit meetings. "I guess a lot of discreet business happens in places like this?"

Orol takes a sip of his cocktail, warily scanning the room. "Most of the authorities in this sector are paid off by those of us who do business here. It's a safe place to make contact when discretion is required. But I meet clients in my office all the time, too."

The door opens, and a tall woman with straight, nearly black hair that hangs past her shoulders enters, glancing around nervously. James makes eye contact with her, noting her freckles. Now, people see them as a flaw and have eliminated them from the gene pool. Each charming dot on her cheeks sets her apart as a reincarnate. She'll need a procedure if they ever expect to pass her off as a person from this time, but that isn't IdenTECH's business. It's his job to get her an identity.

Behind her, an even taller man with dusty blond hair looks on, and James catches his honey-colored gaze for a moment. The man, who must be her owner, leans down, saying something to her that she doesn't quite seem to hear.

"That's her," he says, giving her a subtle nod. Her eyes widen as she stands there, clutching her bag.

Orol leans over. "What's all over her face?"

James shakes his head. "Those are freckles. Not a defect. People from my time considered them to be cute."

"Odd," Orol says.

The woman's indecision teeters for a long moment. *Come on*, James mentally urges.

Her dark eyes sweep over him, making him feel inspected. James isn't sure what she sees. What causes her to take two tentative steps toward them, then suddenly freeze, turn back, and dart out the door.

"Fuck," James says, running a frustrated hand through his hair as he starts to get up.

Orol's hand clamps down on his shoulder, keeping him seated. "Don't bother. You said she was reluctant in your messages. We don't want to pursue her. It will only frighten her more. Reach out again next week after she realizes we haven't sent the authorities after her. Sometimes it takes me a few meetings to establish contact with a client. These reincarnates are probably going to be even more difficult to nail down. Don't be disheartened."

James rubs his sweaty palms down his thighs, mentally cursing the failure of the first four meetings with reincarnates they secured.

Orol's gaze narrows on their glasses vibrating on the table, then shifts to James.

"Sorry," he says, forcing his knee to halt its anxious motion. "Today marks the end of month two. Thirty more days to go. I can practically feel the clock ticking, which would be exciting if it weren't my life in the balance."

"We're close," Oro1 reassures him.

It's not like it's Oro1's life they're talking about. Still, James says, "I know. At least Kate's got month four covered and I'm close to having month five. I'll rest much easier when we figure out how to implant an identity into the system. It's not like I can continue paying the lease year after year indefinitely. Won't GROW notice that someone has kept one of their manupartners for an inordinate amount of time?"

Oro1 nods. "We'll get you an identity long before that happens."

James downs the last of his drink. "Agreed. And in case we don't, I'm going to work on Plan B."

30 – Viper

K8

December 14, 2390, Day 13.

K8 only agreed to go with them to Holiday Boxing Night because James seemed so excited about the big fight night planned. Apparently they are entering two manupartners, and it is in the Holiday spirit, after all. Her attendance has nothing to do with the fact that she wants to finally meet Sable, the physician he's been ~~spending time~~ running a business with. She isn't jealous. It's only that another two weeks have slipped by and she hasn't gotten to see him nearly as much as she would prefer. Spending all night with him for Holiday is going to be wonderful.

Her door chimes, alerting her to their first visitors. Just a dab more of blush . . . perfect. When she breezes into the living room, James is emptying several packages out of the smartwaiter, which she'd prefer to be doing herself because—well, he's very particular about the use of funds—and while they're ~~definitely~~ probably covered—and while he did say she deserved all the things she wanted . . . that does seem like a few more packages than what she purchased.

There's tension in the set of his shoulders as she turns around.

"James?" she asks, testing.

The door chimes again.

"We can talk about this tomorrow," he says.

She slips past him, opening the door, grateful for the distraction.

"Happy Holiday, Katie-Cakes!" Jett calls, rushing over to her to pepper her with cheek kisses. "Lessa won't make it. Morning sickness."

"It's not even morning," K8 says, wondering why her friend hasn't made a better excuse.

Jett waves a flippant hand through the air. "That's what I said." Then he leans in conspiratorially. "It's been over two months since they turned Yansy in, and I might have heard them telling the woman next door that they're staying home and activating a ManuMATE as a little Holiday present for themself."

K8 giggles. That sounds exactly like Lessa.

James approaches. "Speaking of, I wanted to reiterate that I appreciate you leaving Decci at home. I know you would enjoy having . . . it—" James clears his throat, and Jett's grin illuminates how amusing it is to watch James stumble around for his words. "Having him here with you for Holiday."

Jett puts a conspiratorial hand on James's arm. "Believe me, I find this much more amusing." He nudges K8 in the ribs. "Don't you agree?"

She giggles, biting her tongue.

James continues, undeterred that her friend is poking fun at his expense. "When I can, I will compensate you for the time lost, naturally."

"Naturally," Jett says, snorting. As K8 turns toward Oro1, he mutters, "I see you're still clinging to the hyperindependent bullshit."

"It's a process," James replies.

She ignores them and their weird, blunt dynamic in favor of greeting Oro1. "Happy Holiday!"

He returns the greeting, pulling her to his side. From the corner of her eye, she sees James attentively watching as Oro1 squeezes her. Silly man. He says nothing, which is good because she wouldn't tolerate it if he did—another reason she is never jealous. But it still makes her insides warm. Maybe he'll forget about the purchases.

"Sable is running late. NHOS inspectors showed up at the recycle station, which delayed a batch of decommissionings," Oro1 says. "Apparently, since the runaway manupartner, they've made a few unexpected appearances."

"Good thing we got our two loaners for the fight tonight before they came," James says, opening a bottle of Vine. She can't help but notice his stare drift toward the smartwaiter.

K8 retrieves five glasses and watches James pour.

Fifteen minutes before they're about to leave, Sable arrives with the two stocky manupartners.

K8 puts on her most winning grin, offering her hand to the woman like James showed her. She adores the customs from his time. They make her feel like she's a ~~character~~ real person in one of the Old News articles. "Hi, I'm K8."

Sable glances at her hand, then at James, which makes K8 bristle.

"It's called shaking hands," James tells Sable, cutting through the quickly coagulating tension. "I've been showing K8 things from my time."

Sable's dark eyes widen.

K8 is becoming increasingly antsy with her hand hovering in midair between them, but her desire to impress James outweighs her rising discomfort.

Berry-stained lips purse as the physician considers K8's hand. "I don't see why we must touch each other to greet, but if this was your custom." Sable takes her hand and K8 nearly breathes an audible sigh of relief.

"We just move them up and down for a second, like this," K8 says, demonstrating. "Now you say, 'I'm Sable.' Then we both say, 'Nice to meet you.'"

"At the same time?" Sable asks, incredulously.

K8 defers to James, who says, "No," then laughs as they follow the procedure.

When K8 releases her hand, James slips an arm around her waist, murmuring in her ear, "Very nicely done."

K8 beams, hoping his praise means she'll be getting a reward later. It is *Holiday*, for Zephyr's sake. "Now we're friends," she tells the other woman.

"That will throw off my optimal balance," Sable notes, sighing.

"That's what I said!" K8 exclaims, pleased they've found common ground so quickly. "I think as long as we don't become good friends, it will be fine."

Sable studies her for a moment. "You're making a joke?" Her open features can't hide the twitch at the corner of her full lips.

"K8 is very clever. It's one of the traits I like most about her," James says, his warm hand running affectionate strokes down her side.

From the kitchen, Jett makes a retching sound, and she swears she hears him say something about Yansy.

Sable says, "Well, that was interesting. I tend to agree with the man in the kitchen." Then she looks toward the two manupartners patiently waiting by the door. "We should probably go get them entered. I think that one," she points to the slightly taller one, who is twitching, "is malfunctioning."

"What about your Vine?" K8 asks, startled that the seemingly intelligent woman would forget about something so important. It was pre-boxing Holiday *drinks*, after all.

Sable straightens like K8 has caught her interest, then follows her to the kitchen. When K8 hands her the glass, Sable sniffs it, then downs it in one go. She hands the glass back. "Thank you. After the day I've had, I needed that."

K8 isn't sure what to think of the abrupt physician who she's decided has zero interest in James or the people in the ring trying to punch each other.

"Why do you all like this again?" she asks. Is it something she should be concerned about? The stagnant smell from the tightly packed spectators certainly is. Sweat and something metallic—*blood*. Her nose wrinkles as she stares down at the red splatter in the center ring, where workers are actively cleaning. If only she had a perfume-scented scarf to tie around her face.

"I like it because of the Blackmarks," Sable says, pointing to the climbing wagers.

Her new friend has a point. Those figures would go well with her Worldbank account. And keep her from the chastisement her purchases have surely earned her.

An hour goes by before their first manupartner enters the ring. Thankfully, it's the twitching one. Better to get it out of the way first before things get worse.

It steps into the ring clad in the shortest pink-and-black-spotted one-shoulder tunic she's ever seen. It's wearing a scruffy-looking shoulder-length wig, a matching headband, and a pair of boxing boots that resemble gladiator sandals. A detail only the most fashionable during her time would note.

"What is he wearing?" James asks.

"It's supposed to be a cave dweller costume," she says, pointing to the particle pane displaying a picture of the manupartner along with the words "Stone Man." The crowd goes wild as the manupartner walks to its corner.

Jett nods to the manupartner in the ring. "Stone Man's face is twitching in rhythm with the clapping. Should we be concerned?"

Sable's lips purse as her eyes narrow on the manupartner. "He'll last through the fight." She pats her breast pocket. "I can decommission him after if needed. Hopefully, it won't come to that, because I don't know how we would get his limp body back to GROW for recycling without being noticed."

Butterflies erupt in K8's stomach. That doesn't sound good. James must notice her newly erupted nerves because he reaches over, takes her hand, and squeezes. "It will be fine. She's being cautious."

James enters a large sum into the betting platform for Stone Man's opponent. K8 glances at the smaller contestant, who's listed as "Boxer Yoorl." By the anxious glances he's giving his stocky manupartner opponent, he must be human.

"In my time, boxers were categorized by weight, but it seems now they're organized by the potential for spectacle," James tells her. Maybe that means she'll finally get to see the unbeaten Lizard Man. That would be one amusing positive for coming.

The bell rings and the first round starts. The crowd gasps as Stone Man misses three jabs in a row before landing a poorly placed uppercut. It's enough to send Boxer Yoorl stumbling back. The crowd cheers. Loudly. The raucous noise makes K8 grateful she's never attended one of these events before. Between the smell, the violence, and her already-aching feet, she can confidently say she is not a fan of boxing.

But James is wearing a fiercely attractive grin, which makes it worth it—at least for this one night. Though she isn't sure if it's the boxing he's enjoying or the prospect of making unicoin.

Boxer Yoorl rallies, but not before the wagers for Stone Man skyrocket. The seconds drag on with Stone Man landing two more hooks, only taking one himself. The bell rings, ending round one.

It's not looking good. K8 leans over to James. "He's going to win." As the fighters get to their feet, she buries her face in James's shoulder. "I can't watch."

"No, he's not. Look." James takes hold of her shoulders, turning her toward the center ring.

She peeks open an eye in time to see Boxer Yoorl land a precisely executed right hook on Stone Man's inconspicuously presented jaw. He goes down.

The ring master rushes forward. "Ten, nine, eight . . ."

Stone Man stirs but doesn't rise to its feet. Unlike the crowd, she knows it is a carefully planned act.

"Four, three, two . . ."

K8 glances up to the main particle pane to see the ringmaster hold Boxer Yoorl's hand in the air, declaring him the match's winner. If she thought the crowd was loud before, they were hectic now. Angry. Like people who thought they bet on a sure thing, then lost.

Sable nudges past her. "I should probably go collect him."

K8 is eager to escape the frenzied energy. "I'll go too. I need a drink." She also wishes to avoid the guilty niggle the upset crowd is causing her. *Remember, it is illegal funds*. For James's life, it's worth upsetting a few of her peers.

They all end up following K8 and Sable out of the arena to the concessions area. While Sable excuses herself to manage Stone Man, James and Orol take drink orders. Fifteen minutes later, they're standing around a bar-height table, comparing winnings.

"Why have I never agreed to come with you two before? This is fun!" Jett exclaims.

K8 chuffs. "You only think it's fun because of the Blackmarks."

"Nothing wrong with that." Sable raises her glass.

James leans in K8's direction. "You hate this, don't you?"

She tries to hide a sheepish grin, but it's impossible. "A little."

"I appreciate you coming. I promise, once we launch IdenTECH, no more boxing nights," he says.

"I'll let you make it up to me later," she says, running a hand across the hard plane of his stomach. Zephyr, she wants to feel those muscles flexing as he—

"K8," James whispers, removing her hand, which has accidentally slipped between two buttons and may have been petting the fine trail of hairs her fingers found there. He places his device in her lonely palm. "Look."

She blinks as she takes in the total displayed in his Blackmarks account, running the conversion in her mind. "This is your account balance?"

"Yes," he says proudly. "I complete the transfer from my Off-the-Books account after every fight." *In case something were to happen* is implied.

"But—" She is momentarily speechless but recovers quickly. "You have enough to cover the next month's rent. Maybe a second if they offer a promotion."

Relief washes over her, and she almost feels guilty at how glad she is that James has solved his own problems. She won't have to sell her things! Oh Zephyr, does this make her a horrible person? No, James wanted to do it himself and she's letting him. It's respectful and considerate.

"I wanted to surprise you. A few days ago, Oro1 got access to the historical betting data. We determined that Holiday is a prime opportunity for betting," he says.

That explains the large sum he wagered. He knew it would be worth the risk. James shrugs as if the achievement isn't nearly as significant as K8 feels it is. She pushes her drink toward the center of the table. If she becomes any giddier, she might float away.

"I am surprised." She grins, not caring at all about her friend essentially hacking into the illegal boxing club's database for data. She has other things on her mind. Because if James has the next month or two covered, maybe more after the next fight, he won't have to focus as intently. That will free him up to do other things. Namely, her. She can't resist the urge to press herself suggestively against his side. "I'm very impressed." His warmth seeps between their clothing and she can almost imagine the glorious sensations their skin touching would elicit if the fabric weren't there. "Does this mean that tonight you'll—"

Oro1 clears his throat.

She peels herself off James, turning to address her friends. Oro1 is giving her a pointed look. Jett grins knowingly and Sable's face pinches in disgust.

She's about to voice a protest when a voice she never believed she would hear again booms, "It's that mad woman!"

Her blood attempts to flee her body all at once. She's lightheaded as she reaches for James. They turn to the commotion behind her.

Viper is stomping toward her. His long blond hair is bound at the nape of his neck and his copper eyes are flashing with something that frightens her. Is this about her rejection?

The irate man stops two feet from her, and she feels James take a step toward him.

"You. Cursed. Me," Viper hisses.

K8 blinks, momentarily struck speechless. Is he serious? "But curses aren't real."

"My coworkers reported me for your outburst at my workplace. Then my manupartner malfunctioned the day I saw you in the food court with the cat woman," he barks.

Cat woman? "Oh, you mean Sister Xelna?" K8 asks, still confused and a little nervous about where this conversation is going. James puts a steadying hand on the small of her back. Controlled tension radiates off him.

Viper ignores her question in favor of throwing another accusation her way. "And you just happen to show up the night I lose all the Blackmarks in my account."

She shuffles back a step, seeking James's warmth.

Oro1 moves to stand on her other side. "I'm sure whatever this is about can all be smoothed over with a drink."

Viper holds out his device. "A drink I can no longer pay for."

"I'm not sure what your bad luck has to do with K8," James says. His arm slips protectively around her waist. "But I suggest you find someone else to air your grievances to."

"What did I do to you that I deserve this?" Viper demands, ignoring James. He waves the device wildly in the air as if it supports his inquiry. "Tell me."

"I . . ." K8 hesitates. What can she possibly say? It's not like she's going to explain to Viper, in front of James and the newly gathered onlookers, that his participation in a misguided fantasy of hers when she was in her twenties emotionally scarred her. Then she dwelled on it for the next sixty years. Oh Zorg, is that what she did?

Before she can open her mouth to say something, anything, Viper's eyes flick to something behind them. "Sable?" His eyes narrow as they jump between her friends.

The air hangs taut between them, and it's clear that Viper is doing his best to process what he's seeing. This can't be good. In fact, this is probably very bad. She glances back at James. "We should go."

"I see what's going on here." Viper rubs his chin as a startling grin spreads across his pale face.

Sable walks around the table to stand beside James. She squares her shoulders. "There's no rule against me participating on my off nights."

"Except that's not what's you're doing, is it?" When Sable only glares, Viper chuckles. "Interesting. Very, very interesting. The rumor of your ruthlessness isn't wrong." He stuffs his hands into his pockets, then readdresses her. "K8 is your name? Don't worry, K8. I won't forget you this time."

K8's throat tightens.

"Perhaps we could discuss whatever it is you think you know, and how it might benefit all of us, elsewhere?" James asks, so softly the onlookers around them lean in.

We need to leave. We need to leave. We need to leave. The chant goes off like an alarm bell in her mind. But maybe he won't actually remember her or James. He forgot her once before. He'll remember Sable, though. They both work for GROW.

"You can't prove anything," Sable says.

Murmurs erupt around them. Several people track Oro1, who leans over to whisper something in Sable's ear before slipping through the crowd.

Viper doesn't need to answer, but he does. It would have been better if he issued a threat or a warning, but he only says, "See you around, Firelight."

By the time they make it back to her apartment with the two manu-partners in tow and one less Jett, who claimed to have had enough excitement for the evening, K8's tears have dried. Her fingers idly trace the seams of the couch as a numb sensation spreads through her.

In her living room, James paces while he and Sable, also seated on the couch, argue about damage control. Oro1 leans against the wall, observing. Likely thinking.

"We don't technically know what he thinks we're doing," Sable says.

"He knows exactly what we're doing," James says.

"How can you be so sure?" Sable jumps to her feet, like she can't keep still either.

It's odd how similar she and James are. Both driven, calculating, focused, passionate, but James isn't nearly as cold. K8 can see how one might describe the physician as ruthless. Not that K8 thinks Sable lacks emotion. Her emotions are so tightly lidded that she comes across as icy and unfeeling. Would James have turned out like that if he'd been born during her time?

"Can you please just trust me on this? If he didn't guess exactly what we're doing, he has a pretty good idea." James plops down into the seat beside her, placing his head in his hands. "We should have never agreed to use new specimens. Borrowing the ones people turned in for a day or two was far less risky."

K8's attention snaps to Sable. "You grew new manupartners for the fights?"

"I was struggling to find good fighters in the pool of recyclables. I have access to the genetic material required to make the kits, so I presented the idea to the team, and we agreed to try it," Sable says, shrugging like she hadn't just described being engaged in theft. "I was careful. Once I recycle them, there will be no evidence."

This is so much worse than K8 imagined. What is the penalty for stealing from a company like GROW? This is exactly what she wanted to avoid. The authorities will find out her involvement and take away her job, her unit, her Worldbank account, the contents of her closet . . . and James. K8 feels the tension in her face go slack. They're going to get thrown into the social confinement center, and James will become a lab clone before getting recycled. It's all her fault. She really despises Viper now. Maybe she should get in touch with Sister Xelna and see if there really are curses.

"This was stupid. A bad idea," she mumbles.

Oro1 clears his throat. "We hadn't run into any problems until tonight."

The comment feels like a rebuke. Worse than any chastisement she might have expected about her purchases. Tears prick her eyes, and she can't stop them from falling down her cheeks. If only the soft cushions would open up and swallow her whole. "Don't you think I know that?! If I never went with you, he would have never seen me. Then he wouldn't have noticed Sable."

"It's not remotely your fault. It's ours," James says, rubbing a hand down her back. "We knew the risks."

She appreciates the sentiment, but it isn't true. If it were, wouldn't her other friends be agreeing with him? Oh, that's right. FRIENDS. She almost forgot. This is what her life has been reduced to. It only makes her cry harder.

Oro1 walks over and sits down next to her, his body language stiff and awkward. "Please don't cry."

She chuckles through her tears. "Why not? James is the only one who thinks it's not my fault, and that's because he's from the past and he likes to take on every burden himself."

A look K8 can't interpret passes between the two men bracketing her. Then she feels James's hand slip away. Why is he abandoning her? Did her words upset him?

"K8, darling. It isn't your fault," Oro1 says, drawing her attention. "I didn't mean to make you feel that way with my comment. If you would prefer that I exit our FRIENDS group—"

James clears his throat. Oro1's eyes flick past her. She turns in time to see James mouth, *I'm sorry.*

She almost laughs as she realizes what is happening. Like how James is teaching her customs from his time, he's teaching her FRIENDS too. A little stunned, she turns back to Oro1 to wait.

"I'm sorry," he finally says. "May I hug you now?"

K8 leans over into her friend's open arms. "I appreciate you saying that, Oro1. You definitely may not leave our FRIENDS group, you ridiculous man."

Then she turns to Sable, their newest member. Her eyes widen. "Don't look at me like that. I never blamed you." She marches toward the door, muttering, "This many friends is clearly not optimal."

K8 can't help but smile despite the crises they've been plunged into.

"I'm going to keep these two until morning, then add them to my first batch of decommissionings. I'll message when it's done," Sable says, then hesitates, before turning to Oro1. "Thank you for collecting the manupartners. You drew less scrutiny than if I were to have been the one to get them."

"No problem, darling." Oro1 stands, offering to make sure Sable makes it back to her apartment safely.

She rebuffs his offer, adding a biting "Don't call me that."

K8 giggles at Sable's response, feeling a short-lived lightness. But when the door closes, James turns to K8. The way he's looking at her now, like he's dissecting her . . . his stare feels heavy, prickly, but not in a way that makes her want him to remove it. Is he about to bring up her purchases? If so, that's fine. Honestly, it would be a welcome distraction from tonight's events, and now that the next two months are assured, she can explain to him that she trusted that he had it covered. She only wanted to make sure he knew he could count on her. In fact, she hadn't even selected every item she wanted. Something she could do now that she knew they had some cushion.

The sunny scene in the particle panes seems to match her resolve. She'll wait for James to let her know that Sable messaged, and the threat has cleared, and then she'll go out for a bit. Her eyes make a reluctant dance from the cheery screens to James's decidedly darker face.

She's almost a little afraid to ask, but she can't help herself. "What?"

He smiles, but instead of making her feel better, it makes the anxious bees in her stomach swarm more furiously. He seems to sense her reaction. Is he enjoying it? He reaches forward to brush an errant strand from her temple. "K8, sweetheart. Tell me about Viper."

31 – Never Is a Promise

James

James leans forward, waiting for her to answer.

"Who's Viper?" Her voice cracks as she repeats his question. Then she coughs, pointedly avoiding eye contact. "I thought you would want to discuss my purchases."

That is the least of his concern now. "You can't avoid this conversation."

Kate shifts on the couch like she's ready to bolt. "I only thought since the fighting ring scheme had been going so well—"

"Your shopping isn't what I asked you about." By evading his question, she only makes him want to know the answer more. His smile broadens, and he leans forward. "Who's Viper?"

Kate shoots the full packages a longing glance, as if they might save her, but they sit by the wall, conspicuous and unhelpful.

"Quit squirming. I'm not upset or jealous, but I'd really like to know what type of man we're dealing with and what he has to do with you," James explains. That's mostly true. Everyone knows it's impossible to be jealous of people with names like Viper, Glen, Braxton, or Frank—he's getting distracted. "Kate?"

"Logically, it makes sense that you want to know. If our positions were reversed, I would likely feel the same," she says, placating him.

"So you understand why I . . . *need* to know," he says, coming narrowly close to saying *want.*

She shrugs, picking up the remote for the particle panes. A moment later, they illuminate the living room with a sparkling gray skyline scene. "This is nice. Would you like a glass of Vine?"

She starts to stand, but he catches her around the waist, surprising her by drawing her into his lap. "Not so fast, sweetheart—"

She sobs, and suddenly his skin prickles with his misstep.

"Oh no," he says, adjusting her so he can see her face. "I just thought he was an old boyfriend, upset because you broke it off with him at his work or something. I didn't realize . . ." That Viper meant so much to her? He can hardly bring himself to say the words aloud. "Kate, we don't have to talk about it if you aren't ready."

Which isn't ideal since he would really like to know what Viper is capable of, but it isn't worth Kate's tears. "Shh," he says. He strokes her soft hair while she curls into him, nuzzling into his neck. Better than any deal he ever brokered, she feels fucking perfect in his arms.

"He wasn't my boyfriend," she finally says.

That's right. How could he not have considered that? Everyone now had manupartners. His curiosity is nearing its breaking point. Still, for her, he keeps his mouth shut and waits.

"I've never had a boyfriend." She groans, wiping her tears on his shirt. "This is mortifying. Even more so since I know how things were during your time."

He adjusts her once more, partially because he senses she's ready to talk, and partially because he's enjoying holding her a little too much. "I promise, I'm not judging you for the manupartner thing anymore. I told you I understand, and I meant it."

After an extended pause, she exhales. "It was stupid. I was young and still grieving for my parents. I had these ridiculous notions swirling around my head, and when Viper approached me in a bar, well, he promised me everything I wanted."

What she is describing makes James want to knock the other man through a wall. But this isn't about him, so he listens. As Kate's tears fall, James holds her hand until she's expelled the entire awful story.

Later that night, when he crawls into her bed for the first time, he can't help but draw her into the protection of his embrace. She's tearstained and exhausted. Pressed against his side, she falls asleep within minutes.

As the night drifts by, he watches her and turns the story she told him over and over in his mind. What he can't understand is how, with all their conduct courses and social rules, someone like Viper existed still. The man's lack of empathy was shocking. How could he be completely oblivious to the harm caused by his words?

That was one of the beautiful things about Kate. She wore every emotion so openly. Viper had to have seen that Kate thought it was real and got off on it. That told James exactly the type of man they were dealing with. Not flippant and self-involved, like most contemporary people. Viper was the type of selfish person who fed off the emotions of others. He tried to exploit opportunities not for progress or the betterment of those around him, like James, but for pleasure or personal gain. Impulsive and unremorseful.

During James's time, men like Viper were common, but somehow he's come up with the idea that the future is different. But if that were true, why couldn't someone like Kate find the companionship she deserves? Hell, the government has to assign FRIENDS groups. The future is just as bad as he originally thought. At least he has her, and her FRIENDS, who seem to be slowly evolving. Even he seems to be evolving. *Because of her.*

James can't stop his fingers from brushing her hair back from her face.

She stirs. "James?"

Leaning over, he kisses her forehead. "I'm here."

If he were a truly good man, he would keep his distance until he's sure he can deliver on all his promises. But while he's not a sociopath like Viper, he'll always ruthlessly pursue what he wants.

Her voice is soft and sleepy as she asks, "You're not leaving?"

She blinks up at him, and as her heavy lids draw closed, he can't help but want the woman melted into his side and the future he's going to earn for them.

He isn't sure she's still awake when he says, "Never."

32 – The Most Precious Possession

K8

December 15, 2390, Day 12.

The next morning, K8 is able to focus enough to complete a solid ten task orders before lunch, despite her nerves and drifting, anxious thoughts. The day is passing sluggishly as they wait to hear from Sable. With each passing hour, she senses James's energy becoming tauter. Right now, it seems like it might pull tight and snap at any moment.

"Still nothing?" she asks, knowing there's nothing she can say to ease his distress. At least the PalmPrint prototypes arrived, which will give him something to do.

"No. I've messaged her, but she hasn't seen it," he says, grimacing. "I don't like this being out of my control."

"I know," she agrees. "We have to trust that she's taking care of it."

It is incredibly thoughtless of Sable to leave them in a state of concern like that. Reinforcing James's reluctance to depend on others is the last thing they need. Specifically, because K8 wants him to depend on her. Count on and open up to her. Her eyes narrow as she mentally scolds the physician.

"No news is better than bad news, right?" she says, though she isn't sure even she feels reassured. She checks the Flash News app. No reports of a mishap at GROW. That is good news at least.

James grumbles, "I'm sure it's fine."

Her device pings. She glances at the screen, eager for the distraction. It's an email from GROW. The subject reads:

SPECIAL OFFER.

Please let it be a discount, she prays to Zephyr. The inspectors never sent her one, and she was reluctant to broach the subject, afraid it might trigger them to come collect James for testing. She settles into her desk chair to read the message.

"Renew now and receive two free weeks," it reads.

Excellent, she thinks, skimming further. *Well, boo*. It's only valid for another three-month contract. As it stands, she only can afford the next month. But maybe if they were to combine their money. She saw the balance of his account last night. Might as well check and see if they can take advantage of the discount.

She switches her workstation on, and the screens illuminate. The retina scan confirms her identity, and K8 logs into her Worldbank account.

She almost chokes when she sees her unicoin balance. She must have gasped, because James, who is inspecting the PalmPrint prototypes on the kitchen counter, shoots her a glance.

"You okay?" he asks.

K8 plasters on a fake smile. "Sure am." She hopes he'll not see straight through her.

Her focus returns to the screen and the dismal reality of her World-bank account. Thank Zephyr he has the funds. She should probably tell him to go ahead and wash the Blackmarks into unicoin.

Goose bumps trail down her spine at the thought of what will undoubtedly be an uncomfortable conversation. Telling him about Viper the night before was one of the most embarrassing moments of her life. Perhaps the conversation can wait a few more days.

She glances at the calendar, then opens the GROW contract. At the bottom, near her digital signature, is the date her extension payment will come due if she chooses to keep him. Her manupartner will be due back to the facility by noon twelve days from now. In big block letters, it says "OR GROW PERSONNEL WILL BE DISPATCHED TO REPOSSESS YOUR UNIT." She swallows at the aggressive text. Twelve days. Where has the time gone? No problem.

Her stomach churns. Maybe if she were getting paid soon, she could manage month four, then that would give her reprieve from the conversation all together. She searches her calendar, landing on the Fifthday sixteen days from now. Maybe GROW has a by-the-day extension plan? She could buy a few more days, and then if she sells a few things like she's been meaning to but was really hoping to avoid, she could do a longer extension then. Then he would cover month five and beyond, and they'd never have to talk about it. For all he'd know, she had it covered the entire time.

She logs into her GROW account. Three unread alerts are waiting for her:

> Limited Time Offer.
>
> Something Special Just for You!
>
> Ever Considered a Second Manupartner?

She scoffs. Who can afford that? Maybe with one of the off-brand models, but certainly not a GROW.

She clicks on the link that says Plan Extensions.

One month is half her normal monthly earnings. She scrolls down.

Two weeks . . . there's hardly a discount. Clearly, the aim is to get people to purchase longer contracts.

One week . . . is . . . oh Zorg, she's in trouble. Why hasn't she looked at this sooner? It's still over a week's earnings. And there isn't a by-the-day option. Surely they won't repossess him. Then she can pay the late fees or whatever once she gets paid. No more nights out for a while. And there was that pair of shoes, but for James, she'd forgo those, naturally.

K8 creates a quick tally, including columns for her current World-bank balance, a number uncomfortably close to zero. Then her next paycheck. Her monthly expenditures. Finally, the total for a one-month GROW contract extension. She sets the formula and her stomach swirls as the bright red negative calculates.

James is worth it. Not only is he a real man, he's . . . well, he's James, something she never imagined she would think all those weeks ago when she read the articles. She glances over at him. The muscle of his forearm flexes as he types something onto his device. Zephyr, he's beautiful. The intensity of his gaze warms her to the core. Not to mention his talented fingers. His promises.

His shoulders lower as he sets the phone down, turning to her. "Sable was able to include the manupartners in her first batch of recyclables this morning."

"It's well past noon," K8 says, her lips pressing into a frown. James has been a nervous flutter of energy all morning. Needlessly. She feels rather irritated with the physician. Perhaps enough to degrade her to an acquaintance.

He pinches the bridge of his nose. "I know. She says she got busy and forgot to message."

K8 chuffs. "That is not very respectful or considerate." Unlike James, who she is certain will never let her down. She wants to be there in the same way for him. Show him he can depend on her.

Steeling herself, she adds a third column titled Value of Items to Sell. She can do this and preserve her dignity.

With purpose, K8 rummages through her closet. It only takes her an hour to have a sizable pile on her bed. One by one, she takes each pair of shoes, handbag, or luxury scarf into the living room, starting with her least favorite. Obviously. She places them on a little table she's set up opposite a stretch of particle pane she sets to a muted neutral light. Then she takes several photos, a video, and then catalogues it into the tally. She leaves a little breathing room in her figures for meals and possible estimating errors, then assigns an expected value for each item. When the little red numbers flip to black, she lists the selected items online.

Satisfied, she files her unlisted treasures back into her closet. When she picks up a particularly adorable bird-shaped bag by an up-and-coming designer, she clutches it to her chest. "I'm so pleased I was able to save you."

When she's almost finished restoring her closet, her device emits a ping associated with a monetary transaction. She snatches it off her nightstand, eager to see which item went first. Seeing the heels with the heart-shaped embellishments, she sighs loudly. It's tragic, really, but at least she got full list price for them. And if she remembers correctly, she was wearing those that night in X Quadrant when she'd met and subsequently slept with that lovely man all those years ago.

Well, maybe they will do someone else some good. The woman's messaged that she'd like to come pick up her purchase as soon as possible.

K8 is digging them out from the bottom of the pile of items for sale when the door chimes. She fishes out the pair, keeping her device in her other hand so she can confirm the transaction. When she returns to the living room, James has answered the door. A short woman stands before her, and K8 recognizes her cropped, shiny brown hair from her purchaser profile. "Hello," the woman says brightly, showing her the purchase code on her device. "Are those them?"

She makes gimmie hands in the shoes' direction. James watches with a curious expression on his face as K8 instinctively pulls the shoes back from the woman. "Are you sure they'll fit?" she asks her, hoping it doesn't come off as rude.

The woman, for her part, blushes. "I know I'm rather small, but they're a size thirty-eight, correct?"

"Yes," K8 chirps. She can feel her knuckles going white around the straps.

The woman takes pity on her. "They're quite lovely. If you'd like to cancel the sale, I'd understand completely."

James's brow furrows as his assessing gaze drifts between her and the woman. He frowns as he grabs ahold of K8's wrist, squeezing slightly as he pulls the heels from her grip. He hands them to the woman. "These will accentuate your legs beautifully, I'm certain."

The woman is blushing furiously now. "Thank you," she says, sneaking a last glance at James. Then she takes off toward the elevator at a pace that makes K8 wonder if the woman thinks she is going to chase her down to steal the shoes back.

When the door closes, James turns her to face him. "What are you doing, K8?"

She shrugs, looking at her device as if it might get her out of the conversation. Finally, she offers, "Nothing."

"You didn't seem like you wanted to sell that woman those shoes?"

"Well, it was a little uncomfortable, but I listed them for a reason." Despite the fact that their parting is making her feel a bit forlorn. *They're just shoes, K8.* James, focus on James.

"Sweetheart," he says, and she leans into his palm as he cups her cheek. "Why are you selling your things? You don't have to do that for me. I told you I'd figure it out, and I have."

Tears prick her eyes as she contemplates her answer. "I want you to be able to depend on me. I told you I have the next month covered. I just would prefer a little more wiggle room."

She only has twelve days to keep her promise. And if she fails, they'll come get him. Because she did make a few inquiries after he asked, so she knows the full process of decommissioning. They bring the GROWs into a room in batches. A physician, like Sable, does a secondary blood test from a sample collected from the fingertip. An injection is given that lulls the manupartner into a sleep state. Then a second injection is given that stops the heart, much in the same way they used to decommission sick pets.

After that it gets a little messier, since the manupartners are considered recyclable organic material. K8 shudders at the thought of the video she watched. At the vat of glowing orange algae-like liquid, and the large mixer blades that churn the waste bodies and the chemicals that break them down into a usable substance. The video explained that they don't remain in a humanoid form for long after they come in contact with the chemicals, but K8 swears she saw an arm floating around the flesh stew.

A very strong part of her considers whether she should just let James convert the funds and make the payment. It could be James's arm if she doesn't fix this.

But she has twelve full days. There is no reason to be dramatic. If she fails, he has the funds to cover it. It would be crushing to admit she isn't worthy of his trust, but at least he'd be alive. Would that make him retract his promises? Her already nervous stomach swirls, but she plasters on a brave face.

"It's a common practice. Buy something. Wear it a few times. Sell it. Buy something new." It is partly true, so she doesn't really consider it a lie.

"K8, if those shoes were one of your favorites, I'm sure we could have found something else for you to sell."

She shrugs again, looking away. "They weren't a favorite pair."

"Well," he says, running a thumb across her jaw, sending the most delicious sensations skittering down her neck. "If you wore them a lot . . ." He trails off, and she realizes he's stepped into her space.

"I didn't," she confesses, her voice becoming breathy and high-pitched.

"Still, selling your prized possessions for me is very sweet of you, K8." His hands have fallen from her jaw to find a new home on her hips. She nearly whimpers as his lips whisper over the flesh of her neck, which arches for him of its own accord. It's been too long since their encounter in the broom closet, and K8 is already primed for him.

"You've been so patient with me while I work. And I know opening up to me last night was difficult for you. I want to say thank you." He kisses her neck more roughly, letting his teeth graze over her pulse point. "Tell me how I can thank you."

"Do that again," she whispers, and she can feel his chuckle against her neck before he leaves a trail of hot sparking flesh down to her collarbones. If opening up, as he says, was all it took, then perhaps she should have told him all her embarrassing stories a long time ago. His teeth brush an especially sensitive spot on her shoulder. She moans as sensation dances across her skin. Then he's walking her backward, kissing her, tugging, and pawing. Her body tingles with awareness and she can feel moisture accumulating between her thighs.

The cash notification from the device still clutched in her hand sounds. She starts to look, to see which of her prized possessions, as James put it, she'll have to relinquish, but James takes the device from her. His arm snakes around her, and he reclaims her mouth as if he's irritated she ever took it away from him at all. It makes heat blossom throughout her body. The way he's kissing her, like he craves her. As if to him, she's the treasure. As they pass the table, he sets her device aside without ever taking his focus from her.

When the backs of her legs hit the couch, he eases her down onto it, leaning over her. He reaches up, hooks a finger into her top, and slides it down, exposing her breasts. "Look at you," he says, studying her as if she were a prize. "So beautiful."

It doesn't take much nipping and licking at her nipples until she is panting. Spreading her legs wider so his roaming hand has better access. They both gasp as he discovers the wet heat there. Then he looks at her with such intensity that she's almost frightened. Until he says, "I have to taste you."

"Ohhh," she moans, nodding frantically.

He kisses down her body, over her skirt, until he has it bunched up over her hips. She jumps as he bites down on a little pad of fat right near the apex of her thighs. He laves the sting with the flat of his tongue, then he moves further up, licking up the outside of her lace panties before sliding them to the side and repeating the motion. She's so needy for this, for him, she almost combusts at his second pass. She's eager for release, but he likes to work for the things he wants. She wills her body steady and demands, "More."

He groans, then obliges, only coming up for air and to ask, "I saw the box for your little toy, K8. Did it make you feel good?"

"Yes," she pants as his first finger enters her. His mouth moves on her clit as he inserts a second finger. He curls them, making her hips bow off the cushions.

"Better than this?" he asks, his voice husky. Sexy. His mouth is slick as he grins up at her, never slowing the steady pulse of his fingers.

"No, nothing like this," she replies, praying he'll give her his mouth again.

This time, when he rewards her, she can't hold it back. Her release crashes through her, making her insides clench so tight she's sure she's crushing his fingers. As she comes down and her head clears, she looks up to see him on his knees between her legs. His erection is straining through his pants. She remembers the peek she stole when he was first activated. Remembers how perfect it is. How it felt as he ground against her at the party. Has thought about it so many times. About how he would stretch and fill her. She's practically salivating.

Finally, they're going to do this. Right as she reaches a greedy hand for his waistband, her doorbell chimes.

33 – Petty Theft

James

"Fuck," James says, staring down at the very ready and eager woman before him. She tasted so fucking good. Felt so tight, squeezing around his fingers as she came like the time before. Why didn't he do this sooner? Because of The (Stupid) Plan he'd concocted.

But when he realized she was selling her things . . . well, fuck him. She deserves a little reward. She's been so patient since Lessa's party. They both have, really. Had she not been so tired last night after her confession and they weren't sick with worry, he might have fallen into her then. But with their evidence destroyed and the money he's built up in his Blackmarks account, he can relax a little. Because right now his cock needs that tight grip or he thinks he might die.

Fuck whoever is at the door, fuck his plan, and fuck being a good guy. That was all over the moment he tasted her. It's exactly why he wanted to wait. He knew he'd get lost in her. Time for an update.

The Plan, Revision 1: Step 4. Fuck her senseless is now Step 1.

He can multitask. He'll have to because he has to have her now. He'll still carry out Steps 1–3. Date her and all that. He'll just be pleasuring her as he does.

"Ignore it," she says, running her fingertips along his length. *No shit, sweetheart. I plan to.*

Her hand palms him, and he rolls his hips for her. *Yes, grant me mercy*, he wants to beg. He needs those delicate fingers to be on the other side of the fabric. He's about to tell her that when the doorbell chimes again. Then three direct strikes reverberate through the space, followed by Lessa's voice. "Open up, Kate. I'm here to pick up my purchase. And so is . . ." They trail off for a moment before their voice rings loudly once again. "And so is Evlyn."

James groans, running a hand across his mouth, clearing away some of Kate's arousal.

The door handle rattles. "I want my bag, Kate. No take backs."

James leans over a half-satiated, half-desperate-looking Kate and helps her adjust her top back over her amazing breasts. He *knew* they would be amazing.

"She's coming," he yells. "Give us a minute." And he almost winces at the irony. She would be coming again if it weren't for her bothersome friend. At least he was able to get her off once before they were interrupted. Thank their non-deities she'd gotten there before Kate's buyers showed up. He helps her off the couch, adjusting her skirt.

"Do I look like I just had an orgasm?" she asks.

Her straight hair is a little mussed and the fabric of her blouse is stretched a bit from him tugging it over her chest. The pale skin of her chest is pink and blotchy, mirroring her strange yet tantalizing scales, not to mention how kissably swollen her lips are. She still looks utterly fuckable, and he says, "Yes, I'm afraid so."

Her grin is radiant as she says, "Good." Then she points to his mouth, then his needy cock. "You should do something about that, though." Before he can communicate any sort of shock at her bluntness, she flounces toward the door. She gives him a final look, pointing to his bedroom. Then she opens the door.

When James emerges, freshly showered and momentarily and quickly satisfied, Lessa and an unknown woman with a completely shaved head and fierce orange irises are staring at him.

Lessa has a faux leopard fur handbag looped across their shoulders. Their hand is wrapped around the chain too, making James wonder if they also suspect Kate will tear the purchase away from them.

To test the waters, he says, "Nice bag," as he approaches the group. He wishes they would leave, because while he's taken care of himself for now, he's certainly ready to pick back up where he and Kate left off. Her tits are that amazing. It won't take much to get him going again.

Instead of ushering them out the door, he takes a seat beside her, casually draping his arm across the back of the couch so he can twist her hair in his fingers.

"I suppose I have you to thank," Lessa says, holding up their purchase.

"Oh, yeah?" he replies.

"Yes. If it weren't for your . . ." Lessa clears their throat, then leans forward conspiratorially. ". . . *extension issue*, Kate wouldn't be selling all her things, right, Kate?" James isn't entirely sure they're teasing, considering the wary glance they gave him the last time they saw each other. He widens his eyes at them, hoping they'll figure out they need to be more discreet in front of a total stranger.

"I have no idea what you're talking about, but me too!" the woman squeals, lifting her feet, twisting them this way and that so James can get a good look at the multicolor glitter of her shoes. He gives her a tight smile. Because while right now Kate is giving the outward appearance of laughter, he knows she values these items, and this is costing her something. These people are only too caught up in their own worlds to notice. Precisely the reason Kate longed for something more.

"I've been trying to get Kate to part with this bag for years. I even had an alert set up, so if one went up for sale, I'd get a notification. So imagine my surprise when I saw it listed." Lessa smirks at Kate, who only shrugs.

"It's not like I was going to give it to you," she says.

"I told you I would pay for it every time I asked. You didn't want to give it up. But then you got James, and it seems you've turned over a new leaf." Lessa purses their lips into a disapproving frown.

Suddenly, he's defensive. "I told her there was no need." He turns toward Kate, strongly wishing he could spell it out for her, but Evlyn is leaning forward, intently focusing on their exchange. "Why don't you hit pause on the items you are trying to sell? If you decide to *keep me*, we can always re-list them."

She shrugs, eyeing Evlyn. "I explained my reasons. I want to *keep you*."

He sighs, guessing her meaning. She wants to do this for him. He feels the same way—but he's *him*. He must be someone who can stand on their own and take care of those around them. There is no need for Kate to put herself through this for him. But how can he argue with her when she's looking at him like that?

"Trust me," she urges.

Okay, if this is what she wants—what she thinks will make him a better person, he'll try, despite his discomfort. "Okay."

"And stop pushing me about it," she adds.

He wants to groan. Instead, he says, "I'm trying, Kate. This doesn't come naturally to me." But then the irony that he was meant to be a manupartner strikes him. He grins. "You were the one who selected my traits after all. If you didn't want me to be to be like this, then you should have made different selections."

Evlyn giggles. "I have to know what you selected."

Kate playfully rolls her eyes, but her amusement quickly fades when the doorbell chimes. Is she going to get spooked now every time someone comes to the door? Saving her from the act, he quickly goes and opens the door.

Oro1 steps inside. "Ready to test the prototypes?"

He sends a reluctant glance back to Kate. She's perched on the edge of the couch like she's won something.

"Have fun!" Kate says, clearly trying to shoo him out to avoid an argument from him. That's fine. They'll discuss it later, because he refuses to allow her to be nervous about the doorbell. Even if he is trusting her to handle the next month.

Surely Kate will make an excuse to Evlyn about why he's leaving with her friend. She wants him to trust her to handle things, so he collects the prototypes, then slips out of the unit before guilt has a chance to change his mind. "Let's go," he says, and Oro1 falls into step beside him.

It isn't long before they're approaching Y Quadrant's SAT garage.

Their SAT hums as it swiftly transports them through the city, smoothly passing through several interchanges. Occasionally, it slows enough for him to catch a glimpse into someone's apartment or business. People go about their daily tasks, and he wonders about their lives. Who among them has manupartners? Who went out on Holiday, pulling sticky candy from fishes' pouches? Who is plotting with their own schemes on BLACKOUT, trying to subvert the pay bracket system? Does Viper live in this quadrant or another?

"Were you able to find out anything about Kate's old friend?" James asks, unable to say the man's name without cursing, something he's trying and failing to get better about.

"He's worked at GROW for the last seven decades in their marketing department and lives in D Quadrant. I've been able to trace a couple of BLACKOUT profiles back to him. One from a different sports betting application. Another that sells a digital product," Orol says.

"It seems like he's pursuing a variety of avenues to increase his income. How concerned should we be?" James asks.

"I haven't seen anything that makes me think he'll report us to the authorities. Especially considering his activity on BLACKOUT. My guess is that he'll try to get us banned from Off-the-Books Boxing," Orol pulls out the plastic sleeve containing the PalmPrint prototypes. "Maybe other clubs he's a member of too, but I don't think it's anything we should worry about since we don't plan to go back."

"What about Sable?" James asks.

Orol releases a full belly laugh. "Of the three of us, I'm the least worried for her."

James shakes his head, considering the tough woman and what circumstances might have led her to be so guarded and serious when most of the people he meets are flippant and unaffected.

Orol holds out a set of PalmPrint prototypes to him. He eyes them anxiously. "Remind me again why we couldn't test these at a MediSpa in C Quadrant?"

"If they register an alarm, we want to be as far away from where we live as possible," Orol supplies.

James peels away the adhesive on the back and lines his hand up. As he inches closer, he can feel the attraction of the molecules that make up the fleshy palm-shaped sticker. Once his skin touches it, a suction sensation dances across his palm, letting him know it's adhered properly. All that's left to do is peel the plastic protector sheet off the other side. Well . . . and test it.

Fifteen minutes later, they are nearing the front of the line at OXY. Oro1 leans over, whispering, "If yours works and mine doesn't, just go in and act like there's no issue. Then meet me back at Kate's."

James steps forward. The woman with a cropped blue bob gives him a huge grin. "Welcome to OXY, MSP's premier oxygen infusion chamber. Please place your palm here." She holds out a tablet similar to the ones in the SATs. James can hear the blood rushing in his ears as he places his hand on the pad, doing his best to pretend nothing untoward is going on.

The split second the system takes to recognize him lasts an eternity. Finally, it flashes green, and Jett's identification number pops up. "Hello, Jett," the woman says. She's reaching for the aqua velvet rope when the screen beeps, flashing an angry red. Her brow winkles as she examines the response.

A chorus of fucks reverberates in James's mind. Oro1 shuffles behind him but doesn't say anything. "There seems to be an issue with your identification. Please try again," she says, holding the tablet out.

He holds his hand over the imprint scanner. This time, the scanner doesn't tease him with a green response. As the red light flashes, the woman taps her m-volt. "Please send a security—"

But before she can finish, James swipes the scanner out of her hand and turns to dart down the hallway right as a bouncer pops out of the barricaded door. With the stolen device in hand, James runs past the elevators, which appear to be stuck in an emergency open position, to the stairwell. Thankfully, they're only on the tenth floor. James hopes they can't or won't fully lock down the building.

As he races down the stairs, he can't help but think that if he can get away with the stolen device, how useful it will be to have. Oro1 can hack into the system, delete the record of the PalmPrint attempt, and reprogram it so they can test each print as a means of quality assurance. Maybe they can even figure out what triggered it to fail. Each industry's identity verification devices are a little different, and MediSpas that don't require retina scans are the most sensitive, therefore a useful testing measure. James suggested IdenTECH buy their own, but he discovered NHOS doesn't issue the devices except to *legally* registered businesses. His minor crime will be worth it in the long run.

The lobby is crowded as he bursts out of the elevator shaft, slipping into the throng. He only spares a single glance over his shoulder before snatching a mask off the wall and bumping an alarmed woman out of his way. Once he's in her air exchange slot, he breathes a little easier. Despite that, the bouncer has finally caught up. Once he's outside, the towers in this quadrant are so congested it shouldn't be too hard to disappear.

The door opens and James rushes out. He runs until his lungs burn and the inside of his mask is damp from his heavy, hot breath. Finally, when he's made it to M Quadrant, he stops, taking a moment to inspect the stolen device. It comes alive at his attention. A message is displayed on the screen in big bold letters: "Please return to OXY, MSP's premier oxygen infusion chamber. Thank you for your cooperation."

James taps the screen until he figures out how to power it off, shutting down any enabled tracking. Outside, the buzzing sounds of SATs making their way through the city draw his focus. He needs to find one and make his way back to Kate's unit before Orol gets there. He doesn't want her to worry.

Right as he's about to enter the air exchange door of the nearest building, a SAT painted like he's never seen slowly creeps by. Colorful lights and words cover it. They say, in various languages, POLICE. Shit. Even if they're looking for him, they can't see his face underneath the air filtration mask. Plus, he wore an atrocious multicolored jumpsuit for this specific purpose. He blends in with the other brightly clad pedestrians roaming the streets. What a world, where wearing black would be what made him conspicuous.

As it stands, the only thing that might make him distinct is the stolen device gripped in his white knuckles. Before the police car gets too near, he unzips the top of his jumpsuit and slips the device in at his chest. He can just make out the inside of the vehicle and the pair of officers inside. He gives them a nod before stepping into the building. He doesn't dare look back out the windows until he's safely inside. Thankfully, they're gone.

The building's directory hangs on the wall next to the mask deposit. SAT garages are on floor twenty-five of the mostly residential tower he's stumbled into. His heart doesn't stop racing until he's scanned his own palm and is safely enclosed in the SAT, zipping through the city, back to Kate.

34 – Even Pretty Girls Lie

James

James and Oro1 step out of elevators on Kate's floor at roughly the same moment. James reaches into his jumpsuit, fishing out the device.

"Want me to take it so Kate doesn't know?" Oro1 asks.

James scoffs. "No. I'm not hiding things from Kate. That isn't how relationships work. I'm handing it to you because you're the IT guy."

Oro1 chuffs, taking it.

The nondescript concrete walls of her apartment are a welcome sight. Kate is back at her desk, presumably plugging away at task orders with a grin on her face. It's astounding that she enjoys calculating the complex equations, but she genuinely seems to. Told him she found the predictability of numbers relaxing.

He's about to get her attention to tell her all about their adventure over a glass of Vine when he notices the dozen organized piles of clothing and accessories that line the walls and kitchen counter.

"Kate?" he nudges. Oro1 steps up beside him and they share a concerned glance. This goes on for a long time as she loudly clicks away at her keyboard.

Oro1 leans forward, whispering, "She told me once she enjoys the sound."

When he learned about the m-volt's capability, he wondered the same thing, and that is exactly what she told him too.

He angles his head in the direction of kitchen. Oro1 gets out three glasses while James opens a bottle of Vine.

"Sweetheart, why don't you call it a night and come have a glass of Vine with us?" James offers.

"One moment," she says cheerily, though he detects a false ring to it. Both men flick their gaze to the piles, then back to her.

"Kate, darling. James stole a tablet, and we almost got caught," Oro1 says.

She blinks like she's quickly processing what he said. Her eyes never leave the screen as she says, "That's excellent!"

"I think she's intentionally ignoring us," James says, setting the glass on the desk beside her. He and Oro1 move to the couch.

"You should probably go ahead and wash the Blackmarks and pay your lease so she'll stop this," Oro1 suggests.

"I was thinking the same thing." James pulls out his device.

The clacking on the keyboard stops. "I told you I would handle it."

A shiver tracks down James' spine. He isn't sure he's ever heard her be so firm. "Kate, this is clearly causing you unnecessary stress. I know I can depend on you. Please, just take down your listings and let me handle this."

"No," she barks, though he can't help but hear a little quiver in her voice. "This is important to me."

Since he found out she's selling her things that morning, he's been thinking about it and has concluded that she must not have enough money to pay for the upcoming month, despite what she told him. Why else would she be acting so defensive about it? Considering her spending habits and the extra expense of him, how bad is her financial situation really? He wishes Oro1 would pick up on the tense atmosphere and leave so he could have a private conversation with her about it.

"I won't make the lease payment unless you ask me to," he concedes. A few seconds later, the clacking resumes. Sighing, he logs into his Blackmarks account, which he already has linked to the bank that does the washing. "I'll just make the conversion—"

His body goes rigid, which Oro1 must notice, because he asks, "What is it?"

"It won't let me make the transfer."

Oro1 moves closer. "Let me see."

He watches James go through the same correct steps three times before he pulls out his own device, using his m-volt to operate it. Screens change until he recognizes the same Blackmarks depository he uses.

James's heartbeat ratchets up as Oro1 attempts a transfer.

A box pops up, displaying the message *Your transaction is unable to be processed at this time.*

"Maybe they're having a system outage?" James asks. At Oro1's flat expression, James guesses that isn't the case. "Let me try again."

The air seems to be warming. His clingy multicolored jumpsuit isn't helping. He isn't prepared to tackle a crisis wearing this. He should have changed the moment he got home.

The second attempt fails.

At the edge of his senses, he's aware that Kate has stopped working to listen. Fuck.

At the third attempt, a different message populates. *Account has been frozen due to illegal activity.*

"Illegal activity?" Oro1 asks. "Half of all Blackmark transactions are illegal. Washing funds is illegal. I don't understand."

"Maybe it's the platform," James says. Oro1 told him about that happening occasionally.

But Oro1 shows him a message that just populated from Sable. *My Blackmarks account is frozen. Checked with my FRIENDS and theirs are working. Seems like a targeted action. Check yours.*

Below is Oro1's response. *Ours are frozen too.*

James's throat constricts. Nervous to look at his device, he dares a glance and finds the same damning message. "Fuck. This has to be Viper's doing." The man moved quickly. Not a good sign.

Oro1 types, *James thinks it's your coworker, Viper.*

"Don't be too upset," Oro1 says, shrugging. "It was just play funds. You heard Kate. She has the next month covered and by then we'll have sold several PalmPrints. IdenTECH is where the real funds are. Maybe we'll have even sold a new identity . . ." He trails off as he notices what James is staring at. The piles and piles of items she's selling. "Oh."

A thick moment hangs between them. Oro1 says, "I bet we can sell enough . . ." He hesitates, then decides on "even sooner." The implication is clear. Sell them before the next lease payment is due. "Out of curiosity, when is the next month due?"

James winces, but types *twelve days* into his device and shows it to Oro1. His business partner's eyes widen.

Across the room, Kate's chair squeaks as it rolls back from her desk. She stands, facing them with her hands planted on her hips. "You think Viper is responsible?" Kate asks, having clearly overheard every word.

James rubs the back of his neck, trying to decide how to tackle it when Kate blames herself again. Oro1 opens his mouth to answer, but no words come out. Smart, considering his misstep last time he was in this situation.

"I see. All of your funds are frozen"—her voice cracks at the word—"because of me." Kate looks away, and James can tell she's fighting back tears. He wants to go to her, but he suspects reassurance isn't going to help this time. Still, he instinctively stands, ready to do something, anything, to ease her burden.

Her device pings and she picks it up off her desk, glancing at the message. "I can't deal with this right now. I need to leave for Lessa's appointment."

She collects her bag and marches toward the door. At the last minute she turns, fixing them with a fierce look. "I have repeatedly said that I would cover the next month, and I will." She's so resolute as she slips out, he might almost believe her if it wasn't for the fact that she can't make eye contact with either of them.

Oro1 clears his throat, holding out his phone to show him Sable's latest message. *Viper quit this morning.*

Three hours have passed since Oro1 left to discover what he could about Viper, his plans and whereabouts. James doesn't need confirmation to know this is bad, however. Only another half hour until they're down to eleven days. If they could sell at least one PalmPrint, he could transfer what's left of his investment in his IdenTECH account to a new, unfrozen personal Blackmarks account. Maybe with what Kate has set aside, it would be enough. He just needs her to tell him how much exactly that was.

After changing into an outfit as black as his mood, he's been sitting in Kate's desk chair, contemplating his next move.

I'm a valuable resource. And it's not like you haven't done shadier things before, the computer and all its illuminated screens seem to say.

"Like stealing a tablet," James offers.

Disembodied laughter fills his mind. *It won't be enough. No matter how many pretty dresses your girlfriend sells.*

He hates to agree, but he suspects the electronics are right.

Without thinking too deeply about pesky things like privacy and ethics, he activates her computer using the login she created for him. She's left three windows open. One is the Worldbank login. The second is the GROW contract extension page. Kate's login is still active and, from what he can tell with a quick scroll, as expected, the contract is still open to extension.

He is about to log in to her bank account when he glances at the third. A tally. Her balance is there, and to his dread, he sees the bottom line, which is a very precarious amount of unicoin away from being red. And that includes over two dozen sales to make over eleven days.

James undoes the top button of his shirt and rolls up his sleeves.

He doesn't want to be having the thoughts that flood into his mind, but they do all the same. She lied to him. Actually, knowingly lied. Sure, she thought he had it covered as a backup, but that doesn't excuse the fact that she led him to believe she had a full month covered herself. As it stands, without selling her things, he isn't sure she has groceries covered.

"Fuck," he mutters.

He's still sitting there when a giggling Kate breezes back through the door. As if on cue, the particle panes buzz, switching to a pre-programmed night scene. Dark clouds roll across the screens as the light fades. There's no moon to ground the sky, but the stars come out all the same.

The moment she sees him, and then the screens he sits in front of, her face drops.

"What are you doing?" she asks, glancing between him and the screens, which display the direness of their situation.

He should save it for the morning when his head is clear. He knows this, but his mouth opens of its own accord. "This won't work between us if you avoid every difficult conversation." When she doesn't respond, he adds, "You can't lie to me."

She steps back like he's struck her. "I didn't *lie*." She says the word like it's a soggy piece of bread.

Does she believe that?

She shifts her feet, uncomfortable under his gaze. He opens his mouth to argue, but before he can get a word out, she says, "I'm going to bed."

He's too pissed off at her avoidance to say anything else. "Off you go then," he says.

In what he is coming to learn is classic Kate fashion, she plasters on an unconcerned, fake smile and slips into her room.

I guess you'll be sleeping in your own room tonight, the overhead lights mutter.

"Yeah, I guess so," he agrees.

The bed creaks with each of James's contortions. Regardless of how he moves, he can't get comfortable on the stiff bed in Kate's spare room. That his mind keeps drifting back to their argument isn't helping.

He knows it isn't fair to judge her by his standards. Especially since she's been making allowances for him this whole time. He owes it to her to do the same. Never mind that he's been trying to put his trust in someone else to handle something for once.

He takes a few deep, grounding breaths. When he's had time to calm down, he will discuss this with her. For now, he closes his eyes and lets his mind dissect the more urgent dilemma.

Each path leads to one destination: Plan B. Even if she can sell everything she plans to, he isn't sure they'll have enough. It wouldn't be wise to count on selling a PalmPrint, though he'll certainly try.

He takes out his device to message Sable. *Can we meet tomorrow as soon as possible? We need to discuss Plan B.*

Her response comes quickly. *Meet me at the Sports Center in your building at nine.*

Having a plan, even if it's a shitty one, makes him feel marginally better. There's nothing more to do tonight.

He turns over, considering picking up his tablet to distract him. It would be better than the rehashing his mind is intent on doing.

It's only that Kate told him in no uncertain terms that she had the next month covered. Protested adamantly that she wanted him to depend on her a few hours ago. He wants to explain it, but her denial makes reasoning with her feel like a pointless endeavor. He should have kept his mouth shut and dealt with the matter of their relationship after he solved the problem of his lease.

He throws the blanket off, unwilling to let his thoughts control him. The tablet says it's four in the morning. Might as well get the day started.

35 – An Uncomfortable Confrontation

K8

December 20, 2390, Day 7.

Five of the remaining twelve days have passed since the night James found out about what she now mentally refers to as her BIG LIE. The accusation thoroughly stung. So she did a little research, intending to build a case that would prove James wrong. Much to her misfortune, he wasn't.

She even consulted the Respectful and Considerate Conduct Course online manual, which listed over twenty acceptable lies, such as telling one of your FRIENDS their new eye color worked with their skin tone to spare their feelings. Or yes, you absolutely want to eat at Say Yes to Noodles again, to avoid conflict. Despite her best efforts, she failed to classify the misleading information she gave James regarding her ability to pay his lease in any of the categories.

K8 lied.

She isn't sure if *angry* is the exact word to describe how he's been ever since. Exasperated. Resentful. Incensed. Worried. Disappointed. If there is a single word that combined those five, that would be it. It floats in the air between them as they share space and meals on opposite sides of the room in silence.

He is leaning against the counter, calmly, without saying a word, but the glint in his eye is aggressive. He's stewing over something, and the particle panes, which he's set to what she can only describe as a haunted forest, mirror his mood.

She isn't sure if it's the ongoing tension between them or whatever he and Oro1 did earlier in the day that has set him off. He's been staring at her for the better part of an hour while she's been intently focused on her 3key, which makes her feel like it's her. Does this mean he's ready to talk about it? This is worse than any scolding she might receive.

She should never have lied to him about having the funds. It left her with a funny, nervous sensation in her stomach. She's spent hours trying to remember if she ever told an outright lie before. Perhaps in her youth. All children lie. But to lie to him—it makes the air between them thick with distrust. She had wanted him to learn to lean on her, a decision that blew up in her face.

Bravely, she lifts her head to stare back. Her instincts fire, *Look away!* She's already committed, though. Might as well double down. "I told you I have it handled," she says. *By selling my things so I can make the payment in the nick of time* is implied. *Like a hero,* she can almost convince herself. If she can make it true, will it still be a lie?

She only needs to sell a few more things. Ten, in fact. Then he'll have another week.

Suddenly, it occurs to her that this is precisely why people have manupartners. A manupartner wouldn't be looking at her like James is now. A manupartner would be asking her what she would like to do next. Could he ease her discomfort somehow? Order food? Get her a drink? Bring her to orgasm? Turn themself in?

A manupartner would happily march back into the recycle station to get decommissioned to avoid her discomfort, like Yansy and Purpl, and all the others. But not her manupartner. Hers is real. As in really real. He's a man with feelings, and memories, and substance. And abdominal muscles that flex just so as he prowls across the room. And those eyes that seem to see right into her. And that tongue and those fingers. Decommissioning is not an option.

She's not exactly resentful toward James and the awful feeling he's bathing her unit with because Zorg knows she asked for this. But . . . his eyes narrow at her as if he doesn't believe a word she says. This is . . . *uncomfortable*.

"You lied to me," he says, stalking toward her. "And you've yet to address it. I've given you plenty of time."

She rolls the chair backward on instinct, but he reaches for the chair's arms and spins her to face him. He's so intimidating as he leans down into her space. She can imagine it must have been the same in his former life. *Why* he would have been successful. And to have all that brooding attention on her. She feels lightheaded with the intensity of it.

"James," she pleads. The proximity of him, the heat she feels radiating off his body—her fingers reach out as if they're out of her control. Maybe if she brushes her fingertips across his clenched jaw—

"Are you done denying it?" He smirks, and it's like the nick of a razor. Quick and sharp. It stings. She jerks her hand back to her chest like she's been cut.

She wasn't denying it, exactly. It only took her a little while to come to terms with it. Lying may not have been the best choice, but she's made the calculation. "I told you, I have it handled, and I will." She reaches for her device and wiggles it in his face. "I've almost got everything sold." For half of what she'd wanted, but no problem. She'll fish out a few of the items she put back in her closet and list them. In a few days, she'll have enough, then she'll make the payment. Then he'll be safe for a bit longer. Seven days, to be precise.

James stands straight, running his hand through his hair. The action makes her want to wrap her arms around him to reassure him. But she must hold her ground. She doesn't need him to solve this ~~huge problem~~ minor problem of theirs for her. Plus, he probably wouldn't let her near him, anyway.

"K8, we have to establish a few ground rules, okay? You can't lie to me. Honesty is everything in a—" He catches himself.

What was he going to say? In a relationship? His promises and a vision of a future with him flash through her mind. Before her lie and the frozen accounts, she was tragically close to getting everything she wanted. Perhaps if she were to acquiesce this one point . . .

She lifts her chin. "I understand."

Her desk chair catches her as she slumps back into it. Thank Zephyr this is over. Their first fight. Though terribly uncomfortable, it went well. Now she's exhausted. Sleep, then list more items. With that resolved, she rises and paces past him. Before she can make it to the sanctuary of her bedroom, intending to forget this awful feeling, his hand wraps around her arm. She squeaks as he draws her toward him.

"Aren't you forgetting something?" He lowers his face so she can see the individual hairs that make up his stubble.

Oh, of course. What was she thinking? Now that they're in—dare she say—a relationship, he expects a goodnight kiss. How nice. She reaches up on the tips of her toes, pursing her lips. Her eyes slip closed, and she waits for the firm press of his lips.

He gives her arm a gentle shake and her lids snap open. He's glowering down at her. "Are you mad?"

She blinks. "Of course not. Our conflict is resolved. I thought you wanted—"

"An apology."

"An apology?" she squeaks.

"Yes, K8. The gesture one offers when they've wronged someone. Remember before, when I offered you one?" His expression is a little angry, but at least he's grinning. Is he enjoying making her squirm?

She recalls the morning he apologized to her for being a *dick*, as he'd described himself, which feels like ages ago. But listening to him admit he was wrong did feel pleasant.

K8 takes a deep, steadying breath. *You can do this.* "I suppose I'm sorry for lying to you. That must make you feel undervalued. But I'm fully confident that I will sell enough—"

"You, sweetheart, are clueless. Words like *suppose* don't fit well with apologies. Neither do caveats."

K8 huffs. How dare he correct her? First off, she wasn't finished. She had a point she still needed to make. Secondly—an awful thought strikes her. Is this because of the intimate nature of their relationship? Does he think she's so eager for him that he can control her apology? She can't hide her shock. "Is this because I let you explore my body sexually?" She jerks out of his grip, but his hand already snapped open like it was wrapped around a hot pipe.

"If you for one moment think you can correct me and demand things, because you, what? Gave me an orgasm. I'm not so lonely and desperate as to—"

"Please quit talking," James says. His large hand covers his eyes, and he's massaging his temples. "I don't have time for this right now, K8.

I have exactly no time to solve a rather monumental problem. I can't get a fucking win, and now you're accusing me of what, exactly?"

She stands there stunned, mouth hanging open, as each of his words ricochet in her mind. Her hand trembles as she brings it to her mouth, like she might dip in a bucket and draw a response from it. But the well is dry, and the bucket comes up empty.

"I can't do this with you right now." Without another word, he turns, collects his things, and walks out the door.

K8 grabs her device from her desk and stumbles into her bedroom, where she collapses onto the bed. Denial, he accused. Is she really in denial of her behavior? Is that why she has an urge to research what makes a proper apology? The desire to prove him wrong and absolve herself of guilt? She swallows the building lump in her throat. That doesn't stop her from picking up her device and thinking the command for her system to explain what defines a proper apology to her as if she were a child.

By the end of the explanation, tears are streaking down her cheeks. He was right again. A sob bursts from deep in her chest. Is she even capable of having a relationship? James seems to know what to do, but he's from the past, where relationships were a given. Or is their entire conflict because he's from the past? Would someone from her time accuse her of lying and then denying it? She is going to go mad if she gets lost in this thought spiral again. "I don't want a manupartner!" she screams at the softly glowing ceiling. "I want James." *But he doesn't want me.*

He couldn't have been any clearer when he said, *I can't do this with you . . .*

She lays there for the rest of the evening, contemplating how she messed up her one chance at companionship so thoroughly. At least now she can say she had a boyfriend, even if it was short-lived. She laughs bitterly as she makes her way into the bathroom.

What will he do when he gets an identity and therefore is free from her? He'll probably find another reincarnate who meets his very strict relationship standards and settle down with her. All the while, K8 will be in her unit with three months' worth of memories, her slightly more in tune FRIENDS, and a closet full of beautiful things.

Her tearstained reflection stares back at her as she cleans her teeth. *What is wrong with you?* she asks it. Her reflection doesn't answer.

36 – That's Just Kate

James

December 23, 2390, Day 4.

Days have passed since their argument, and James is still at a loss. He left Kate's apartment more than a little disheartened. Considering how logical she is about so many other things, he didn't expect their conversation to go so poorly.

The only thing he could think to do was read the entire Respectful and Considerate Conduct Course manual, all four hundred and fifty-nine pages, in an effort to understand her better—time he realistically didn't have. He knows he should wait to rehash the conversation until after he solves the problem of her lease, but he's been watching her. If he doesn't take action soon, he's afraid things will get worse between them.

And what did she accuse him of? Taking liberties, which made no sense. She was clearly trying to shift the blame away from herself. Earlier during lunch, he asked Jett for insight, but he wasn't helpful, saying little more than, "That's just Kate."

He's missing something. Tonight, he will talk to her about it after his meeting with Orol and the reincarnate they're poised to sell a PalmPrint to.

Orol picks up his glass, shaking it so the ice clinks pleasantly. "So is Kate still planning on helping you?"

James told him about their fight. Not all the details. Just that they had one and they weren't entirely on speaking terms. "I think so. Assuming she is, if we can make this sale, plus what she's making from selling her things, I should have enough for another month. And if not, there's always Plan B."

But he's due for a win. Especially considering the failed meeting with the reincarnate he met earlier at Bird Tea. She seemed to be ready to purchase up until the point the PalmPrint's cost came up. Then it became "I'll think about it."

"Do you think the reincarnate is going to show?" Orol asks.

If he does, it will be a second meeting. "Unless he's wasting our time, I think he will. Then it will be up to us to convince him."

He can understand the reincarnates' reluctance to meet with them. It is their life they are dealing with. It takes a certain leap of faith to meet a complete stranger and admit such a damning bit of information.

But he and Orol have their own brand of certitude. They are fully confident that their future clients will eventually concede that the benefit outweighs the risks, and the other benefits of their company are even more far-reaching. Once he's earned some significant capital, he plans to find other ways to branch out. Multiple income streams will be vital. Especially considering how easily Viper got their accounts frozen.

The man they are meeting with today is one of the few they met early on who got spooked. Yesterday they got a message from him. *You haven't turned us in.*

Oro1 replied, *No, we haven't.*

But James understood this isn't about trust. It's about establishing motivation. James added, *That would be bad for business.*

James glances up from his device to the man approaching them from across the bar. A woman follows him. When she spots them, she stiffens, but the man puts his hand on the small of her back and guides her forward. She must be his *owner*, though they really should come up with a better word for the future people who accidentally end up with reincarnates.

Considering he's bringing her, he must be ready to make a purchase. Finally, a fucking win. Time to start stacking them up.

"Lucas," he says, reaching to the reincarnate. "Good to see you again."

Lucas takes his hand, then Oro1's, before introducing the woman. "This is Astra. The woman who found me and offered me refuge." He takes her hand and kisses it. Then he looks lovingly into her blue eyes. "And so much more."

She blushes furiously before awkwardly mimicking the handshake. "A pleasure."

"So you aren't his owner?" Oro1 asks.

Astra taps the tip of her nose with a red polished fingertip. "No. That is an unfortunate story."

"My owner, as you say, kicked me out when he realized I was one of GROW's mistakes. It took a considerable amount of begging to convince him not to turn me in. I wandered the halls in A Quadrant, hiding wherever I could until Astra found me two days later. She suspected I was a reincarnate, so she took me in. Gave me food and water. Now here we are," Lucas says, entwining their fingers.

James eyes the movement, noting the clear transference happening, but who is he to judge? He can't keep Kate off his mind, so it's not like he's much better.

Astra beams. "Getting to know Lucas has been quite the adventure for me."

How long would it last until she became tired of him and tossed him to the side in favor of something new? Not James's problem.

But out of curiosity, he asks, "What happened with his lease?"

Astra chuckles. "His owner was being investigated by collectors from GROW from what I gather. He finally managed to convince them Lucas ran away and he hasn't seen him since. It's been quite the drama in our tower. That is one of the reasons I agreed to get Lucas a PalmPrint. We have to be very careful. We have an appointment next week to have his facial structure altered. Wouldn't his eyebrows look better if they were raised slightly? And his nose could be a little smaller."

James has to take a drink to keep from cringing. Waking up to Kate in the future was a huge blessing.

"Just enough change that I won't be recognizable," Lucas chimes in.

"Of course," she says, patting his hand.

They complete the transaction, and they show the couple how to use the prints and maintain them. When they leave, James turns to Oro1, feeling accomplished.

The latter orders another cocktail to celebrate.

"They gave me an idea while they were talking. Do you think we could create some type of contact lens that could trick the retina scanners?" James asks when Oro1 gets back to the table.

Oro1 pats him on the back, chuckling. "Your mind doesn't ever quit, does it?"

"No," he says. "I guess not." For once in this unfamiliar future, he's feeling unashamed about his drive. With the funds having already landed in the IdenTECH account, relief slowly starts to wash over him. Knowing Kate, even if she's still upset with him over their conversation, she will use her funds to help him. It's one of the things he admires about her.

"We can tackle that once we get IdenTECH's identity replacement division officially launched. For now, we celebrate our first sale." Oro1 raises his glass in cheers like James taught him.

They clink glasses, and James can't help but allow the warmth of the liquid and his first success to flow through him. Meeting that couple was the reminder he needed about his luck. "How about that story?" he muses.

It was a wild story, which made his and Kate's feel much less tenuous. He can't wait to tell her about it. He takes out his device to send her a quick message that he'd like to talk when he gets back, but finds a message from her already waiting for him.

Going out tonight. Don't wait up.

37 – A Quick Fix

K8

Earlier the same day.

K8 bolts upright in bed, suddenly wide awake. After wasting three days stewing, clarity strikes her. Why did her realization take so long? There's only four days left. But all isn't lost. Well, the opportunity to have a relationship with James is lost, and therefore so is her sanity, but she can still do what she promised. She lied. She got lost in denial. She accused him of—internally, she groans. Clearly, he wasn't trying to dominate her or whatever story she grasped onto to avoid her own faults. How embarrassing. No wonder he wants nothing to do with her.

But she has an opportunity to move the needle in the right direction. One variable she can control. Improve, even if it is too late to get the result she wants. K8 is going to fix herself.

The hot water is invigorating as she quickly showers. She rushes to her closet, throwing on the closest outfit. Does this even match? It doesn't matter. She ties her hair into a no-nonsense ponytail, throws on a little blush, some mascara, lip gloss . . . maybe a touch of glittery eyeshadow that would really pull the look together. There—she's ready to tackle the day.

With determination, she approaches the stacks of still-unwrapped packages. Most of the items are still narrowly within their return window. Incredible Bill will be fine without her purchases, and she will be fine without the latest winter line. James, however, if she doesn't do this, won't be fine.

When she peeks her head out the door, James is nowhere to be seen. Perfect.

Loaded up with everything she can carry, she slips out of her unit on a mission.

Four hours and three trips back to her unit later, she's sitting at a table in the center of the food court, processing what she's afraid to identify as grief. But at least refunds will be issued in three to seven days. So even if she can only afford a one-week extension, between her next paycheck, the remaining refunds, and the rest of her gently used sales, she'll afford the next full month. Then she will have kept her promise, and the rest will be up to him. As he wished.

In her peripheral vision, a man coming around the corner catches her attention. It's James. Her heartbeat ratchets up, and she sinks behind the two remaining packages that the shopgirl told her weren't refundable. A store credit would be of no use to her, so she decided to keep the items—including a shimmery little dress she might treat herself by wearing out tonight. She is getting tired of lying around, heartbroken and morose. Plus, it is the three-month anniversary of her eighty-sixth birthday. And she deserves to celebrate her accomplishment of becoming a better person. Maybe Jett will go with her.

Speaking of, Jett follows James around the corner. They pause and talk animatedly for a moment. Then they shake hands, and Jett walks off. James stands against the wall, glancing at his device every few minutes. He's waiting for someone. Oro1 perhaps?

Zorg, hopefully he won't see her.

Then a striking brunette approaches him as if she's met him before. K8's stomach pitches. The woman leans forward, and K8 can tell they are speaking in hushed tones. Then the woman walks into Bird Tea, with James following behind her. Of course he's meeting a beautiful woman at the place she originally wanted for them to have their fake meeting.

Her heart is in her throat as she picks up her device and messages Jett. *Have you seen James?*

We just had lunch, Jett replies. *Why?*

K8 takes a measured breath. *Do you know if he was going somewhere after?* The question is innocuous enough.

Yes. The next response takes longer to come, and while K8 waits, her knees bounce uncontrollably. *He said he was meeting a reincarnate. If you messaged him, he probably hasn't seen it. You know how focused he can be.*

She'd laugh if her stomach wasn't in such a tight knot. As if he'd want her to message him. Apparently, James hasn't told Jett about the dissolution of their relationship. A sensation that feels a little too close to shame crawls up her neck.

She replies, *Okay thanks*.

Robotically, she pushes through the crowd to the bank of elevators, clutching her remaining packages. When she gets to her unit, she changes the particle panes to a rainstorm scene. The position she takes on the couch gives her an equal view of the door and the thunderstorm.

After four hours of stewing, he hasn't returned to her unit. She's sure she's going crazy, because she's done denying things. She's jealous. He's out with a woman from his time who makes sense to him. A woman who's capable of providing the type of relationship he desires. A woman who isn't K8.

There's only one thing for it. She needs to get James out of her system like she did Viper. As she gets ready for a night out, she sips a glass of Vine to calm her nerves. The slinky silver dress is more lovely than she imagined. She's sure to get the attention she deserves wearing it.

Her palm is only a little shaky as she places it on the SAT palm print reader before picking up her device to message Jett. *Going to Bubble Bar if you want to come.*

Then she messages James. *Going out tonight. Don't wait up.*

38 – Lovers at Last

James

Does *Don't wait up* mean what he thinks it does? Maddening woman. He can only imagine the narrative playing in her mind.

He shoots Jett a quick message, and he gets a location in response immediately.

Standing, he claps Orol on the shoulder. "Kate needs me. I've got to go."

Orol's brows crease. "Everything okay?"

"No, but it will be." He downs the rest of his drink and leaves, determined.

James can't get to the bar that Jett gave him the address to fast enough. Bubble Bar—God, the future makes his brain hurt.

The woman at the host stand gives him a placid smile. "Welcome to Bubble Bar, MSP's most effervescent simulation chamber."

He offers her an equally stupid grin, a technique he's mastered in the almost three months he's been forced to play the role of a manupartner. "My Kate wishes me to surprise her."

The woman feigns a gasp, raising her brows to the customers waiting behind him. "Oh, how exciting! Just enter her identification number here."

He does, and when the screen flashes green, he exhales a relieved sigh. She lets him in.

Glowing orbs in dark blues and purples assault his senses. As he makes his way further into the space, the undulating dark floor makes him wish for something to latch on to. Overhead, there are spheres hanging at different levels, with ladders leading to them. A track circles the room behind them, and he sees servers marching between spheres carrying loaded drink trays. Several of the bubbles are blacked out so he's unable to see inside, but more are transparent.

Inside, people sit around circular couches, chatting and—there's a couple fucking in the nearest bubble. The woman sweeps a sheet of auburn hair over her shoulder and his heart stutters. Then the woman glances up from her position splayed over an armrest on a moan and catches his stare. It's not Kate. She gives him a come-hither look, like he is more than welcome to enter their bubble to join their fun. He can't tell if her lover is a manupartner or a real man. It doesn't matter. He shakes his head to communicate that he'll pass.

Looking away from the public display, he makes his way deeper into the main room, noticing that the bubbles and catwalks rise several stories. Is Kate in one of the bubbles? Is she alone?

Colorful lights pulse throughout the circular space much in the way they did in clubs from his time. They are offset by enormous particle panes displaying disorienting images of floating spheres. He doesn't get the impression that this is a sex club, but if one wanted a hookup, this would be the place. The soft electronic music is ethereal and strange, but after almost three months he's used to the strange.

He climbs a ladder that leads to the first catwalk, passing several servers who eye him curiously, but don't say anything. There's no sign of her in any of the transparent bubbles, so he makes his way up to the next level where there is a common area in the back with a bar and another host stand.

Bodies are crowded on and around the path that leads to it, and he has to push his way through. As he passes the host stand, he hears the host tell a small group that the bubble will go dark when the door is locked.

As he scans the space, he spots another flash of auburn hair toward the back of the common area. His stomach sinks as he realizes it's her. The man she's with looks too much like a perfected version of himself, and he knows what she's doing. She's distracting herself with a less complicated version of him. Will she actually go through with it? He isn't curious enough to find out. This isn't what either of them want, and he isn't about to stand by and let it happen.

He watches the man lead Kate down a dark catwalk, presumably to a bubble he's already secured. James debates for a moment before his control finally snaps and he's following them. If Kate wants him, then she'll have him. Not some over-tweaked replica. They just have a few things to settle first.

Kate emits a feminine giggle as the man presses her into the railing, burying his face in her neck. Then James has a fistful of his shirt and is tugging him backward. The man gives him a few rapid blinks as he tries to determine what is happening, then his lip curls into a snarl.

James releases him, saying, "Nothing personal, buddy, but the lady's spoken for." He's almost proud of how civil he's being.

"Excuse me?" The man looks as though he's going to step a little too far into James's personal space, and that won't do. "You mean to say she's with you?"

"That's precisely what I mean," he says.

Kate pushes herself off the wall, angling toward the man. James catches her hand, pulling her to him so he can get an arm around her before she can reach her new *friend*.

She tries to shove him away. "You can't tell me what to do. We've been through this. Besides, you ended our relationship."

He takes her chin in his opposite hand and holds her still long enough to place a kiss on the tip of her nose. "You're adorable, you know. And you have a lot to learn about being in a relationship." When Kate's resistance melts at his words, he turns to the man. "Don't make a scene. I'm sure another suitable *friend* won't be too hard to find."

He looks at Kate, and James can tell he's struggling to remember her name. "But women like her don't come in here that often. I thought—I mean, where am I supposed to find—"

A replacement. Someone of Kate's caliber to stick his dick in. He might murder the man if he says anything else, so he cuts him off before he can make the mistake. "She's not an object, you moron. She's a fucking treasure. Go away before we have a problem."

The man lets his eyes drift to Kate again. "I guess if this is what you want?"

Kate is speechless and blushing at his words. James, knowing it will needle her, answers, "Trust me. It's what she wants."

"You can't just do that," she protests, pushing weakly against his chest. By now, the man has decided it isn't worth the trouble, and they're alone in the hall.

"I just did, and you like it." James grabs ahold of her hips as he walks her toward the railing. When her back hits, he takes both wrists and holds them behind her back. She doesn't resist. He leans in, lowering his voice to say, "If you need a distraction, I'll be the one distracting you. And if you need to get fucked that badly, I'll be the one fucking you. Understand?"

She nods vigorously.

"Good. And so we're clear, I'll be the only one fucking you."

She nods again.

"Use your words, sweetheart."

He licks up the line of her neck as she says, "Yes."

A chuckle escapes against her heated skin. "Say, 'Yes, James. I understand that if I need to get fucked, you'll be the one doing it.'"

Her voice is breathy when she says, "If I say it, you'll do it. Promise?"

With his free hand, he grabs a handful of her tit, grinding his hips into her soft flesh. "Promise."

Her voice is sweet, almost contrasting with the words as she says, "Yes, James. I understand that if I need to get fucked, you'll be the one doing it."

" 'Even when I'm bad and you're mad at me,'" he says, and her eyes widen.

"Does this mean you're still my boyfriend?" she asks, trying to repress a grin.

"Say it," he growls.

She swallows. "Even when I'm bad and you're mad at me."

"Very good." Her nipple peaks to a hard point as he runs a thumb across it. "Yes, I'm still your boyfriend. That was a fight, sweetheart. Not a breakup. Now, where would you like to get fucked? Here or at home in your bed."

"Both, please," she says, shifting her hips against him.

He chuckles again. "Very well."

Grabbing her wrist, he drags her down the hall, glancing through cracked doors until he comes to a bubble with only a few people inside sipping drinks. This will have to do. James barges in, barking, "Get out."

The group looks up, startled. A man with spiky green hair jumps up, protesting their invasion. "But this bubble is already rented—"

"Out," James points toward the door, practically vibrating now.

The group is no match for his demanding tone. A woman rises and sheepishly tugs on the man's shirt sleeve, dragging him out the door. The two others follow, eyeing James suspiciously. When they're gone, he slams the door and locks it. The bubble dims, and James is sure that means no one can see in.

"That wasn't necessary," Kate says, but before she can add anything to her protest, he's kissing her.

When he pulls away to tug down the straps of her dress, exposing her breasts, he says, "They're fine. And that was one way to get a man's attention, sweetheart."

He walks her back until her knees hit the back of the couch.

"Are you still mad at me?" she asks.

He chuckles, dragging her dress up over her hips so it hangs on her waist. "A little, but that doesn't change anything." He eyes her panties. "Take those off."

As she slides them down her thighs, he shrugs off his jacket, tossing it to an adjacent couch. A quick flick has the buttons at his wrists undone and he's rolling up his shirt sleeves. With a hand to her shoulder and a gentle shove, Kate falls back onto the couch. Then his hand is at his belt buckle. When his cock springs free, Kate stares with wide eyes. "This is what you wanted?" he asks.

She nods, looking pretty and a little dazed.

"You just couldn't be patient, could you?" he asks.

The corner of her lips ticks up, and he would pay a handsome sum to know the thoughts floating through her head.

Her shiny auburn hair falls in a straight sheet down her back. He gathers it in his fist, then tilts her head so she's staring up at him.

"You drive me crazy," he says.

She moves forward like she wants to take over, but he keeps her hair, holding her back. His dick gives a twitch as she grins up at him.

"You like it," she says, smirking.

"While that is oddly true, what we're about to do doesn't mean we're going to skip our much-needed conversation later, understand?" he asks.

She licks her lips, and he almost passes out. "If that is what it takes."

James doesn't break eye contact as he guides her head forward. As his tip brushes against her lips, a bead of pre-cum smears across them. Her rosy tongue sweeps out, tasting it. "Mmm," she murmurs. Thick, dark lashes flutter and an involuntary groan escapes James's mouth at the sight.

As his grip on her hair tightens, her mouth opens, and he presses himself inside. "Fuck, Kate. I've dreamed about this. Your fucking mouth." Then he eases his grip, letting her take over. Her hands tighten around his thighs, her nails digging in as she works her way up and down his length, licking and sucking. Her mouth is hot as sin, but it feels like heaven. When he gets too close, he tugs her hair, pulling her away. "You're way too good at that."

She grins at the praise, saying, "Thank you. You could have had that a long time ago if you weren't so stubborn."

He shakes his head, laughing as leans forward, kissing the corner of her lips before pressing her backward until her back hits the seat. "As if I'm the only stubborn one in this *relationship*. You ready for me?" he asks as he reaches between her legs to confirm.

"Zephyr, yes, you ridiculous man," she ekes out between heavy breaths.

Her thighs spread, and he can see the glistening mess she is. Then he's hovering over her, lining himself up. "I would take my time, but I'm sure security is on their way."

"Fuck," she says as he presses in. He can't help but feel proud at her use of the word. Not to mention turned on.

He works in methodical, pulsing strokes, thumbing her clit in the way he's learned she likes. Her body tenses and her teeth sink into his shoulder as she quakes beneath him. Feeling her flutter is fucking heaven, and it takes his full concentration not to follow her over the edge.

He keeps moving, determined to cement his position as the man in her life. Her second one comes as he pulls her atop him, making her play with herself to get there as she rides him. All the while, he buries his face in her perfect tits, nipping and caressing while he mentally chants a prayer for strength. He refuses to let their first coupling to end before he can give her a third.

Footsteps sound outside, and angry voices float through the door. Damn. There's always later. Assuming he survives.

No. Fuck that. He lifts her off him, spinning her so she is facing bubble's wall. They look out over a crowd of swarming bodies who can't see them. "Hands on the back of the couch and widen your knees."

She does as he tells her, and he settles himself between them before sliding inside. "God, you're even wetter than before."

There's more rustling outside the bubble, then a knock which reverberates hollowly. Kate glances behind him at the door.

"Don't focus on them. Focus on me." Over his shoulder he yells, "Fuck off."

Then he goes to work on number three. By now Kate is quivering, barely able to hold herself up, so James snakes an arm around her waist to bear some of her weight. A guttural moan escapes him as he yanks her viciously back onto himself.

Between Kate's throaty pants, he can hear whoever has been knocking on the door punch a code into the exterior lock panel. Then the lock and the door hiss open. With how his mostly clothed body is positioned, he's covering Kate's nudity, though he isn't entirely sure she'd mind being watched.

"Eyes forward," he instructs, wrapping a hand around her throat from behind to angle her jaw. Then he glances over his shoulder. A man in an official-looking uniform stares at them from the doorframe, mouth agape. "Get the fuck out," he spits through gritted teeth, having no doubt the man will comply. At least for a little while. He doesn't stop moving. It's not like people aren't having sex in every corner of this weird establishment, anyway.

Finally, the man loses the battle of wills with a sigh. "Five minutes," he says.

"Ten," James counters, which gets a little shiver out of Kate.

The door clicks shut, and James resumes his punishing pace. It doesn't take long before Kate's inner walls grip him tight. Thank goodness he only has a few minutes because he isn't sure he could last any longer. Pure bliss has almost sent him flying over the edge half a dozen times. Gripping her breasts, he slams in a last time before his vision darkens, and an obscene pleasure burns through him. When he finally comes back to reality, he realizes he's clinging to Kate as if she were the sole life preserver from a plane that's crashed into the sea. Ironic, because in so many ways, she is.

He kisses her shoulder and her neck as he slowly releases her.

"James, that was . . ." Kate trails off.

"I know," he says, softly kissing her lips as he turns her to face him. "I think we both needed that."

He takes the napkins from his pocket that he collected on the way in and cleans up the mess he's made between her thighs. She's staring at him with awe, and he wonders if his expression is the same.

"I'm glad to know sex is an option for making you compliant," he teases, giving her a wink as he helps her off the couch.

She returns an eye roll, saying to no one in particular, "My *boyfriend* is ridiculous."

It earns her a chuckle.

Her legs tremble slightly as he helps her adjust her dress. Because he knows she'll like it, he says, "You look thoroughly fucked, sweetheart."

She offers him a giddy, half-crazed smile, and he can't help but pull her in for a kiss.

"Beautiful," he says, brushing a stray strand of hair from her temple.

Her grin becomes smug as the door behind him opens, and he can't hide his amusement as he snatches his jacket off the couch, tossing it over a shoulder. He offers the opposite arm to Kate. She takes it, leaning on him as he leads them out of the bubble. As they pass the security guard and the four stunned patrons, he notes their envious glances. He's pleased her. Now he can only hope he'll have enough time for his body to recover before she's ready for the promised round two.

On the SAT ride back to her unit, a contented Kate leans into his side. "James?"

"Yes, sweetheart?"

"The woman you met with today—she was from your time?" Kate tenses, waiting for his answer.

He sighs. "She was, but I don't think she had the money to make the purchase." That put the woman in a similar position to him, which he didn't like at all—for either of their sakes. Unfortunately, there was nothing he could do about it until he figured out his own precarious situation. A fact that in his past, he would have blown right by, but now

. . . now it bothered him more than it should have. "She said she'd be in touch."

Kate's body relaxes. Was she jealous? Was that why she was with someone else when he found her? One fight and she thought they broke up. Surely she's got the message now. Never hurts to double down. "Kate, you are the only woman I want, okay? If that changes, you will be the first to know—explicitly—but I don't think it is going to."

She nestles into his side, humming pleasantly.

He gives her thigh a squeeze, clearing his throat. "And you'll let me know explicitly if things change for you, right?"

She sheepishly grins up at him, saying, "Yes, I will do that," before tucking back in.

Back at her apartment, he changes the particle panes to a starry night sky scene, noting the two packages sitting by her desk. He stifles an exasperated sigh, because if it were during his time, he'd already be making sure she had enough money to do whatever she liked. But as it stands, he is still a work in progress.

He tells her about Astra and Lucas from A Quadrant and the Palm-Print they bought.

"I doubt they'll last a year," she says, and he readily agrees.

She keeps stealing glances at the two packages as he rushes through the rest of his story. Clearly, she has something on her mind.

"Yes?" he asks when he finishes.

She points to the packages. "Those are the only two I was unable to return." A proud grin lights up her face. "In three to seven days, I will have enough funds to pay for an additional month. Maybe more, depending on if you sell another PalmPrint."

His chest squeezes tightly, and he wraps an arm around her waist, drawing her close. "You're dying to say I told you so, aren't you?" he teases, but he can't help but feel staggering gratitude.

She shrugs, reaching up on her tiptoes to kiss him.

"I don't deserve you," he says.

She gives him a look that says, *Not that again.* "This means we can finally relax. Now you have breathing room to get IdenTECH off the ground, and maybe even solve your identity!"

She's so hopeful that he can't bring himself to mention Viper is still out there, capable of causing trouble, though James can't think of what else the man could do besides turn him in . . . But how could he have known James is a reincarnate? He couldn't. Getting their accounts frozen is as far as Viper can take it. They are probably in the clear.

"Sure, a little downtime won't kill me." He smirks, and her eyebrows twitch at his attempt at humor. "Once enough of the returns go through, we'll make the extension. Go change into something more comfortable." He makes his way to the kitchen to pour them a glass of Vine. His thirty-five-year-old body needs time to recover. He plans to spend the entire night making sure she knows how much she means to him.

He's closing the cold storage when his device pings. It's a message from Sable. In all caps. Hairs on the back of his neck stand on end.

JUST FOUND OUT INSPECTORS ARE COMING IN THE MORNING. THEY'RE TEMPORARILY SHUTTING US DOWN FOR AN INVESTIGATION AND SENDING EMAILS TO ALL GROW CUSTOMERS REQUIRING THEM TO TURN THEIR MANUPARTNERS IN BY CLOSE OF BUSINESS ONE WEEK FROM TOMORROW. DECOMMISSIONINGS WILL BE HALTED. IF WE WANT TO INITIATE PLAN B, WE'VE GOT TO DO IT FIRST THING!

James's heartbeat stutters. It shouldn't have come to this. They were supposed to have three more days. With Kate's sales, her returns that would show up over the next couple days, and the PalmPrint they sold, they could have made the next payment in plenty of time. Were there other reincarnates like him that would get caught up in the recall, too?

He shakes his head. There's no point considering it since he can't do anything to help them. He can't help anyone if he's dead.

Viper? he asks Sable.

Plan B was a big risk, but what choice did he have?

Possibly, she responds. *Too many recent violations. They want to inspect the entire facility. If he alerted the authorities, it would be enough to push them to act. We need to get you out of GROW's system before they shut us down.*

His mind flashes between the image of Kate beaming at him, proud of herself for returning her precious purchases, which somehow signifies everything meaningful in this new version of his life and the very real possibility he might not survive this.

He types, *Did you find a candidate ready for a Peaceful Passing Procedure?*

I identified a 298-year-old lab tech. I've already messaged him. 07:00? Sable asks.

He takes a deep breath. Sable has kept her word until this point, becoming a friend, albeit the strangest one he's ever had. Well, besides Jett. She wouldn't let him get decommissioned, and she was upfront with him about the risk. His stomach rolls, and he's uncertain if he can handle the Vine he takes a sip of.

"James, is everything okay?" Kate leans on the counter, studying him.

He clears his throat. Although she's tentative, there's a hint of cautious optimism that looks so good on her he's unable, possibly unwilling, to dampen it. "Small setback, but nothing to worry about."

While he feels a little hypocritical about the lie, "Sparing the feelings of another" was number seven of acceptable reasons to lie in the Respectful and Considerate Conduct Course manual he devoured.

"Give me a minute to send a message. I'll join you in a moment." He slides a wineglass to her, and as she walks away with it, he watches her hips sway through the gauzy fabric of the nightgown she slipped into. If only he'd come to his current conclusion months ago—but he doesn't have time for regrets. Plan B could fail, and he could die a second time. The last hour has given him emotional whiplash. It takes all his focus to stay grounded in the present moment.

He will not fail himself or her. Still, tonight, he will make love to her, absorb every shiver, every breath, every touch—everything that makes Kate special—because there is a very real possibility it could be their last time.

39 – The Measure of a (Wo)man

K8

December 24, 2390, Day 3.

K8 wakes with James's body wrapped around hers, his face nestling into the curve of her neck. He stirs, and she can feel him grow hard against her thigh. "Good morning," he says.

Two armies of butterflies battle in her stomach. The first set, a fiery red army with luxurious fluttering wings, eagerly wants to feel him once more. The second army of butterflies are much more ominous, made up of frozen accounts, scoundrels named Viper, and anything and everything that could go wrong. She imagines they're black and dangerous. They fly around, taking aim with their dagger-sharp wings, trying to eliminate the red army.

Best to ignore them. As soon as she gets up, she'll check her account. The Blackmarks from the PalmPrint sale should get washed, then transferred today. And maybe a few returns will show up early. Then she could pay the lease and never have to worry again. At least for another month.

But when James says, with a roll of his hips, "I can hear you thinking. Focus on me, sweetheart," the black army disappears in an explosion of color. He makes love to her slow and sweet. It is in that moment she realizes she could do this a thousand more mornings. More, and never get tired of it. It isn't just the sex, though James is an excellent lover. It's him. He approaches making love to her like everything else he does. With his sole focus and determination. It makes her feel like the treasure he says she is.

Afterward, James exits the bathroom, hair wet and slicked back from the shower. His clothes are still in the spare bedroom, so he wears only a towel as he approaches her. He leans over the bed where she is resting after their morning activities.

"What time is it?" she asks on a yawn. For her to be this tired, it must be early.

"It's 05:30," he says, and kisses her sweetly. "Go back to sleep."

"What are you doing?"

"In my past life I used to be an early riser," he says. The way his stare keeps retracing her sheet-clad form like he's unable to peel his eyes away makes warmth flood through her. She stretches, luxuriating in his gaze, before turning and nestling into her pillow.

She feels the heat of him as he leans over, brushing his lips below her ear. "You are perfect, exactly as you are."

"Mmm," she sighs, savoring the perks of her new relationship as she hears the door click shut behind him.

The doorbell chimes, and she wakes with a start. She glances at the clock, noting the time: 07:50.

She draws in a deep breath, trying to calm her racing heart. She must have been having a bad dream. The doorbell chimes again. "James!" she calls as she jumps out of bed to throw on a robe. He must have run out.

The dark army of butterflies revisits her when she opens the door to a frazzled-looking Lessa. Their gunmetal hair is tied back in a messy knot and their wan color of their usually glowing skin makes them appear as if they haven't been sleeping well.

"Is it the baby?" she asks, ushering them inside. Trying not to panic.

Lessa gestures at their overall appearance, which includes a bland tan jumpsuit. "Yes, this is the baby, but that isn't why I'm here. I've sent you a dozen messages. Where is your device?"

K8 bites her lip. "I put it on Do Not Disturb last night." She runs to her bedroom, but it isn't on her nightstand. She returns to the living room to find Lessa plucking it from between the couch cushions. They hold it out to her like it's dirty.

"Don't ask," K8 says, taking it.

Lessa clutches her stomach, glancing away for a few seconds. K8 tries patiently waiting, but not knowing why her normally aloof friend is waking her up at eight in the morning is making her have morning sickness, too.

She scans the messages as Lessa rushes to the bathroom.

Check your email. Can't sleep. Just got an email from Worldbank.

They're looking into the accounts of anyone who has done business with GROW recently.

K8's heart skips a beat. She keeps reading.

My account is flagged with a note that says vendor transactions may take an extra 10 days to process due to the review.

K8, why aren't you answering my messages?

I got myself a GROW for Holiday, by the way.

This can't be legal. It says we can still receive payments and use our existing and some pending funds. I'm looking into it now.

K8, aren't you concerned about paying James's lease?

Jett told me you were counting on a few returns to cover it. Did you already pay it?

There is an hour between messages. Then:

K8, I'm coming over.

K8 is standing at her desk, stunned, when Lessa returns from the bathroom. Offhandedly, she asks, "Is there something they can do for the vomiting?"

Lessa shakes their head. "Nothing they've given me is working." Crossing the space, they plop down onto the couch and scan the living room. "Where's James?"

K8 shakes her head. "I don't know. He was gone when I woke up. Probably at the Sports Center with Oro1." Panic hits her all at once. "Does this mean my account is being reviewed too? My returns! If they take longer to process—we're counting on them to pay James's lease!"

Lessa rubs their temples, and K8 is aware she's shrieking.

"That's why I came over. You should check your account," they say. "And pay the lease as soon as possible. If NHOS is investigating GROW, you want to have as long of an extension as you can afford covered. GROW won't want to refund the longer leases, so they'll have their legalese team work something out with the officials. The more you can pay, the better."

If only she had a way to pay more. Quickly, K8 logs into her Worldbank account, finding the same note tagged on her account. James's transfer and two of the twelve returns are showing as pending, which is a relief. She may not have enough to pay one month if her remaining returns take an additional ten days. She needs to have this uncomfortable discussion with James—which would make him proud of her growing relationship acumen. If only he were here.

She's about to message him when her device chimes. Ah, it's probably James. She glances at the email. It's from the Birthing Agency. Her heart backflips. Despite her rising panic at James's undisclosed whereabouts, she clicks the message. She's never received an email from the Birthing Agency, and there's only one reason they'd contact her.

It reads:

Congratulations, C-K8lyn-MSP-00023468!

The NHOS Sector MSP Birthing Agency has identified you as a citizen candidate for reproduction. Please use this unique registration code to set up your appointment with a representative from the Agency.

MSP-BA-CC-K8lyn-00023468-9EJ0753

While you are preparing for your visit, it is important to consider the method of copulation a candidate may utilize. Many candidates choose to select a DNA donor from the Birthing Agency's registry list and implant the zygote medically. However, if the candidate can provide a suitable genetically approved donor or partner to copulate with, the candidate must provide this information to their assigned representative at the registration meeting.

At your visit, your representative will collect a blood sample. Once the candidate's identity is confirmed, your representative will remove your Reproduction Prevention Implantation Chip. Once the candidate's chip is successfully removed and your ability to conceive is confirmed by our highly specialized—

There are several paragraphs left, but K8 quits reading. She's been selected. Against all odds, she's been selected. After Lessa, she never thought she'd get the chance. Tried to put it out of her mind, but being a citizen candidate of the Birthing Agency has been her dream for as long as she can remember. It's the only plausible hope she had for finding a real partner. But then she got James.

She's too stunned and worried to feel any excitement. She needs James. She thinks the command to call him. *Answer*, she mentally decrees. There is a buzzing coming from his old room. When she enters, the first thing she sees is his device is lying abandoned in the center of the neatly made bed. Her dread carves out a pit in the depths of her stomach. It isn't like him to forget it. "Oh, James, what have you done?"

Lessa comes to stand beside her, glancing from the device to K8.

Her body feels cold as she sits down on the bed, cradling the black-market device in her lap. If only she knew the code to get in. But because of the nature of these devices, they're notoriously difficult to hack into. Perhaps Oro1 could do it in a few hours, but she has a sinking feeling that tells her she's too late. Something's amiss.

The bed creaks beside her as Lessa sits down. Then in an uncharacteristic move, Lessa puts her arm around her shoulders. K8 holds up James's device. "What does this mean?"

"I don't know," they say.

Tears spring forth in K8's eyes, falling unhindered.

K8 sniffs. "What? No jokes about wrinkles?"

Lessa shakes their head. "I can feel you hurting and I don't like it."

She looks at her friend. "Lessa, that's called empathy."

"Is there a pill for it?" they ask, giving her a crooked smile.

K8 chuckles despite her aching heart. "Probably, but you don't want to take it. Empathy is a good thing."

Lessa chuffs. "If you say so."

Right then, the other device in her hand pings. Another email. From GROW this time.

K8 swallows the tight lump in her throat as she opens it.

She doesn't read past the first line:

Thank you for turning in your GROW manupartner at the K Quadrant
Recycle Station. We hope you had a pleasant—

She gasps. "He turned himself in."

Lessa looks over and reads the email. "Why would he do that?" they
ask.

"I don't know, but there had to be a good reason." Tears fall freely
down her cheeks as she attempts password after password with trembling hands until she gets his device locked. Now only a retina scan will
open it. "Fuck," she says, tossing it on the bed. Zephyr, that made her
feel a little better. She messages Oro1, but he replies that he doesn't
know of any plan. "Maybe it is something to do with Sable?"

Did Sable get caught and then reveal his identity to the authorities
to get out of trouble? Did they come get him, or did he turn himself in
voluntarily? It doesn't matter—because they have him!

Oh Zorg, they're going to kill him. She knows. She knows, and she
has to do something. The non-deities can't be cruel enough to give him
to her only to take him away, can they? Her stomach tumbles. She's
going to be sick. She rushes to his bathroom, heaving over the toilet,
but nothing comes out. Still, her body makes a grand effort at going
through the motions. Salivating and surging until fresh tears leak from
her eyes.

K8 wipes them as an idea strikes her. Surely they haven't decommissioned him yet. According to her research, they put them in batches
and decommission them in groups. He'd be at the end of the line,
so there's still time. If he turned *himself* in, there would be no retina
scan from her authorizing his decommissioning, like they made Lessa
do when they turned Yansy in. Technically, K8 still owns him until
the legal contract period is over. She can get him back and make

a substantial payment. And now, *now* she has something of value. Something huge.

K8 rushes to her workstation and logs in. As she works, every minute that ticks by feels as if the walls of her unit are inching closer, ready to sandwich her between them. Ready to crush her. She takes entirely too long to find a BLACKOUT site that will accept her merchandise. And too long to write and place the listing.

Lessa comes to stand behind her. "K8, what are you doing?"

She grins, finally feeling some control amidst the panic. "I won the birthing lottery, but I'm going to sell it."

"But isn't that what you always wanted?!" Lessa asks.

K8 shakes her head. "No, companionship is what I always wanted, and now that I have even more than that, I'm not letting it go."

"Which means?" Lessa leans down to read K8's listing. "You're selling your chance to have a baby?! You can do that?"

"Yes," she says resolutely.

Over the last few weeks, K8 has spent time observing. That's what scientists do. In addition to the PalmPrints they invented, they've been working on these little fleshy rubber fingertip pads that held a small sample of blood. They sounded risky to her when James told her about them, but now she sees their benefit. She adds the use of them to her description along with as much of her blood as they'll require for the check-ups. All nine months' worth. She adds a few helpful suggestions, like always seeing a different Birthing Agency physician, even venturing to different quadrants, and scheduling appointments during the busiest times of the day. When she's confident her listing is perfect and covers any potential pitfalls, she publishes it.

Three months ago, she never would have imagined herself in this position. Never could have imagined herself giving up something so monumental. A baby or James. After she had time to process her reaction to Lessa's news, she realized she hasn't been entirely honest with herself about her desire to win the Birthing Agency lottery. Especially after all the baby fun she's been having with Lessa. The opportunity to bring a child into the world would be almost as beautiful as what she's found with James.

Behind her, Lessa paces. "I can't believe you're doing this. I think it might be too late. Then you'll be left with nothing."

The thought gives her pause, but only for a moment. A baby would be . . . amazing, she finally admits to herself. But James's life is at stake.

"Don't worry, Les. It's not too late. As soon as this sells, I'm going to GROW and I'm going to get him back."

Despite the massive shift brought about by that realization, she finds her decision surprisingly easy. With the price she's set, they'll be able to afford two full years of James's lease, which should be long enough to make them overlook her flagged account as Lessa suggested. And surely there's someone out there with the unicoin who wants to have a baby bad enough it will sell quickly. She thinks of the woman who invented the hangover chewable. Someone like that could easily afford it. She only needs it to happen in time to get him back.

The clock at the bottom of her screen reads 09:21. Time creeps by like smog-heavy clouds. Lessa pulls up a side table to sit on, seeming determined to show their solidarity.

K8 sits for ten minutes, staring daggers into the screen, internally screaming, *SELL—SELL—SELL*, as Lessa watches on. Finally, a notification message pops up.

SOLD!

40 – Decommissioning

James

At 08:10, attendants escort James and a dozen relinquished manu-partners from the recycle station garage in M Quadrant to a lobby where dozens more are lined up in neat rows, grinning and blinking. Unaffected by the holding pattern they're caught in. He joins them, taking his place among them. He tries not to fidget or let his thoughts spiral as he waits for Sable to come collect the day's first batch, which, with any luck, will include him.

Every couple of minutes, the garage attendants walk another group through the building, past the full lobby he waits in. Movement down the hallway grabs his attention—a man in an oversize green jacket whose insignia he can't make out greets another man in a sleek cobalt three-piece suit. The material of the suit looks like a synthetic Napa leather; its luxurious quality signifies the vaguely familiar blond man's financial status. Maybe he's one of the two owners of GROW here to oversee the inspectors. James might have seen his face in a news article or on their website. As the men pass, the blond man eyes the rows of manupartners. James's heart jumps when his honey-colored eyes snag on him, then narrow. He holds his grin, willing his gaze to go distant. Eventually, the man moves on.

An agonizing twenty minutes later, Sable appears with two technicians beside her. "We have a lot of work today, so let's make this quick." She counts off the first thirty manupartners, of which he's one, then commands, "Follow me."

The group shuffles forward, falling in line behind her and the female technician. The male tech, whose name, Sable told him, is Nixon, takes up a position at the rear of the procession. He's the one who will take James's place on the table.

Sable leads them to a large stark space that reminds him of an operating room, but ten times the size. Three rows of metal tables stand neatly in the center of the room, and there are dozens of what he thinks are steel refrigerator doors along the back wall.

"You have five minutes to disrobe," booms Nixon, who is about James's height and build. "Place your discarded garments in the bins at the front of the room." He points at the row of bins already piled half full of fabric and footwear. "You'll find a biodegradable gown at the foot of each table. Please put it on and lie down atop the table. At the end of five minutes, we'll begin the procedures."

James notes his voice, wondering if he can mimic the slightly nasal baritone. He plasters a dumb grin on his face and complies as the female lab technician approaches Sable, who nods, giving her instructions he can't hear.

Nixon taps his stylus on his tablet as he looks on. His hand is trembling slightly, and James can only hope he doesn't withdraw at the last moment. Plan B is dependent on him. James glances over at Sable, who now leans against the wall by the door, appearing unconcerned.

Quickly, James takes off his garments and tosses them in the bin. He has to weave through a sea of nude and partially clothed manupartners to get to the agreed upon table labeled Fifteen.

A woman on the other side of the room is whimpering slightly. He glances at her. Her dishwater blonde hair is disheveled, partially obscuring her red-rimmed eyes. She lifts her gaze and they make brief eye contact. He wills his expression to become dumb and glassy. To his relief, she looks away. Of all the batches, there has to be a reincarnate in his. *Fuck*.

He slips on the paper-thin pale blue hospital gown they provided, then lies on the table, which will be the last of the first tray of injections. The crisp metal bites into his skin and the bright overhead lights make him feel like a cadaver. The sensation makes the words *I don't want to die* echo like a memory in his mind.

You screamed that once before, the overhead lights say. *Care to recall the memory?*

The dread that hits him is nearly enough to make him convulse. This is not the time to have a mental breakdown, and he's fairly certain recalling his death in this circumstance would cause one. *Not now. Not now. Not now*, he mentally chants.

A few rows down, the woman is quietly repressing sobs. Quick little gasps of air slip out as the seconds tick by. "He said he'd come," she mutters.

Her distress is enough to distract him from his devolving thoughts. *You can't save her*. If he were the hero, he could. But James is no hero. Yet the thought occurs to him, if this works and they can figure out how to solve people's identity problems, isn't that precisely what he'll be doing? Granted, they'd have to initiate some type of background checks to make sure they aren't helping actual criminals.

Criminals like you? the lights question, and a part of him wants to correct them. Technically, nothing he did in his past life was illegal, but he gets their point.

As he lays there waiting, he wonders about the woman and the rattling table that he assumes is her doing. Who was she in a past life? Was she a good person? Did she have children or a family? Will she freak out when her turn comes? Will someone, like she says, come to save her?

A third set of footsteps enter the room. Everything in him wants to lift his head to look. To discover the person's identity. They take several steps followed by creaking wheels before both sounds stop.

"Let's begin," Sable says loudly, possibly for his benefit.

There is a rustling, then a tablet says, "Identity Confirmed."

"The top row is injection one. The second—"

"Isn't it always like this?" The ice in Sable's voice sends a flood of warmth through him as she reprimands her charge. It's oddly endearing witnessing her be unapologetically herself, and somehow it makes him confident Sable is going to come through for him. She has to.

The technician must have nodded because Sable barks, "Then why are you wasting my time telling me something I already know? Get moving."

He knows she's hurrying to get the batch completed before the inspectors show. God, should he be nervous? No, she assured him she had everything on her end taken care of. But this is his life that hangs on her word. Nerves in a situation this risky are perfectly reasonable.

He hears Nixon sigh, saying, "Time of decommissioning, 08:45."

Time passes like it's being dragged through thick and sticky tar. Still, he lays there not flinching at every clink, scrape, breath, or footstep. Nor when the tablet repeats, over and over, "Identity Confirmed."

Not when Nixon says, "Time of decommissioning, 09:00."

Not even when the woman starts sobbing in earnest. "Please don't. Please. I want to live."

"Hold her down," Sable says. Something clatters to the ground. "Damn it, Avrel. You're wearing my patience thin."

The sobbing suddenly ceases. James is queasy, and he has to keep reassuring himself he's doing the right thing by not getting involved. The woman's owner didn't come and now she's dead. She had to be a sacrifice for the greater good. It was inevitable.

Sable and her two technicians keep working until they are within two tables from him. "Identity confirmed!" He almost jumps when the tablet goes off next to him.

From the corner of his vision, he sees Sable eye the girl with a look so irksome, it almost makes him flinch. "Why are there no more syringes left in this round?"

"Y-you used two on that female unit and the other fell off—"

The table James is lying on reverberates loudly as Sable's hand smacks down on it.

"I don't want your excuses. You should have prepared enough in case such a thing were to happen." James can see Sable's angry finger fly toward the door she must have entered from. "Go, quickly prepare two more, and collect the next batch."

The woman glances between Sable and the door, seeming frozen to the spot. "Now," Sable hisses, and it's enough to set Avrel in motion.

When the door closes, Sable leans over James and smiles. "Having fun yet?"

"You're terrifying," James says, sitting up.

"Change quickly," Sable instructs. "I've been timing her, and it will take about seven minutes for her to refill the syringes and get back here with a new tray." From her pocket she pulls out two of the little fleshy finger pad prototypes, which are filled with James's blood. She gives them to Nixon, helping him put them in place.

When Nixon takes his position lying on the table, she says, "Any final words?"

Nixon shrugs, grinning. "Don't be such a bitch?"

James can hardly bite back the laugh as he puts on Nixon's personal protection. He imagines with the goggles, mask and hair shield he resembles the man Nixon closely enough that the other frazzled technician won't notice.

"I promise I'll try, though I'm afraid it might not do any good," Sable says.

"Will it hurt?" Nixon asks, taking on a more serious tone.

"Not a bit. It will feel like you're dreaming. Much better choice than walking out into the atmosphere, I assure you," she says. "And since you couldn't afford a Peaceful Passing Procedure, we've offered you the perfect solution."

With that, Nixon plasters the same dumb manupartner grin on his face as James wears. A second later, Avrel rushes back into the room with a fresh tray. Eagerly, she passes the first syringe to Sable. "Please confirm his identity," she instructs James.

A brief panic lights up his nerves as he moves around the table. Sable barks an encouraging, "Get on with it."

He turns the correct palm over and depresses the needle into the practically seamless finger pad containing his blood. Then he lifts the finger and squeezes it into the little receptacle. A moment later, his own face pops up on the screen along with his and Kate's identification numbers. He angles it away from the other technician to be safe. They share the same basic features and he's certain Sable has the other technician so rattled she didn't notice him enough to identify him. Still, it was a risk.

The tablet chimes, "Identity confirmed!"

James's heart leaps. Sable doesn't waste any time with the first injection. Then he watches as the girl stares at a device, presumably a timer, on her wrist. After about fifteen seconds, Nixon's eyes slide closed.

"Time," the girl says right as the doors burst open.

Sable freezes as she reaches down to pick up the next syringe.

"Please stop what you are doing and line up against the back wall," says the man wearing the green jacket with the now legible letters: NHOS Inspector. Several others follow in behind him and fan out across the room.

James is exceedingly grateful for the personal protection hiding the sweat now beading across his forehead.

They know about you, the bank of refrigerators at the back of the room announces. *You're all but caught*.

James ignores them, sharing a glance with Sable, while Avrel does as they instruct.

The inspector frowns deeply. "Today's decommissionings were called off. We sent notifications to all senior-level personnel last night."

"I didn't see the notice," she lies, sighing as if the inspector's annoying her. "I just need to complete this procedure." Her tone is firm and even.

"GROW is under investigation for a dozen suspected violations, ma'am. Our official mandatory injunction authorizing our inspection states that all operations must cease until the recall is over and our inspection has been completed. Keep your hands where we can see them and move to the wall," the inspector instructs.

Sable moves her hand away from the tray and Nixon twitches. Will he wake up if the second injection isn't administered? Before he can consider the consequences, James grabs the final injection and unceremoniously sticks it into the man's arm, depressing the plunger.

The inspector marches over. "What do you think you're doing?"

James turns to face the man. "Leaving this manupartner between injections could cause it unnecessary suffering. The Hippocratic oath I took—"

"The what oath?" the inspector asks, becoming increasingly irritated.

"As a physician, we take oaths—"

Sable cuts in. "He's trying to say it's unethical. And if either of us were caught performing unethical procedures, we could have our licenses revoked."

"Right," James says, coming to stand beside her.

The inspector's eyes dart between them and Nixon, then he sighs as if he has enough on his plate already. "The three of you, follow me."

As they follow, Avrel leans over toward him. "You don't sound like Nixon."

His nerves are so rattled all he can think to do is lean toward her and say, "I'm in the middle of a voice transition procedure." He has no idea if that is a real thing, but Avrel perks up.

"Oh, I've always hated my voice, but I didn't know I could have it altered," she says.

He adds in a whisper, "Almost anything is available on BLACKOUT."

The inspectors line them up with a dozen other GROW employees. "Please remove your protection gear so we can see your faces." Then he leaves them in the large room to do as instructed.

Are any of the other GROW employees paying enough attention to notice that he isn't Nixon? But he has no choice. He slips off the protective gear, hoping Avrel's voice doesn't ring out, accusing him.

His jaw flexes as he feels the young woman lean close. She sucks in a sharp inhale, whispering, "I guess your voice isn't the only work you're having done. Though it appears to still be in progress," she says, tapping her nose.

James clears his throat, wishing their conversation doesn't draw more unwanted attention. "Full tune-up."

"How old are you again?" Avrel asks. Is she flirting with him?

"Two hundred and ninety-eight," he says.

"Wow," she replies, and he notes the awe in her voice. "I guess wrinkles are inevitable, eventually. Still, I need the name of your doctor."

Over the next hour, different inspectors come in, delivering other GROW employees.

Sable's shoulder bumps his drawing his attention. "What's the plan if Viper is here to identify us?" She asks the question quietly, so Avrel won't hear.

"Run?" he suggests.

Avrel angles toward them like they're friends now. "What do you think they're looking for?"

"No clue," he lies, deciding it's best to remain friendly with her.

The three of them take a position in a row toward the back and wait. Eventually, three inspectors march back into the room, running through the lines of workers. They make sure everyone has compliantly taken off their goggles and masks. Then someone says, "This is everyone on this level. They're ready. Show the inspectors in."

James's throat tightens, and beside him, Sable shifts.

They are going to catch you. You'll be dead, and your friend who risked everything for you will get thrown in jail, the lights singsong.

If he survives this, he is going to get his head checked, or this irritating habit is going to drive him insane.

Sable whispers, "Isn't that the owner of CHOICElover? I think his name is Res6?"

James studies the man in the cobalt suit from earlier who makes his way to the front of the room, followed by—

Oh look, Sable was right. It's Viper! a melodic voice from overhead points out.

Fucking fuck.

"This is bad," Sable mutters.

"Stay calm," he urges, leaning closer to brush her shoulder reassuringly.

Viper's platinum hair is down, brushing his shoulders. He's also wearing a smug grin as he stares directly at them. That he sees them and doesn't directly point them out confirms what James deduced about the man's character. Like a total sociopath, he wants to draw out the spectacle of the investigation.

"Quiet!" the lead inspector booms. The murmuring in the room grinds to a halt. "It is each citizen's duty to come forward if they become aware of NHOS violations. As most of you are aware, GROW is being investigated for . . ." the man continues speaking for several minutes, but James tunes him out.

Res6 scans the rows of employees, looking for someone. His gaze passes over James and as it pauses, it suddenly occurs to James where he saw the man. He was hovering behind the woman with the long black-brown hair and, most notably, *freckles* in Z Quadrant before she darted into the hallway. A look of recognition is shared between them. The corner of Res6's mouth twitches, though James isn't sure if it's to grin or frown.

Under his breath he tells Sable, "That man you say is Res6 . . . he's a potential client. He brought a woman to a meeting with us, but they bolted."

"The one with freckles you told me about?" Sable guesses, and he nods. "A trap?"

"I doubt it. The woman seemed genuinely frightened."

"Hmm," Sable hums.

Res6 leans over and converses momentarily with Viper, who nods vigorously, aggressively eyeing James. When Res6 glances back, Viper is scowling. Probably because he just confirmed their identity and Res6 is going to get all the credit for identifying them. James can only imagine the headlines.

MSP Citizen and CHOICElover founder identifies corruption at competitor GROW.

CHOICElover founder won't stand for unethical business practices from competition.

NHOS discovers Citizen Hero in CHOICElover founder.

Res6 sees this as a marketing opportunity. Viper, instead of going directly to the authorities with his tip, must have sold it to him. Upon receiving such an opportunity, Res6 didn't waste it. Clever—he has to give it to the man.

James tunes in to the inspector, who is finishing his monologue. ". . . going down the rows of employees to identify the perpetrator, who may or may not be in this very room." More murmurs break out, but louder, and the inspector shouts, "Quiet, please! Both identifying the guilty and clearing the innocent from suspicion hold equal importance. Once you've been cleared, we ask you to exit the room and not speak of today's proceedings, as this is an ongoing investigation. A notice from GROW detailing the status of your employment benefits during our investigation will follow."

A petite blonde woman steps up to Res6. James reads her lips as she says, "Let's begin with the first row."

The blonde woman, Res6, and Viper make their way down the row, clearing GROW employees, who file out of the room. James can't help but notice the spring in their steps and he wonders if, like his first phone conversation with Jett months ago, this is an amusing break in the monotony of their lives.

His stomach twists as they move on to the second row, quickly making their way through it. Then the third, getting nearer and nearer to their position toward the back.

Shouting comes from outside the door, and he can barely make out the words, "I'm sorry ma'am, but this area is restricted to employees only."

Has the dead reincarnate's owner finally come for her? James shivers involuntarily.

Res6, Viper, and the inspector are one row away now. Sable shifts beside him, then his blood runs cold as he hears a familiar voice say, "But I still own him. I can pay—I have the funds!"

Sable reaches out, grabbing hold of his wrist, but as the men work their way down their row, she releases it. James risks a glance at Viper to see if he recognizes Kate's voice. He doesn't, moving steadily down the line, stopping before each employee to study them.

He leans over to Sable, whispering, "When they confirm it's us, we run. Go straight to the bar Scraps in Z Quadrant. I'll find you."

From outside the room, someone calls, "Seize her. We can't let her go in there while an active investigation is underway."

Every fiber of his being hates Kate's distress, but she might unknowingly provide the distraction they need to get away.

On the offense, Sable barks, "Is someone going to deal with that mad person, or shall I?"

The blonde inspector turns, staring right at Sable. "I'm certain the situation is being handled by the appropriate GROW personnel."

They move to stand in front of Avrel. "Identify yourself."

"F-Avrel-MSP-00034489," she says, wringing her hands like she has something to worry about. The gesture highlights her youth, and he would almost feel sorry for the young woman if he weren't so busy trying to keep his cool.

Res6 shakes his head. "Not a match."

Tension flows off Avrel as she rushes for the exit. "I'll wait for you guys outside," she says over her shoulder before the door closes behind her. But as she passes through the door, he spots a flash of auburn hair and a delicate finger in the face of a burly security guard.

His heart squeezes so violently he nearly doubles over. The men step up to James next and he gives them his attention. Viper's scowl is now a deep frown as he eyes him. James flicks his eyes to Res6, who is studying him.

The inspector says, "Identify yourself."

"C-Nixon-MSP-00010672," he says, repeating the numbers he memorized. He doesn't break eye contact with Res6 as the moment stretches on. *I know you have a reincarnate*, he wants to say. More like wants to threaten. With a subtle glare, he tries his best to wordlessly communicate the message *You turn us in, I'll turn you in. And if I have to run, I'll find you and bribe you, which will be worse.*

Finally, Res6 says, "Not a match."

James's head spins, making him feel like he's floating as he walks to the door. How he's going to get outside without Kate seeing him, he has no idea.

"No need to wait for me," Sable calls. "Take Avrel and go back to the decommissioning chamber. We have a mess to clean up." Her gaze flicks to the personal protection he's holding. He quickly puts it on. "I'll deal with that woman and follow shortly." He assumes she adds the last part for his benefit, which is mildly reassuring.

The inspector clears her throat. "If you're quite finished, identify yourself."

Sable's voice follows him out the door. He can only imagine the frightening grin CHOICElover's owner is receiving as she says, "E-Sable-MSP-00031475. A pleasure to meet you."

41 – I Still Own Him

James

As James paces down the hallway, following Avrel back to the decommissioning chamber, he hears her hysterical voice.

"It's that woman," Avrel says.

They must have convinced Kate to move to a different room. He motions for Avrel to slow so he can peer around the corner. Kate is standing in front of a desk with her finger in another man's face. Even though he's down the hall, he can see her usually flawless makeup smudged and her cheeks shining with tears. Her stick-straight hair looks as if she's been nervously running her fingers through it, and it needs a good brushing. Seeing her like this has his heart in his throat. Orol wouldn't have told her about his and Sable's plan. She must have gotten a notification from GROW.

He didn't tell her about Plan B because he thought he'd make it home before she knew anything was amiss. And if he'd gotten caught, better that she was not privy to the details. Oro1 explained the possible ramifications. She could have been fined and suspended from her position. This way, she could honestly tell them she didn't know he was turning himself in. He never expected her to find out like this, though. She must think he's already been decommissioned.

As he absorbs the scene, Avrel pokes her head out beside him. "Oh, drama!" she whisper-shouts.

"Shhh," he insists. Seeing Kate so frazzled and upset is almost more than he can take. The urge to go to her is so strong he nearly gives in.

"I have the money. I have it and you can't do this," she yells at the poor confused man. "I still own him."

How could that be true? She didn't have the money when he left.

"Ma'am, we've repeatedly told you that once a GROW unit is turned in for reprocessing, we are unable to reverse the transaction. This would be true even if it weren't for the recall. It's against company policy."

"But I read the contract. I am supposed to get three notices," she cries. "Three!"

"Your unit was voluntarily turned in this morning as a part of the recall, ma'am."

"But I can pay for two years," Kate sobs.

The man stares at her, grimacing. "We have made it clear there are no exceptions. Especially considering all units, regardless of their lease term, are included in the full company recall."

She tries a different approach. "Can you see if he is still alive? Tell me they haven't decommissioned him yet. At least tell me that."

The man makes a series of taps on his screen and James sees the corners of his lips turn down. "This is completely against protocol, but if I tell you, will you promise to leave?"

Kate vigorously nods, and the man taps on his tablet. "Hmm. It seems they processed a batch before the inspectors arrived. Looks like the manupartner called James was decommissioned at 09:34—"

The swinging metal door opens behind him and Sable walks out with something clenched tightly in her fist. She's followed by security guards. Kate blinks as Sable steps in front of her. "He's dead?"

From around the corner, he watches shock pour over Kate's beautiful form. It drowns every inch of her like she's being dipped into a vat of it.

A small hand grips his arm, and he turns to see Avrel biting a knuckle. "Do you think she fell in love with it?" His brows lower in confusion, and she expands. "It happens sometimes."

"It never occurred to me," he answers honestly, a little taken aback. How had he never considered that she might have fallen in love with him?

"So tragic!" Avrel is still whisper-shouting.

Even from a distance, he can see Kate trembling and taking quick, shallow breaths.

The man, not recognizing Sable's wrath, calmly explains, "I just explained to our Valued Customer that her unit was decommissioned about half an hour ago. I know it's against protocol—"

Sable lifts a hand, silencing him. Kate sways, placing her hands on the desk.

His instincts are firing so loudly he can barely think. *Go to her, go to her, go to her.* Is that him or the overhead lights again?

He almost does it, consequences be damned, but Sable barks, "Get out of our way!"

The man scurries to one side and Sable and the security guards dart around the desk.

James glances back to Kate in time to see the two burly guards steady her as she stumbles. Then Sable's hand, clutching the object—*a syringe*—shoots out.

"NO!" Kate screams in a final rebellious outburst, but a second later, her body goes limp.

Sable turns to the shocked man. "Sometimes when they can't afford to renew their lease, they become hysterical. The recall is probably going to cause a lot more of this, so you should be prepared. Sedation is the easiest way to deal with them. They come to their senses when they wake up refreshed."

James's heart thunders as he steps back from the corner to continue on their original path, ushering Avrel to do the same. As they retreat in the opposite direction, the last thing he hears is Sable saying, "Take this woman to her unit unharmed and I'll consider not docking your pay for forcing me to do your job."

"Sable is scary, huh?" Avrel says.

James chuckles. "Tell me about it."

Not understanding the colloquialism, Avrel prattles on about different Sable encounters, which James tunes out.

All he can think about is her earlier words: *Do you think she fell in love with it?* Kate came here to save him. She did something drastic—sold something—to save him. Because she has some great affection for him? James knows she enjoys his company. That he provides the companionship she's always longed for, but it hasn't occurred to him it might be more. Deeper.

But it must be real. Kate seemed almost callous as she'd watched the woman succumb to the atmosphere on the day he woke up, so he knew it wasn't life in general she'd been aiming to preserve. It was for him.

Kate loves him?

Kate loves him.

Kate loves him!

It takes everything in him to pry himself away from the scene and make his way down the hall. He has to trust that Sable knows what she's doing with Kate. That's what friends are for.

But Sable killed the crying manupartner. Are you sure you can trust her? the lights of the elevator he quickly approaches hiss at him.

Taunt me all you want, he thinks, unfazed because he is choosing to put his trust in Sable and the rest of his new friends. Soon, he'll be home with his new identity and all will be well. Because Kate loves him.

42 – A Fateful Reunion

K8

K8 wakes up in her bed in a blind panic. Zorg, she can't get enough air. Her fingers slip beneath the neckline of her jumpsuit, tugging. It's so tight. Constricting. Suffocating. Why is she still in the outfit she put on this morning? *No mind. It's not important.* The last thing she remembers is the man at GROW telling her James was decommissioned. James. Her James. ~~Decommissioned~~. *Dead!*

But it can't be true. It can't. She would know, right?

She surges out of bed and rushes out of her bedroom. She has to get to GROW. She has to get to him.

Someone's in her living room, but she pays them no mind. "K8, sweetheart. Where are you going?"

She has to get to James. But someone drugged her, or was she dreaming this whole time? It would have taken less than an hour to exchange the Blackmarks into unicoin. Of course, the transaction would be traceable once it hit her account. The NHOS Banking Commission Officials might ask her about it, but there isn't anything inherently illegal in selling her Birthing Agency code. At least, she doesn't think there is.

Earlier, she checked her Worldbank balance, noting the pending transaction, which meant she could use the funds. Despite the note that her account is flagged, the transaction was processed rather quickly. She assumed that meant the non-deities were on her side. Now, the amount of unicoin she has is staggering. And there's nothing she would rather spend it on.

"I got the money! I got the money! I'm going to stop them, James, don't worry!" The man steps between her and the door, blocking her path. Instinctively, she reaches up onto the tips of her toes, swaying slightly. Then she gives James a firm kiss on the lips. *James*, she thinks, sighing into his warmth. "Wait! What are you doing here?!"

Her hands run up his chest and over his face. He's alive? Is she dreaming? "How is this possible?" she says on a sob.

"Oh, K8, I'm so sorry." He grabs her shoulders and draws her into his chest. "I really fucked that up."

Tears bead in the corner of her eyes. How could one person cry this much? Her eyes are exhausted, and she's pretty sure she's aged at least a year. But he's here, holding her. She's elated and relieved and angry. And fully crying again now. But her orientation to her current situation becomes clear. "You're not dead."

"No, I'm not dead."

"But how?" Before she can think better of it, her anger takes over, and she pushes away, smacking the butt of her fists into his chest over and over. "You're a bad man. I can't believe you left without saying goodbye. You made me worry, and I yelled at that man. And I've never yelled at anyone!" She's yelling now.

Finally, James gets a hold of her wrists. When she's calm, he wipes her tears away with his thumbs. "You're right. I'm such a bad man and I'm so terribly sorry that I caused you to go through that. I got the email about the recall and you were so happy and I didn't want you to worry. Sable and I had a backup plan worked out to get me a full legal identity and out of the GROW system for good in case something went wrong, but—"

"But you fucked up!" she shouts.

"I know. I fucked up big time. I should have told you. I wanted to protect you because I'm totally and utterly in love with you. You are perfection personified and I'm a hypocrite and an idiot. Please forgive me?" he begs.

Her heart stops. Did he just say what she thinks he did? It can't be real, can it? He stares at her like he's waiting for a response, but she has no idea what to say.

After a minute of stunned silence, she shrugs. "I guess at least we have lots of unicoin now."

"Sweetheart, tell me what you've done," he says. "How did you get the money?"

She grins. "I won it. The lottery."

She replays the last few minutes. She's pretty sure he said he's in love with her—but does he even realize he said it? There's no way she's deluding herself again.

"The lottery?" James looks at her incredulously. "Oh shit."

Just wait, and he will say it again. As confirmation. Then she'll acknowledge it.

She shakes her head, feeling the grin turn into a full-fledged smile because she has so much to be happy about. "Yes, from the Birthing Agency. I got the notice this morning after you left, then I got the notice that you turned yourself in. But then I logged on to BLACKOUT like you showed me and I sold it, James. For you."

"Oh, K8, you could have had a baby like you always wanted, but you sold it for me?" he asks.

Warmth floods through her as James stares at her with awe. "I'd give up anything for you." She'd sell her prized clothing and accessories collection, her lottery win. Anything. She nods, wiping away happy tears. Zephyr, she is only now realizing what a fright she must look. "I forgive you, but more importantly, you're here and alive."

"Come here," he says, pulling her into his arms again, and she can't help but relish the sensation of him. The sensation she thought she may never experience again. "We'll find a way to fix this, okay? Together we'll fix this."

She nods into his chest, running her hands over his back, needing to feel him, to know he's alive. He runs his hands over her hair like he needs to do the same, only making a few passes before the doorbell chimes.

A knock follows, and James groans. "We're uninstalling that as soon as we get rid of whoever that is. And then we're getting a sign for the outside of the door that says, 'Go away.'"

43 – Real, Like Me

James

James and Oro1, who arrived moments after Sable, quietly watch on, letting the two women argue from opposite ends of the couch in Kate's apartment.

"You had no right to sedate me," Kate says, seeming like she might start growling at any moment.

"You weren't being reasonable," Sable counters, wrinkling her nose like she smells something off-putting.

"I thought James was dead! I thought—"

Sable, who has clearly had enough, jumps in. "You thought that I'd let him turn himself in and get decommissioned?"

Kate throws her hands in the air. "Why would I think anything otherwise? You have no reason to risk yourself to save him."

"That's not true," Sable spits, looking as offended as James has ever seen her.

"Care to explain?" Kate crosses her arms, waiting.

Sable glances at the sunny particle panes, and James can barely hear her as she says, "Because you guys are my friends."

"I thought you had your own friends, and we were throwing off your optimal balance," Kate snaps. Her hand flies to her mouth, and Sable flinches like she's been struck.

James is about to intervene when Kate jumps to her feet and rushes over to Sable. "That was awful of me." She looks at James, who gives her an encouraging nod. Then she takes Sable's hands, the latter only momentarily resisting, and says, "I'm so sorry, Sable. That was cruel and I didn't mean it. You're absolutely our friend. The optimal balance thing is stupid. I should have known you wouldn't let anything happen to James."

James isn't sure he is entirely following their logic, but at least they've quit arguing.

Sable's lip trembles as she turns back to Kate, but she draws the emotion in before it fully slips free. "It's only that my current friend group is underwhelming. I'm tired of switching them every year, so I thought it would be prudent to unofficially join yours . . ."

The women carry on apologizing for various things, including the sedation, and James wonders how likely they are to start an *I'm sorry* trend. He doesn't think he'll ever fully acclimate to the future. But at least he's found something here he never had before.

"Well, this is an interesting turn of events," Oro1 mutters.

"Agreed," James says.

Oro1 fishes out four glasses and takes a bottle of sparkling Vine from the cold storage. "Just because Sable's learned how to apologize doesn't make her any less frightening," he says, uncorking and pouring it.

"Agreed," James repeats.

"I heard that," Sable snaps, releasing Kate from a long, slightly awkward hug.

Both women wipe tears away from their eyes, though Sable's might have been a speck of dust.

Feeling the urge to stand up for Kate, James says, "You decommissioned that reincarnate, so Kate's assumption isn't entirely outlandish." Having borne witness to Sable's callousness so often, he doesn't bother feeling bad about confronting her. And perhaps he wants to double confirm they haven't partnered with an actual psychopath.

Sable barks a laugh. "I should have told you. That woman was a manupartner, not a reincarnate. They're so eager to please, so I planted a little seed for the scene."

"Be more specific," James demands, not entirely convinced.

"She was one of the first to get turned in, so I pulled her aside and told her that her owner's last request was for her to act distraught as she was being decommissioned. I told her I would report it back to him and it would make him feel cared for." Sable shrugs. "It will end up in Avrel's report."

Orol chuckles. "That is incredibly cunning. If you're ever accused of harboring reincarnates, you can point to your cold heart and ruthless history."

"Exactly," Sable says. "See, I have no qualms about decommissioning people from the past who shouldn't be here. It's *unnatural*." Her eyes track to James, then she winks, which makes his arm hairs stand on end. Frightening woman indeed.

Kate moves back to her place on the couch, patting the cushion beside her. James places the glasses of sparkling Vine on the coffee table and takes the seat beside her, and she nestles close.

Kate holds up a glass. "To James and Sable for winning the day!"

They raise their glasses and take a sip.

"Now that I'm officially a free man with a girlfriend with lots of unicoin, what are we going to do while the inspection is ongoing?" James asks. "And what does the recall mean for all the reincarnates out there?"

Oro1 holds up his tablet. "The recall has the reincarnates scrambling. I've already got a dozen messages."

"And I might have a solution," Sable says, waving her device in the air. "I got Res6's contact information before I left. He saw Kate freaking out in the hallway and I think he must have recognized her, so I went after him. He seemed more anxious to get out of there than anything, so I pressed our advantage."

James chuffs. "He was probably worried about covering his own ass. I bet he let us go because he recognized me and realized I knew he's hiding his own reincarnate. Oro1, do you remember the woman with freckles who got spooked?"

"She was his?" Oro1 asks, rubbing his chin. "What a hypocrite."

"Tell me about it. Imagine if it leaked out to the public," James says. "He'd have a PR nightmare on his hands."

Sable gasps, her eyes lighting up. "I smell an opportunity!"

"Hold on. I thought the reincarnates were limited to GROW," Kate says.

"Apparently GROW isn't the only one tinkering. Maybe CHOICElover undergoes more rigorous testing before they put out a new release," Sable suggests. "Maybe his reincarnate is an unintended result."

"That makes sense," James says, nodding. "What if we could convince Res6 to make replacement manupartners using the reincarnate clients' DNA? Then the client can turn the replacement manupartner in for the recall in their place."

Sable bolts to her feet. "That's exactly what I was thinking."

"So he essentially creates blanks that can be turned in instead of the reincarnate, which gets them out of the GROW system. But what about an identity?" Kate asks. "Doesn't the Peaceful Passing Procedure candidate getting turned in solve that better?"

"Well, they can participate in the borrow program until I figure out the programming for the full identity replacement, which will be much less risky," Oro1 says, refilling glasses. "I considered outsourcing for some of the work. Maybe when we get some initial contracts, we can pursue that."

James watches as Kate takes a long sip. "If you need an investor, let me know. I've recently come into quite a fortune," she says.

James chuckles as Oro1's brows raise. "You don't want to know," he says, shaking his head. "You're keeping every single one of those coins and using them for whatever your heart desires, understand?" he asks. She nods in agreement, and he takes her chin and kisses her firmly.

When he turns back, Sable is eyeing them like she's watching a building collapse. "I hope whatever you two have isn't contagious."

As much as he wants them to leave so he can enjoy some time alone with Kate, he's enjoying working with them, too. This is the type of action his mind thrives on. Making plans and anticipating problems. "Wait, if manupartners take a week to grow, doesn't that conflict with the deadline?" James asks.

"They can be grown quicker, but less grow time means more glitches, which shouldn't be a problem for a unit ready to be turned in," Sable explains.

"Sounds like all you guys need to do is get this Res6 person to meet with you," Kate observes.

"And convince him," Oro1 says.

Sable snorts. "More like blackmail him."

"I'll take care of that when the time comes," James says.

"Actually, I've got this one. I'll keep you in the loop, though." Sable stands and collects her bag. "It's been quite the day. I'm ready for a nice long jog in the lake trail simulation chamber."

Before James lets them go, he has one more thing he needs to do. Even though he now knows the decommissioned woman wasn't real, he can't shake the image of fake tears streaming down her face in the decommissioning chamber. Did that happen to the reincarnate from the news story they caught when he first arrived in this world? The nagging sensation feels like a call to action. He was helpless then, but he isn't helpless now. It's time to voice the idea that's been marinating in his mind for weeks now. "What if someone in need can't afford our services?"

Oro1 leans forward thoughtfully, while Sable cocks her head as if this is an odd thought. Kate gives him a warm, encouraging smile, asking, "You want to help them?"

He squeezes her thigh as his gratitude swells. He knew she'd understand and be his biggest champion. "Yes, I want to help them."

Sable's lips curl downward. "But if they can't afford—"

He interrupts Sable, stating in a firm voice, "I *need* to help them. Don't get me wrong, the unicoin is a strong motivator, but if we can do both, I think we should." He needs to do things differently on his second chance. Kate asked him to be a better man, and at first, he wasn't sure if it was possible. But here he is with a golden opportunity. Imagine: James Alexander Fletcher—humanitarian. Or would it be philanthropist? Either way, take that, Timothy Borne!

"Okay," Oro1 says. "Then we'll help them. Come to the office tomorrow and we can work out the details."

Satisfied, James stands, scooping Kate into his arms in a single movement. "Great. Now will you two please get the fuck out of here? Kate and I have some celebrating to do that's been a long time coming."

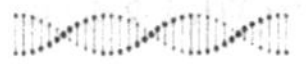

December 25, 2390, After.

Overnight, as sleep eludes him, the details of those last few days of his life slowly trickle back to him, like his second near-death encounter has broken something loose.

Kate stirs. "Why aren't you sleeping?"

"Memories," he says. "Go back to sleep."

"Tell me about them," she counters.

She nestles into his chest, and he speaks.

"When I first woke, I thought I'd just met with an investor, but that was the day before. I was with my team celebrating before I went to the airport." He recalls vague images of their faces smiling ear to ear, congratulating him on the payoff of his bold plan. "I just closed a deal with one of the Broch children, Evan, I think. We had very similar ambitions. He and his brothers owned a full city block in Brooklyn. Another on the Upper East Side. Another in Chelsea. I pitched the demo of the entire block and the planned development of mini communities. My team even suggested repurposing some of the salvaged building materials, so it would have an authentic feel. Sadly, a few beloved community establishments had to go." Kate clears her throat, interrupting him, so he adds, "Which I would now be more considerate about demolishing?"

Kate giggles. "Good enough."

He continues. "Evan came ready to sign, and I think I was practically drooling when the blue ink met the paper. That day was the happiest of my life—until now."

How he was before makes him cringe. It's only been a few months, but he feels so removed from that version of himself. The future has changed him. *Kate* has changed him. And he is better for it.

"That's sweet," Kate says, yawning, and he wonders if she understands the significance.

"It was the biggest moment of my career, and I'd trade all of it again for the life we'll build together," he says, but at this point her even breathing suggests she's fallen asleep again. He chuckles, drawing her close.

His purpose has inextricably shifted. He has his relationship with Kate, friends—*real* friends. Not the NHOS issued Project: LEN FRIENDS garbage Kate told him about. And he has a business that provides services that actually help people—save lives, even. He didn't know life could be like this.

When he wakes next, Kate isn't beside him.

"Kate?" he calls, hoping she hasn't gone far. The bathroom light illuminates the room with a soft yellow glow.

She pops her head out, and his heart seizes.

"Hi," she says.

"Hi," he replies.

"So, you'd trade it all, then?" she asks, giving him a heart-melting smile.

"All of it," he says, sitting up, taking her in as she steps into the bedroom. She heard his late-night confession after all. His heart is in his throat as she makes her way to him.

Her auburn hair tumbles in uncharacteristic flowing waves down her bare shoulders. Her makeup is minimal, which only makes her look hotter. The white cotton panties and the impossibly soft-looking camisole show only an inch of stomach, and her feet are bare. "Holy fuck."

"Do you like it?" she asks.

"Fuck yes, I like it, Kate. You are my waking fantasy."

She gives him a bashful grin, and he can't help but wonder how she doesn't know how insanely gorgeous she is. How sweet and smart and perfect. How she doesn't need all the elaborate and ornate clothing of this time to enhance what he sees. He's so glad she hasn't picked out any of that. What she's wearing suits her perfectly.

"I did a little research about lingerie from your time, and I thought you might like this."

Sweet fucking Kate. He is rock hard, and they aren't even touching. Like she knows she's utterly paralyzed him, she walks forward. He crawls to the edge of the bed, kneeling as she comes to stand before him.

"James?" she asks, hesitating.

"What's the date?" he asks.

She grins. "December 25th."

"Did you know that during my time, today would have been Christmas?" he asks, just now placing them on the calendar.

"I may have read that," she says, coyly.

"Kate, this is the best Christmas gift I've ever received," he says, letting his gaze drift over her. "Thank you."

"I'm glad you like it." A delicious flush crawls up her neck, and he can't wait to follow it with his lips. But the way she's staring at him is so unguarded. Appreciative and affectionate. Admiring even, like he'd be her choice regardless of her options. It makes him feel—

"I love you!" he blurts, and his eyes dart between hers for a perilous moment. He accidentally let it slip yesterday, and she was so angry she didn't seem to notice. He prays he hasn't misjudged. She has to feel the same. She has to.

He isn't sure he can take another breath without dying. Are the windows broken? The air is getting in.

"James," she says, and her voice is like a breath. It soothes him. Coaxes his heart into a steady, confident rhythm. Finally—finally he's getting used to the overwhelming new emotions the future is causing him to have. He thinks maybe he can live this way, especially because Kate makes it so easy. Even if she never says it back.

His hands hook around her thighs and glide up her smooth skin until they slide beneath the fabric of the panties, so he's cupping her ass. He leans his head into her chest, holding her to him. Kissing her soft skin.

"I didn't know women like you were real, Kate. That it could be like this." He sucks in a breath. "I thought I was in hell, in purgatory in this new time. But now I know better."

His words are coming out incredibly cliché. He refuses to give her anything less than what she deserves. He prays to God he doesn't scare her with what he says next. But he's confident she feels the same. This time he knows it's not an impulse or a slip. Perhaps this is the first time he's ever been real. "What I mean to say is, I believe I've been brought back to this time to love you, Kate. I love you."

Then he tilts his head back, and he braves a look at her. Her chest heaves as she sucks in a breath. "Really?" she asks. "You mean it?"

James barks out a laugh. "Of course I mean it. I'd move mountains to prove it to you."

She giggles, grinning down at him. "No need. You've already made the impossible happen."

"What's that?" he asks.

Kate looks away, grinning. When her sparkling eyes finally flick back to meet his, there is such vulnerability within them; it cleaves into him, finding a permanent home in his heart. *Say it back*, he mentally demands. But instead of speaking, he gives her time to build up the nerve.

She stares at him as if he's brand new, shaking her head in disbelief. "I can't believe this is real." Her fingertips reverently brush across his forehead, then his crooked nose and cheek, then his lips. Finally, she says, "I love you too, James."

As he stands, he scoops her up, and her legs wrap around his waist. "You deserve everything, sweetheart. A lover, a friend, a confidant, a co-parent." He squeezes her ass at the last one and she jumps, eyes going wide. "Let me give it to you, Kate. All of it. *Real*, like me, and all for you."

44 – A New Man

James

January 14, 2391, a few weeks later.

James reviews the notes in his device for a final time. He's counting on tonight going perfectly.

Lessa helped him rent out a smaller room in the space in B Quadrant where their conception party was held. They, Orol, Jett, Sable, and a few other new faces are already gathered by the time he arrives with Kate. Their friends stand around bar-height tables sipping on drinks as they enter the intimate space.

Instead of baby-themed particle panes, James has arranged for three of the four walls to display varying images; falling rose petals, a beach-front gazebo, an ocean with swaying palm trees, and something the party planner called sparkle effect. Even the floor itself is a particle pane that is programmed to resemble sand.

Kate gasps as she takes in the atmosphere before turning in question to James. Right as their eyes meet, James drops to a knee. Behind him, on the fourth particle pane, a message is displayed.

James stares up at the woman who's stolen his heart. Who's given him a reason to be something more. Who he'd move mountains to please. Who he's worked every single day for to prove that he is worth her time, attention, and affection. Who accepts him for exactly who he is, imperfections and all. He doesn't have a flowery speech planned. Words aren't his thing. He'll show her every day what she means to him. Now there is only one thing left to say.

"Kate, will you marry me?"

Kate's hand flies to her mouth as her gaze flicks between James, on his knees, extending the ring Oro1 helped him procure, and the image behind him. Then her brow wrinkles and, for a moment, terror hits him. He knows legal marriages aren't a thing anymore, but he thought she would appreciate the symbolic gesture. He thought they would have a ceremony and everything. People of this time love to find every excuse to celebrate, after all. And even if it isn't a governmental transaction, it means something to him. Maybe he's misjudged.

Kate clears her throat. "James, you know I spell my name K-8, right?"

"What?" he asks, a little dumbfounded. At the table in his periphery, Jett and Lessa are sharing a snicker, as if they knew this is how Kate would react and that the joke is on him. He shoots them a glare. Oro1, for his part, is only smirking as if he finds the whole thing amusing.

"K-8," she repeats. "How can I possibly fake marry you if you can't spell my name right?!" The corner of her lip quirks up, and it's enough to send a flood of relief through him. Then it occurs to him that one of their friends couldn't keep a secret. Lessa, most likely.

James chuckles, rolling his eyes at the strange but perfect life he's built. "This whole time I've had it wrong. Well, in that case, marry me, K. 8.?"

K. 8. shakes her head.

"No?" he asks, raising a brow.

"No. No, not *no*. No, that's not it. It is still pronounced the same. But you don't spell it like that." The smile splitting her face makes his chest want to explode. "Ask me again," she says. "But get it right this time." She tips her chin to the pane behind him. Her name has changed from Kate to K8. Like from *K8lyn* in her identification number. It's so obvious now. He should have realized this a long time ago.

His thirty-five-year-old knees are getting stiff. There's probably a treatment for that he needs to look into. James lets out a playful groan. "Please stop torturing me and say you'll marry me, K8."

Now she's nodding and crying. But instead of kissing him as he rises, her gimmie hands are out, reaching for the ring, and he can't help but laugh at her antics. She's perfect.

He holds it back. "You didn't actually answer the question."

A cute smirk plays on her lips and her eyes glaze for a moment as if she's remembering something. "If I say yes, will you give it to me? Promise?"

"Promise," he replies, recalling that those were the same words she used to coax promises out of him in the private Bubble before they had sex for the first time.

"Yes," she says, but she moves past the ring, momentarily wrapping her arms around his neck. He can taste the salt of her tears as she repeats into his lips, "Yes."

The moment he releases her, her hands find his. She's snatched the ring from his grip and is attempting to put it on her fingers, moving between them, trying to figure out where it's meant to fit. Apparently, this is another dead custom. James takes the ring from her, holding her hand as he slips it onto the correct finger. It fits perfectly.

"There," he says, and she beams. His K8 glances between him and Lessa, and he understands she's dying to show it off. "Go on."

With that, K8 dances away, and James can only watch with love threatening to burst his chest. Grateful for the unbelievable second chance that has made him something more, better than what he was before. Now and finally, James is real.

Epilogue – Res6 and Electra

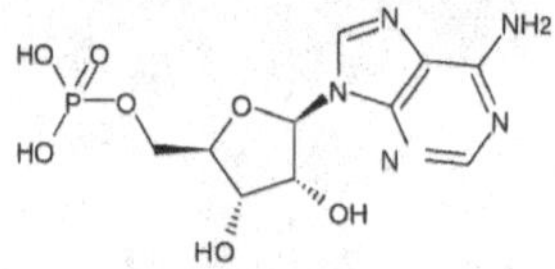

James

January 17, 2391.

Days earlier Sable messaged, *Res6 is ready for his favor*.

The deal was, he didn't identify them during the GROW inspection, and they kept quiet about his freckled reincarnate. He grew them replacement manupartners to turn in to GROW in place of their reincarnate clients, thus helping them gain their freedom. They provided Res6's reincarnate with an ID.

Would this back and forth go on forever, or would this exchange mean their score is even? Granted, that doesn't mean James is opposed to doing business with the man again in the future, even as hard to pin down as he is. Just not with such a heavy weight hanging over their heads.

Giving a last glance to K8, his fiancée, who's basking in the afterglow of their lovemaking session, he quickly dresses, then hops in a SAT heading for Z Quadrant. When he strides into the private meeting room they've rented, Res6 and his reincarnate are already there.

The man stands, nearly stumbling as he reaches out a hand. "Res6."

"James," he says in return, not releasing the man's hand. The question that's been nagging him pops into his mind again. "You know, I still can't figure out your motivation. Especially considering her." He inclines his head toward the frowning woman. "I see the marketing angle of getting a competitor shut down—a tactic that only lasted a week, mind you. That can't be your only reason."

Res6 tugs his hand away and returns to his seat, not too subtly glancing over to the freckled woman. "Perhaps I have other reasons."

"Are you going to keep me guessing?" James asks.

"I didn't realize we were friends," Res6 says.

James chuckles. "My partner, Oro1, will be here any minute." He turns to the woman. "You must be the reincarnate. Like me."

Their stares snap to him.

Electra stands, taking James's hand. "Electra Lynch," she says. "Born 1998. Died 2027. I've been back for a few months now. I'm glad to finally meet another normal human being." She nods in Res6's direction. The man scoffs, making James want to press the issue of his motivations. Clearly there's some lingering animosity between them, which Sable hadn't mentioned.

"Good, good. And I know what you mean. Trust me," James says, chuckling, which seems to set her at ease. "You've come to the right people. If a discreet identity is what you're looking for, we've got you covered."

She gives him a warm smile.

James studies the man. His scowl makes James slightly on edge, but he isn't sure it has anything to do with him. "You turned us in for using reincarnates in the fighting ring, but by then, Electra would have already been in existence. Now you're going to great lengths to protect her. I'm still trying to understand why."

Res6 shifts uncomfortably and the pair share a charged glance. The tension between them is palpable. Were he and K8 like this in the beginning?

The woman beside him smirks, confirming the source of the man's scowl. Her dark eyes flash with challenge. "Good luck with that."

Does this man have any idea what he's gotten himself into? For a moment, James can only smile fondly.

Nope, he has no idea.

Thank you for reading GROW times a million! Need more of James and K8? Read a bonus scene on my website:

www.jennifermwaldrop.com/grow-bonus-scene

Ready for Electra and Res6's story? Check out *Love, Manufactured: Volume 2 – CHOICElover* on my Amazon author page: https://bit.ly/4ll7yjn

Acknowledgments

Thank you for taking the time to read *GROW (Your Own Boyfriend)*. I hope you enjoyed K8 and James's story—it's my favorite book baby and was the most fun I've ever had writing!

If you enjoyed it, even a little, I would be honored if you'd head over to Amazon or Goodreads and leave a review. I know leaving a review can be time-consuming, but it helps us indie authors more than you know and may help other readers discover our work. Also, if you happen to mention that I made you laugh, that wouldn't hurt either, because I'm actively trying to convince my husband of how funny I am . . . haha.

I'm the type of writer who takes a village, so I want to say thank you to a few very special people whose support, insight, and feedback were invaluable to me in the writing and publishing process.

First, Casey Harris-Parks—when we got on our call and I told you about this harebrained idea that I spawned from a bizarro, spice-induced fever dream, you said, "STOP EVERYTHING AND WRITE THAT NOW!" I did, and with your coaching, we brought *GROW* into the world. You're the best champion an author could ask for, and if it weren't for you, *GROW* might still be living in the ether of my mind. Thank you.

To Srishti Rathour—who fell in love with my vision and told me in no uncertain terms, "I want to help you make this into a masterpiece!" I said, "Umm, yes, please!" You helped me break the story down and tediously rebuild it, making it the best story it could possibly be. I couldn't be prouder of the result of our efforts. Thank you.

Thanks to Erica Peck for copy editing and Nicole Kincaid for proofreading. You two had the arduous chore of keeping all my i's dotted and my t's crossed, of catching my copious errors, and of making sure my word tenses and usage make sense within the bounds of conventional English grammar standards. Thank you.

Finally, thank you to my husband, who is the inspiration, in some small way, for every book boyfriend I write. You're the stable shore against which my wild waves crash (or something poetic like that). Basically, I have an ADHD brain and keep you on your toes—which you lovingly tolerate. You're the partner with whom I've started businesses, traveled the world, and even moved countries. If it weren't for you, my life wouldn't be nearly so magical.

About the Author

*Image by @tiadawnphotogra-
phyokc*

Hey, I'm Jennifer. I write stories that explore the human experience—searching for clarity in the chaos, meaning in the unexpected, and connection through the characters we come to love. My work spans from lush fantasy romance to quirky speculative fiction, all rooted in emotional truth, hidden layers, and a touch of the unexpected.

Whether I'm exploring love, death, or the weird magic in between, I'm here for readers who crave stories that surprise, resonate, and stay with you long after the final page.

Find me on Instagram @authorjmwaldrop or TikTok @authorjmwaldrop and my website www.jennifermwaldrop.com for: my newsletter sign up, updates on my current WIP, bonus content, and more.

www.jennifermwaldrop.com

My Amazon Author Page